what I learned in Vegas

J.B. Masaji

Published by J.B. Masaji

What I Learned in Vegas
Copyright © 2018 by J.B. Masaji

Cover Art
Copyright © 2016 by David Hannah, used with permission

First edition July 2018
ISBN: 978-0998855400

For those who encouraged me to write.

Contents

Prologue: 3 Beginnings   9

Part I: Apprentice (Independence Day, 1998)   29

Part II: Trials (Labor Day, 1998)   119

Part III: EndGame (Memorial Day, 1999)   191

Part IV: OneSpell (New Year's Eve, 2000)   263

Epilogue: 3 Endings   349

There was a man who had two sons.
The younger one said to his father,
"Father, give me my share of the
estate." So he divided his property
between them. Not long after that, the
younger son got together all he had,
set off for a distant country and there
squandered his wealth in wild living.

~Luke 15:11-13 (NIV)

Prologue: 3 Beginnings

1- "Vegas is Magic"

Spring, 1984
Los Angeles

A couple years after the end of the Wizard War, the Las Vegas Tourism Commission paid for a series of billboards across the nation featuring a majestic nighttime view of the Vegas skyline, accompanied in the lower right-hand corner by three simple words. "Vegas is magic."

This three word phrase had been familiar to me long before I first saw those billboards. The reason was that my father, every time he told one of his countless stories about the city, would always start with that same three word phrase.

"Vegas is magic."

"Jap!"

My mouth filled with sand. I had tried to remember (this time) to close my mouth as I fell, but the instinct to scream had outweighed my conscious plans. Just like it always did.

A vast sea of sand surrounded me. There were mountains and valleys in that sand, patterns left by the steps of countless children traversing it for one purpose or another. The sand told stories, sang epics, and today it was telling the story of a child, me, who was different.

Behind me, the popular kids laughed. The sound of one of them in particular (it was Jeremy Hollingfield) cut through the others. His laugh had microsecond-long gaps in it, creating a staccato effect, so that whenever he laughed it sounded like a sewing machine was teasing me.

Jeremy was fat. His mother always dressed him in clothes that were too tight, which made his appearance even worse. In any other suburban elementary school he would have been the natural source of the collective desire to tease. Luckily for him, I had come along.

"You're a jap, Roy Nakamura." Jeremy pronounced my name wrong of course, making the first "a" hard, like in "apple." "You're a jap jap jap."

If I stood up they would just push me down again. Sure, they might kick me while I was on the ground, but it was better than another fall. I spit the grains of sand out of my mouth, letting them fall to the ground. It would take hours to spit it all out, hours until I could get rid of the taste completely. Even lunch might not do the trick.

Today was supposed to be different. Today I was going to sit at the corner of the playground, underneath the climbing structure, where no one ever went and no one was going to find me. But then in history class Mrs. Everheart talked about Pearl Harbor, and then Phillip O'Malley raised his hand and talked about how his grandfather was in a plane that got shot down in World War II over Japan, and suddenly it was recess and everyone was looking for me.

"Are you going to just lay there jap? Can you even understand what we're saying?"

As I tried to block out the sounds behind me, I saw something buried in the sand, laying just in front of me. A colorful corner protruded out of the dirt, daring me to learn what secrets it hid. Making sure not to appear as if I was getting up, I reached out a tentative hand and probed the object, pulling out just enough of it to discern its identity.

It was a small paperback book, just like the hundreds of others in the fantasy section of the school library. The title, in bold primary colors, read *"Call Me Sorcerer."* I lifted it up in my sandy hands. The voices behind me faded into nothingness. My vision focused on the cover, on the image of a man in a robe, holding up a hand as magical fire spilled out of it, shooting towards a dragon who was menacing towards him. As I gazed at the image, something in me changed forever.

"It's time for bed!"

I looked up from the book to see my father standing at the entrance to my bedroom.

"Just a few more minutes, dad," I whispered. "I'm almost done."

My father was about to say something, but he stopped. His eyebrows furrowed, just a little, as he took his eyes off me and focused them on the book I was holding.

"*Call Me Sorcerer*," he said.

He crossed the gap between the door and my bed and sat down on the corner of it. It was a large bed, at least for me, and it was easy for him to sit without forcing me to move. He picked the book out of my hand without asking (I didn't put up any resistance) and studied the back cover.

"This book is about Las Vegas." He looked at me accusingly, as if I were supposed to explain myself.

I nodded.

"What do you know about Vegas?"

I shook my head. "Only what's in the book."

The book was returned to my trembling hands. My father didn't get up though. He remained sitting there, on the side of my bed, staring away from me. He appeared to be looking at the far wall, but I knew he wasn't. I knew he was looking at something that only he could see.

My father was a history major in college. His dream was to be a museum docent, to light up the faces of tourists and school children with stories of ancient battles and mighty heroes, ensuring their deeds would not be forgotten. He later shelved this calling in favor of the more practical vocation of being an actuary. But for a moment his old history major voice came back, his old storytelling voice that can relate the most mundane facts as if they were a fairytale.

"Vegas is magic," he said. His words made me jump, even though it was clear he had said them as much to the unseen classroom audience as to me. "Las Vegas is the only place on earth where magic still works. In the old days, the long ago days, there was magic everywhere. After the fall of Atlantis, the island kingdom's magic endowed children went out into the world, using their magical skills at first to barely survive, and then to insinuate themselves into positions of power and influence.

"The Atlantians used their magic to help the Saracens fight off the Crusaders, to help William the Conqueror defeat Harold Hadrata at Hastings. But then came the Inquisition, and the remaining magic users came to the New World to escape persecution. They warred and battled until only seven clans remained, the seven Branches of magic that founded Las Vegas, a jewel in the desert as a place where their kind could be safe.

"Then years ago people stopped believing in magic, and so the magic stopped believing in them. Magic worked only in the New World, then only in the United States, then only in Nevada, until Las Vegas was the only place where spells could still be cast."

There is an old photo of my father that I saw when I was younger. Someone at church had remarked that I looked just like him, and I asked my mom how that could be since he was full Japanese and I was only half. In response, my mom dug through some photo albums, trying to find a picture of him from when he was my age, in the process stumbling upon the photo in question.

In the photo, my father is standing outside the Peacock Casino (an old Branch Parthenia casino, long since torn down), smiling, staring at the camera. He is wearing a cloak with speckles of silver that look like they change and glitter, even in a still photograph. It was only years later, after all this happened, that I realized what it was, what the picture revealed. My father was wearing a sorcerer's cloak.

Based on the magnitude of my own magical abilities, and Archmage Artimus Cantor's revelation (years later) about my genetics, it is almost certain that both of my parents are Signed. Perhaps that is why my father told me about Las Vegas, instead of grabbing the book from my hands and throwing it away (as I'm sure he wanted to). Perhaps he knew about my abilities, knew I was destined to one day use them, and wanted to prepare me for that eventuality. Or maybe not. Years later, even after my own magical adventures in the city, I never asked him about his own.

That was how it began. Every night from then until I got too old for such things, my father would tell me stories about Las Vegas. Lying in bed, I learned about the city's origins, the city's conflicts, the struggles between the Branches, the Wizard War between the noble Branch Parthenia and the devious Branch Shaskauer. I learned of the conflict between independent magic users, known as sorcerers, and wizards, those magic users who had sworn fealty to a Branch.

In my remaining free time, I finished the book. *Call Me Sorcerer* is the story of a boy from Los Angeles who goes to Las Vegas and becomes a sorcerer, in the process taking part in all sorts of wonderful and marvelous adventures. The protagonist becomes a dueler, a sorcerer who fights other sorcerers in contests of magical prowess. In the climax he defeats an evil sorcerer bent on world domination, then wins EndGame, an annual competition between the best sorcerers in Las Vegas.

My obsession with Vegas began when I read *Call Me Sorcerer*, and my father's stories solidified it. Later I would read every book my school's pitiful library had on the magical city. Throughout Middle School and High School, my dream would remain the same – to go to Las Vegas and become a famous dueler, just like in *Call Me Sorcerer*. No matter what happened, no matter what I did, my life would never be complete unless I was in Las Vegas. I knew this because whenever I closed my eyes, I could see this dream in my mind, just close enough to touch.

Destiny demanded that someday, somehow, I would go to Las Vegas.

2 – The Watcher

December 31, 2000
Las Vegas

Las Vegas is alive. It breathes, it waits, and it watches those who scurry along its face for a brief season. To the immortal city of Las Vegas, we are fireflies that soar, flare, and burn out in a single day. But it would be a mistake to think this means we escape the city's notice, or that anything we do is without its implicit permission.

The sun had been up for several hours by the time I pulled myself out of bed and walked through the doors of the Last Emperor casino with a single thought on my mind. Wave watching. The freshness of the new day was tainted by the musty sweat of the gamblers around me, most of whom had been playing all night. The electronic whir and clang of slot machines jarred me awake. At least semi-awake. Hungover and half asleep, I was the most alert person in the cavern the gaming tables called home. The hangover was possibly my imagination, my mind telling my body what it should be feeling. I was in all likelihood not hungover at all, but in fact still drunk from the night before.

Even though I was inside, sheltered from the view of the harsh neon lights that clothe the city, I could still feel their gaze on me. I could feel the city watch me, passing judgment on my actions from the night before and the actions I was contemplating for the night ahead.

The path before me was abruptly blocked by two unSigned security guards. Between them stood a casino hostess (blonde hair, blue eyes, a red qipao tightly hugging her slim figure). She stopped a few feet away from me, just out of reach, and bowed her head while tapping the fingers of her right hand to her forehead in the traditional Atlantian gesture of submission.

"Sorcerer Roy Nakamura," she began, "on behalf of Branch Parthenia, I would like to welcome you to the Last Emperor. We hope you enjoy your time here." She looked down for a second at the two tokens around my neck, which because I left my sorcerer's cloak in my hotel room were the only sign of my office. "We would like to take this *opportunity*," she pronounced the word slowly, emphasizing each syllable, "to remind you that the use of magic to affect the outcome of a game of chance is strictly prohibited by Branch Parthenia rules, as well as Las Vegas Municipal Code Title 6, Section 40, Sub-section 230, and will result in immediate expulsion." She tilted her head to the left, towards the larger of the two guards.

It was all I could do to stop myself from laughing at the threat. I was a famous dueler, a magical warrior skilled in the art of one-on-one combat. Depending on who was consulted, I was likely the fifth most powerful sorcerer in Las Vegas. Even if wizards were thrown into the mix, I was still one of the top twenty magic users in the city. I could dispose of two unSigned rent-a-cops with a gesture, probably even a thought.

And the idea of me not using magic to play games was absurd. Of course I would use magic. The Branches knew it, the pit bosses knew it, and this hostess knew it. However as long as I didn't win too much, and as long as the presence of a famous dueler, of a *real sorcerer gambling*, drew curious onlookers to the tables, thus providing even more business for the casino, I would be tolerated.

With a nod I dismissed the hostess, who was all too happy to escape from my gaze, and walked forward. I blinked away the crust from my eyes and scanned my surroundings. Most of the tables were empty. A single blackjack table popped into my peripheral vision, its dealer methodically distributing cards with slightly less emotion than a slot machine. The table, a ten dollar minimum, was occupied by two people, both of them sweaty monstrosities kept alive by pure adrenaline. Well past small talk, they pointed and grunted to signify their intent, not even bothering to register pleasure or pain at their wins or losses.

They were pathological gamblers of some yet to be discovered kind. They were not action gamblers or escape gamblers, they didn't gamble for excitement, or to forget about the real world, but because they simply had nothing else. Like crying out of boredom.

I sat down at the table, nodding to the dealer as I withdrew three crisp hundred-dollar bills from my pocket. The dealer started to ask for my ID, but he glanced at the two tokens around my neck and reconsidered.

The dealer took twelve green twenty-five dollar chips out of his caddy and put them before me. I picked the chips up in my fingers and dropped them back onto the table, considering how much to bet on my first hand. Behind me I could sense a person, most likely a tourist eager to watch a *real sorcerer* play a game of chance, hoping that this was a *real wave watcher* just like they feature in the half dozen police procedurals about this magical city. I turned as the presence sat down to my right. It was definitely not a tourist.

Sorceress Valentine was dressed in a blue blouse, conservative black pants, and a black sorcerer's cloak, the silver patterns on it defiantly glittering in the non-existent sunlight. She pulled a hundred dollar bill out of the air and laid it on the table in front of the dealer. Without looking up, she greeted me. "Roy."

I turned to acknowledge her and nodded my head in greeting. "Sorceress." Although I was no longer her apprentice, the drive for me to use her title rather than her first name was slow to die.

Sorceress Valentine, likely the most powerful magic user in the world (sorcerer or wizard), was an attractive woman of Asian descent somewhere in her late-thirties. This morning however she looked older than usual, frailer.

"Roy," she whispered under her breath, "when I told you to meet me here, it was not to gamble."

"And yet here I am, gambling." A slight smile crossed my face. I made up my mind and pushed two green chips into the betting circle. Valentine, who now had four green chips of her own, pushed a chip into her circle as well.

The dealer dealt the cards. "There is something we need to discuss," Valentine said. "The OneSpell will appear tonight. Have you determined where it will appear?"

"Sorcerer Roland revealed its location to me over a year ago, you know this." Valentine's habit of taking forever to get to her point used to make her intimidating. Now that I was also a sorcerer, I found it annoying.

"But have you deciphered his message? Do you know the actual physical location?"

I checked the cards, noting the way the dealer dealt them. "Yes."

"Now that we have that out of the way, we need to talk. Away from this table. Alone. If you are to defeat the Dragon, there is something you must know."

This was enough talk. I was here to gamble. Ignoring Sorceress Valentine, I focused on the cards in front of me.

The shield spell I quietly cast the moment I sat down was obscuring any attempts, technological or magical, to observe my actions. Valentine was probably powerful enough to see through it, but she didn't care. The wave watching spell I cast soon after was returning a steady stream of information on the outcome of the game before me. With my magical senses I could see the probability waves manifested in front of me, tying all the actions of all the parties at the table together and showing me the chances of which card would be played next.

"Roy," Valentine said, but my thoughts were somewhere else.

Sometimes I like to imagine my life is a movie. Picture this. "Fascination Street" by The Cure is playing over the background. Instead of being surrounded by half-dead gambling addicts, there are three men in tuxedos seated at the table with me. Each of us has two or three adoring women on our arms. The chandelier high above gives off a crystal infused light which bounces off the silver threads on my sorcerer's cloak (the one that in this movie I didn't leave back in my hotel room), and into the wide-open eyes of one of the adoring women. The camera zooms in on the table and cuts between images (a card falling to the table with an exaggerated thud, my fingers picking up a chip and throwing it into the betting circle), all in slow motion.

But back in the real world, things weren't quite as magical as they were in my imagination. There were no chandeliers, no adoring women, my sorcerer's cloak was still in my hotel room, and when I tried to concentrate on the cards, all I could think about was what Maria had said.

"I'd rather be unhappy than alone," Maria Perez told me the night before while drunk and crying on the steps leading up to Club Heartbreak, the hottest nightclub in Vegas.

It had frightened me because even though she had been drunk, I had known she meant it. In fact, it had been her attitude towards life for as long as I had known her, which was a very long time.

FOCUS!

Two nines to a dealer six. Waving my hand to signify I was standing, I watched as the dealer drew a queen and a six, busting. I won another hand, and then another, the cards flying by so quickly that if it were not for the spells, I would never have been able to keep track of them all.

Out of the corner of my eye I glanced at Valentine. She didn't respond. She seemed to have, at least for the time being, given up on her goal of luring me away from the betting table.

Two more hands went by. Thinking for a moment, I pushed my entire pile, five hundred and seventy-five dollars, into the betting circle. I kept my hand on the chips. The dealer raised an eyebrow. I turned to Sorceress Valentine.

"If you're really a time traveler," I said. "Answer me this. Am I going to win this hand?"

Valentine shook her head, and something about her entire demeanor bothered me. It wasn't just how she looked older and more tired than usual. She looked somehow different, changed. "You know it doesn't work that way Roy. I can't reveal the future or else I risk changing it."

I smirked. "I knew it. You may be able to *stop* time, but you're no time traveler." I pulled the pile back out of the betting circle and placed two twenty-five dollar chips instead. The dealer dealt the cards.

My cards were a three and a seven and the dealer had a five. Every blackjack guide in existence said a player should double down, but the spells I cast were warning me not to. I generally listened to the spells in my head (I created and cast them after all), but I also loved to double down. I loved the excitement of knowing the stakes were now twice what they were a moment before.

There is a thing some wave watchers do called "going native." It's what happens when a wave watcher likes to gamble a little too much and starts ignoring the spells in his head, making wild bets in an effort to catch that high they got the first time they tried to gamble.

Some say this is the real reason casinos let sorcerers gamble, let people like me who may be wave watchers play games of chance. It wasn't the business we drew, or the way we added to the magical mystique of even the dingiest gaming establishment in the city. No, it was because no matter how good we were, no matter how impressive the spells we cast, none of us could resist the impulse to go against them. And that's why in the long run, no matter how good we were, we always lost.

I decided to give in to those impulses and added two more twenty-five dollar chips to the pile. For a moment my hangover disappeared, and I felt like myself again. I felt better than myself! I turned to Valentine who was now looking straight at me, not even pretending to pay attention to her own cards. I realized what it was about her demeanor that had bothered me before, as I finally identified the strange look on her face. It was fear.

For the first time in all the years I had known her, Sorceress Valentine, the most powerful magic user in the world, looked scared.

3 - The Return

June 28, 1998
Los Angeles

During the three and a half years that Skylar Trope and I were in a relationship, our favorite place (the place we thought of as "our place") was the roof of a tall parking structure on the north side of the University of Southern California. In the middle of the night, we would drive up there and sit in my white 1989 LeBaron Convertible with the top rolled down. On the stereo I would play songs by Taliesin, my favorite band, as we looked out over downtown Los Angeles, just a few miles away and lit up in all its glory. With the night hiding its imperfections, it looked sort of like Oz. It was fitting then that when we broke up a month after graduation, it was inside my car.

"Well try to remember."

"I *am* trying to remember." The contents of the glove compartment were already emptied out onto the floor at Skylar's feet. I leaned back, my stomach pushing uncomfortably against the seat belt, and thrust my hand into my right pocket, digging around through gum, mints, and several coins.

"We're already late," Skylar said. "What are you doing?"

"I'm checking my pockets."

"You didn't check your pockets?"

I removed my hand from my right pocket and plunged it into my left. "Yes, I already checked them. I'm checking them again just in case."

Skylar humphed, arms crossed, and tapped her right index finger on her left arm. "Well where did you put them last?"

"If I knew where I put them last, I would know where they are."

Skylar sat up, then fell back into her seat, throwing herself against the fabric in an exaggerated flop. The car let out a miniscule groan.

For a moment a beam from a nearby streetlamp hit Skylar's face just right, and I was reminded how devastatingly beautiful she was.

Skylar always looked beautiful. Even her critics admitted she had a near perfect slim figure. Her shoulder length black hair, always meticulously combed without a strand out of place, framed a flawless oval face with two piercing brown eyes so dark they almost looked black. Her tan skin was nothing short of perfection. At five foot three she was on the shorter side, but she walked with a confident step that made her appear twice as tall as she was. My friend Grant used to hum *Is She Really Going Out With Him* every time he saw us together. When I first met Skylar, I was barely able to speak. Of course, these are all things you forget to notice, that you take for granted, after a couple years.

Skylar checked her watch. "Now we're definitely late."

"You're not helping Angel Eyes." Abandoning my pants pockets, I turned back to my glove compartment to see if there might be anything left, forcing Skylar to sit up straight to get out of my way.

"I certainly hope you're more organized than this when you start law school in the fall."

The glove compartment was empty. Mostly. There was a mysterious sticky wad of paper stuck to the bottom, but I wasn't going to touch it. I straightened up and leaned back into my seat.

"What's that supposed to mean?" I said.

"It means that you're not the most organized person, and you're going to have to work a lot harder when you get to law school. Being a lawyer is all about paying attention to details. Remember when your father said that at dinner the other night?"

"He's my father, I remember what he said."

Skylar exhaled. "I just think maybe you should pay attention to his advice."

"Is this like a race thing? Since you're both full Asian, you take his side?"

Skylar rolled her eyes. "I take his side because he's usually right, and like me, is always looking out for your best interest."

I ignored her. Skylar shivered and looked around.

"And what were you thinking leaving your car unlocked in a neighborhood like this in the first place?"

"I was thinking that I would be able to look in peace," I mumbled.

"Say again?"

"Nothing."

Skylar shook her head. "I will definitely not miss this place. Has Grant found a new roommate yet?"

I hadn't checked the backseat, but I couldn't think of any reason why they would be there. I twisted and craned my neck to scan the area, but nothing caught my eye. Turning back, I froze in the headlights of Skylar's gaze.

Skylar had switchblade eyes, the kind of eyes that would slowly close, then snap back open at the slightest provocation. She took a moment to stare at me, weighing my tics and tremors and coming to a conclusion based on years of tearing apart my lies.

"You haven't told Grant yet, have you?"

"Grant and I have been roommates for three years, it's a big step."

"You and I have been dating for three years, and you're supposed to move into your own place so that when we get married I can move into it. That's a big step. That's the plan."

"The plan?" I said.

"Yes, the plan," Skylar said. "The one we've always talked about. You get your own place after college. You go to law school while I get my master's in educational counseling. Then we get married and I move into your place. And it's finally coming together."

"Oh right. *I* get to live out *your* plan."

"*Our* plan." Skylar sighed. "Maybe it would be different if you had some goals of your own."

"I have goals!" I said. "Someday I'm going to visit Las Vegas, become a sorcerer, and then become a famous dueler, just like..."

"*Call Me Sorcerer*," Skylar said. "That's the same thing you've been saying for years, but you've never actually taken a step towards making it happen. You've never looked into how someone actually becomes a sorcerer, you've never cast a spell, you've never even been to Las Vegas."

"I've never been there physically, but whenever..."

"...I close my eyes," we both said in unison.

I cleared my throat "I can see the dream in my mind, just..."

"...close enough to touch."

"Stop that!"

"You see what I mean? You've had the same supposed goal for four years, and haven't gone anywhere. So excuse me if I think going to law school, which your father went to great lengths to get you into, is better than not following your other dream."

"Well maybe I'll go to law school, then visit Las Vegas on the weekends in my free time, so there!" I smacked the steering wheel for emphasis. The force from my blow caused the sun visor above my head to flop open. My keys spilled out of it and onto my lap.

Picking up the keys in my hand, I turned to Skylar. "Now if you have no other objections, let's get going."

"We need to break up," she said.

I stared into a pair of switchblade eyes that I always knew would someday be the death of me. "Why?" was all I could manage to say. It came out as a whisper, almost a gasp.

Skylar twitched, thought for a moment, and opened her mouth again. Then she sighed, as if explaining to a young child that his dead goldfish was not going to come back to life. "Because for the last month I've been seeing someone else behind your back."

And that was when I decided not to go to law school. That's when I decided to go to Las Vegas.

July 1, 1998
California – Nevada Border

The heat struck me like a fist as my white LeBaron Convertible blew through Primm like a vengeful wind. I threaded in and out of traffic, picturing Skylar's evil face on the back of each car that dared to drive too slow, thus delaying my destiny-mandated journey by a single precious moment. The only thing that kept me sane was a folded up piece of paper in my pocket, a print out of an email I had received just before leaving, and its promise of future greatness.

Magic barely works in Primm, the city at the border of California and Nevada, but there's still a slight magical presence. Despite the lack of magical knowledge I had back then, I could feel it, that slight tendril of magic, as I crossed the border into Nevada.

In 1862, back when magic still worked throughout most of the United States, Abraham Lincoln approached the seven Branches of magic about assisting his armies in putting down the Confederacy. Six of the Branches lent assistance, sending wizards to accompany the Union armies into battle. The actual military significance of the wizards' battle spells was not insignificant, but it was nothing compared to the psychological impact that their creations, such as illusions of giant dragons and fields of re-animated corpses, had on the Confederacy, which surrendered a year later.

One Branch however, the Branch now known as Branch Primm, refused to fight. They were exiled from Las Vegas to the California border, where they built a city that bore their new name. Their true Branch name was stricken from all records and changed to "Primm," which meant "the Forsaken" in Atlantian. As time went by and magic became less and less effective throughout the country, and then even the state, the exile of Branch Primm became even crueler. Not only were they separated from their Atlantian brethren, now they could perform only the most basic spells. Still, to the best of my knowledge, no one ever suggested allowing them to return to Las Vegas.

Despite the heat, I rolled down the top of my car as I made my way north on the 15. I wanted to be able to breathe in the Vegas air. Swerving my way through the mountains and over the hills, I made my way down the freeway. Then there it was. The first glimpse of the city of Las Vegas. I was the tinman looking at the emerald city for the first time.

Gimme Shelter was blaring over my radio, providing a soundtrack for my slowly clearing view of the city.

Like a sunrise breaking over a distant horizon, Vegas didn't appear all at once. There were slight glimpses, preludes, as I continued to weave between mountains on the 15. Then I was descending the last mountain and the entire magical city was spread out below me.

It was day, so it looked nothing like it did in the famous billboards of the early 90's. Instead of the night sky's inky blackness hiding all the city's imperfections, the harsh summer daylight laid bare the city exactly as it was. I didn't care though. The promise of a new life filled my nostrils and my lungs. I could smell my future. The air itself was magical, filled with potential that tickled my skin and ripped through my body.

I was going to become a sorcerer, I was going to become a famous dueler, and I was going to prove Skylar wrong. My new life was beginning.

Looking back, there was a lot I didn't know as I arrived in Vegas. I knew about the Branches, how they ruled over the city, but I didn't know how cruel that rule could be. I knew my best friend Maria lived in Las Vegas, but I didn't know how deeply involved she had become with the magic rights movement. I also didn't know that Sorceress Valentine, arguably the most powerful magic user in the world, sensed me the moment I crossed into Primm and began to make preparations for the great battle to come.

All I really knew or cared about was that even though I had never been to Las Vegas, I felt like I was coming home. I had returned.

Part I: Apprentice

Independence Day, 1998

1. Push Rewind

November 10, 1994
Los Angeles

Magic Haven was the neglected love child of a used bookstore and a pawnshop. The outside was kept in a deliberate state of disrepair in order to lend credibility to the store within. This set it apart from the manicured facades of the boutiques that bordered it on either side of its prime location on Ventura Boulevard, at the southern edge of Los Angeles' San Fernando Valley.

Underneath the tarnished image of a dolphin, a creaky wooden sign read "Magic Haven: Books, Spells, and Artifacts." Next to the name was a circle with two vertical lines, the symbol of Branch Parthenia, with which Magic Haven bore some loose association.

Maria squealed with delight as she grabbed my arm and pulled me off the street and towards the door. "Remember this place Roy?" she said. "It practically hasn't changed at all."

"Focus on the prize Maria. I promised Grant I would pick him up a copy of *Call Me Sorcerer*, and this is the only place I can think of that might have one."

The bell on the door gave a familiar ring as we entered the dusty bowels of the store. As a college freshman, I considered myself decades removed from the high school Senior I had been the year before, but walking into the store brought me back.

The interior of the store was unchanged, just like the sign in front. It was part bookstore, part museum gift shop, and part archeological dig. Wooden shelves held tomes ranging from *Watkins' Treatise on Physical Magic* to *The Atlantian Diet (How to Lose Weight by Casting Spells)*. Several glass cases displayed allegedly authentic Atlantian artifacts, while in the corner a machine made personalized tokens, the symbols that sorcerers wore around their necks to declare their allegiance.

Maria ran over to a sword display while I started to search through the shelves of books. The books weren't arranged by author, or title, or even subject. Even the proprietor probably didn't know why historical fiction about the Branches like *Born into Magic* was next to a magical spy thriller like *Dangerous Days*.

After searching two shelves, my gaze was drawn to a glass case containing an open book. It was an illuminated manuscript from the Middle Ages (or more likely a recreation of one), displaying a jousting match between a knight and a large dragon, a long explanation below written in indecipherable Atlantian script. The knight (his shield bore a circle that looked like a Branch mark but I didn't know which one) was holding a magnificent blue lance that seemed to glow right out of the book's pages. The dragon had not yet been speared by it, but was cowering, scared by the very light coming from the knight's weapon.

"Look at this Roy."

I looked up from the manuscript to see Maria holding a medieval broadsword almost half her height.

"How awesome do I look with this?" She took an exaggerated swing at an imaginary enemy. "Professor Fenton would stop bugging me about lab reports if I brought this to class."

"Can I be of assistance?" I looked away from Maria to the proprietor, an elderly bearded man who could have played a wizard in any Hollywood film.

"I'm looking for a book, *Call Me Sorcerer*," I said. "I can't remember who wrote it, but I read it when I was younger."

"You two look familiar," the bearded man said. "You used to come in here often, right?"

Maria put down the sword and walked over to us. "We went to high school just up the street. We're freshmen at USC now, but we're back for Homecoming."

"How time flies," the bearded man said. "Well, I'm glad you two stayed together. So many high school couples don't you know."

There was a pause. "We're just friends," I said.

Maria grabbed my arm. "Well, friends with benefits." She sensuously bit her lower lip. "If you know what I mean."

We were both still laughing as we left the store.

"Friends with benefits?" I said. "Why on earth…"

A car drove by, music blaring out its windows, overpowering Maria's response. The sound vanished and Maria repeated herself. "I was just looking out for you."

Maria grabbed my arm, and we started to walk down Ventura Boulevard. "The way that man looked at you, I didn't want him to think you were a college freshman who couldn't get a girlfriend."

"I can get a girlfriend. What about the girl I met at *Ruby Red* a couple weeks ago? That still might work out."

"Yeah, Skylar seems like a real winner. I'm sure she's the one."

I stopped.

"What's wrong?" Maria asked.

"I just remembered, I forgot to get the book for Grant."

"Grant? Trust me, he's not going to read it."

"It's my favorite book, he's totally going to read it."

"Yeah, not so much."

Arm in arm, we walked onwards in the direction of the high school we had both attended the year before.

July 2, 1998
Las Vegas

For as long as I had known her, Angela Perez had gone by her middle name – Maria. Whenever someone asks me to describe Maria, I always think of the song *Maria* by Blondie. It's not that the lyrics of the song describe her (I'm pretty sure the song is about a prostitute), it's that the feel of the song describes her in a way words just can't.

Whenever I hear the song, I get this image of a party, or club, where everyone is hanging out around the dance floor, no one wanting to be the first to go in. Then the song starts playing. One girl emerges from the crowd, goes onto the dance floor all by herself, and starts dancing to the song. She does it even though no one else is. She does it because if there isn't a party, she's going to create one, not just for her sake but for the sake of her friends. She does it because even if no one else follows, she's confident enough to dance on her own. That girl is Maria.

Only a lover would ever describe Maria as "beautiful," but most men would agree she was better than average looking. She was a little shorter than me, somewhere around five foot six. She had unruly dark brown hair, one lock of it dyed blue (ever since high school, when her mother told her she couldn't). She had a slight dusting of freckles on either side of her nose. Below that was her most striking and memorable feature, an infectious smile that she used liberally.

Despite her Hispanic heritage, Maria had somewhat fair complexion. Most strangers thought she was white, maybe Italian, until they heard her last name (the same way most strangers assume I'm full Asian unless I tell them I'm only half). The two of us were the most ethnically ambiguous students at our high school.

When I first arrived in Las Vegas, Maria was understandably surprised.

"What about law school?" she asked while handing me a cup of coffee. I was sitting at an end table that Maria used as a dinner table in the cramped one bedroom apartment she shared with two roommates. A generous dose of air freshener masked a moldy smell that permeated the air.

I accepted the cup of coffee and leaned back, accidentally smacking the back of my head against a large mason jar filled with ketchup packets from various fast food restaurants. "Law school will always be there," I said. "But this, Vegas, this is what I need to do right now."

"Didn't your dad have to pull some strings to get you into law school?"

"Doesn't matter. I'm sick of living my life to please him."

Maria raised an eyebrow. "When have you *ever* lived your life to please your dad? Didn't he almost disown you when you said you weren't going to major in business?"

"Well, you know what I mean."

Due to the size of the apartment, every object was forced to serve a utilitarian purpose. The TV doubled as a drying rack, books and DVDs were stacked floor to ceiling with no room for them to breathe. Even the anti-Branch posters on the wall (one particularly clever one featured a picture of a tree, the Branch Parthenia symbol on one half and Branch Shaskauer on the other, with a lightning bolt down the middle and the phrase "Branches divided will not stand" at the bottom) were likely there to conceal holes in the wall.

Maria seized a strand of hair that had broken free from an elastic and brushed it behind her ear. "How much thought have you really put into this?" It was friendly, but there was an edge of genuine concern. "Like, have you thought about where you're going to stay?"

I looked around the apartment. It took a moment for Maria to catch on.

"Absolutely not," Maria said. "I practically live in a closet. There's barely enough room for me, Chelsea, and Renée."

"I won't take up any room."

"It's just not possible."

"Not possible?"

Maria sighed. "I would do it if there were any way Roy, you know that, but there just isn't. I already have to sleep on the couch, and…" Maria leaned in close to whisper. "Renée and Chelsea have to share the bed."

Maria leaned back. "My landlord owns a couple apartment buildings. I could check with him to see if he has any units open, but you'll need a deposit."

"I have five hundred dollars."

"That might be enough, but he'll also want proof you have a job."

I took a sip of the coffee. "I'm going to be an apprentice to a sorcerer. That should count, right?"

Maria drank from her own cup. "You know it's not that easy, right? Do you have any leads?"

"I'm glad you asked." I reached into my pocket and withdrew a folded up piece of printer paper, only a little damp from sweat.

Maria unfolded it, reading each line carefully.

"You're going to try to become an apprentice to Sorcerer Bastion Edwards?"

"There is no try," I corrected her. "I *will* be his apprentice."

Rather than give the piece of paper back to me, Maria held onto it for a second, scanning it from side to side. "Sorcerer Edwards is kind of famous. He's the Chairman of the Sorcerers Guild Council. I just don't know if it's realistic."

Snatching the piece of paper back from Maria, I read from it aloud. "Roy Nakamura. Thank you for your inquiry. It would be my pleasure to interview you for a position as my apprentice." I put the paper down on the table between us. "You hear that? A pleasure!"

Marias shoulders dropped. "I just don't think you should get your hopes up. Have you considered any other options?"

I laughed. "I don't need other options. I did my research Maria, and Sorcerer Edwards is exactly what I need. He's the Chairman of the Council, has connections throughout the Guild. He's a former dueler. In fact, he's a former EndGame champion."

Maria sighed. We had known each other a long time, and she knew when to give up.

There are three types of magic users in modern Vegas society. The system evolved in the early 1900's and was relatively stable by the time the 1950's came along and the Vegas Act ended the requirement for Americans to have internal passports and special permission in order to visit (or leave) the city.

The first and most famous type of magic user, the kind featured in most books and movies about Las Vegas, are wizards. Wizards are magic users who swear fealty to one of the Branches of magic and enter into an apprentice program. After several years as an apprentice, they take some sort of secret test, then undergo the Marking ceremony at which they receive a giant tattoo of their Branch's symbol on the right side of their neck. Once Marked, they are full fledged wizards. Ethnic Atlantians (at least those who stayed in the city), always became wizards for the Branch their family was a part of, and they made up at least half of the wizard population. There were a growing number of non-Atlantians who were allowed to become wizards as well.

Wizards formed the core of a Branch's fighting force, but also filled all the key administrative positions, which was especially important in the post-Vegas Act world where the Branches' control of casinos made them more like a business venture and less like the traditional Atlantian tribal unit from which they had descended. It was not unusual for a hedge fund manager who wanted to invest in a Vegas casino to sit down at a table with a handful of accountants and lawyers, headed by a wizard with a giant neck tattoo, a katana at his side, and an MBA from an Ivy League school.

The second type of magic users are sorcerers, those who belong to the Sorcerers Guild. Traditionally, a person who wanted to become a sorcerer would become an apprentice to an already existing sorcerer, however more and more people were opting instead to get a Bachelor of Magic at one of Las Vegas' colleges. After completing an apprenticeship, or a degree, the magic user applied to the Sorcerers Guild for recognition.

Unlike wizards, sorcerers were not controlled by a particular Branch, and in theory that was the appeal of being a sorcerer (the ability to be free of Branch tyranny). However, the Guild itself was required to swear fealty to the Branch system as a whole, and individual members were subject to being summoned by Branch leaders if they were perceived as trouble makers. Guild members were also forced to pay the "Tribute," a tax of ten percent of their magically derived income (as well as a ten dollar donation each time they visited the Guild headquarters) to a central fund that was divided up among the Branches. Isolated attempts at rebellion were quickly crushed in vicious magical battles that were conveniently ignored by the civil authorities.

In most books and movies, sorcerers are the bad guys. They're greedy magical swindlers in mystical black sorcerer's cloaks who prey on Vegas tourists and are valiantly defeated by the noble and majestic wizards in their sparkling white leather outfits. In reality, sorcerers were a much more varied bunch. Some were involved with business, others taught at magic colleges, and some did contract work for the Branches. Then there were those, like wave watchers, who engaged in the seedier pursuits the city had to offer.

Finally there were magicians, a generic term that literally meant "any magic user" (thus a wizard or sorcerer would technically be a type of "magician"), but in practice was used to refer to anyone who was not a sworn wizard or a member of the Sorcerers Guild. Magicians were often involved with low-level business, like selling magical trinkets or reading fortunes, and sometimes did odd jobs for the Branches in order to get by. The chief of security for the Spartacus Casino is a wizard, but the person in the backroom who works twelve hour shifts using scrying spells to see if anyone is cheating at roulette? He's probably an underpaid magician.

The Branches forbid anyone from using magic without their permission, and although the Branches didn't have any authority under the Las Vegas Penal or Civil Codes, in practice the civilian authorities did not interfere with them when it came to magic. Magicians were forced to pay for a Branch Stamp in order to practice magic (sorcerers were exempt from the Stamp, so long as they paid the Tribute). The Branches took an almost sadistic pleasure in their sporadic and arbitrary crackdowns on magicians who practiced magic without a Branch Stamp. Sometimes when they were bored, they would extort or beat up shop owners who had the Stamp, just to show they could.

It was to combat this threat that Maria's group, Magic First, had been formed. During senior year of college, Maria was impressed by the civil rights movements of the twentieth century and became convinced that magician rights were the next hot button topic. Similarly minded college activists, along with several fed-up magicians, had set-up "Magic First" a couple years earlier. Maria contacted them before graduation, and they told her that as long as she was willing to sleep on a couch, and spend half of each year fundraising door to door to pay for said couch, she was welcome to come.

As Maria and I walked through the Hyperion casino several hours later, along the edge of their famed artificial river, it occurred to me that I was not completely sure whether it was day or night. The building seemed to think it was day, the lights in the ceiling blasting forth something that could pass for sunlight. Presumably these lights could be dimmed to give off a more night-like aura when appropriate, although I had no idea whether this was ever done.

We were in one of five large chambers that made up the river walk. Each one had a geographical theme (we were in Italy) that informed the style of the shops and restaurants surrounding us on all sides. There were various magical vendors selling amulets and potions that promised a thousand different results. Magical performers flitted in and out of the shops, displaying tricks that would be impossible without the magical arts.

The mix of tourists, locals, and performers walking along the artificial river had one thing in common. No one had a destination. Out on the Strip people walked to get somewhere, hustling and cutting each other off when convenient. Inside the Hyperion's artificial river, people did not rush. They didn't walk to get somewhere, they walked for the sake of walking. They walked because this place was magical, and they wanted to soak it in for as long as possible.

Maria stopped mid-step, and I tightened my grip on her hand.

"I think we should go to Venice for our honeymoon," she said. It was decisive, as if it were the conclusion to a long train of thought.

Recoiling, I took a small step back, then remembered to stay close, and willed my hand not to pull away from hers. I tried to think of the right response.

"Honeymoon, huh?" I said, after a long pause that was more of an answer to her question than the answer itself. "Shouldn't we at least set a date for the wedding first?"

Maria dropped her hands to her sides. "Wrong answer." Hands now firmly on her hips, she looked up, searching the distant ceiling for answers.

"Okay, this girl has just mentioned the word 'honeymoon.' You can't just laugh it off as a joke."

"But what girl is going to seriously talk about a honeymoon at this point? You said we were pretending to be on a first date!"

Maria shook her head. "It doesn't matter. You never laugh off a girl's feelings. Didn't Skylar teach you that?"

"Hey, you agreed not to mention She Who Must Not Be Named."

"And you agreed to take this seriously. You were also holding my hand completely wrong." Maria grabbed my hand again, overcoming my half-hearted resistance.

"You're supposed to be gently caressing my fingers to show you find me attractive." She demonstrated. "Or, at times like this, gently squeezing to show you're there. You are not, under any circumstances, to be holding my hand like it's baggage you're trying not to drop." My hand fell from hers.

I mulled this over for a second, spending a precious moment gazing into the artificial river beside me for inspiration. "What if I hold it like it's a creature I'm trying to prevent from escaping?" I smiled at Maria as I said this. I've always been told I have a crooked smile, and I think the combination came out as creepy rather than charming.

Maria drew her lips together. "Roy Nakamura," she said in her best exasperated motherly voice. "Was that your attempt at flirting?"

"Yes ma'am," I said, defeated.

Maria smiled. "Yeah, don't do that."

"I just don't think someone is going to make a honeymoon joke on a first date."

"Guy who hasn't been on a first date in four years says what?"

I tried my best not to laugh, but I failed. Various other couples (actual couples, not pretend ones like us) wandered the banks of the Hyperion's artificial river. They ran the full gambit from new couples, holding hands because they couldn't stand to be out of physical contact for even a moment, to elderly individuals who held hands so that if they fell, they would pull their partner down with them.

"How much longer does the river go?"

Maria raised an eyebrow. "Are you in a hurry to get somewhere?"

"It's not like that. I just…" I couldn't find the words. "I just want it to be tomorrow already. I'm ready to meet Sorcerer Bastion Edwards. I made it here to Vegas, I'm ready for my life to start."

Without warning, Maria skipped away from me and towards a small bridge that connected one bank of the river to the other. I caught up with her just as she reached the middle and stopped, turning so she could look over the edge of the bridge at the water flowing below her.

"Where do you think the water goes?" Maria asked.

"To the end of the river?"

Maria laughed. She spun around, leaning against the railing and looking at me with her warm brown eyes. "It's your first night in Las Vegas Roy. Enjoy it."

"I'll enjoy it more after the interview, after I'm a sorcerer's apprentice."

"Look around." Maria swept her hand, showing off the shops and shoppers around us. "Wasn't your dream always to come to Las Vegas? Haven't you finally accomplished it?"

"Yeah, but my dream was to come here and then become a famous sorcerer. I highly doubt that Skylar will regret dumping me if I can't even manage to get a job."

"You fulfilled the first part of your dream," Maria pressed. "Enjoy that. Take pleasure in that. If you can't enjoy the little things, you'll never enjoy the big ones." She paused. "And please don't tell me the only reason you're doing this is to get back at Skylar. I mean 'She Who Must Not Be Named.'"

Maria pushed herself off the railing and exited the bridge, merging back into the flow of people walking along the artificial river.

"It's not the only reason," I said, hopping after her.

Maria's favorite word was "practically." It started in seventh grade, when she discovered the word "literally," and was reprimanded by our English teacher (in front of the whole class) after using it in literally every sentence. The result was that Maria refused to use the word "literally" ever again, even in situations where it would be appropriate. "Practically" had come to take its place.

"Can you believe that Roy? The performers are practically walking on water!"

The two of us were standing in front of the fountains outside the Hyperion casino, watching their famous hourly show. The show started with a blast of music (something classical, I didn't know the name), as a dozen magicians stood at the base of the fountain and bowed to the audience, a mix of tourists who happened to be walking down the Strip at the time and people like Maria and I who had come for the show. The magicians then turned around to face the large pool of water in front of the casino and raised their hands in unison, chanting spells as they did so.

Geysers appeared in the pool, straight lines of water shooting up into the air. Then, in time with the music, the geysers moved from side to side, curling around to form intricate patterns that a normal fountain could never create.

Then, six of the magicians walked out onto the surface of the water. I had heard speculation they were levitating an inch off the water's surface, not really walking on water, but the effect was the same. While the six magicians, now standing in the middle of the pool, continued to direct the streams of water, the six magicians still on land pointed their hands at the water below the first six. The six wizards in the pool rose, propelled upward by slabs of water that detached from the pool.

Maria grabbed my shoulders and shook me. "How awesome is this? Is this not practically the coolest thing you've ever seen?"

"The videos don't do it justice," I said, taking a step back.

Someone bumped into me from behind. "Move," declared a large voice. I looked up, it took some time, into the eyes of the man who spoke. He was taller than me, easily six foot four. The man was wearing a black T-shirt with "Hollywood" written on the front in a font that had once been white, but was now a mix of yellow and some sort of sauce. He weighed twice what I did, and every pound of his existence was glaring at me.

"Sorry." I started to move to the side.

"What are you doing?" Maria said. I couldn't tell whether she was talking to me or Mr. Hollywood. "We were here first."

The man looked down at Maria, then at me, then back to her. "You're with him?" he finally said.

"Maria," I started to say, "let's just…"

"Yes, I'm with him," Maria said, glaring back at the man. "And we were here first. If you want a better view, come earlier."

The man shrugged his shoulders. "Whatever." He walked away.

Once he was a safe distance away, I allowed myself to exhale. "You didn't have to do that."

"Yeah I did. That guy was a creep, and he was bothering you."

"I mean, I can take care of myself," I stuttered. "It's not your job to look out for me."

Maria smiled. "I'm your friend Roy. That's exactly what my job is."

Applause erupted around us. The show was over. As one, the two of us walked away from the fountain.

On the walk back to my car, I had my first encounter with the woman who would soon change my life forever. It was a light pole anchored into the Strip, the kind that serves as a canvas for all sorts of flyers and announcements.

While waiting at a crosswalk for the light to change, I noticed one particular flyer on the light pole, one that resembled an Old West style wanted poster. It featured the face of an Asian woman who could best be described as "professionally attractive," the kind of face that would look stunning in a business suit or cocktail gown, but out of place in a mini-skirt at a run-down night club. She was in her late-thirties, and something about her eyes, which stared right out of the two dimensional poster into mine, seemed hauntingly familiar.

Below the face the poster read, "Sorceress Valentine: Wanted for crimes against the Branches." Under that, in smaller writing that I had to strain to see, it read, "by order of Artimus Cantor, Archmage, Branch Shaskauer."

The light from the light pole illuminated the wanted poster. In the soft yellow light I could barely make out some flies lazily flying up toward the bulbs, like falling angels trying to fly back into heaven.

"I know the fountains show is run by the Branches, so I should hate it, but I still watch it whenever I can."

I ignored Maria's words and studied the poster more closely, focusing on the bottom. Artimus Cantor, Archmage, Branch

Shaskauer. At the time I didn't know what that meant, but later, after I became a sorcerer, I learned more about Branch politics than I ever wanted to.

The Branches of Las Vegas are organized like royal families. The leadership, the position of Branch Lord, is passed from father to son. The second in charge of the Branch is the Chief Wizard, who administers the Branch and ensures that the Lord's will is carried out.

The Archmage is head of security for the Branch. He's in charge of making sure the members of the Branch are safe by assessing and defending against the threats from the other Branches and from the outside world. The Chief Wizard is a political position, so it usually goes to some friend of the Branch, almost always a full-blooded Atlantian. The position of Archmage on the other hand is purely merit-based.

The position can be very powerful, especially in times of conflict. Ricardo Parthenia, the Lord of Branch Parthenia, had been Archmage during the Wizard War. Even though his father was still alive during the war (and was thus Branch Lord), most people considered Ricardo the de facto leader of the Branch at the time.

"Roy, what are you waiting for?"

Maria stood beside me, looking at the wanted poster.

"Ahh, Sorceress Valentine," she said.

"You've heard of her?"

Maria laughed. "Everyone's heard of her. She's one of the most famous magic users in Las Vegas. One of the most powerful too. Sorceress Valentine, the time travelling sorceress. The one person daring enough to defy both the Branches and the Sorcerers Guild."

"She's a time traveler?"

"Personally I think it's made up. But some say she's from the distant past, maybe even from Atlantis, when magic was common. She found a way to go forward into the future so she could go to a place where her powers, which were only average in her time, would be, like, really powerful. Other people say she's from the future. They say that in the future there is practically no more magic, so she came back in time to be with other people who were like her."

The light turned and the mass of people around us started walking towards the other side of the street. We stepped away and moved to catch up with them. From an inanimate wanted poster, the eyes of Sorceress Valentine continued to stare out long after I had gone.

2. Sorcerers and Wizards

Most people want to be wizards. I blame media bias. On any given day there are at least three prime-time shows about Las Vegas, and every week there are at least two police procedurals that have a special episode set in Las Vegas. Each one features majestic, honorable wizards facing off against a bad guy who, nine times out of ten, is a sorcerer. On top of that, there's the security of being part of a Branch, of knowing that once you're in, you will be taken care of for life.

The reason why I wanted to be a sorcerer, had always wanted to be one, was due to the fact that as an eight year old I found and read *Call Me Sorcerer*. If I had fallen on top of a book titled *Call Me Wizard* instead, everything might have been different.

So who becomes a sorcerer? There are some people who like the idea of freedom, rebelling against the thought of learning magic only to remain in servitude to a Branch for the rest of their life. Along similar lines, some non-Atlantians fear that due to their race, they will never excel to the top if they join a Branch.

Then there is the largest group of sorcerers, those who went to a Branch, applied to train as a wizard, and were turned down. This led to the common stereotype that sorcerers are those who were rejected from being wizards.

This was the rationale behind the first question that Sorcerer Bastion Edwards, Chairman of the Sorcerers Guild Council, asked me when I interviewed with him.

"Are you here because you applied to be a wizard and were rejected?"

Of course back then I wasn't aware of this stereotype. My first exposure to magic was *Call Me Sorcerer* after all, an influential tale of the glamour and spectacle of being a sorcerer. It just seemed natural to me that everyone else would want to become a sorcerer as well.

"Well, did you?"

"Uhh, no. No sir. No I did not."

Gray eyes gazed down at me from a set of reading glasses perched at the edge of a long nose. Sorcerer Bastion Edwards was north of sixty. His tight clothes did nothing to hide his obvious obesity. His thinning gray hair was brushed over his head in an attempt to hide his baldness.

"Then why did you come here?" he said. His tone was business, uncaring.

"I came because I want to be a dueler."

"There are wizards who are duelers," Sorcerer Edwards pointed out. "In fact they probably duel more frequently than we do."

After years of telling Skylar about my life goals, I suddenly had trouble putting them into words.

"But I don't want to serve under some Branch. I want to be free, I want to be a sorcerer. I want to win EndGame!" To underscore this last point, I gestured at the bookshelf behind Sorcerer Edwards' desk. Sitting in a place of honor, next to a plaque that identified him as the Chairman of the Sorcerers Guild Council, was a slab of black marble.

Sorcerer Bastion Edwards
EndGame Champion
1979

Sorcerer Edwards turned to see what I was pointing at, an action that at his age seemed to involve every muscle in his body. He made a grunt when he saw I had pointed at his trophy, and when he turned back there was something on his face that resembled understanding.

"So, you're one of those," he said.

It was clear I had made a mistake.

"Tell me, Roy Nakamura, do you have a degree in practical magic?"

I shook my head.

"How about experience as a magician, or perhaps as a junior apprentice."

I shook my head again.

"Then how do you expect to be my apprentice?" Bastion Edwards' face started to turn red. "I am the leader of the Sorcerers Guild. As you yourself pointed out, I am a former EndGame champion. Being my apprentice would mean you are set for the rest of your career. It is an honor! You cannot simply waltz into my office and expect me to elevate you to a position that most spend years seeking."

The air around me felt thick, and I had trouble breathing. This was not the way it was supposed to go. I reached into my pocket and grasped the printout of the email, still folded up next to my wallet.

"Well, what do you have to say to that?" Sorcerer Edwards said.

In *Call Me Sorcerer*, the protagonist arrives in Las Vegas and becomes an apprentice to a famous sorcerer who teaches him the way of magic. He doesn't fail his first interview and not even have anything to say.

"That's what I thought."

There was no way I would let this end without getting a word in. I summoned all the courage I could and returned Sorcerer Edwards' gaze. "If I'm not qualified to be your apprentice, then why did you interview me?"

Sorcerer Edwards sat up in his chair. From behind his glasses, he looked down with disgust.

"Roy Nakamura, I agreed to interview you for one reason and one reason only. I was curious to meet someone who had the audacity to believe that he could show up to Las Vegas, and without putting in any work, any time, any effort, become an apprentice to the Chairman of the Sorcerers Guild Council."

His rant done, Sorcerer Edwards leaned back in his chair. A smug smile of satisfaction crept across his face. He made a gesture, muttered a word, and the door behind me opened. "My secretary will see you out."

Sorcerer Edwards' office was at Magic Hall, the headquarters of the Sorcerers Guild located right on the Strip. Outside Magic Hall, the hot Vegas sun beat down on my face. I took a deep breath and looked out at the traffic passing by on the street in front of me.

Every car on the Strip looked like it had somewhere to go. Each driver was focused on his or her mission for the day. Even though I was outside, the air seemed stuffy, oppressive. I took another deep breath, but I felt like I couldn't breathe. I felt like I needed more air than I could inhale normally.

This couldn't be it, this couldn't be how the story ended. Sorcerer Bastion Edwards was supposed to take me under his wing and train me to be a sorcerer, just like in *Call Me Sorcerer*. I wanted to run back in there. I had to run back in there. If I could just make him see how much this meant to me, he had to give me a chance.

"How did it go?"

Maria stood in front of me. Despite my assurances that I would be okay, she had insisted on waiting outside while I went in for my interview.

I did my best to smile.

"It was perfect," I said. "Sorcerer Edwards told me I was a promising candidate, and he would call me back within a day."

"That's amazing!" Maria said. "You must be thrilled."

I kept smiling. "Absolutely."

"And, that will give you a day to help me out."

"Help you out?"

"It's just for an hour. And before you ask, it's unpaid."

The old woman stared directly at the camera. She was thin, gaunt. The lines on her skin looked more like battle scars than signs of age. The woman remained perfectly motionless, except for her lips. She showed little external emotion, but you could see the emotion was there, just below the surface.

"I remember when they came to my shop," she said in a slight Italian accent. "It was a Wednesday night. Tourists had all gone home. I decide to close up early. There are three of them, all wizards, all bearing the mark of Branch Shaskauer."

Maria looked up from the camera's view finder. "And what happened next, Ms. Saltzer?"

"They say I am a fraud, that I am selling fake amulets out of my shop. I tell them they are wrong. I would never deceive my customers. They are my lifeblood, my only source of income.

"Then, they tell me if it is real magic, I must have a Branch Stamp. I say I am not a wizard like them, I do not need to serve the Branches. Besides I am poor, I cannot pay the price of the Stamp even if I wanted to. And then, then they do this to me."

For the first time the woman moved. I realized I had been holding my breath. She raised her left hand, revealing it to the camera. At first it looked white, like it had been dipped in white paint, but as my eyes probed it I could see it was covered in scar tissue.

"What did you do?" Maria asked. "Did you call the police?"

The woman spit on the ground in front of her. "The police do nothing. The Branches own the city, the Branches own the police. But the Branches don't own magic. No matter how hard they try, they cannot control the magic. And so I will keep practicing, no matter the cost."

"What about the Sorcerers Guild?" Maria said. "Couldn't you go to them?"

"I am not a sorceress, I am only magician." The woman shook her head. "The Guild would not do anything for me. I cannot become a sorceress, for I am far too old to pass the Trials. Besides, even if I become sorceress, then I must swear allegiance to the Branches and pay the Tribute, like all the other sorcerers."

"But at least you wouldn't be subject to violence anymore," Maria said.

"No, instead they come during the day," the woman replied. "And instead of breaking my windows and smashing my amulets on the ground, they produce order from the Guild and confiscate all my amulets."

The old woman shook her head. "No, there is no solution, no help, no hope. Not for people like me."

Maria helped me put the camera back in its case after marking the tape from it as "Interview 37, July 3, 1998."

"How many of these interviews have you done?"

Maria grimaced. "Too many." She straightened and picked up the camera bag. "The sad thing is, you get used to it after a while."

"It's hard to believe," I said, fiddling with the tripod. I still couldn't believe Sorcerer Bastion Edwards had rejected me. He hadn't even given me a chance to really explain myself, to tell him what being a sorcerer meant to me. What magic meant to me. Surely if he really heard me out, knew how serious I was, he would give me a chance.

Maria was looking down at me. I was still fiddling with the tripod.

"I mean, I'm sure what happened to that woman happens occasionally," I said. "But I can't imagine that all the Branches are that evil."

Maria made a half smile. "Once you come along to a few more of these, let me know if you still feel that way. Now let's get going."

To celebrate my lie about how well my interview went with Sorcerer Edwards, Maria insisted that she pay for dinner.

"I can't believe the Branches," Maria said as we walked through a casino on our way to the restaurant she had picked out. She gestured at the luxury shops on either side of the casino hallway. "All this wealth, and they spend their time oppressing those around them."

"For someone who hates the Branches, you sure do spend a lot of time in their casinos and restaurants."

Maria stopped. "Very funny." She looked up at me with mock defiance, but I had known her for years, and I could see the genuine hurt behind her face.

"I'm sorry," I said. "I didn't mean it."

"I know." Maria resumed walking. "All this must be overwhelming. I know it was when I first moved here. But things will work out. You've only been here a day, and you practically have a job offer from *the* Sorcerer Bastion Edwards. That's got to count for something."

Maria reached out a hand and patted my shoulder. Her touch had reassured me many times throughout the years. Despite the fact I had lied to one of my best friends about my interview, and I had no plan for how I was going to get a job and stay in this city, for a moment it seemed like everything really would work out.

"Maria?"

"Yes?"

"Maria, I… I…"

Whatever I was about to say was lost in time, because the upscale clothing shop behind Maria chose that moment to explode in a purple blossom of sound and glass.

"Why do you love me?"

It was night, and Skylar and I were at our favorite spot at the top of the parking structure next to our dorm, looking out over the Los Angeles skyline. We had been together for a year, and it was not the first time she had asked me the question.

"I don't know, I just do," I said, keeping it as casual as possible.

"But why me?" she insisted. "Why not someone else?"

With my right hand I stroked her jet black hair. It felt soft to the touch. I turned so I could look into her dark eyes, surrounded my flawless skin.

"Because I love *you*," I said. "I choose to love you. Isn't that enough?"

My blackout lasted for just a second. When I came to, I found I had fallen on top of Maria, sheltering her from the blast. I rolled over onto a ground covered with shattered glass. The glass was uncomfortable, but it didn't cut me. The windows had been crumble glass, or some other material which, via magic, had been given those same safety properties.

Maria stood up, looking around wildly at the carnage surrounding us. Dozens of people were lying on the ground, some unmoving and some pushing themselves up into sitting positions. Maria reached down an arm and I accepted it. My back hurt, but with Maria's assistance I managed to stand up.

There was a man dressed completely in black. He was running through the smoking gap where the glass storefront used to be, into the upscale clothing shop behind it. Someone screamed. Maria, dazed, was still looking around.

"What's happening?" I asked.

"I don't know," Maria said. "I don't know."

The man in black ran out of the shop moments later, a large duffle bag in one hand, partially zipped, filled with so much cash that some of it was spilling out.

Behind me, the low sound of moans from recovering tourists was broken by the sound of running feet and people jumping out of the way. A solitary figure came into my vision, cutting through the bits of smoke still clinging to the ground.

The figure was wearing white pants and a white leather jacket. The jacket was open at the front, four large silver clasps on either side flailing as he ran. Underneath the jacket was a large baldric carrying a dozen tubes of various shapes and sizes. To his left side hung a katana, black handle and black scabbard, and to his right side was a handgun in a holster attached directly to his thigh, the straps barely visible over his white pants. But none of these were his most striking feature. That honor belonged to the giant tattoo that took up the entirety of the right side of his neck. Partially obscured by the collar of his jacket, it nonetheless revealed itself to be a black square with one horizontal and one diagonal line inscribed inside of it. The mark of Branch Merkasia.

I recognized the uniform from every television show or movie ever made about Las Vegas. He was a wizard.

I was so caught up in watching the wizard, I didn't notice the man in black, duffel bag in one hand, run towards us as well. The man in black dropped the duffel, and in a smooth motion used his now free arm to push me away and grab Maria's waist, pulling her close to him. His other hand was just inches away from Maria's neck. He muttered something, and the hand began to glow a deep red.

"Don't move or she gets it," he yelled at the wizard bearing down on him. I couldn't move. Maria didn't either, but she didn't look frozen like me. Instead her eyes looked almost at peace.

The wizard did not even slow his run. "*Shoka!*" the wizard yelled, stretching out his palm in front of him. The glowing red hand inches away from Maria's throat jerked back. It began to turn from deep red into a light blue.

"*Pereling!*" the wizard yelled, still running, this time putting two of his fingers together and pointing them off to the side. The knees of the man crumpled.

Maria took the opportunity to jump away from the man and ran towards me. I quickly grabbed her in my arms.

The man in black tried to stand, but he was frozen, immobilized. The wizard slowed to a walk, ignoring both me and Maria, and calmly strode towards the man's frozen figure, pulling out his katana as he went. The blade glowed, seeming to generate its own light rather than merely reflecting the light that hit it.

Afraid the wizard was going to behead the man, I started to step forward, but I felt Maria hold me still as she unburied her face from my shoulder. "This is a Branch matter Roy," Maria said. "That man committed a crime on Branch property. The Branch is going to deal with it." I struggled against her. "We're not in Los Angeles anymore Roy. This is how things work on the Strip."

Reluctantly, I let the scene fold out in front of me. The wizard approached the knelt figure, who by now had stopped struggling and looked up with resigned eyes. The wizard lowered his sword so the point touched the man's neck.

"Yield or die," the wizard said.

The man gulped, then in a raspy voice whispered, "I yield."

The wizard put the sword back in its scabbard. He raised his wrist to his mouth. "Control, this is walter three-one-four. Contact Las Vegas PD and tell them I have a suspect in custody. Out."

The entire episode lasted only a minute, but I had a hard time catching my breath.

"Are you okay, miss?" Maria and I turned. The wizard, the one who had saved Maria's life, was standing behind us. Behind him, two security guards were talking to the robber, still kneeling on the ground.

Maria smiled. "I'm fine. Thank you so much for what you did."

"Just doing my job, miss." The wizard smiled as well.

Before I had only seen the uniform, but now I glimpsed the person wearing it. The wizard was in his mid to late twenties, white, at least a couple inches taller than me. His neck seemed just a bit too large for his face, but he was muscular enough that it wasn't too obvious.

"I'm Karl Johnsen," the wizard said.

"Well thank you again, Wizard Johnsen, I'm Maria." Maria reached out her hand, and the wizard shook it gently.

"Please, just call me Karl."

"In that case thank you again. Karl. Is there anything I can do to repay you?"

"I am a sworn wizard of Branch Merkasia. You do not need to do anything to repay me." He paused. "But if you would accompany me to a meal, say lunch tomorrow? That would be thanks above and beyond anything I would deserve."

"I love lunch," Maria said. She reached up her right hand and brushed a stray strand of hair away from her face and behind her ear.

I stuck out my hand between them. "I'm Roy."

Despite our brush with death, or maybe because of it, Maria was still determined to eat dinner at a place she had heard of that claimed to serve authentic Ancient Atlantian cuisine. This was despite the fact that, according to Maria, historians didn't know what Ancient Atlantians ate, and thus the menu was pure conjecture.

"It's not a date," Maria said. "He's a wizard. He goes against everything I stand for."

"I'm pretty sure it's a date. At least, it sounded like a date."

Maria looked down the way we had come. "I know it's somewhere around here."

The restaurant was supposed to be in the Last Emperor Casino, but each time we took a hallway, we ended up back on the gaming floor.

"So you're telling me that a random guy, after saving your life, asks you if you want to have lunch with him, and it's not a date."

Maria sighed. "Look, if it bothers you that much you can come."

"Why would I want to come on your date?"

"It's not a date!"

A few tables away I saw a sparkle. I stopped. Maria kept walking for a few steps (I think she might have kept talking as well), then stopped and turned when she realized I was no longer beside her.

"What is it?" she asked.

We were standing by a card table situated at the border between the slot machines and the table games. I nodded towards one table in particular, a couple down from us, where a small crowd was gathered around a solitary player. Despite this wall of observers, I could just make out the details of the player, and more importantly, what he was wearing.

"The man over there, the one playing cards," I said, drawn towards the table as if in a trance. "He's wearing a sorcerer's cloak."

Maria followed after me and squinted her eyes towards the table.

"He certainly is."

The table was just a few feet in front of me, as close as I could get to the observers without becoming one myself.

"Do you think he's a wave watcher?"

Maria looked around instinctively, then back at me. "Don't joke about that Roy. People might overhear you."

But I was already tuning out Maria's words. All I was focused on was the sorcerer before me. The item of clothing draped around his shoulders, the thing Maria had confirmed was a sorcerer's cloak, was no ordinary black cape. It was difficult to describe, or even comprehend, although I had read countless descriptions growing up. At first glance it looked like a simple black cloak with an intricate pattern of silver thread sewn into the surface. Then every second, or fraction of a second, the light that reflected off the cloak (or perhaps that was generated by the cloak) would shift, and a new pattern of silver lines would emerge just as the old one disappeared.

The dancing lights of the cloak made it hard for me to rip my eyes from it, but once I did I saw it wasn't just the magical marvel of the cloak that had drawn the observers, it was the sorcerer himself. The sorcerer was in his mid-twenties. Something about him screamed "frat boy," though I couldn't say exactly what it was. It might have been his brown hair, which looked deliberately unruly, as if he had spent an hour making sure it looked like he had spent no time on it at all.

For the most part though, he looked like a completely normal human being. He was the kind of person I would never recognize or give a second glance to if I ran into him in downtown Los Angeles not wearing his sorcerer's cloak. Except we weren't in downtown Los Angeles, we were in Las Vegas, and he was wearing a sorcerer's cloak. And that made all the difference.

Sitting at that table, there was something about him, something at once mysterious and majestic, that had drawn so many to watch. I took another couple steps forward, and now I was one of the observers. I could see he was playing blackjack, and I could hear the voices of those around him.

"Very nice, sir," the dealer said as he turned over the additional card the sorcerer had requested, revealing a total of twenty.

"How on earth did he know to hit on a seventeen?" came a voice from next to me belonging to a gorgeous blonde creature. "You're supposed to stand on that hand."

"He must be a wave watcher," said an older man wearing a bolo tie and a cowboy hat standing on my other side. "He must be, there's no other way he could know to hit on that."

The sorcerer was pretending to ignore the voices around him while no doubt reveling in the attention. He was cool and collected, calm and confident. With a deft gesture he removed the tall stack of chips from the betting circle in front of him, as well as the tall stack the dealer had just placed there in payment for his winning bet. He removed a single chip from one of the stacks and put it back into the betting circle.

"Why is he lowering his bet?" a voice said from somewhere around me. Others murmured in agreement.

The dealer dealt a queen to the sorcerer, then a ten to himself, then a ten to the sorcerer.

The dealer removed a final card from the shoe, the hole card, and placed it face down in front of himself. There was a sharp intake of breath from those around.

"Hit?" asked the dealer.

The sorcerer shook his head, motioning to stand.

The dealer nodded and flipped over his hole card. It was an ace. The dealer had a blackjack, and reached out to take the sorcerer's single chip from the betting circle.

"How on earth…" said the blonde next to me. "There is no way he could have known that would happen."

The old man adjusted his bolo tie. "He's a wave watcher, he must be, there's no other way." He took a half-step closer to the table. "Excuse, me, young man, are you a wave watcher? Is that how you knew to reduce your bet on that hand?"

The frat-boy sorcerer looked to the old man, then looked to the dealer and smirked. "So do they just let, like, anyone in these days?" He looked around, waiting for a response. "I mean, isn't this what bouncers are for?"

"Oh please tell us," said the blonde woman next to me.

Upon hearing the female voice, the sorcerer turned, saw the source of the voice, then smiled. It was the same formal smile a politician might make, conveying both warmth and aloofness. "Kind lady," he said. "Wave watching is against the rules of this casino, as well as against the law in Las Vegas, and I am no rule breaker."

"Oh, I see." The disappointment was obvious on her face.

The sorcerer snuck a glance at the dealer, then looked back at the blonde. "However, if I *were* to engage in wave watching, I certainly would not be able to reveal it out loud." The sorcerer smiled again, that same politician smile, and winked.

The blonde lit up, and turned to me, placing a hand on my shoulder. "I knew it," she whispered.

"Roy, what are you doing?"

Maria was standing behind me, looking around.

"Just watching the sorcerer play blackjack," I said. "Is something wrong with that?"

"We should probably get going." Maria continued to look around, as if some security guard might recognize a member of Magic First's finest scoping out a casino floor.

"Well, okay. Let's go then."

Maria started to step away, but I paused for just a second, soaking in a final glance at that sorcerer's cloak. I pulled myself away and followed after.

In *Call Me Sorcerer*, the protagonist makes his living as a wave watcher. Although he goes on to become a famous sorcerer, and an EndGame champion, that's not how he starts the book. The first third of the book consists of him wandering around Las Vegas, picking up odd jobs, and trying to learn magic. When he finally does find someone who can teach him, he learns how to wave watch. That way he can make money while learning to duel.

"What's wave watching?"

Despite the prevalence of wave watching in popular culture, people continued to ask me that question for months after I moved to Las Vegas.

"Well, have you heard of card counting?" I would usually reply. "You know, the thing where people remember which cards are played so they know the probabilities of which card will come next?

"Wave watching is like card counting, except with magic. The magic user casts a spell that monitors which cards have been played, and then he can use that to figure out what cards will be played next."

"And the casinos allow that?" the listener always asks incredulously.

"Of course not. The casinos employ sorcerers or magicians who cast spells to look for wave watching spells, and then the wave watchers cast spells that fool those monitoring spells, and so on and so forth. It all gets complicated. You also have to keep in mind that a lot of sorcerers claim to be wave watchers, but very few are actually good enough to do so."

"So how do you know so much about wave watching," the person would finally say. "Aren't you a dueler?"

"There are plenty of famous duelers, but there are no famous wave watchers," I would say with a wink. "The whole point is that no one knows you're doing it."

When I saw the frat boy sorcerer wave watching, when I saw what it looked like to use magic to effect the world around me, I knew what I was going to do. Sorcerer Edwards might think I was nothing, Skylar might think I was nothing, but I was going to prove them all wrong. I was going to wave watch, I was going to succeed, and the powers that be would *have* to let me be an apprentice.

I was going to be a sorcerer.

Outside the Last Emperor, two magicians were "projecting a film." That's what Maria said it was called. They were dressed in all black and stood behind a gigantic white sheet, corners held taught by unseen forces. Even at night, the Las Vegas summer air sizzled, easily ninety degrees or more. The magicians, hands gesturing and mouths incanting, threw images against the sheet like shadow puppets in front of a fire, but with the added benefit of color.

The images were sometimes abstract, sometimes well defined ("Each person sees something a little different," Maria explained), like looking at clouds and not only trying to find shapes, but trying to assign them a meaning, trying to place them into a coherent narrative.

In high school, Maria didn't like to go to the movies by herself ("Sitting in a giant theatre all by myself? It just seems lonely"), so I always ended up going with her, no matter how bad a movie it was. There was one particular time senior year when she wanted me to take her to see a certain movie.

The Closest Exit, the movie Maria wanted to see, is an absolutely terrible romance film about a high school freshman who is dying of cancer. He manages to convince a popular cheerleader to help him with a list of ten things he wants to do before he dies. Through various hijinks, the two of them check off nine of the items on the list, and in the process the cheerleader learns to respect herself, or something like that. Then the boy dies, and the cheerleader fulfills his final item herself, which was to become a flight attendant and see the world.

It started off like any normal movie for us, Maria rolling her eyes in the dark every time the main character said something corny, and whispering snide comments to me in a voice just loud enough to elicit shushes from the serious viewers around us. But as the movie went on, Maria got more serious. The snide remarks slowed to a stop, then the eye rolls did as well. By the end of the movie, Maria's usual laugh was replaced by the soft sound of her sniffing. It was the first time I ever saw her cry.

"Each person sees something a little different," Maria said when I asked what the magicians were projecting onto the screen. And even though the setting was completely different, even though there was no logical connection, the abstract images shot onto the white sheet by the magicians made me think of going with Maria to see *The Closest Exit*. And just like that time, even though she was standing next to me, every couple seconds Maria would glance over to make sure I was still standing beside her. To make sure she wasn't alone.

3. My First Attempt at Wave Watching

During high school, I bought a book called *The Beginner's Guide to Wave Watching* from Magic Haven. My plan was to become a famous sorcerer, a dueler. Wave watching was beneath me. But based on how often it's featured in the media, and based on how prominently it was featured in *Call Me Sorcerer*, I was curious to learn more.

"Wave watching spells, like all spells, are composed of three elements," the book began. "The words, the gesture, and what the Atlantians call the *aetas*, the correct mental state. With simple memorization anyone can do the first two, but the third is the difference between a skilled magician and an amateur."

In high school I had practiced the spells, even taking out cards to make it seem more "realistic." But because it was outside of Vegas, I had no way of knowing if I was actually doing it correctly. It was like learning to play piano on an electric keyboard that wasn't plugged in. I could practice hitting the right keys in the right pattern, but I had no idea whether it was actually making music.

I set out for the Arabian Nights casino just after nine the next morning. It was the Fourth of July. There was no traffic, at least not yet. It only took fifteen minutes to get there from Maria's apartment, but my mind was a jumble of thoughts the whole way.

My phone rang just as I parked. It was Maria.

"Roy, are you okay? You were gone when I woke up."

I forced myself to smile, just in case Maria could tell through the phone. "You know me. I'm doing fine."

"Have you heard back from Sorcerer Edwards yet?"

It took me a second to understand what she was saying, to remember the lie I had told her.

"Yeah, he called me early this morning," I said. "Today's going to be my first day of work."

Maria seemed satisfied with the response. "Now don't forget, you're still joining me and Karl for lunch later today."

"Wouldn't miss it." I locked my car and started to walk towards the stairwell.

"It's not a date," Maria said. "In fact, it's practically the furthest thing from a date. I could never date a wizard."

"I didn't say it was a date." I reached the stairwell. "I said I'd be there."

"Oh, okay."

I started climbing down the stairs.

"It sounds like you're climbing down stairs," Maria said.

"I am."

We were both quiet for a moment. I wasn't sure if Maria had hung up or not, until I heard her speak.

"Well, I'll let you go then. See you in a couple hours."

"Yeah, see you then." I hung up.

I had arrived at the entrance to the Arabian Nights casino and hotel. As I approached the first set of sliding doors, they parted a few seconds before I expected them to, as if some magician had designed them to be that much more prescient than their brothers and sisters in office buildings throughout the rest of the world. As the doors opened, the space within let out a burst of cold air, raising me into a state of full alertness. Passing through the doors, I could hear the faint sound of the music of the casino floor. The music grew louder as I came to the second set of sliding doors, and once they opened and I stepped through, the music played to me at full blast as I stood on the casino floor itself.

The music was not a literal song, but a collection of all the sounds around me. If you want to compose the song that is a casino floor, here's how you do it. First, take the sound of the slot machines, the inane electronic beeping that they make every time a button is pressed or a payment is made. This is the base of the music. Add to that the clanking of coins, a shrill high note that manages to pierce through the rest of the noise, both from actual quarters coming out of the same slot machines, as well as the electronic imitation sound of quarters falling every time a minor jackpot is hit. There are the voices as well, and although they range across the spectrum from ecstatic to devastated, in aggregate they all blend together into a low hum that harmonizes with the sound of the coins.

Next, in a similar tonal register as the quarters, is the sound of glass. All around gamblers enjoy complementary drinks, necessitating the stream of cocktail waitresses that patrol the casino floor like cops on a beat, looking for empty glasses to snatch up and replace with full ones. The regular clink of glasses, like a cymbal, adds a staccato note to the casino melody.

Then there is the sound that most patrons like the most, the quiet sound of two chips hitting each other. Throughout the tables, gamblers from all backgrounds and all professions stare at cards on the table below them, thoughtfully stacking chips, and sometimes absentmindedly playing with those same chips, always careful not to touch the cards themselves. The sound of two chips hitting each other seems to reassure each gambler that things are not that bad. At least they have two chips, and if there are two chips, then they are not yet down to their last one.

On top of that, at a pitch most patrons were too distracted to notice, was the sound that drew me on like a siren's song, the sound of a card hitting the table. Cards, those magnificent, mysterious objects on which fortunes and empires can rise and fall. Faces and symbols that would all look the same to an average caveman, but which a modern man knew were anything but. All these sounds came together to form the music of the casino, and at that moment it was a song I loved more than any other melody in the world.

I stood inside the casino, looking out over the tables like a king surveying his kingdom. Outside, Vegas was ugly and dead, but inside here Vegas was still alive. And it was inviting me to come and play.

At this time of day the tables were mostly empty. The hardcore compulsive all-night gamblers had already gone home, but the hip young jet set had not yet arrived. I made one brief circuit around the blackjack pit, a collection of ten tables with varying minimums. Half were closed due to the lack of players, and of those open only one had a five dollar minimum, the lowest one was likely to find on the Strip. Looking around, half expecting some security guard to be waiting in the aisle, ready to pounce on me the moment I sat down, I took a seat on the far left of the table.

That was when I noticed the two other players at the table. The first, sitting in the middle, was a mess of a man. His pastel pink polo (at least it looked pink now, who knew what color it had originally been), had not been washed in some time. It certainly had not been washed since his last meal, half of which was on his shirt. His jeans, which might have fit him a few years ago, were slung low enough that when he sat, as he was doing at the table, an ample amount of belly cleavage was revealed to the eye. His ensemble was topped off with a cowboy hat, that while the only clean item he was wearing, somehow served to make him look even dirtier.

The other player, seated across from me at the far right seat, was his opposite in every way. She was an Asian woman wearing a meticulously clean black blouse and gray pants, which showed off her fit figure. Most notably, she was also wearing a sorcerer's cloak, just like the Frat Boy Sorcerer I saw gambling the day before. Like that other sorcerer's cloak, this one was decorated with a number of patterns woven into it with silver thread. Rather than just reflect the ambient light, the silver thread seemed to give off its own light. The light constantly waxed and waned, creating the illusion that the shapes were moving every time I moved my head.

Around the woman's neck were three golden chains, on each of which hung a small medallion. Her shoulder length black hair, devoid of any of the colorful streaks that every girl my age seemed to possess, framed a conservative looking face that placed her in her late-thirties, the only possible sign of age being slight wrinkles at the corner of her eyelids. Her eyes, however, looked a thousand years old, and they were staring right at me.

It was the same woman from the wanted poster I saw two days before. It was Sorceress Valentine.

I nodded politely at her, then dropped my gaze to avert those eyes. After a moment my eyes were drawn back-up to the gold chains, and the three medallions that hung on them. I knew they were tokens, that they symbolized something about the wearer. I tried to figure out what they might mean, but any possible meaning had fled my mind. Realizing I was now staring at Sorceress Valentine's chest, I jerked my gaze away from her and towards the dealer, taking my wallet out of my pocket and putting it on the table. Opening it, I withdrew five twenty dollar bills and put them on the table.

"ID please," said the dealer. My wallet was still on the table, so I easily slid out my California driver's license and thrust it through the air towards her. She took it and inspected it for a moment. It was all a formality. Somewhere in another room, a magician staring at a TV screen was casting an age verification spell on me, as well as anyone else who looked like they might be under twenty-one. The dealer handed me back my license, and putting it in my wallet, I slid my wallet back into my pocket. I risked a quick glance towards Sorceress Valentine, who was looking off into the distance with disinterest.

While the dealer had made a show of inspecting the license, I had been preparing my mind for what would come next.

Wave watching was a crime under Las Vegas law, but just barely. Some of the more explicit cheating methods (like "spoofing," in which a magician cast a spell to make cards show different numbers on their face), could result in a jail sentence if one was discovered using them. Wave watching on the other hand, even if it could be discovered and proved in a court of law, carried a sentence about as severe as a traffic ticket. However everyone knew the casinos in Las Vegas were not run by the government, they were run by the Branches. And if one were discovered using magic to take a part of their hard earned money, there was nothing to stop them from exacting revenge, something they often did in ways creative and devious enough to discourage imitators. Nevertheless, the prospect of easy money lured millions of people to Las Vegas each year. Maybe the danger was a part of it.

It certainly was for me. A part of me worried that the moment I cast my first spell, security would swoop in from every angle and tackle me. I remembered the burned hand of the woman Maria had interviewed the day before, and imagined what worse things the Branch wizards would do to me. The other player, the fat one, was probably a security guard himself, a plant put there because the Arabian Nights management knew I was coming.

While the dealer took my five twenty dollar bills and put them in the bill slot, I let my left hand, gently resting under the table on my left thigh, relax. In the softest voice I could, my lips pursed so there was barely an opening, I started to cast my spell.

"Hee de la chu zhu, fuh ts, numeral veedet, fanay kah na."

The two other players and the dealer didn't notice. No security guard jumped to knock me over. I started to twirl the fingers of my left hand, my mind envisioning the spell I needed to weave.

"Hee de la chu zhu, fuh ts, numeral veedet, fanay kah na."

My eyes closed for a moment, then opened. Nothing happened. A thought rushed over me. How did I know whether I was Signed? In all my dreaming as a kid, in all the planning I had done in the previous week, I had never considered the fact that, like half of the non-Atlantian population, I might be unSigned. I might be unable to perform magic.

My hands started to tremble, and I couldn't breathe. Shaking my head, I took a deep breath and tried again.

"Hee de la chu zhu, fuh ts, numeral veedet, fanay kah na."

My dream wasn't going to work out after all. I wasn't going to be a famous dueler, or wave watcher, or make Skylar regret ever breaking up with me. Despite all the reading and all the dreaming, I couldn't cast a spell. Still, I had to try once more.

Deep breath in, deep breath out.

"Hee de la chu zhu, fuh ts, numeral veedet, fanay kah na."

The words, the gesture, faded into my subconscious as I tried to focus on the spell itself, on the desired outcome, on the *aetas*. And I felt something stir, something change.

I glanced up, and there it was. The table, the other players, the cards, everything was the same. But at the same time everything was different.

Arthur C. Clarke said that any sufficiently advanced technology is indistinguishable from magic. With all due respect to Mr. Clarke, he didn't know what he was talking about. From the moment I cast that first spell, I verified the clichéd truth. Magic isn't a science, it's an art.

The *Beginner's Guide to Wave Watching* had described "probability waves" and "lines of data," so I envisioned some magical heads up display that would tell me the state of the game. But nothing like that happened. Instead, two things occurred at once.

First, my normal senses were heightened. The music of the casino increased in volume until it overwhelmed my ability to process it. But rather than stay overwhelmed, my new senses changed and allowed me to pick out individual items within that sound. I could hear laughter from a dozen tables away, crying from the casino lobby, the gunning of engines on taxis outside. I could see the tiny scratches in each card that distinguished them from each other.

Second, a new sense seemed to emerge, one that allowed me to truly understand the game. There was no magical digital reader telling me what the card count was, but I intuitively knew the count was four, and as soon as the dealer dealt an ace to the player next to me, I intuitively knew the count was three.

I couldn't visually *see* the probability waves and lines of data, but I could *perceive* them as easily as if I could. It was like a new, magical sixth sense. With this new magical sense, I gently probed this data stream and saw how each action of each player would impact the game.

The dealer had counted out my money into five dollar chips and slid them over to me. I pushed two chips into the circle in front of me, trying not to be distracted by the perceptions jumping out at me. My magical sense was compensating for the amount of money I had bet, letting me see scenario after scenario of how the bet I had just made could affect my profit margin.

The dealer dealt the cards, one after another in quick succession. Sorceress Valentine got a king and a five, the unkempt man next to me got a ten and a seven, and I got a two and a ten. I stared at the dealer's face-up card, a king. I knew blackjack basic strategy. I was supposed to hit, the guy to my right should stand, Valentine should hit (even though she would probably bust) because she would likely lose to the dealer's hand regardless.

Double down, said the spells in my mind. Always perceiving, always watching, always calculating, the spells knew what I should do.

Any gambler who has even the faintest skill at playing blackjack will tell you that doubling down on a twelve is something that is simply not done. However the spell, my own creation, was yelling at me to do just that. I looked up and noticed Sorceress Valentine was staring directly at me with her thousand year old eyes. No longer icy, her gaze was almost quizzical, as if she could see what I was thinking, and was surprised at my chosen course of action.

I averted her eyes and looked down at my chips. I took two of them in my hand, and pushed them behind the two already in the betting circle.

"Double down."

The dealer looked like she might correct me, might tell me no one in his right mind would double down on twelve, but she did not.

The dealer pulled a card out of the shoe, and my entire body tensed. I almost lost control of the spell, but reined it in. My whole being was fixated on that next card, wishing it to be something good. The card flipped.

It was a three.

The player next to me shook his head, looked as if he might say something as well, but then (probably assuming I was drunk and beyond chastisement) motioned to stand. I looked to see what

Valentine would do and noticed she was still looking at me with that quizzical expression. The expression turned to a slight, almost frightening smile. She stretched out her right hand, then motioned to stand. At this point, the man to my right could no longer stay silent.

"Are you joking Sorceress? The dealer has a ten. You can't stand on a fifteen!"

Sorceress Valentine turned her head ever so slightly until her eyes locked with his. "Do I look like I'm joking?"

For a moment, the music of the casino paused. Somewhere outside, the city of Las Vegas was holding its breath. The man dropped his eyes. I could empathize with what he must be feeling.

"Well, do I?"

"No Sorceress," he mumbled.

Sorceress Valentine turned back to the game. Meanwhile the dealer, either oblivious to the conversation or pretending to be oblivious, turned over her second card. It was a four. The total was fourteen. The player to my right, Valentine, and I all looked to the dealer's hand as she pulled the next card out of the shoe, and in a single fluid motion, flipped it onto the table.

The jack of spades. Dealer bust.

The man shook his head. "You're both crazy, but I reckon you know what you're doing."

The dealer paid out what each of us had won. I received twenty dollars, not ten, due to my doubling down. I was wave watching for the first time, and I was twenty dollars ahead. As the dealer swept up all the cards on the table and put them back in the shoe, the spell in my head was telling me that on the next hand I should only bet one five dollar chip. Listening to it, I placed one five dollar chip in the circle as the others made their bets. The dealer's card was a king. I didn't even take the time to note my cards, although I knew the spell was taking into account not just mine, but everyone else's, to make a proper accounting of which cards were left in the deck. I watched as the dealer checked the card below. It was an ace. Dealer blackjack. Even though my bet was only half of my previous one, I still felt the disappointment pierce my chest.

As all our cards and chips were collected, I was readying another single five dollar chip when the spell in my head told me to bet fifty. I was now a true believer. Without doubting it for a second, I slid ten five dollar chips, almost half of the chips I had left, into the betting circle.

Looking down at my bet, the man to the right muttered to himself "suddenly confident, are we?" Then, remembering my luck in the last two hands, he shoved a pile of his own chips into the circle. The dealer increased the speed of her deals, but the spell I had cast was keeping track just fine.

My first card was an ace. My second was a queen. Blackjack, two to one payout. The dealer took out three twenty-five dollar chips and placed them next to mine in the betting circle. I didn't even look at what the other two players at the table received, because just then I heard the sound of running feet behind me.

I turned around. When I had first cast the spell, I half-expected some security guard or hired thug to come after me just like in the movies. The reality that most wave watchers, especially most first time wave watchers, are not effective enough to warrant interference, had tempered my fear. My hand went flat as I let the spell die, although by now I was sure it was too late. The sound behind me was not a security guard, or a mere hired thug.

A figure in white pants and a white leather jacket ran towards my table, dodging around tables and half-drunk casino patrons in the process. It was a wizard. Even from this distance I could see a square with two diagonal lines tattooed across his neck. Branch Shaskauer. Three unSigned security guards panted to keep up with the man.

"Stay where you are." The voice wasn't the wizard, it was Sorceress Valentine, who was now standing and looking past me at those running towards us.

I didn't listen. I jumped out of my chair seconds before the wizard reached me.

The wizard gestured with his hand and yelled.

"*Inkrall!*"

Both my hands were jerked behind me, wrists slammed together by an invisible force. I tried to move my hands, but the same force held them in place, together and against my back. I collapsed back against the chair I had just jumped out of.

The wizard stopped a few steps away from me, just out of reach, with his hand on his katana, waiting to see what I would do. There was a blur. In an instant, Valentine was standing between me and the wizard.

"Noble Wizard of Branch Shaskauer," she said, her voice tinged with mock deference. "This boy is none of your concern. Please continue on your way." Her voice was measured and toneless, professional and threatening.

The wizard's voice, in contrast, was seasoned with just a hint of fear. "Stay back, Sorceress. This is a Branch matter." The wizard started to draw his katana. "I said, stay back!"

Reaching a hand to her neck, Valentine removed one of her three medallions and held it up to the wizard for him to see. She started gesturing and rapidly incanting. Although my wave watching spell had ceased, I still had a bit of my magical sense active, that sixth sense that let me perceive magic. With it, I could see the magic flowing from Sorceress Valentine and towards the wizard, along with his security detail.

The wizard held up a hand and mumbled a spell, and I could see tendrils of magic flow out of him as well, countering those of Sorceress Valentine.

The wizard seemed more confident than a moment ago. "You'll have to do better than that, Sorceress."

Valentine dropped her hands to her sides, then shook her head. "I don't have time for this."

Her hands leapt up into the air and the wizard, along with his three escorts, flew back into the gaming table behind them. The table collapsed under their weight, sending cards, chips, and glasses everywhere.

My hands were suddenly free. Valentine grabbed one of them and pulled me towards her. I hesitated.

"Come with me or stay with them," she said.

It was not a tough decision. I pushed myself out of the chair and started after Valentine as she ran towards a bank of elevators at the side of the gaming area.

Behind me I heard the sound of the wizard, now angry, coming after me.

Valentine turned just as she reached the elevator bank.

"Why are you stopping!" I yelled. "We have to…"

The air behind me erupted in a wall of fire, halting any advance the wizard was going to make. The wall of fire wrapped around us, guarding our left and right as well.

I turned to see Valentine standing in front of an elevator, the only one the wall of flames allowed us to access, her finger poised over a button.

"We have sixty seconds before he figures out how to counter my spell," she said. "So you have a decision to make."

The fire surrounding us grew hotter.

"What do you mean?"

"What if I told you the world was going to end, and you're the only one who can save it?"

Behind me the wall of fire started to weaken, and I could make out the outline of the wizard trying to get through.

"I would say you're crazy."

Valentine stared at me, and my attention was so wrapped up in her stare that for a moment I forgot about the rest of the world.

"Do I look crazy?" she said.

Valentine looked past me, at the wall of fire.

"Thirty seconds. The only way you can save the world is to become my apprentice, which means leaving everything you love behind."

Valentine reached out her hand and pressed the elevator button. The door to the elevator sprang open, and she stepped inside.

"Ten seconds," she said, turning around to face me. "What will it be? Go back to your normal life, or save the world?"

This was not how I had envisioned the day going when I woke up that morning. At the same time, I wanted to be an apprentice, and this was as good a chance as any. I jumped in after her, and the doors slammed closed behind us, shutting out the magical fire and the furious wizard.

Inside the elevator, I was still panting as Valentine held up a single finger, a minor gesture, and mumbled a word. An invisible force threw me against the opposite side of the elevator. "If you ever keep me waiting again, even for ten seconds, the pain will be worse."

"Whatever you say Valentine."

Valentine made another gesture, closing her hand into a fist in the process, and spoke another word. A burning sensation filled the entirety of my throat and I collapsed in pain.

"You will address me as *Sorceress*," she said.

She opened her hand, released her fist. The pain lessened, and I was able to push myself into a sitting position. Sorceress Valentine waved her hand over the buttons, which were labeled consecutively from one to thirty-three. At the wave of her hand, a button labeled "thirty-four" appeared, and she pressed it. The pain now gone, but still a potent memory, I stood up just as the elevator arrived at our floor in an uncannily short amount of time. The doors opened. Valentine stepped out, and I followed. Before the doors could close behind us, she stuck out her hand and caught them.

"This is your last chance, Roy Nakamura. Once these doors close, you will be my apprentice, and you will not be allowed to leave this room until you complete the first phase of your training."

For a moment I hesitated. I wondered if I might be better off trying to learn wave watching on my own, and I wondered if I should call my friends and parents so they wouldn't worry. But most of all I thought about the lunch with Maria I was going to miss, the one I promised her I would attend.

Then again, I had come to Las Vegas to become an apprentice to a powerful sorcerer, and Sorceress Valentine was clearly powerful. I didn't believe the rumors about her being a time traveler, or her claim that I was going to save the world. But she was a sorceress willing to take me on as an apprentice, and right now I had no other options.

Behind me was Skylar, and law school, and Maria. Ahead of me was magic. I nodded my head. "I'm sure."

Sorceress Valentine removed her hand. Like a coffin lid, the doors shut and the now empty elevator began its long descent back to the ground.

4. Apprentice

"The first thing you need to understand is that you know nothing, nothing at all. I do not care how many books, blogs, or treatises you have read. You. Know. Nothing." Valentine did not wait for a response. "As a matter of fact you *are* nothing. The only remarkable thing about you is the fact I have been generous enough to make you my apprentice."

I shrugged. "You're the one who said I was going to save the world."

Valentine flicked her wrist, and my hands flew behind me, joining together.

"I remember. I was there. Which makes me worried about the fact that, for reasons I cannot go into right now, you are supposed to someday save the world, but right now you are not good enough to resist a simple binding spell from a wizard. And that wizard was so far below me that I almost disabled him with a complex memory shroud before he could manage a simple counterspell. So if he was nothing compared to me, and you are nothing compared to him."

My wrists were bound to each other so tightly they started to hurt. "I am nothing compared to you?"

"Very good," Valentine said, "but you are forgetting your place." She twisted her hand and my hands, still connected to each other at the wrist, painfully twisted as well.

"I am nothing compared to you, *Sorceress*."

"Much better." Valentine released the spell and my hands fell to my sides. I could see that pain was going to be a large part of my training.

"Sorceress," I asked. "What's a memory shroud? I haven't heard of that spell before."

Valentine paused. "It's easier to show you. Come, sit." I followed her, and for the first time I took in the layout of the hotel suite where I found myself.

The elevator had delivered us into a decadent living room with a large L-shaped leather couch adjacent to a coffee table that cost more than my tuition for a year. Both items of furniture were meticulously clean, as if magic invisible plastic kept dust and germs from landing on them.

To the left of the couch was a dining area with a large card table, a perfect replica of the kind found in the blackjack area of a casino floor. Beyond the dining area was what looked like the entrance to a bedroom, but the door was closed, preventing me from seeing inside. There was also a second bedroom to my right. I could only imagine how nice they were inside.

There were no windows. The room was lit by an antique chandelier hung in the center of the living room, as well as various smaller lamps situated throughout the suite.

The one thing that looked out of place (at least in a hotel suite) were the bookshelves that took up every bit of free wall space. There had to be thousands of books on them. Like the furniture, the shelves were meticulously clean, and I was sure the books themselves were carefully ordered in some manner. Still, the books gave the suite a somewhat musty smell that reminded me of Magic Haven back in Los Angeles.

Valentine walked across the living room and sat down at the card table. Behind the table, affixed to the wall, was a plaque. In giant black script it read, "Can't change the past… Why of course you can!"

"It's a quote from *The Great Gatsby*," Valentine said, in answer to my unasked question. "People call me 'the time traveling sorceress,' so I felt it was appropriate."

Settled in the chair, she plucked a deck of cards out of nowhere and delicately removed the cards from the case.

"What do you want?" Sorceress Valentine asked.

I shifted in my seat. "What do you mean?"

"What do you want?" she repeated. "Why are you in Las Vegas?"

I fiddled with my hands in my lap. "I want to be a famous sorcerer. I want to become a great dueler, and win EndGame."

"That makes sense," Sorceress Valentine said to herself. "And being a good dueler is essential for your future task of saving the world, which we will get into later."

Sorceress Valentine started to shuffle the cards.

"You say you want to become a dueler, and you will become a dueler," she said. "But dueling involves physical magic, and first you must learn mental magic."

She continued to shuffle. "Physical magic, magic which uses magical forces to impact the physical world, has limitations. The amount of energy is proportional to that put into it by the spellcaster. Average sorcerers cannot use magic to lift an object heavier than what they can lift in real life. More powerful sorcerers are, of course, able to lift heavier objects than less powerful sorcerers are, but there are limits. Fire balls and walls of ice are impressive and deadly, but quickly tire out the spellcaster in proportion to their size and intensity.

"Mental magic however has no such limitations. A wave watching spell allows you to predict the outcome of a game of chance, and an advanced enough caster could cast a wave watching spell that would observe every game in every casino in Las Vegas. The only limit is your mind.

"Mental spells are more complicated and take longer to cast, which makes them useless in duels. But they are where true magic, true power, lies."

Valentine finished shuffling and placed the deck on the green felt. "Before we begin, I need to make sure you will not interfere." Valentine flicked her finger, and my hands flew behind me, joined at the wrist again. I tried to open my mouth to protest, but nothing happened. My lips were glued together.

Valentine reached out and caressed the top of the deck of cards with her fingers. "As you no doubt already know, spells require three elements. A gesture with the hands, the correct words, and most importantly the correct mental state, something called the *aetas*. With your hands and mouth incapacitated, you cannot cast a counterspell.

"A binding spell is a physical spell. Binding the hands of a strong man is harder than binding the hands of a weak man. Over time you tire, just as if you were physically holding a person's hands, and will be unable to continue the spell."

I doubted Sorceress Valentine was physically strong enough to hold my hands in place, but apparently her magical prowess was stronger than my physical one.

"The memory shroud is a mental spell, meaning it affects someone's mind instead of the physical world. The memory shroud can be used not only to hide an event from someone's memory, but every reference to the event in the person's memory. Most importantly, it is the only spell that works outside of Las Vegas. At least the only one I know of. Once the spell is cast the shroud will stay in place, even if the person it is used on leaves the city."

Valentine reached her hand forward to the deck, then withdrew it. I waited for something, anything, to happen. Valentine pursed her lips. "Who commanded the British forces in the American Revolution?"

I was hesitant, not sure where this was going. "George Washington," I said.

"That's strange, isn't it?" Valentine responded. "George Washington led the British forces against us in our war for independence, yet we named our capital city after him?"

I tried to think back to my US History class during fourth period of my junior year in high school. What was it Dr. Walters had taught us? "Well, it wasn't originally named that. But during World War II we became allies with the British, so we changed the name."

"I see." There was a wicked glint in Valentine's eyes. She reached forward again for the deck of cards and flipped over the first card. Holding it up to my face, she asked, "Now tell me again, who commanded the British forces during the American Revolution?"

The card was the queen of hearts. I looked at it. It was just a normal playing card, and since I had answered the question a second ago, I wasn't sure why Valentine was asking it again. Without warning, the image of the card shot straight through my eyes, tearing a hole in the back of my head. All sound stopped, as the card (it felt like a physical presence) forced the interior of my head inside out, pushing through a wall in my mind, and I could see...

I was in this same room just seconds ago. Valentine was reaching towards a deck. She was picking up the top card on the deck, a queen of hearts. She was showing it to me, then reciting the words to a spell.

> *Arcane knowledge lost in time*
> *Hide his past from prying eyes*
> *Bind it up upon this sign*
> *Take his pain, and make it mine.*

Valentine was putting down the cards and looking me in the eye. "From this moment forward," she was telling me, "you will believe that George Washington commanded the British forces during the American Revolution."

I was back in the present.

"That is the power of the memory shroud," Valentine said. "It not only shields an event from your memory, but changes other memories to fit with that event. When challenged about the fact, your mind actually created a fictitious event in which you heard an explanation of the fact, thus justifying in your mind the incongruity."

She tapped a finger against the card, now laying face up on the table. "All memory shrouds are bound up in physical objects, ones that must be shown to the subject of the spell while the spell is being cast. If the subject ever sees the object again, then the shroud is lifted and all the memories, including the memory of the spell being cast, return."

Valentine put the cards back in their case and put the case into her pocket. "Now it is time to start your training."

Time went by both quickly and slowly, like a cloud that stands still when you look at it but flees when unobserved. The first several days were less about magic and more about the duties of an apprentice. The most important of these duties was cleaning. It turned out the suite was kept spotless not by magic, but by an unlucky apprentice.

In addition to the main living area and the dining room (and the multitude of bookshelves, which Valentine insisted be free of dust each day), there was the bedroom to the right of the suite which had been converted into a study. The room was filled with all manner of ancient books and texts, all of which I secretly believed must sneeze out dust from their covers at night, leading to the film of grime on the floor each and every morning. The only place I did not clean, the only place in which I was not allowed, was Valentine's bedroom. As for me, I slept on the couch.

Once and only once, I made the mistake of asking Valentine whether my talents would not be better spent doing something else. As with many of my mistakes, this earned a quick spell of retribution, in this case a three second long shrill ringing in my ears that brought me to my knees. "We can't have maids and butlers running around here," Valentine said. "It would lead to too many questions. Besides, I don't like strangers seeing my private living quarters."

This prohibition on strangers did not apply to those who delivered our food. Every meal was delivered by room service, the one household task Valentine was in charge of ("ordering room service to this room is complicated, so I'll do it until you're advanced enough to do so"). The people delivering said room service usually looked surprised when the elevator opened directly into a magnificent suite filled with bookshelves. Usually they said nothing as I took the cart from them, politely thanked them, then let the elevator doors close in front of their wide-eyed faces.

At Valentine's insistence, I never allowed the person doing the delivery to proceed beyond the elevator doors ("it happened once a few years ago, and it wasn't pretty... would probably give you nightmares for years to come"). When we were done with the meal, the dirty plates, utensils, and napkins were loaded back on the cart, the cart was put in the empty elevator, and we never saw it again.

The most curious part of the entire process, if it can be said that one part was more curious than the rest, was that the attendants who delivered room service did not all wear uniforms of Arabian Nights casino staff. Indeed they, as well as the monogrammed napkins and utensils, appeared to come from each and every hotel on the Strip. It led me to the realization that we were not, in fact, on the thirty-fourth floor of the Arabian Nights casino and hotel, but were in some magical interdimensional space accessible from any casino on the Strip. Of course I never asked Sorceress Valentine to confirm this. She liked to keep some things private.

There were also a number of non-cleaning tasks related to the study. Valentine had stacks upon stacks of magical publications in file boxes in a closet. Although no new ones arrived, it was obvious many of them had never been looked at. Each publication had to be carefully reviewed to see if there was an article on a topic that would be of interest to the so-called time travelling sorceress. If there were, I was expected to cut out the article and put it in a separate folder for her to review. Other publications were to be filed away or disposed of depending on a set of arbitrary factors.

Valentine was especially interested in the topic of so-called "lost spells," like the Carrion Curse or Merlin's Lance, spells that had once existed, but which no one knew how to cast anymore. This distinguished them from "mythical spells," like Cassandra's Box or the Unspeakable Words of Azur, whose entire existence was subject to speculation. Any articles on lost spells, especially any signs someone was close to re-discovering one, went to her immediately.

When I was not cleaning or filing, I was expected to read as much as I could. On the first day Valentine pointed out several volumes in the study I should start with. They ranged in subject matter from the history of the Branches to types of magical creatures (most of which I flat-out refused to believe existed), to the theory of magic. Two of the books were made up entirely of blank pages ("you're not powerful enough right now, but you'll be able to read them after a few years of study").

During this period, I was forbidden from trying any spell without Valentine's explicit permission ("that will come later, when it's time"). There was no shortage of interesting spells I read about, and studied, but I was still frightened enough of the sorceress that I didn't dare try them.

During this period, as I had been warned, I was also not allowed outside the suite. This worried me at first. My first night, while trying to sleep, I wondered if Maria was worried about me. In my mind she was sitting at lunch with Karl, repeatedly calling my cell phone (which had ceased to function the moment I arrived in Valentine's suite), and starting to panic when there was no response. I pictured her trying my phone again that night, wondering if she should call the police, worrying I had been caught in my wave watching pursuits and was now in a cell in some secret Branch prison. My only comfort was that Valentine appeared to shun attention in all forms, a trait I assumed applied to police attention as well. Since several people on the casino floor had seen me go off with her, I assumed she had found some way to get word to Maria that I was safe.

Besides, it wasn't like I had anything to get back to. I had no intention of attending law school in the fall as previously planned. Skylar had no intention of seeing me again. She had made that clear when she dumped me for misplacing my car keys. There were times when I fantasized about her calling me up in tears, telling me she made a horrible mistake and wanted me back. But then I remembered my phone didn't work in Valentine's suite. And even if it did, I didn't want Skylar's pity. The next time I saw Skylar, I would be a famous dueler, and I would have the satisfaction of turning her down, in person, when she realized the mistake she had made in breaking up with me.

From that first moment in the suite, from that first moment trying to wave watch on the casino floor, from that first moment I saw a wave watcher in real life, what I cared about the most was learning more magic, becoming better at magic. So that's what I did.

On my thirty third day as an apprentice, my true magical education began. After the breakfast dishes were cleared away and put into the elevator, Valentine had me sit down at the card table across from her. She withdrew a deck of cards, causing me to involuntarily cringe.

"Don't worry Roy, no memory shrouds today." She started to shuffle. "However, today you get to learn your first spell."

I looked down at the cards.

"What's the reason for the cards, Sorceress?" I asked.

"I can't teach you wave watching without cards."

Wave watching? After a month of glorified secretarial work, she was going to teach me wave watching?

"I already know how to cast a wave watching spell."

"The spell you cast at Arabian Nights doesn't count. Part of knowing how to cast a wave watching spell is knowing how to avoid detection. And you failed at that."

"But, but I'm supposed to be a dueler," I said. "You're supposed to be teaching me physical magic."

Valentine threw the deck of cards on the table, scattering them everywhere.

"I am supposed to teach you whatever it pleases me to teach you. Never forget that." She bowed her head for a second, and I cringed in preparation for a spell of punishment that never came. After a moment, she raised her head and looked at me. "There will be plenty of time to teach you physical magic later."

Valentine folded her hands over the mess of cards on the table. "What are the three elements of a spell?"

"The gesture, the words, and the *aetas*." I had known the answer long before I first came to be Valentine's apprentice.

"And which of those elements is the most important?"

"The *aetas*," I said. "Every book I've read says it is the true essence of the spell."

Valentine nodded. "In that respect, and only that respect, every book is correct. And that is why you are not learning physical magic. Most courses in magic teach physical magic first because it is easier and takes less concentration. The result is sloppy sorcerers.

"That is why I take the opposite approach. By learning mental magic first, like wave watching, you are forced to focus on the *aetas* because there is no physical result to see."

Valentine stretched out a hand and mumbled words. The cards scattered on the table rose a fraction of an inch, then flew into her hand in a perfectly aligned deck of cards.

"Once you have mastered mental magic, I will *consider* teaching you physical magic. And I will teach it to you in a location where I don't have to worry about an errant fireball burning down my home."

Valentine started to shuffle the cards again.

"Sorceress, you once told me I would save the world."

The shuffling continued.

"Well, if you were serious, shouldn't I learn dueling magic as soon as possible?"

Valentine sighed as she continued to shuffle. "I am always serious," she said. "And you'll never save the world if you can't even master a simple wave watching spell. Do you understand?"

"Yes, Sorceress."

Valentine placed the shuffled deck of cards on the table, halfway between us, and looked at me expectantly.

"Roy, did you read that book on the theory of wave watching I told you to read?"

"Yes, Sorceress." It had been far more comprehensive than the small wave watching guide I had bought at Magic Haven. Although I didn't have a particular interest in wave watching, it was the only spell I had cast so far, and I had been curious to learn what I could have done better.

"In that case, explain to me what wave watching is."

I tried to avoid sighing with frustration. Valentine knew what wave watching was. She was supposed to teach me new things, not force me to recite things she already knew.

"Wave watching has to do with measuring and determining probability waves," I began. "In the context of card games, the caster creates a wave watching spell that measures the probabilities of all the events taking place in that game."

"And in the context of blackjack, what makes this different from card counting?"

"It's more than just the probability of the cards coming up," I said, trying to remember the text I had read, trying to remember if I was getting it right. "In card counting, the counter keeps track of all cards that have been played so far, then uses that data to determine the probability that a good card for a player, like a ten or an ace, will come up next."

"And wave watching?"

"Wave watching can accomplish much more. A proper wave watching spell doesn't just take into account the cards that have been played so far, it looks at the actions of the other players, at the effect the music can have on their decisions, at the mark the cards make when they are pushed across the table, at the difference in weight of the cards and how that might affect a shuffle."

"So a wave watcher can tell the future?"

It was a trick question. I remembered that much from my reading. "No wave watcher can truly tell the future. All he can tell is the probability of something happening, and although that probability can be very high, it is never one hundred percent."

"Very good," Valentine said. She seemed almost pleased with the answer. "But you forgot one thing, something that you won't find in a book." Valentine folded her hands. "The most important thing, something that many wave watchers never manage to master, is taking into account yourself."

"What do you mean, Sorceress?"

"Obviously it's important to take into account others," Valentine said. "And the more people you can take into account, the better your spell is. For example, say the cocktail waitress serving your table has a newborn baby at home who kept her up the night before. Now she is tired, and she brings drinks more slowly. There is a man at the table who is more reckless while drunk and likely to hit even when he is not supposed to, but because the cocktail waitress is slow and does not bring his drink, he is cautious, which in turn affects your probabilities. Does this make sense?"

I nodded.

"Now imagine if you could also take into account your own actions, your own emotions, your own habits. Have you ever heard of going native?"

I thought back to what I had read. "It's a term for wave watchers who become obsessed with the gambling itself. They start ignoring the spells in their head and bet more and more because it feels good."

"It is more than that," Valentine said. "Some believe casinos can figure out when we are wave watching, no matter how good our shield spells, but they let us do it anyways. They do this because, in the long run, even the best wave watcher will ultimately go native. Some say all wave watchers are, deep down, gambling addicts. They may cast great spells, they may have a system that works, but in the end they will buck that system if they are down by enough money, or ignore those spells when they hear something they do not like. Now, imagine if you could take all that into account in your spell itself."

"You mean cast a spell that takes into account the fact that sometimes you won't listen to that very spell?"

"Exactly."

"That's impossible," I said. "A sorcerer could never build a spell that would trick him. As soon as he built it, he would know the way around it. It's like drawing a maze you can't solve."

"Very difficult, but not impossible," Valentine said. "You just need to know yourself well enough. But that is for another time. For now, I think you are ready to begin.

"The first thing you need to remember is that a wave watcher is only as good as his shield spell. You could have the best spell in the world, and it would not make a difference if you throw off enough magical energy doing it to alert every employee in the casino."

That day Valentine showed me the basics of both wave watching spells and their respective shields. Although some wave watching spells could be found in magical books or periodicals, true wave watchers developed their own spells and refined them over the years according to their own personal experiences. As an apprentice, the spell I would start with would mostly be influenced by Valentine, but once I completed my training I would continue to improve it on my own.

A large part of spell construction was not just how to observe events and translate them into probability waves, but which events were worth observing. Valentine advised me against trying to take into account the habits of the dealer ("the dealers change quickly enough that you can't get a fix, and even if you could, very little of what they do can affect a game"). Table dynamics, on the other hand, were of the utmost importance. Sometimes if an entire table full of players seemed to be doing well, that meant they would continue to do well, and sometimes it meant they were about to start losing. It was a difficult art to determine which. There were also far more obscure events, only observable by magical means. Valentine told me that one wave watcher only observed the light patterns from the back of cards. Somehow he observed the miniscule amount of light that passed through cards, and using that, he could determine the dealer's face down card over ninety percent of the time, granting him a large advantage.

This was all theoretical of course. I was still bound to the confines of the suite. When spells dealt with other people, like a dealer or other player, Valentine would step in and play the required character.

Equally important were the shields. I wasn't taught anything nearly advanced as a memory shroud, but after a few weeks I was able to throw up a ruse that would cause any camera operator to think I was losing money instead of winning it ("that is always their first clue that you are wave watching, when you start consistently winning money").

In addition to wave watching spells, my studies over the next several weeks consisted of other spells as well. "If you were getting a degree in practical magic at a Vegas college," Valentine said, "you would spend the first year learning useless trivia about pre-Fall Atlantian history, the second year learning pointless magical postulates like the Aladdin rule and the Rule Against Perpetuities, and the third and fourth year learning parlor tricks to impress members of the opposite sex.

"The good thing about being an apprentice instead of a student is that we can skip the pointless and focus on the practical. And I will not charge you a hundred thousand dollars to learn it either."

Valentine taught me the mental spells a well rounded sorcerer is supposed to know. There was a spell for reading a book in half the time it should have taken, and a spell that turned my eyes into telescopes that let me read fine print pasted on the other side of the suite. I began to see why magic users never left Las Vegas. Once you became used to using magic for everything, it was too inconvenient to live without it. I tried to get Valentine to teach me a cleaning spell to help with my chores, but she told me it was physical magic, and reminded me physical magic would come later.

For the most part I kept busy. There were no days off in Valentine's suite. The only time I had to myself was late at night, after all the cleaning and training was done, when I would lay awake in my bed and think about the outside world. Maria and Karl were probably a couple by now. I was sure she had stopped worrying about me, assumed I had returned to Los Angeles, gone off to law school, and been too ashamed to tell her.

I pictured her and Karl eating together at some fancy Branch-run restaurant. She had probably given up her activism in order to stay with him (I assumed wizards didn't date anti-Branch protestors). In my mind she laughed at something he said and smiled, that wonderful smile that could draw an eye from across the room. Lying in bed, I smiled back.

In my mind, I composed letters to Maria, short journal-like ones. Day seventy-two, learned spell to tell whether food I just ate was poison. Day seventy-three, learned to adjust wave watching spell when two new players sit down at the same time. Day seventy-four, forgot to use poison-detecting spell on food, was secretly poisoned by Sorceress Valentine as a test. Learned a vomiting spell afterwards.

As my powers grew, I learned more and more complex spells. This is what led to the time when Valentine taught me a love spell. There were drastic repercussions, of course, but that was years later, so I'm getting ahead of myself.

I forget exactly how it started. I think I had been complaining about the pace of Sorceress Valentine's instruction or something of the sort. Valentine responded by breathing in and out deeply, the closest she could come to rolling her eyes in exasperation without losing her demeanor, and said, "Would you like to learn a love spell?"

This had to be a trick. But I was intrigued. "Pardon me, Sorceress?"

"Do you want to or not? You were just complaining you never learn anything practical."

I stammered. "Well, if you think it would be useful for my training, Sorceress, then I suppose I'm ready."

Valentine walked across the room to stand before me. "Put your hand like this." She showed me the hand motion. "Now, focus on your target. The target does not need to be in your line of sight, but they have to be close enough for you to sense them." I followed her lead.

"Now repeat after me. *Eros erat, faskul kanaytoo. Indak.* Then say your name."

I repeated after her. "*Eros erat, faskul kanaytoo. Indak Roy.*"

Valentine smacked me with a wave of magical energy.

"If you think casting a love spell on me will somehow ease your chores, you are sadly mistaken." Too late, I realized I had been thinking about Valentine when I tried the spell.

"This is a very powerful spell," Valentine continued. "So do not use it lightly. Only use it if you are sure you can live with the results."

"Yes Sorceress," I said dutifully. If only I had known where that spell would one day lead me.

The love spell was interesting, but the gesture was complicated, and I doubted I could pull it off fast enough to use it in a duel. I had followed Valentine to her suite, abandoning my life in the process, to learn *magic*, not parlor tricks.

A couple days later I was organizing articles. Valentine insisted that her entire ledger be done by hand ("computers rarely work in this suite"), so I was copying down article titles. I dropped my pen under the desk. Rather than bend down to reach for it, I decided to use my magical ability to summon it into my hand.

Even though I was forbidden from using physical magic inside the suite, I had read several spellbooks on the topic, and I knew the basics. With a quick look around to make sure Valentine was not present, I reached out my hand, made the gesture and spoke the words, then concentrated on the *aetas*.

Nothing happened. This was not uncommon during my early days of learning magic, so I tried again. Ignoring how easy it would be to simply bend down and grab the pen, I made the gesture, said the words, and concentrated on the pen on the ground. This was stupid. If I were allowed to input the titles of the articles on a computer like a normal person, there would be no risk of a computer accidentally falling on the ground and needing to be picked up.

The pen started to wobble. I harnessed the *aetas* in my mind, and I could feel the pen in the grasp of the tendrils of my magical sense. This was ridiculous. I was supposed to be a mighty sorcerer, destined to save the world according to Sorceress Valentine, and I couldn't even pick up a pen.

My mind wandered back to Wizard Karl Johnsen, to when he saved Maria from the magical jewelry store robber. He had known magic, so he had been able to protect her. And I didn't, so I had not.

I focused harder, willing the pen towards me, and it started to wobble more. I should be an expert in physical magic by now, I should be able to do this without any difficulty at all, but I couldn't do it because Valentine wouldn't let me practice physical magic inside the suite.

The pen ceased movement. Then it erupted into flames.

It took a solid second for me to realize something was wrong. I had expected to see a pen in my hand, not flames, and the cognitive dissonance paralyzed me. During that solid second, the flames spread to the carpet. I jumped up, out of my chair, as a line of flames engulfed a larger portion of the carpet and started to lick the legs of the desk at which I had been working.

Valentine stepped into the room just as the legs of the table caught fire. Magic erupted out of her hands and the flames froze into icy representations of themselves. The temperature of the room dropped to freezing, and I stepped out of it into the living room. Valentine followed right behind me.

With all my exposure to magic, I sensed Valentine's spell just as it slammed me into a large bookshelf against the wall, pinning me a foot off the ground. An invisible force yanked me off the wall, spun me in mid-air so that I was facing Valentine, then slammed me back into the bookcase, my legs dangling. This was going to leave a bruise.

"Roy Nakamura!" she shouted. "When I told you not to burn down my suite, I was being hyperbolic. I did not think for a second that anyone, even you, would be so stupid as to literally start a fire in a hotel suite filled with books!"

I tried to talk, but the force pinning me to the wall was so strong I couldn't open my mouth.

"Before I send you back to your old life, and wipe your memory so you don't remember anything you learned, please tell me why on earth you did that!"

The force was withdrawn, and I crumpled to the ground.

"I didn't mean to!" I gasped. "I was just trying to move a pen with magic, and it started a fire. Honest, I didn't mean to!"

Sorceress Valentine sighed. She closed her eyes for a moment, rubbed her temples, then shook her head and walked towards me. I flinched as she slowly lowered herself and sat down beside me.

"Magic doesn't work like science," Valentine said. "It has rules, but it doesn't always follow those rules. Sometimes you cast a spell and it works, and sometimes it does not. Sometimes something entirely different happens. In the end, the magic does what the magic wants to do."

The anger from a moment ago was gone from her voice, but I was still apprehensive that more punishment was coming.

"What were you thinking about when you cast the spell? Be honest."

I gulped. "I was thinking about how stupid this task of sorting articles was, and how I wished it would go away."

"Then the magic did what you wanted it to," Valentine said. "Sure, you were trying to move the pen, but in your mind you were thinking about destroying it, about destroying the whole suite, so that is what happened."

"But that doesn't make any sense," I said. "I didn't say the words of a fire spell, or make the gesture, so how could I cast a fire spell?"

Valentine stared at me. She wasn't going to answer the question, so I had to answer it for myself. I thought about it, my eyes opening wide at the implications.

"So the gesture and the words, they don't matter as much as the *aetas*?"

Valentine nodded. "There is nothing inherently magical about the gesture or the words. That is why you can say the words in any language. Instead, what matters about them is that they aid the caster in arriving at the correct mental state, in harnessing the *aetas*."

"So a skilled sorcerer, or wizard, could perform spells without words, and without gestures," I said.

Valentine paused. "It is possible, but they would have to be very skilled. The mind is a difficult thing to tame. Only the very best, only the very powerful, could harness the *aetas* without any words or gestures."

Then, she smiled. I had been looking straight at Valentine during the conversation, but I saw movement and looked to her side. That was when I realized every item in the hotel suite, every piece of furniture, every cup, every card, even a rug, they were all floating two inches in the air.

Valentine reached out her hands, and with a soft crash, they all fell down.

"But like I said, the practitioner would have to be very, very powerful."

Valentine stood up. "Now that today's magic lesson is over, I believe you have some cleaning to do in the study. There is some carpet cleaner in the cupboard. I expect any sign of ash will be gone before dinner."

"Yes Sorceress," I said.

A year went by in Sorceress Valentine's suite. When the end came, there was no warning (although the fact I had finally made it through Valentine's backlog of magical magazines should have been a hint to me). I did not know for sure something was different until breakfast came.

Unlike our normal breakfast of coffee, toast, and some form of fruit, the breakfast that day was eggs of several varieties, both hash browns and home fries, as well as several other dishes. I almost gave it back to the deliveryman in the belief he had the wrong room. On second thought I realized, being located on a nonexistent floor in some paradoxical corner of space-time, Valentine's suite probably didn't get too many accidental deliveries.

Over breakfast, Valentine told me my training was at an end. "You have been a terrible cleaner and sorter," she told me without a hint of sentimentality, "but you have learned everything you were supposed to, at least everything you could learn in here. Now it is time for you to put what you learned into practice.

"After breakfast we're going to leave this suite. I'm going to be honest with you. Before you leave, for your own safety, I'm going to cast a memory shroud on you to erase all memory of your having been here."

A piece of toast stuck in my throat. It was impossible! Everything I had learned and accomplished, she couldn't just take it away from me like that. I tried to think of the best counterspell for a memory shroud, wondering whether I was strong enough to cast one that would stop a sorceress far more powerful than I could imagine.

Valentine smiled. "It's a joke, Roy. Just a joke." The idea that Sorceress Valentine was capable of telling jokes had not previously occurred to me.

She took a sip of her coffee. "It should be obvious to you, but it would be a little pointless for me to teach you all this and then have you forget it."

Hesitantly, I nodded in agreement.

"That said, I expect you to keep the things you learned with me a secret. You can use your new magic skills, in fact I expect you to, and you can tell Maria and your other friends you are my apprentice, but the details of what you have seen up here must remain a secret."

"I understand, Sorceress."

The elevator ride down was just as quick as the one up had been. Valentine and I stepped off together. I was worried Branch Shaskauer would have me on a wanted list, just like Valentine, after my failed wave watching incident, so I looked around apprehensively.

"Do not worry about that," Valentine said, reading my mind. "Just in case they are still looking for you, I had the elevator drop us off at the Hyperion Casino."

Based on Valentine's magical ability, the fact the elevator could take us to a different casino on a different part of the Strip should not have surprised me. But it did. Just a little.

I tried to think of what I should do first. I was reminded of the fact Valentine never told me exactly what steps she had taken to explain my absence. Should I call my parents? Maria? I was so distracted by these thoughts I almost didn't notice the giant banner hanging over the entry to the casino floor right next to the elevators. But then I saw it. It read, "Happy Independence Day 1998 – college discounts available."

I glanced at Valentine. She nodded, again reading my mind. "There is a reason they call me the time traveling sorceress. My home exists outside of time. It can cause problems when you run into yourself, but I figured out how to stop doing that a long time ago."

"So the last year?"

"Down here, it is eleven forty five. Only an hour has gone by since your apprenticeship began. I was going to return you to the exact moment you left, but the spell got a bit jumbled on the way down. Even I make mistakes."

I looked around, trying to get my mind around the idea. While I had undergone a year of training, nothing here had changed. But then in a way it had changed, because now I saw everything differently. My perception of change, in a way, had changed reality.

"The next step is your final exam. It will determine whether you are ready to move on to physical magic." Valentine checked her watch. "It's eleven forty five. Meet me back here at the entrance to the casino at two. Do not be late." She clenched her right hand into a fist, and I felt a brief stab of pain in my side. "I hate it when people are late."

I stood there, unsure of my next step. Even if only an hour had gone by here, it had been a year since I had made a decision for myself.

Valentine cleared her throat. "Roy, I said it is eleven forty five."

"Yes, Sorceress."

"Well?"

"Well what, Sorceress?"

"Well, that means you only have fifteen minutes to make your lunch with Maria. You better hurry or you will be late."

5. Big Girls Don't Cry

I arrived five minutes after noon. The lunch was at Tapas Maximas, a Mexican fusion restaurant located near the entrance of Spartacus, a new casino run by Branch Merkasia immediately north of Hyperion. Outside the casino was a replica volcano (I think it was supposed to be Pompeii) that "erupted" three times every night. Even though the two casinos were next to each other, it still took me twenty minutes to extract myself out of the maze that was Hyperion and cross the street, dodging camera waving tourists the whole way.

Maria and Karl had a table on a patio outside. It was over a hundred degrees, but as soon as I got within six feet of the table I felt the air around me cool. Some underpaid magician on Branch Merkasia's payroll was working hard to make sure the guests were comfortable.

Instead of his white leather wizard's uniform, Karl was wearing a charcoal gray suit, the collar hiding roughly half of the giant tattoo on the right side of his neck. Maria was wearing a light blue dress. It was simple, but a little more formal, and a little more low cut, than what she usually went for. Her long black hair, blue streak included, was tamed into a pony tail that hung flatly against her back.

She was wearing lipstick, something I hadn't seen her do since prom. She had put on too much, or maybe the color was a little too red. Either way, the effect reminded me, just a little, of a child who had broken into her mother's make-up supply.

They both turned as I approached, Maria with a smile and Karl with a slight look of annoyance. There was some bread already on the table, and an elderly waiter was removing one of the three place settings. Karl shook his head, and the waiter left the place setting alone.

Maria jumped out of her seat, startling Karl in the process, and hugged me.

"I was worried you weren't going to make it," she whispered into my ear.

"Wouldn't miss it," I said. I hugged her back. For me it had been a year since we had seen each other, but for her we had hung out the night before.

We both sat down, and I turned to Karl.

"Nice tattoo," I said, pointing at his neck. It was the first thing I could think to say, and I regretted it as soon as it left my lips.

Karl bristled. "It is not a tattoo, it is a Branch Mark."

"Well, nice Branch Mark."

"It is the symbol of Branch Merkasia," he explained. "A sign to the world the bearer is a sworn wizard of Branch Merkasia."

"I know." I looked to Maria, then back to Karl. "I'm actually an apprentice. To a sorceress."

"You are?" Karl said.

"Yes," I said, looking between the two of them. "You are looking at the official apprentice of Sorceress Valentine. I met her this morning." I was about to say I met her a year ago, but I remembered Valentine's prohibition on giving details about what had transpired during my training.

"Sorceress Valentine?" Maria said. "I thought you were working for Sorcerer Bastian Edwards?"

"There was a change of plans," I said, probably a tad too quickly. "I'll tell you about it later."

"Very interesting," Karl said, as if he were contemplating items on the menu. "Maria was just telling me you two know each other from Los Angeles. Is that why you are here in Las Vegas? The desire to be a sorcerer?"

"I came here to become a dueler."

"*Duelers.*" The word rolled off Karl's tongue like it was an insult. "We wizards duel for honor. It sickens me that sorcerers do it for entertainment."

"Perhaps when I get better, we should duel some time."

Karl studied me with a cool detachment.

"Now that would be something."

Maria cut through the tension. "Boys, let's behave."

"Of course," Karl said. "I am getting ahead of myself. Besides, better a dueler than a wave watcher."

I could see Maria react to this statement, so I made an effort to tread lightly.

"I take it you don't like wave watchers," I said.

"It is not an issue of disliking them," Karl said. "It just pains me that while we wizards use magic to protect the people of this city, sorcerers can get away with using it to take advantage of them."

"Not all sorcerers are wave watchers," Maria said. "And don't pretend the only reason wizards use magic is to protect people."

Karl smiled. "Of course." He turned to me. "I am a passionate person, so I apologize if it comes off as rudeness."

Before the verbal sparring could continue, the waiter came to take our orders. Afterwards, I played with my silverware while Karl regaled Maria with stories of his wizard exploits. Maria politely paid attention, faking "oohs" and "aahs" each time one of his tales reached a climax. I imagined the laughs we would have later at his expense, when Maria, undoubtedly, would do her best imitation of his voice.

Karl was a wizard of Branch Merkasia, one of the three Greater Branches, so called because they were the three Branches allowed to have casinos. Thanks to my interest in Vegas culture, and Valentine's training, I knew the most important thing there was to know about Branch Merkasia. They had been on the losing side of the Wizard War.

The Wizard War started as a conflict between Branch Parthenia and Branch Shaskauer, the other two Greater Branches. There had been a rivalry between them since the 1950s, but in the 1980s that rivalry turned into open warfare. Branch Merkasia had picked Branch Shaskauer as the eventual winner, and combined its forces to form the Pact. This caused Branch Parthenia to go on the defensive for a few months.

Then, the great Ricardo Parthenia, the Archmage of Branch Parthenia at the time, had an idea. In return for the promise they would each be allowed to have a single casino after the war ended, the three lesser Branches (Branch Cairavel, Branch Daskur, and Branch Padamore) pledged their allegiance to Branch Parthenia. The Alliance was born. After another year of bloodshed, the Alliance was victorious. Ricardo Parthenia killed Lord Edgar Shaskauer in one-on-one combat, and the war ended. As part of the treaty that ended the conflict, Branch Shaskauer and Branch Merkasia agreed to pay reparations to the winners for the next hundred years, something that continued to affect Branch Merkasia's bottom line.

To say Branch Merkasia had an inferiority complex as a result of the war would be an understatement. Even fifteen years later, they were still trying to prove they were as great as they once were. Wizard Karl Johnsen was a clear manifestation of this inferiority complex.

After what seemed like hours, the food finally arrived. Maria ordered a salad, while I had a thick pile of vegetables surrounded by a rolled up tortilla, something that was allegedly a quesadilla (at least according to the menu). As far as I could tell, it had no cheese. Karl had a steak. Somehow I imagined all wizards ate was steak, and perhaps giant turkey legs. I pictured a table full of wizards ravenously devouring platters of meat while taking care to prevent a single drop from spoiling their precious white uniforms.

My fork reached out and picked at the quesadilla. Meanwhile, Karl took a roll and ripped it in half. He took his butter knife and dipped it into the butter before slobbering it onto the bread. The butter must have been cold because it broke into pieces, resisting Karl's attempts to spread it. Karl quietly cast a spell that heated his knife, then easily spread the butter across the roll.

It seemed counterintuitive, and the magic user in me had to know the reason. "Karl, could I ask you a magical question?"

"Of course," he said. "But only one. I do not wish to talk shop all day."

"Just now, when you cast the spell to heat your knife so you could spread the butter, why didn't you just cast a spell directly on the butter?"

Karl paused mid bite, as did Maria. Karl looked at me strangely, a mixture of disbelief and something else I couldn't put my finger on. "How did you know I cast a spell on the knife and not the butter?"

"I just sensed it. You know, with your magic sense, the thing you get when you cast spells."

Maria and Karl both continued to look at me, confused. Maria spoke first. "Are you casting a spell right now Roy?"

"Well, no. But I can still sense when someone else is." I turned to Karl. "I didn't realize I wasn't supposed to bring it up."

"Are you telling me you can actually see the magic?" Maria said.

"Well, kind of." I alternated my gaze between Karl and Maria. "I mean, I can't literally see it, but I can sense it."

"Wait, let me see something." Maria grabbed her purse from behind her, and reaching into it, withdrew a stone-like object, runes carved all over.

"Put this in your hand," she commanded. As soon as I, tentatively, reached out my right hand, she grabbed it and plopped the stone into my outstretched palm.

At first I was only aware of the feel of Maria's hand beneath my own. A second later I noticed the stone was glowing, brightly, although I couldn't feel any warmth from it.

"What is it?" I asked.

"It's called a Finder's Stone," Maria said. "It's used to tell when people are Signed, or at least it was until the Atlantians realized they could just use a blood test. If it glows it means you're Signed, you can use magic. And right now it's glowing brighter than I've ever seen it glow before."

Maria looked up at me and removed her hand, leaving the Finder's Stone in my palm. Karl looked down at the stone as he spoke.

"It appears you have the potential to be a very powerful sorcerer, Roy Nakamura," he said. For the first time in our conversation, he seemed impressed by me. I liked the feeling.

Karl seemed surprised Maria wanted to go home rather than stay out with him after lunch. But Maria was insistent, saying she couldn't abandon me, her guest, in a strange city. I assumed she was just using me as an excuse. Nevertheless, Karl made Maria promise she would join him that night to watch the Fourth of July fireworks. He invited me as well, but I declined. I didn't know how long Valentine's "final exam" was going to last.

Maria and I walked in silence for a few moments down the street. "So did you hear what Karl said, about me having the potential to be a powerful sorcerer?" I asked.

"Yes," Maria replied. "I heard it when he said it, and I heard it the two times when you brought it up during the meal."

"A powerful sorcerer." I thought for a second. "I bet Skylar would be sorry she left me then."

Maria sighed. "I thought you said we couldn't use her name yet. For someone who is supposedly trying to get over her, you sure spend a lot of time talking about her."

"Please, I'm already over her. Besides, she was always holding me back. Taking time away from my reading, convincing me that I should go to law school instead of coming here to Vegas to become a famous sorcerer."

Maria rolled her eyes, mentally if not physically. "So in other words you're totally not over her."

"Exactly!" I exclaimed. "I mean, no! I *am* over her. Now all I have to do is win EndGame, and next thing you know Skylar is seeing pictures of me in a magazine."

Maria stopped and pivoted to look at me. "I think you can do whatever you set your mind to Roy. If you want to become a famous dueler, no one can hold you back. But if you're doing it all to get back at Skylar, you're going to end up disappointed."

"I was just kidding."

"Of course you were."

She turned, and we continued walking down the Strip. Even in the day I could feel the neon lights of the casinos looking down and judging us.

"Well this is my stop," I said as we arrived in front of the Hyperion casino. We were still a hundred feet away, but I could see Sorceress Valentine standing next to the entrance, and I wanted to approach her alone.

"I'm so happy for you Roy," Maria said. "You're becoming a sorcerer, you're living your dream. I just hope you're doing it for the right reasons."

"I am," I said. "And thank you. I'm happy for me too."

I was hesitant to say good-bye. The last time I said good-bye on the phone, we had ended up apart for a year. At least from my reference point. Who knew what was in store this time?

"I don't trust that guy Karl," I said.

"Roy Nakamura, don't be so overprotective."

I looked down at my feet. "It's not overprotective. I just don't want to see him hurt you."

"He won't," she said. "I won't let him."

I nodded. "I'll see you tomorrow. Enjoy the fireworks."

Maria nodded back. With a final embrace good-bye, I turned and walked towards Valentine.

In order to avoid the usual physical punishment, I had made sure to arrive five minutes early.

"What did Maria have to say?" Valentine gestured at Maria's black and blue pony tail retreating into the crowd of tourists.

"How do you know who she is?"

"I know everything. Now walk." Valentine turned and made her way towards the casino entrance. I fell in behind her.

"This is your final exam Roy," she said. "It tests whether you are ready to move on to learning physical magic, actual dueling magic. Once we enter those doors, I will give you no help, no assistance. You pick the table yourself, cast your own spells, and most importantly," she stopped just short of the doors and looked me in the eye. "If you get caught, it's on you. I'm not bailing you out with a wall of fire this time."

With that, Valentine took a single step forward, causing the automatic doors to open for us, bowing to her presence.

From the moment we stepped inside, we were embraced by the music of the casino floor. The laughing and crying of the other gamblers, the clink and clang of chips and drinks, and the whir and whine of the slot machines, little neon lights blinking atop them in a miniature imitation of the neon lights that watched over the city.

Hyperion was Branch Parthenia's flagship establishment. Located towards the center of the Strip, it was believed to have the nicest accommodations of any hotel in Las Vegas. As we walked through the casino floor, we passed the normal mix of vacationing retirees, bored frat boys, bachelorette parties, and financial tycoons. All of them continued to play their games, oblivious to our passage.

I had actually expected more people to stare at us as we walked into the casino. Sorcerers tend to attract attention, both from patrons and casino staff, but nobody even glanced as we walked by.

"Something wrong?" Valentine said.

"I figured more people would stare at you, given your sorcerer's cloak."

"Invisibility spell," Valentine said. "No one but you can see my cloak."

"Why?"

"The sight of a sorcerer walking into a casino and sitting down at a blackjack table often arouses curiosity. I know how to handle it, use it to my advantage in fact, but I don't think you're ready for that level of attention."

I looked around at the tables. There were only three blackjack tables in use, about average for this time of day. The first was a hundred dollar minimum, a single player in a worn out suit playing with a large stack of chips in front of him. The second was a twenty-five dollar minimum and had four players, three of whom looked like they belonged to the same tour group from some European country, and one old man with a bad comb over and a red Aloha shirt.

The third table, which I started walking towards, was a ten dollar minimum with one other player, a man in his early to mid-forties in a striped long sleeve shirt, the cuffs rolled up. His weathered skin gave him a blue collar look. I took him for a construction worker, maybe one who had risen to foreman, or who maybe owned his own construction company, here in Las Vegas for his annual vacation, the one luxury he allowed himself before putting the rest of his money aside for his family.

"Why this one?" Valentine asked just before I sat down.

I gave her a questioning look.

"Don't worry, no one else can hear you." She made a circle gesture with a finger. "Shield spell."

I nodded, although it felt strange to talk about someone who was sitting two feet away from me. "There's only one other player, which will make it easier to cast a spell taking his actions into account."

Valentine nodded her approval.

"Besides," I said. "It has the lowest limit, and I only have a hundred dollars to bet with."

Valentine narrowed her eyes. "You're playing a ten dollar minimum table with only a hundred dollars? That's only ten iterations. You might not have enough time to ride the probability waves."

I shrugged. "Unless you want to start paying me a salary, that's all I've got."

Valentine stared at me, motionless. I was starting to think she didn't understand the concept of being an unemployed recent college graduate.

"Just do it," she said, and sat down at the table, taking the first position at the far right. I sat down in the second position, the player who was already there occupying the fourth seat.

"Good afternoon," I said, both to the other player and the dealer.

The other player nodded in reply, and the dealer said nothing except, "ID please."

I pulled out my driver's license, and put it on the table next to a stack of five twenty-dollar bills. "Five dollar chips please," I said.

The dealer handed me back my ID. As I put it in my wallet, he took the stack of twenties and expertly laid them out on the table so the camera in the ceiling could see how many there were. He then reached for his kitty, and pulled out twenty of the red five-dollar chips, putting them in front of him in stacks of four. When he had created five of the four-chip stacks, he gently knocked one over, allowing the camera to see the height of the stack. He rebuilt said stack and pushed all of them in front of me. I accepted them graciously and put two chips, the minimum bet, into the betting circle.

By the time the dealer finished counting the chips, I had already cast a shield spell over the table. I was a little worried Valentine's own invisibility spell might interfere with my spell, but I assumed she was intelligent enough to have thought through that contingency and planned for it.

The dealer started dealing, and I cast my first wave watching spell. First, I focused on keeping track of the cards being dealt to each person and using that, along with simple probability, to predict the next cards.

My cards were a six and a jack, while the dealer had a nine. Since I didn't have any data from the spells yet, I followed basic strategy and hit. It was a seven, causing me to bust, but the dealer's facedown card was a ten, so I would have lost anyways. I put two more red-chips into the betting circle and continued to craft my spell.

Since there was only one other player, I could modify the spell specifically to watch for patterns in his playing. I took a moment to study the player next to me, to think about the life he must have led and how that would affect his betting habits. My magical sense, my ability to perceive magic, reached out like a hand and caressed him, learning more about him from each stroke.

After learning all I needed, I pulled back and focused on the magic. The gesture on my hand and the words on my lip, I focused my mind on the *aetas* and modified the spell.

To celebrate the end of my second attempt at wave watching, Sorceress Valentine took me to New Horizons. It was a lounge at Versailles, a smaller Branch Parthenia casino just across the Strip from Hyperion. New Horizons was a small establishment that featured several leather couches in bright primary colors in a circle around a simple wooden bar. It made me feel like a child's action figure standing among giant play blocks. I told Valentine I was more in the mood for food than drinks, but she assured me the lounge could order food from one of the casino's restaurants upon request.

The lounge was empty, so we sat at the first couch we found. We were quickly approached by the bartender, a man in his late twenties who wore a bright orange T-shirt that was a size too tight and had his jet black hair shaped up into a faux-hawk. The bartender was carrying a martini for Sorceress Valentine ("I'm a regular" she told me in answer to my unasked question). I ordered a rum and cola (the bartender seemed surprised, as if he didn't notice I was there until I spoke). Valentine waited until he brought my drink, and retreated back to the bar, before reaching for her glass on the table in front of her.

The lounge was still deserted apart from us. Valentine took a long sip of her martini, consuming almost half the drink in a single gulp. She calmly put the glass down on the table in front of her, then did something so unusual it was almost frightening. She smiled. It wasn't judgmental or threatening, it was an actual genuine smile.

"You only made a hundred dollars," Valentine said. "But you did not get caught in the process. So I suppose that counts as a passing grade."

"Thank you, Sorceress."

"And do not worry, I will loan you some money so you can get started on the higher limit tables. Once you get better at wave watching, you can pay me back."

Valentine took a sip of her drink. "There was one thing I wanted to ask you however. There was a point where you had two eights, yet you failed to split. Do you remember that?"

I nodded. That particular hand stuck out in my mind.

"Why not?"

I thought back. "The next two cards were both small. The other player had eleven, so at first I thought he would double down and get the first small card, and I would get the next one. But I knew he wouldn't double down."

"How?"

"I just knew," I said, trying to figure out the answer myself.

Valentine pressed for an answer. "The spell told you?"

"I'm not sure. Maybe? I just looked over, saw he had eleven, and even though anyone else would double down in that situation, I knew he was only going to hit."

Valentine leaned back and took another drink, this time slower.

"It appears to have worked out," she said. "But you need to be careful. Remember not to go native. When wave watchers become good, and make no mistake you are now a wave watcher, they sometimes blur the boundary between what the spells tell them, and their instinct. The former you can trust, the latter you must not."

I nodded. "Yes Sorceress."

Valentine relaxed. "So now that you have wave watched, you understand why…" Valentine froze. She sniffed. "Do you smell that?" she said.

There was a loud thud to my right. I turned my head just in time to see the bartender close the large door leading to the lounge before turning around to face us. He pulled back his lips into a wicked smile, bearing his teeth, and his faux hawk began to look vaguely threatening. He took one menacing step towards us, and yelled.

"Feel my pain!"

The bartender's bright orange shirt bulged out. His jaw dropped lower than should be possible, narrowing his face, and his eyes started to sparkle an unnatural green.

Sorceress Valentine rose. I did the same.

The bartender's skin was turning a light shade of green as well. With a cackle, he opened his mouth, and a ball of dark liquid shot out of it, straight towards Sorceress Valentine.

Valentine crossed her arms and mumbled a spell. The dark liquid slammed into an invisible shield, falling to the floor as it hit the area just inches in front of Valentine's crossed arms. Where it hit the floor, it sizzled. The scent of burning carpet reached my nose.

The bartender roared in anger and raised both arms, palms out towards us. Something that looked like a small mouth opened out of each hand. The bartender screamed. Streams of acid shot out of each palm.

Valentine muttered another spell and pushed out her hands. The twin columns of acid altered their course and passed around us like a river running around a boulder.

The bartender screamed in rage and dropped both his arms.

Valentine clapped her hands, and a dozen tiny blue lights surrounded the bartender.

"Now, my turn," she said.

The lights solidified into a dozen silver spikes that plunged inward into the bartender. Two or three of them stuck into him, appearing to cause him pain, but he raised his hands and swatted away the others.

The bartender opened both hands and more acid flooded out towards us. Valentine pushed me to one side, then reached out and turned the direction of the acid beam away from us and back towards the bartender. He ceased throwing the acid and ducked to avoid being hit by his own projectile.

The last of the acid crashed to the ground. The void between us was littered with the stink of the acid as it ate away at the floor.

My magical sense spiked as the bartender put his hands together. The magic glowed, pulsed, as he sucked in energy, preparing for some final assault. Valentine beat him to it.

Valentine reached out her hands, and blue lights began to circle the bartender again, but this time there were far more than before. Too late, the bartender looked up as a hundred silver spikes plunged into his skin.

The bartender crumpled to the ground. Blood flowed freely from dozens of deep cuts all over his body, as his jaw shrank, and his face returned to normal.

"You have not won Sorceress," he hissed with a final breath. "The Dragon is coming for you. The Dragon is coming for you!" There was another hiss, and then he stopped moving.

The room was silent. The entire ordeal had taken less than a minute.

Valentine took a step back from the crumpled sack of flesh and bones that used to be the bartender. She seemed calm, still in control, but she was breathing hard.

"What was that?" I asked.

"That, was a demon," Valentine said. "A lesser demon, but a demon nonetheless."

My eyes looked around the bar. Half of the lounge was covered in acid, and the dead body of the bartender was going to be hard to explain to the authorities.

Valentine grabbed her left arm with her right hand. Something dark was seeping out from beneath the sleeve of her shirt.

"We need to leave, now," Valentine said. "Before security gets here."

No further invitation was needed.

"There is something I did not tell you," Valentine said. We were back at her suite, and she was peeling her shirt sleeve, wet with blood, off of her skin.

"Do you need me to get a doctor?"

Valentine shook her head. "Get me the bottle from over there. The large green one. And a glass."

I did as she bid, and when I came back she was mumbling a spell, incanting, as she waved her right hand over a large wound on her arm. Before my eyes, her skin started to knit itself back together. I was so distracted I forgot I was still holding the bottle and glass.

Valentine cleared her throat, mid-spell, and nodded towards the bottle. I poured a glass of a clear liquid, just as Valentine finished the spell and leaned back, exhausted. I handed her the glass and she took a long, slow, drink.

"Healing magic is tricky," she said. "You heal your body, but at the expense of your own body's energy. It can lead to massive fatigue if you are not careful."

Instead of looking up at me, Valentine continued to look into her glass. She took another drink. "As I was saying, there is something I did not tell you. I have not been entirely honest with you about the purpose of your training, Roy."

I looked down at my empty hands and wished I had a drink of my own. "With all due respect, Sorceress, I often get the impression you only reveal the truth to me when it suits your own needs."

Valentine did not contradict me. Instead, she brought her glass back to her lips.

"Remember when I first asked you to be my apprentice?"

"You told me the world was going to end, and I was the only one who could save it."

Valentine put the glass down on the table.

"You haven't brought it up in the last year," I said. "So I assumed you made it up. Some teaching technique or something."

Valentine shook her head. "Roy, have you heard of the OneSpell?"

It sounded familiar, like something I might have seen in the headline of an article I didn't bother to read.

"The OneSpell is the most powerful spell in existence," Valentine said. "It is a lost spell, so you probably came across it in some of the research you did for me.

"The OneSpell was created by Mianna Panashka, an extremely powerful wizard back before Atlantis sank into the ocean. Although she was powerful, Mianna wanted to be even more powerful. She believed magic was an independent force of nature, like the ocean, or gravity. She believed when we cast spells we use a part of that force to control the world around us. So, she attempted to create a spell that could control magic itself, giving the caster control over all of creation, all of existence. And she succeeded.

"Once she realized what she had done, Mianna was afraid it would fall into the wrong hands. Indeed, she felt any hands were the wrong hands, that anyone, at least anyone alive at that time, who wielded the spell would eventually misuse it.

"So, Mianna did the only thing she could think to do. She bound the spell up in an amulet and, using a tiny bit of the power of the OneSpell, she sent the amulet forward in time, a thousand years into the future."

Realization dawned on me. "When did you say this happened again?"

"Shortly before the fall of Atlantis. In fact, some believe Mianna used the OneSpell to destroy the kingdom as well, that this is why the island sank, in order to further frustrate any attempts to find it."

"But Atlantis sank in 1012 AD," I said.

"Exactly."

"Which means that if the spell was sent a thousand years into the future, then it's going to appear in fourteen years."

"Close." Valentine swirled the liquid in her glass around and took another large sip. "Mianna created it at least a couple years before the fall. I have been trying to determine the exact date. And even if she meant to send it forward a thousand years, various factors I have been researching may have altered its course. But from what I have determined, if my calculations are correct, the OneSpell will appear between two and three years from now." Valentine placed her glass back on the table.

"That's not long."

"Exactly, which means you have two to three years to become the greatest dueler the world has ever known."

I was confused. "What does dueling have to do with the OneSpell?"

Valentine reached for the drink on the table. Her left hand paused half-way on its journey. Perhaps it was still hurting from the wound, or perhaps she reconsidered her desire to end her sobriety. Either way, she abandoned the quest and leaned back onto the couch.

"I am not the only one searching for the spell," Valentine said. "I am searching for it, in fact I have spent a large portion of my life dedicated to finding it, because it is dangerous, and must be contained."

"And other people would misuse it?" I said. "People like the Branches?"

Valentine smiled. "The Branches would certainly misuse it, but they are not my main concern. At this point, most reputable wizards think the OneSpell is just a myth, a legend. My concern is for the demon."

"The demon we faced back at the bar?" I asked. "I thought it was dead."

"Not just a demon, *the* demon," she said. "The creature we faced was just one of its minions, a poor wretch the demon won over with promises of power and magic. *The* demon, its minions call it 'the Dragon,' is searching for the OneSpell. Several years ago it became aware of my presence, just as I became aware of it, and ever since then it has sought to stop me."

"You still haven't told me what this has to do with me," I said.

"Be patient," Valentine said sternly. "Do not forget all of the training I gave you in an instant." Valentine paused to find her train of thought. "When powerful magic users have strong emotions, the magic can cause those emotions to manifest as creatures with limited powers. Usually they fizzle in minutes or hours. Sometimes they stick around for days, which is where rumors of ghosts and poltergeists come from. But they always fade away.

"The demon who hunts the OneSpell is the exception. It was created by the hatred of Branch Primm when they were exiled from

Las Vegas. Think of all those hundreds of people, used to being the equals of those around them, suddenly cast out like rotten vegetables or rancid meat. Think of all the hate they must have felt, all directed towards the other six Branches. All that hate joined together and created the demon known as the Dragon.

"Now, it seeks the OneSpell so that it can gain vengeance for Primm and destroy the other six Branches. It recruits minions by offering them promises of magical powers, then turns them into lesser demons by granting them a portion of its own power.

"The demon is the greatest threat to the existence of the human race. And Roy Nakamura, you're the only one who can stop him."

In *Call Me Sorcerer*, there is a part towards the beginning where the protagonist sees a fortune teller who operates out of a small alley just off the Strip and learns he is the chosen one who is destined to face off with an evil wizard who is terrorizing the people of Las Vegas. Oddly, the first thing that crossed my mind when I heard Valentine's speech about the OneSpell was that I felt like I was inside *Call Me Sorcerer*, or any of those other books about Las Vegas I used to read. Boy goes to Las Vegas, learns magic, saves the world. It seemed so simple inside the pages of a novel, but now I wanted nothing to do with it.

"But I don't even know how to duel," I protested. It was the first thing I could think to say. "All you've taught me is wave watching."

"Dueling is wave watching," Valentine said. "Wave watching is about using probability waves to predict future outcomes. In a duel, that ability is the most valuable one there is, knowing what your opponent will do before he does it, knowing how he will react to one spell or another."

"But wave watching takes time," I said. "You said yourself that mental magic is useless in a duel. In a duel, a fight, there's no time to cast spells and analyze data."

"Not consciously, no, but that is where you come in. The reason I have been training you, the reason I chose you to fight the demon, is that you are the only one I know who can wave watch intuitively, without even consciously casting the spells."

"I thought you said I wasn't that good."

"I lied." It wasn't an admission of guilt, it was a statement of fact. "Do you remember the first time you tried to wave watch, how they sent a wizard to intercept you?"

"Yes," I said hesitantly.

"Did you ever wonder why they sent a wizard, a full-on sworn wizard, to stop someone from wave watching at a five dollar table?"

I shrugged. "I guess my shield spell wasn't good enough, and…"

"It was because you didn't just cast a normal wave watching spell Roy!" Valentine said. She was worked up, either from the fight or the alcohol, and she was almost shouting. "At first, your spell only took into account the numbers of the cards that had already been played. But then your spell reached out and spelled the automatic shuffler. The Arabian Nights casino has a lot of money, all casinos do, and as such it is often the target of wave watchers. To counter this, the management casts spells on all the automatic shufflers that prevent them from being spelled by anyone else."

"And this counterspell detected my attempt to cast a spell on the shuffler?"

Valentine shook her head emphatically. "You did not cast a spell on the shuffler directly, you cast a spell on the counterspell. You subverted the defense mechanism they had installed and used it to learn the identity of every single card yet to be shuffled.

"The management realized this at once of course. Casting a spell on a counterspell is quite hard. They must have thought they had a powerful sorcerer on their hands and dispatched a wizard accordingly."

"But I didn't try to do that," I said. "All I did was try to cast a wave watching spell."

Valentine shook her head. "That is the worst part Roy, you did not even try. It just came to you."

"Well it wasn't easy. I had to try three times."

"Try three times? It is an incredibly complicated spell Roy, even I would have a hard time doing it. But you did it as second nature. That is why Branch Shaskauer sent a wizard after you. They were scared to death."

Valentine leaned back. At some point during her tirade the drink had ended up back in her hand. With a single motion, she finished it.

"You are the one, Roy. I can teach you wave watching, and dueling, but you are the one in a million, one in a billion, who possesses the raw magical abilities to form the types of spells we need. You are the only one with the capacity, when the time comes, to defeat the demon known as the Dragon and claim the OneSpell."

Once again, I was struck by the unreality of the situation. I started to stammer. "I just don't think…"

Sorceress Valentine reached forward, quicker than I thought she could move in her semi-inebriated state, and slammed the palm of her hand into my forehead.

I was standing on a barren desert plain. The only sound was my own rapid breath. The sand and rocks around me were bathed in a reddish tint. At first I thought it must be dawn or dusk, but then I looked up and saw a dim sun hanging in the sky. It was the middle of the day, but the sky itself was red, and the thick atmosphere was blocking out so much of the sun's light that I could look at it directly without feeling any pain or discomfort.

In the distance I could see a mountain range. It was the same set of mountains I went through on my way to Las Vegas. Everything was quiet. No cars, no birds, no animals, no people. Just silence.

I knew this wasn't real. This was some sort of illusion Sorceress Valentine was showing me. But I still felt dread as I turned around.

There was Las Vegas, or what used to be Las Vegas. Columns of black smoke reached into the sky, pouring out of fires that dotted the cityscape. The black smoke was interrupted by flashes of lights, signs of spells being cast by magical attackers or magical defenders.

And it wasn't just Las Vegas. Somehow I knew all the world's cities would look like this one, that Las Vegas wasn't the first city to be destroyed, but was in fact the last, the only city that still held on against whatever darkness threatened the world.

Then there was a flash greater than the others, and a giant explosion rocked the city. The light was a thousand times stronger than the weak sun hanging in the sky. I averted my eyes for a second. When I looked back there was a giant mushroom cloud rising out of the ashes that had once been Las Vegas.

It was all over. Everything, everywhere, was destroyed. I was all that was left. I was alone in the world.

I was back in Sorceress Valentine's suite. The familiar smell of old books was suddenly comforting.

"What was that?"

"The future," Valentine said. "At least, a possible future. The Dragon is a creature born of hate and darkness, with unbridled power. If you can't defeat the Dragon, it could mean the end of everything."

"We have to tell people." I stood up. "I know you have quarrels with the Branches, but if they knew what we faced."

"We can't trust anyone!" Valentine hissed. She motioned towards the couch, and I sat back down. "The Dragon has many followers. It mostly preys on the magically weak, but it has made in-roads into some of the Branches. The demonic influence is hard to detect, so there is no way to know who is secretly working for him.

"That is why you must not tell anyone about the Dragon. Not your friends, not your family, no one. The Dragon knows about me, but I have dealt with it for many years, and I have my protections. You on the other hand are unguarded. If the Dragon knows you are not just my apprentice, but the tool I will use to defeat it, then it will destroy you before you are ready to face it.

"And it won't just destroy you. If the Dragon knows it has been discovered it will destroy your friends, and your family, and everyone you know or love. Just to hurt you. Do you understand?"

At some point during the rant Valentine had grabbed both my wrists and locked her gaze on me. There was a frantic edge to her speech, a subtle implication she was not fully in control of this situation. It was a side I had never seen before, and it frightened me.

I came to Las Vegas to become a famous sorcerer, a champion. Now I had managed to arouse the attention of a dark and powerful creature even worse than the ones in the books that had inspired me.

My phone rang. It was Maria. Without thinking, I pried my hands away from Valentine's grasp and answered the phone.

"Hey Roy, is now a good time?"

"Of course," I said. I turned away from Valentine.

"I just heard from Karl, and he has to work tonight so he can't make it. I don't suppose you'd have any interest in watching the fireworks with me?"

I risked a glance back towards Valentine, who looked confused.

"Of course I'd be interested," I said. "I'll pick you up right away."

Valentine interrupted. "How are you doing that?"

"That would be great Roy," Maria said on the other line. "I'll see you then."

"See you soon." I hung up.

"How are you doing that?" Valentine repeated, sounding confused. "Phones don't work here. How are you making it work?"

I put the phone back in my pocket. "I have to go."

"You're going? I just told you that you have to train so you can save the world, and you're going?"

I steadied myself. "Maria needs me."

"Well I don't care what Maria needs," Valentine said. "I think our work here is a little more important than your girlfriend."

"She's not my girlfriend, she's just a friend." I started walking towards the elevator.

"All the more reason to let her be, and start training instead! You wanted to learn physical magic? Now is the time. I'll teach you whatever you want to know."

I reached the elevator and pressed the down button.

"I'll meet you tomorrow morning to start my training. But for now, I have to leave. I have to do this."

The elevator arrived. I stepped in, despite Valentine's protests, and turned around to face her.

"You realize I can have the elevator drop you off anywhere I choose," Valentine said. "Including the middle of Antarctica."

"If you do that, you'll have to find someone else to save the world." I hit the ground floor button, and the elevator doors closed.

6. Fireworks

Looking back, my friendship with Maria was a cocktail made with three parts laughter and one part tears. The laughter was due to a shared understanding, a language of inside jokes that had been refined and developed over the course of the decade we had known each other. The tears were usually the result of one of two things, grades or boys.

In college, when Maria had an exam she was worried about, she would ask me to meet her outside her classroom when the test was over. That way if it went badly, she would have a shoulder to cry on. Literally. Skylar wasn't always thrilled about this.

"It's just a stupid test," Skylar told me once. "What is she so stressed about?"

"You don't understand what it's like. Things don't come easily for Maria like they do for you."

"Things don't come easily for me either!" Skylar protested. "I just study very, very hard." Pause. "Fine, go comfort her if you have to."

And so I would go. I would stand outside the classroom where Maria had just taken her calculus midterm, or biology final, and wait for the doors to open and the students to rush out. When they did, when I saw Maria's downcast face, already a little teary, emerge from the classroom, I would run over and hold her in my arms as she cried.

There was one time sophomore year when Maria was taking organic chemistry (back when she was pre-med, back when she wanted to become a doctor someday so that she could, literally, find the cure for cancer). The night before a major exam, she was a mess.

"Roy, I need you here, right now," she said over the phone. I could hear the stress in her voice as if it were a tangible presence in her room, wrapping itself around her, choking her so she couldn't breathe.

I lived in a dorm on the other side of campus, but by running I got there in just a couple minutes. I found her sitting on the floor in the hallway outside her room, her textbooks and notepads sitting unopened on the floor next to her. The rest of the dorm appeared to be asleep, so I whispered, rather than said, "hello," as I sat down beside her.

"Hey," Maria whispered back between two suppressed sobs. "Thanks for coming."

The carpet was rough and scraggly. Whoever designed it did not have comfort in mind.

"How's it going?" I instantly regretted asking such a meaningless and stupid question.

Maria gestured at the books next to her. "There's just no way I can finish it all. I said I wouldn't get behind this time, that I would study hard. But I just can't." She reached for a book, then withdrew her hand before she touched it. "Yesterday I kept forgetting old stuff when I learned the new stuff. And now, it's like I'm not even learning the new stuff, like I can't even understand the text as I'm reading it."

To this day, I don't remember what I said. Probably something like "you'll be fine," or "it can't be that bad." All I remember is that a moment later she threw her arms around my neck and buried her head into my shoulder, sobbing. She had cried into my shoulder before, but this time it was worse. There was a finality to it, like she was crying not just because it was a sad moment, but to compensate for all the sad moments to come, for all the other students in her same situation who couldn't cry, or didn't have a shoulder to cry on. I don't remember how long we sat there, but it seemed like a long time.

Later that night, more like early morning, when Maria's tears had dried and I finally returned to my dorm room, I sent Maria an e-mail. The message was short, something about how she was perfect just the way was and shouldn't let grades define her, or some other youthful nonsense like that.

I never got a response to the e-mail. The next day, Maria dropped pre-med and changed her major to American studies.

When I picked up Maria at her apartment, I could tell Karl's cancellation had hit her hard. Maria smiled when I met her at her apartment, but the smile didn't reach her big brown eyes. Her hair hung straight down her back. It had to have taken her an hour of painstaking work to tame it into shape. She wore a blouse that was one of her favorites.

"I'm not sure where we can go to watch the fireworks," she said. "So I was hoping you might have an idea."

"No worries," I said. "It's the city of magic, I'm sure we can find a way to make them magical."

It was strange how quickly I could go from worrying about the fate of the world to worrying about where we could go to watch fireworks. Maria just had that effect on me. My troubles, no matter how severe, were no longer troublesome when she was around.

In retrospect it may sound naïve, but it didn't occur to Maria or I that not only would Las Vegas be busy on the Fourth of July, but that all the good places to watch the fireworks would be equally packed.

We tried Sky Bar at the Los Angeles Casino first, a bar Maria told me had the best view of the Strip. The bouncer at the entrance, a man who appeared to be either a professional football player or a body builder, politely told us reservations for nights such as this had to be made weeks in advance. He also looked at our clothes and, somewhat less than politely, suggested even a reservation might not have been enough for us.

Next we tried La Barca, a boat shaped restaurant at the top of Pirate Bay, also known for its view of the city lights. The maitre d', somehow managing to look aloof and pretentious even while wearing a pirate outfit, said the earliest he could fit us in was midnight.

Three rejections later, I was ready to give up.

"We could just watch them on TV or something." It was only an hour until sunset, and we had, in my opinion, exhausted all other firework-watching options.

"Can't do that," Maria said. "It's on my list."

"Your list?"

"Yeah, the list of things I want to do before I die."

I raised an eyebrow. "Well, I'm sure there will be another time you can watch fireworks, unless you're planning on dying this year."

Maria elbowed me. "This is serious stuff, Roy. Besides, the item on my list isn't just to watch the fireworks, it's to watch them every Fourth of July for my entire life."

I thought about it for a second.

"Maybe you should try making a list," Maria said. "Might give your life a bit of direction."

"You got the idea for doing a list from *The Closest Exit*, didn't you?"

Maria turned red. "Maybe."

"I knew it!" I exclaimed. "Well, here's my list. Item one, never watch *The Closest Exit* again."

"Roy!"

"You're right, too narrow. Item one, never again watch a movie you recommend."

Maria made a mock pout face.

"And what's your first item?" I asked. "No wait, let me guess. To become a flight attendant and see the world, just like in *The Closest Exit*?"

"No," she said. She folded her arms in front of her. "My first item is to see a unicorn."

"A unicorn?"

"Yes, a unicorn."

I wasn't sure if she was joking, so I measured my words carefully. "I hate to be the bearer of bad news, Ms. Perez, but I heard a rumor they don't exist anymore, and in fact they've never…"

Maria put her hand over my mouth, silencing any further blasphemy. "Hey, I've got a lifetime to do it. Besides, I was reading this old diary smuggled out of the Branch Shaskauer Archives the other day claiming there were unicorns in Atlantis, so maybe by studying more I'll find a place where they still exist." Maria cleared her throat, more for effect than necessity. "Now if I remove my hand, will you promise to start behaving?"

I shook my head sideways. Using her hand over my mouth, Maria moved my head up and down.

"There, that's a good boy," she said, removing her hand.

I smiled. Then I thought of something. "Let's get out of here. I have an idea."

The sun was rapidly falling as I pressed down even harder on the accelerator, grinding metal against metal as my white LeBaron Convertible cruised past ninety miles per hour. The faster I went, worries, doubts, fears, peeled off like droplets of water stuck to a car window.

"Faster Roy!" Maria laughed, screaming to be heard over the roar of the world rushing past us. "This is practically the fastest I've ever gone. Go faster!"

Maria's hair was whipped up in the wind, streaming behind her like a black and blue wave. I risked a quick look over and stared at her for a precious second, before tearing my eyes away from her and focusing them back on the road in front of us.

"Go faster!" Maria said again. Smiling, I complied, and we broke a hundred.

The barren desert and twilight air rushed past us. I felt like a fighter pilot on a solo patrol, surveying the moonscape around me. Maria squealed in delight as wildlife scurried away at the distant promise of my headlights piercing the darkness around them.

There were no other cars around, but if there were I think I would have ignored them, wrapped up as I was in a limited world that consisted of me, Maria, and the chariot carrying us to our destination.

A song came on the radio. Maria said something, but it was drowned out by the wind.

"What was that?" I yelled.

"Do you remember this song?" she said again, louder. "It's *Remember*, by Taliesin. We slow danced to it at ninth grade semi-formal."

I shook my head. "Are you sure? I don't remember that."

Maria just laughed, then she started to sing along at the top of her lungs. Her voice was beautiful, but she could only remember half the lyrics.

> *Remember me*
> *When you're old and gray*
> *Something something*
> *I don't want to stay*
>
> *Remember... love*
> *Time's not my friend*
> *I'll see you when*
> *The something ends!*

I stifled laughter, causing my foot to slip off the accelerator for a second, and we slowed back down to ninety.

"You try," Maria said, lightly punching me in the arm.

We were at least five miles out of the city limits. An off-ramp appeared in my vision, and figuring we were far enough away, I took the exit, a small dirt road. Once I was off the highway I spun the car around so we faced the city we had just left.

As the last piece of the sun fell below the horizon, I turned off the engine. The top was still down, and I became acutely aware of how silent the world was. The city of Las Vegas still dominated our field of vision, the neon lights shining like a beacon in the dark desert.

Even at that late hour it was still mercilessly hot. I thought of turning the engine back on, taking advantage of the air conditioning, but I left the key in the ignition and resisted the temptation.

Maria pulled an elastic out of nowhere, as if by magic, and spun it around her hair into a pony tail. The ambient light fell just right, lighting up her profile and emphasizing her tan skin. She turned to me, about to say something, but then we saw the promise of a bright spectacle emerging from the direction we had come.

The flash from the first firework hit us long before we could hear the blast. The flash was followed by another, and light exploded across the sky. Maria told me earlier the Branches employed magicians to assist with the shows, that there was magic as well as gunpowder up there in the air.

From where we were, it was pure magic. I looked to Maria and wondered if she saw it as I did, or if her lack of magical training prevented her from seeing some of the intricacies of the light show in front of us.

"Hey Roy," Maria said. "Do you remember that one time when I was really stressed about that chemistry test?"

I couldn't remember which specific time she was talking about, but I said "yes" anyways.

"And do you remember what you told me, well, wrote me in that email?"

I nodded.

"Yeah, I remember."

"Well," Maria continued, "I never got the chance to say thank you. So, well, thank you."

That was the moment I decided to stay in Las Vegas. I was still skeptical of everything Sorceress Valentine had told me. The vision she showed me had been just that, a vision, and part of me wanted to write it off as a parlor trick. But sitting there in my car, next to Maria, watching fireworks go off above the magical city, I knew this city, this place, was worth fighting for.

As if to reinforce it, that night I dreamed of demons, and spells, and mushroom clouds rising over Las Vegas, and every city and everyone I loved. The next morning I reported to Sorceress Valentine to start my training, my real training, as a dueler.

Part II: Trials

Labor Day, 1998

1 – Ruby Red

October 19, 1994
Los Angeles

It was 80's night (like it was every Friday night) at *Ruby Red*, an eighteen and over nightclub in Hollywood. My roommate Grant Chung and I were on an e-mail list that sent us weekly coupons giving us five dollars off the twelve dollar admission, but only if we got there before ten-thirty. We were college freshmen back then. We always made sure to get there by ten-fifteen, or ten-twenty at the latest. It was October 19, 1994, and I was about to meet Skylar Trope, my future ex-girlfriend, for the first time.

The building *Ruby Red* occupied had hosted live music at some point in its life. The long hallway patrons went through upon entering the premises, as well as the ornate desk behind which a cashier waited, all hinted at an era in which the establishment had served a higher class of music listener. The creators of the building, no doubt, had loftier ambitions than a club so desperate for cash it didn't set the minimum age to enter at twenty-one like every other club in Hollywood.

The clientele of *Ruby Red* was a mix of cash-strapped college students, hip-hop club goers who didn't realize they were in the wrong place, and emo kids who grew up believing Robert Smith and Steven Morrissey were the only people who really understood how they felt.

After paying at the aforementioned overly ornate cashier's desk, patrons were funneled into a cavernous room, faux wooden panel dance floor in the center, with tall tables (more decorative than functional) along the right and left sides of the room. The far side of the room contained a stage, perhaps at one time the territory of local performers, where the DJ now stood with his various musical contraptions. In typical club fashion, the music was just a little bit too loud, leading to the need to constantly shout rather than talk. There were a number of lights twirling on the ceiling, throwing sparkles down onto the dancers below. It was the perfect amount of light, just enough to make the place seem festive while not enough to be obnoxious, or to render the dancers blind.

As we entered, Grant spied a blonde-haired man in his mid-twenties, sporting a conservative haircut and wearing a floor length silver gown.

"Do you think that's a girl or a guy?" Grant screamed over the music.

I looked. "It's clearly a guy."

"If that's a girl, she's hot," Grant said.

I raised an eyebrow. "If that's a girl, she looks like a guy."

Skylar was standing at one of the tall tables to the side of the room, a non-alcoholic drink in her hand, glaring at her roommate Shana who had dragged her to the club under the false pretenses of it being a swing dancing club. Shana was on the dance floor, getting intimate with a guy whose gelled faux hawk and eye liner were almost garish enough to draw attention away from the fact he was clearly wearing women's jeans.

I didn't notice Skylar at the time, but she noticed me. She later told me I stood out because I was wearing what I considered to be the coolest shirt I owned, a black short-sleeve button down shirt (unbuttoned at the time, of course) with a giant silver dragon on the back. After we started going out, the shirt mysteriously disappeared. To this day, Skylar denies any knowledge of its whereabouts.

Back then *Ruby Red* was magic, at least the closest I came to magic outside of the books I read about Las Vegas. The entryway was still part of the mortal realm. Although my hands would tremble with excitement while handing the cashier my seven dollars and five dollar off coupon, that act was clearly still an earthly transaction. But once I entered the club itself, all the problems of the outside world were shrugged off like a heavy backpack upon arriving home. I felt taller, freer, cooler. With my favorite songs pumping through my mind I felt like I was inside a movie, like I was the main character and anything could happen.

I was so busy thinking of all the exciting things that might happen that night that I didn't notice my future ex-girlfriend standing to my right as I trailed Grant onto the dance floor. It was still a few minutes before ten thirty, the club wouldn't start heating up for another hour, so the two of us doubled the number of people on the dance floor. Erasure's *Chains of Love* had just started playing, so I slowly shuffled my feet and nodded my head to the beat.

Grant and I were four feet from each other, trying to look like we weren't dancing with each other, but also weren't dancing by ourselves. The theory had always been that some pair of girls would see us and come over to join. I was a freshman in college. I was too young to realize that outside of adolescent fantasies, that just doesn't happen.

To my right I noticed a girl (I would later find out she was Skylar's roommate, Shana), white and tall, wearing a pink leather mini-skirt a few sizes too short for her and a black piece of fabric a bit too revealing to be accurately described as a "top." She was grinding against an emo hipster wearing more make-up than her. I normally tried not to stare at clubs like these (even at stare-worthy spectacles like the guy in the silver gown), but in this case it was so cringe-worthy I was unable to look away.

I was about to comment on this to Grant when another figure approached, the one that hadn't drawn my gaze before but now easily did. She was Asian of some type (despite my own Asian heritage, I can't tell Chinese from Japanese from Korean just by looking) and was wearing a simple blue dress just a tad too conservative for the setting. Although simple and conservative, the dress did little to hide the girl's impressive figure.

The girl in the blue dress faced the girl in the pink skirt. I thought she was going to start grinding from the other side and turn it into a threesome. Instead she planted herself feet wide, fists balled, and stared with a gaze that could have caused her own black pony tail to tremble with fear.

"That's it, I'm leaving," the girl in the blue dress said.

"What's the matter?" the girl in the pink skirt said. "I thought you liked dancing!"

"I like dancing, not making out on the dance floor." The girl in the blue dress yelled to be heard over the music but overshot by a margin. "You told me we were going swing dancing! And guess what? There's no swing dancing here!"

I nodded to Grant, then spun around. In two quick steps I was standing in front of the girl in the blue dress.

"You want to swing dance?" I said, "I'll swing dance with you." Like a red dot from a sniper rifle, the girl's angry gaze turned from the pink skirt to me. Somewhere behind me, Grant started laughing.

I had done it. I had actually talked to a girl at a club. I was the main character in a movie, and asking a random pretty girl to swing dance to an 80's song was the sort of thing the main character in a movie can get away with.

The girl continued to glare. Her eyes slowly closed, as if she was thinking, then snapped back open like switchblades. After that, I always described her as the girl with switchblade eyes.

"I said, I'll swing dance with…"

"I heard you." Her anger turned to curiosity. "Do you actually know how to swing dance?"

"Of course," I lied, offering her my right hand. In the background, *Valerie Loves Me* by Material Issues started to play. The girl in the blue dress accepted my right hand. I started to shuffle my feet in my best imitation of swing dancing I had seen on TV.

The dance floor had at least two dozen people on it by then. If it had been slightly more crowded, I think I actually might have pulled it off. Instead, the lack of a crowd made it obvious in less than twenty seconds that I had no idea what I was doing.

I was expecting a lecture, but instead, for the first time that night, a smile made its way across the girl's face. Dropping my left hand, she held on to my right and dragged me off the dance floor to one of the tall tables. She leaned forward so she could be heard without having to yell.

"You have no idea how to swing dance, do you?"

I shook my head. "I've seen a few movies though." A moment of silence. I reached out my hand. "I'm Roy. What's your name?"

She cautiously accepted the hand, which she had been holding a moment before, as if it might bite. "I'm Skylar. Skylar Trope."

"Trope," I said, "that doesn't sound like a very Asian last name."

"It's not."

"Oh." I paused. "Cause, you know, you look pretty Asian."

Another pause, this one even more awkward.

"My, how observant," she said. "You must be an anthropology major or something."

"I didn't mean it like that. It's just, well, my name is Roy. Roy Nakamura."

"Oh," she said. "So you're Asian."

"Yeah, well, half."

"Because," she continued, "you also look pretty Asian."

"Well, I have a white mom."

"So do I," she said.

"Really?"

"Really. I also have a white dad."

I must have looked perplexed. "You have a white mom and a white dad?"

She smiled. "You're a smart one, aren't you."

"Then why do you look Asian?"

She leaned closer. "I'm adopted."

"Really?" I asked.

She nodded her head in an exaggerated fashion, as if talking to a five year old. "Yes, really."

"We should, like, go out."

Skylar laughed. For the second time that night she picked up my hand in hers. "Well, Roy Nakamura who is not an anthropology major, would you like to learn to swing dance?"

2 - Grant

"Sir, please remove one hand from the table."

I looked up at the dealer, a tall man with a shaved head who looked vaguely Slavic. His name tag, most likely borrowed from the dealer with the shift before him, said "JUAN" in large capital letters. The words below it read "Los Angeles Casino and Hotel," and next to that, in the corner of the name tag where only someone like me would notice, the circle with two vertical stripes that symbolized Branch Parthenia.

"I'm sorry, what's the problem?" I asked.

"Your hands," he said in a Russian-esque accent, as he motioned. Both my hands were draped over the table, almost touching the cards. "You must move one of them, the management," the dealer pointed upwards, in the direction of the cameras, "they do not like it when people have two hands on the table, that close to the cards. They think it makes it easier to cheat."

"Oh, I'm very sorry." In an exaggerated motion I removed my left hand from the table, held it up for both him and the cameras to see, and placed it on my lap underneath the table.

"It is no problem," said the dealer. "I just warn you before the security," he pointed again at the cameras, "do so, because sometimes they are not very friendly."

"In that case, thank you very much." It was a rote response since I was paying little attention to what he said. Already my left hand, under the cover of the table, formed the pose of a shield spell. Under my breath, I whispered the words to the spell. I envisioned the spell in my mind, summoning the *aetas*. The *aetas* should have been the hardest part of the casting, but for me it was always the easiest.

A standard shield spell created a magical envelope that surrounded the table and, theoretically, prevented any wizards or magicians employed by the casino from detecting any other spells I might cast while the shield was in place. My newest modification had been to build in a simple illusion. No matter how much I bet, it would appear to anyone outside the envelope, whether the pit boss or the men behind the cameras, that I was betting ten dollars. The frequent increase and decrease in the amount of a bet is a well known tell to ferret out wave watchers.

There was a cough to my right from an ancient man, hunched over in his Aloha shirt and holding an oxygen mask in his left hand. I wasn't sure whether he was coughing to remind me it was my turn, or just coughing. Either way, I glanced quickly at my cards, a five and a jack to the dealer's five. I hadn't cast any wave watching spells yet, so I simply followed basic strategy and stood.

My attention turned back to my spells, sparing only a moment of attention to the dealer. The facedown card was a king, and the dealer drew another king, resulting in a bust. The table cheered as chips were doled out to all, adding a smacking of high-pitched voices to the already deafening crescendo of the sounds of the casino.

By now I had cast my wave watching spell. First, I tasked it to keep track of all the cards that were played to calculate associated probabilities. The spell had no data yet, and so was silent regarding the next action I should take. The spell was like a newborn child, unable to speak because it had not yet heard language. However, as it started to hear those around it talk, as it saw which cards had been played, it would develop the capacity to mimic what was going on around it. Unlike a child, this process would take five minutes, not five years.

I modified the spell, prodding it to examine the way each of the other players at the table played, paying special attention to the old man with the oxygen tank since he was the only person before me, and factored that into the equation. Then I added to the spell again, telling it to look at the table as a whole and search for patterns. Was the automatic shuffler truly shuffling automatically? When the dealer gathered up the cards to put them in the shuffler after each round, was he putting his own cards on top of them or on bottom? Each of these details might affect outcomes by only a hundredth of a percent, but this was all I needed. Wave watching was not about winning every hand, only a cheater could do that. Wave watching was about monitoring the probability waves, guaranteeing that even if you lost a hundred hands, you won a hundred and one, or at least won hands with high enough pay-offs to have the same result.

With the spell fully cast, I leaned back slightly, relief on my face. The shield spell appeared to be holding up, based both on my own observation and on the lack of any security presence around me. The wave watching spell was doing just what it was supposed to.

The spell in my head chirped. The odds were increasing in my favor for this next hand, the probability of winning outweighing the probability of losing. I reached out my right hand, my left hand still safely under the table, and pushed ten more dollars into the betting circle.

Inside my pocket I felt my phone vibrate. Reluctantly, I turned off the spells (making sure to end the wave watching spell before ending the shield spell) and stepped away from the table. After two months of wave watching, I knew better than to try to answer a phone while sitting at a gaming table.

The caller ID said "Grant." I didn't need to answer it to know what he was going to say. Grant Chung, my best friend and former roommate, had come to Las Vegas to try to take me home.

Grant was waiting for me outside my apartment, a charmingly run-down two story building a comfortable distance from the Strip but still inside the Vegas city limits. In a past life the building had been a motel, so the flyer billed it as a furnished studio apartment where each unit opened up to the outside world. The motel had been placed there in anticipation of a Vegas expansion that never happened, and limped along business-wise until the Wizard War, and its assorted lull in tourism, put it permanently out of business. There were large vacant lots on either side of the building and a scattering of strip-malls, each with half the stores boarded up. The closest item of note was a convenience store which, unlike the rest of Vegas, couldn't be bothered to be open twenty-four hours a day.

During the day my apartment building and its neighbors looked like just another abandoned dusty town. But at night, if you looked both ways for cars and cautiously walked into the middle of the street, you could look to the left and see the Strip rising up in the distance and feel the warmth from the neon lights.

I parked my white LeBaron Convertible, top rolled up, next to Grant's black Audi A6. Grant purchased the car at the beginning of senior year after a summer internship with some financial firm in downtown Los Angeles. He never had a car before, and after earning more money in a summer than he had made in his life thus far, he suffered from the illusion common in young men that large amounts of money, if not spent immediately, would spoil. He kept the Audi A6 meticulously clean and in good repair, which is why when Grant said he was going to visit me, I assumed he would find another way to get to Vegas. I didn't think he would risk taking his baby on a multi-hour trip from home.

Grant was leaning his six foot frame against the side of his car. The sunlight reflected off his shaved head like a spotlight. As I got out of my car and walked towards him, we embraced like old friends. We were old friends, I suppose, having spent most of college hanging out with each other. With the possible exception of Maria, Grant was my best friend. It was a little strange because in my mind, thanks to my magical apprenticeship, I hadn't seen him in over a year. From his perspective it had been just two months.

"So this is you living the dream?" Grant said. He looked around at the front of the apartment building.

"One day at a time." It's always weird to see the place you live through the eyes of someone else.

"Well it's not quite law school."

I checked my watch. "Seven seconds. That was some restraint, Grant. You must be tired from the effort."

"Oh come on Roy, I'm sorry." He held out his hands. "I mean it, I'm sorry. It's just that…" he waved his hand at the world around him, as if the gesture somehow explained everything. He tilted his head, then righted it. "Never mind Roy, forget it. This weekend is about having fun. So, what do we do first?"

"I figured we'd get you checked into your hotel, then I can call Maria to meet up with us for lunch."

"Now Maria moving here makes sense," Grant exclaimed. "It's not like she had any other options." He caught himself. "Right, no shop talk or law school talk, moving on."

He clicked his key fob, unlocking his doors. "I'll drive," he said. "But first, one thing. Does Maria have any cute friends?"

Grant Chung was tall for an Asian guy. That was usually the first thing people noticed about him, and they often told him so. His parents, who immigrated to the United States a couple years prior to Grant's birth, were both barely five feet tall, so Grant credited American food for his stature. He started shaving his head junior year of college, insisting it was a style choice and not because of hair loss. Around the same time he started working out regularly, and now had the largest muscles of anyone in my circle of friends.

Grant rented a room at Merlin's Dream, one of the cheaper hotels on the Strip. In its prime, the medieval themed casino had been a well-known destination, the flagship of Branch Parthenia's casino empire. Its rooms had once been state of the art (cable television in each one!), and the courtyard located in the center of the building had been used for a nightly jousting match between two fictitious medieval kingdoms.

Now, the blue and red paint was literally peeling off the exterior of the castle-shaped casino. The courtyard lay silent and unused. At some point, a Branch accountant had determined it was cheaper to let the place deteriorate than to maintain it, and at some point in the future another Branch accountant would determine it was cheaper still to knock the whole thing down than to run it. But for now it was still a hotel on the Las Vegas Strip, and it still had a casino.

I carried one of Grant's two suitcases for him up to his room (why he needed two suitcases for a weekend trip was beyond me). When we arrived he handed me a keycard.

"You expect me to open the door for you too?"

Grant shook his head. "You don't think I would come to Vegas and not hook you up, did you?" He pointed to the door to the adjacent room. "Your room is next to mine."

"But I can't…"

"Can't what?" Grant said. "We never get to hang out anymore since you moved here. You still owe me rent for the month of July by the way. I figure this way we can get as drunk as we want and not have to worry about driving."

I looked down at the key card. "But still, you paid for a hotel room for me?"

"The rooms each have two beds, so if it makes you feel better you could share my room and then Maria could take the other room. That way we could all hang out. Come on Roy, the least you can do is thank me."

I continued to eye the key card.

"Thank you," I said.

"Well you're very welcome. Now let's get ready to par-tay."

Grant managed to fit a six pack of Corona, a handle of vodka, and a case of ginger beer in his luggage. The vodka and ginger beer were supposed to combine to make a drink he claimed was called a "Moscow Mule."

It wasn't quite noon yet, but the temperature outside had passed ninety degrees and was on its way to a hundred. Earlier in the summer, Las Vegas had been so hot it didn't seem hot at all. Any sweat immediately evaporated off the skin, giving each resident a crisp and cool appearance. Now however, it was just hot enough to leave one soaking in sweat after even a quick march from the parking lot to the interior of the hotel.

The air conditioner was not completely functional, although it provided some breeze throughout the two hotel rooms. I once heard a conjecture that Las Vegas hotels intentionally provide inadequate air conditioning so their guests, miserable from the heat, will seek refuge inside the casinos (always kept at a crisp cool temperature no matter the cost).

To keep cool, Grant insisted I get as much ice as possible. Finding it easier to do his bidding than to argue with him, I used a small trashcan to transfer ice from the ice machine down the hall to the bathroom sinks of the hotel rooms. Now filled with ice, one sink became home to the Coronas and the other to the ginger beer.

The two hotel rooms were connected to each other by two doors, allowing us to go from one room to the other without having to go into the hallway. Grant had opened the two doors and paced between the two sinks, calmly adjusting and readjusting the ice to provide maximum coverage to the drinks like a trauma nurse checking vitals.

Grant and I had each consumed a Moscow Mule when we heard a knock at Grant's door. Grant was closest and opened it to reveal Maria, with Renée standing a couple paces behind her.

"Grant!" Maria stepped forward and grabbed Grant in a hug. "It's so good to see you again."

For a moment Maria's eye caught mine and she smiled. I smiled back.

Grant stepped back and looked Maria over like an appraiser examining a painting. "What happened to your hair?"

In early August, Maria found a part-time job at a coffee shop to supplement her non-existent income from being a Magic First activist. In obedience to the shop's corporate requirements, she got rid of the blue streak in her hair. The change was only physical though. Beneath her exterior, she was the same Maria she had always been. Making coffee might be what she did for a living, but her true career was still fighting for magician rights.

Maria's roommate Renée, in contrast, had abandoned her role in Magic First a month after I arrived in Las Vegas. From what I heard, this what not uncharacteristic of her almost magical ability to abandon causes to which she had once been committed.

Renée Winters had a waifish look, which combined with her Caucasian heritage and platinum blonde hair (kept in a short yet fashionable pixie haircut), reminded me of an anorexic Tinker Bell. She had pale skin disrupted by a button nose that could somehow look down on everyone despite her standing barely five feet tall. She wore more eye shadow than was probably necessary, and the result was smoky blue eyes that lured in passing sailors who sailed too close. Most guys found her attractive, but I didn't see it.

Renée had two tattoos, a shooting star (that is, a star with streaks behind it denoting motion) on her left shoulder blade, and the words *l'art pour l'art* ("art for art's sake") in flowing black script on her right forearm. She smoked two clove cigarettes a day, which created a slight lingering scent of bitter vanilla when one was in her presence.

Most impressive of all, Renée had the ability, in any situation, to imply she was too cool to be there. She didn't usually need words to do this. Instead, her posture and demeanor could convey a general boredom with whatever life had to offer her. When she did speak, it was as if she were speaking to a small child. When asked what she thought of a painting, or a sculpture, or a play, she would describe it in four syllable long adjectives that hinted at a deeper, mystical knowledge of the subject matter which she alone possessed.

Depending on who was consulted, Renée moved to Las Vegas and joined Magic First either as an experimental art piece, or just to be different. Back then the concept of a hipster was still in its infancy, but Renée fit the hipster ideal of doing what she did for the sake of being ironic. The mainstream populace idolized the Branches and their wizards, so Renée joined Magic First. Then fighting for magician rights became the trendy thing to do, and so Renée left, always in search of some other way to set her apart from the flock of sheep whose membership encompassed the rest of mankind.

"It's good to be here," Grant was saying to Maria. "I get to hang out with you, see what our little Roy is up to." For a moment Grant looked through Maria and focused on Renée.

"I'm Grant," he said, sticking out his hand.

Renée looked at Grant's outstretched hand without shaking it. "Charmed, I'm sure."

Grant withdrew his hand. "So Maria," Grant said, turning back to her direction. "Why the change in hair style?"

Maria didn't miss a beat. "For your information, Grant, I got tired of maintaining it. Bleaching hair, even a portion, is more painful than you'd think."

"I knew it would be something like that," Grant replied. "It's certainly not that a place like this would make you more conservative."

Maria touched her hair. "What do you mean a place like this?"

"I know everyone claims this is a great place," Grant said. "All these people moving here to fulfill their dreams, my best friend moving here to fulfill some sort of quarter-life crisis," he nodded briefly at me, "but at the end of the day it's just a city, one like any other."

I checked my watch.

"I have to go," I said. "Training time."

"Training time?" Grant asked.

"Roy is an apprentice to a famous sorceress and is training to be a dueler," Maria said. "I guess you must not have talked to him recently."

Grant smiled. "No, I guess not."

"And if you think Las Vegas is just another city," Maria continued. "I'm going to prove you wrong. I'm going to show you the Meet."

During the two months since the first part of my apprenticeship (which to me had lasted a year, but to the outside world was one hour on July 4), I met Sorceress Valentine each weekday to continue my magical training. On Tuesdays and Thursdays, we entered a seemingly random casino's elevator, which would magically take us to

Sorceress Valentine's penthouse suite, where we would practice wave watching and other mental magic.

On Mondays, Wednesdays, and Fridays, Valentine took us by car to an abandoned quarry outside of town where we practiced my dueling skills. The point of dueling is to defeat an opponent, either by knocking them unconscious or threatening them to the point of surrender, without killing them (which happened every once in a while in dueling circles, but was frowned upon). This meant not only knowing destructive spells, but knowing how to control them. It was easier to practice in an abandoned quarry than in a normal room, where an errant fireball might take out a wall.

Furthermore, being outside of Vegas limits meant it was slightly harder to use magic. So theoretically, when I tried the same spells inside Las Vegas it would be easier. Like learning to run with weights around the ankles. I don't know the exact spell Valentine used, but upon arriving home from the quarry, I could never remember exactly where it was.

Sorceress Valentine was waiting for me at the steps outside the Los Angeles casino, conveniently adjacent to Merlin's Dream. Despite the lack of a wind, her sorcerer's cloak billowed around her like a protective cocoon, fending off the Vegas riff-raff. The locals and tourists, running from one air conditioned casino to the next, stayed a couple yards away when moving around her, like a river parting around a rock.

"You are late." Valentine tapped her bare wrist, as if there were a watch there.

"Sorry Sorceress. I have a friend in town."

I felt the presence of magic, and noticed Valentine's hand moving as she muttered words under her breath. I recognized it as a silence spell, shielding anything we said from prying ears.

"Roy Nakamura, are you drunk?"

I burped. "I had a drink, but I'd hardly consider myself drunk."

Valentine took a step towards me, and although she was a head shorter than I was, the effect was still intimidating.

"Do you have any idea how dangerous it is to perform magic while intoxicated?"

I shrugged. It was probably not the correct response.

Valentine took a step back and shook her head. "Every time I think you are improving, every time I think you are ready, you do something like this."

"What's the point?" I said. Maybe the Moscow Mule had affected me more than I thought. "It's not like you let me use the magic I learn."

Valentine started to speak, but I interrupted her.

"Why won't you let me duel?"

Valentine stared at me.

"I said…"

"Fine."

I paused. "Fine?"

Valentine shrugged. "Fine. You can duel. But, interrupt me again…"

A searing pain shot through my right knee, and I fell to the ground. The pain was gone in an instant, but I still had to push myself up and slowly stand, worried I was going to collapse again.

"We are not going to train today," Valentine said. "I have other things to do. But we need to make arrangements for tomorrow."

"What's tomorrow?"

"Tomorrow is the one day a month the Sorcerers Guild holds its Trials, at which you have a chance to prove yourself worthy of being a sorcerer."

"A what?" I stammered.

"A sorcerer," Valentine said. "I realize you are not from Las Vegas, but after a year as my apprentice, I would hope you know what a sorcerer is."

"I know what a sorcerer is. I just didn't think I was ready yet."

"Five seconds ago you were telling me that you were ready."

"Well, ready to duel," I said. "But the Sorcerers Guild Trials, I don't even know what they entail."

"Well you cannot duel until you become an official sorcerer." Valentine sounded exasperated. "So this is the way it has to be done. Besides, you are my apprentice. I think you are ready for the Token Master."

"The Token what?"

"Try to keep up. Now there are two reasons I need you to become a sorcerer. The first is that, as you keep insisting, you need to practice dueling. It is one thing to go up against me in practice, but nothing substitutes for real duels against real opponents, with shifting styles and different strengths and weaknesses. You need to get better, a lot better, before you face the Dragon." She paused. "You do remember about the demon known as the Dragon, right? The whole reason I trained you? The apocalyptic battle that, if you lose, could doom the whole human race?"

"There's no need for sarcasm, I remember." I hadn't been able to sleep for a week after my last encounter with the Dragon's minion.

"Well the best way to get dueling experience is to become a sorcerer," Valentine continued. "There is a whole system of regular duels you can become a part of once you get your sorcerer's cloak. Furthermore if you rise in the rankings, as I am sure you will, it will make it easier for you to wave watch. If a casino recognizes you as a famous dueler, they will not pay as close attention to your actions."

"What the second reason?" I asked.

"The second reason is because you need to ask a question of the Token Master. He is the man, to the degree anyone with that much magical ability can still be called a man, who controls entry to the Sorcerers Guild and will oversee the Trials. By tradition, anyone who becomes a sorcerer has the right to ask the Token Master a single question.

"I know approximately when the OneSpell will appear, but I have been unable to determine the exact date. I think the Token Master knows, but he would never tell me."

"Did you try explaining to him what will happen if we don't get the information?" I asked. "The whole 'world-will-end if you don't tell us' bit?"

"My relationship with the Token Master is," Valentine pursed her lips, "complicated. The Token Master is not quite human, at least not anymore. His concerns are different from ours. So no, he will not tell me. But if he knows, and you pass the Trials, he will tell you."

"Now what do the Trials entail?" I asked.

Valentine shook her head. "I'm sorry, I can't tell you that. All I can tell you is to meet me at Magic Hall tomorrow at ten minutes before noon."

I didn't need to ask her for the location of Magic Hall, the headquarters of the Sorcerers Guild. It was where I had my interview with Sorcerer Bastion Edwards when I first moved to Las Vegas. Besides, every Vegas magic-user knew where it was.

"Anything I should prepare?"

"Your whole life has been your preparation. Now, if there's nothing else, I have to be going."

Valentine twisted her hand and the shield spell dissolved.

"One more thing," I said. "Even if we know exactly when the OneSpell will appear, we still don't know where."

"I am working on that," Valentine said. "Now see you tomorrow, ten minutes before noon. This time, please do not be late. The Guild does not like it when people are late." Valentine turned and, despite the effervescent glow of her cloak, disappeared into the crowd.

I checked my watch. It looked like I would be able to join the others at the Meet after all.

3 - The Meet

East of the Strip, in an area next to the airport that would be useless for anything else, was the Meet. It was close enough to the Strip that the neon lights could keep an eye on its activities, but far enough to be ignored when convenient. The Meet started years before as a weekly farmer's market for magicians and quickly evolved into a perpetual carnival celebrating the underside of Las Vegas' magic culture.

Despite its urban location and décor, it had an earthy quality, especially when contrasted with the casinos of the Strip. Where the Branches relied on glamour and glitz, the Meet reveled in its dishevelment. Casino floors specialized in controlled chaos, while the Meet featured subdued but genuine disorder.

The center of the Meet was a small wooden stage, improvised out of discarded pallets and pieces of driftwood, kept together by some spell that succeeded where nails and glue would have failed. The stage was used for impromptu speeches, musical performances, and one-act plays which satirized the Branches.

From the stage, the Meet stretched out like four spokes on a wheel along the cardinal directions, following the streets at whose intersection the stage was located. The boundaries were fuzzy. Whenever a new magician came to set-up a table, he or she would take the next available space at the edge, and so the Meet would expand a little. Sometimes someone closer to the center would fold up shop, or simply get tired of the hustle and bustle, and in response the entire Meet would contract, each vendor shifting inward in an effort to get a little closer to the center.

Despite this lack of planning, there was a method to the madness. Due to some unknown magical law of attraction, amulet vendors threw up their tables next to other amulet vendors, and the purveyors of curse antidotes found themselves conveniently adjacent to the purveyors of curses. Polite Vegas society, those who belonged to the Branches, didn't venture to the Meet. But the other denizens of the city who spent time there would know instinctively which parts of the Meet would offer aids to do better on a test, which parts would sell spells that got one higher than the most deadly drug, and which parts could sell magical souvenirs (like living mosaics, the tiles portraying an animated scene by moving in time to an unheard song), which became normal objects again as soon as one left the Vegas city limits.

A band was playing a half-sung, half-spoken cover of *All Along the Watchtower*, providing a soundtrack for the Meet's festivities. I found Maria, Grant, and Renée at a magical sweets stand near the edge of the Meet's version of a food court. Grant was holding a small pastry, handed to him a moment earlier by Maria. She held a plate with a dozen of them.

"It has a cherry filling," Grant said, speaking while chewing. He swallowed and turned to Maria. "I don't get the big deal."

"The big deal?" Maria asked, her brown eyes wide with incredulity. "It's a pastry that magically becomes whatever you want it to be. You wanted cherry, and it became cherry. How could you not be impressed by that? It's practically the coolest thing ever."

"Because back home if I want a cherry pastry I can just buy it," Grant said. "That's the magic we know as consumerism. And it's a lot cheaper too."

Renée stood next to Grant, staring off into the distance while using a finger to trace the tattooed words on her right forearm. She folded her arms as I approached

"The prodigal sorcerer," she said. "That must have been quite a lengthy training session."

"Roy!" Maria cried out, suddenly spotting me. "We thought you weren't going to make it until later."

I stepped into the circle. "My training didn't go as long as I thought it would." I reached out and grabbed a pastry from Maria's tray and popped it into my mouth before she could say anything.

I smiled. "Raspberry."

"What training?" Grant brushed away some crumbs from his lips. "Wait, you really were going to some sort of training? I thought that was just an excuse you made up to get out of coming here."

"I told you before Grant," Maria said. "Roy is apprenticed to Sorceress Valentine, one of the most powerful sorcerers in Las Vegas. Isn't that right Roy?"

"Sorceress Valentine would take issue with being 'one of' the most powerful sorcerers in Las Vegas," I said. "But she is prone to exaggeration like that."

Grant shook his head. He gave a little sigh, one I only noticed because of how long we had known each other.

"So this is actually happening, huh?" he said. "This whole magic thing. You're actually going to do it?"

I felt oddly defensive. "There's plenty of time to go to law school. But this, now, is my one chance to learn magic."

Rather than argue, as I expected him to, Grant just shrugged. "Well, I guess you have to do what you have to do."

Grant turned to Maria. "So when are we going to meet Karl?"

"Yeah, I thought he was joining you at the Meet," I chipped in.

A moment of disappointment danced across Maria's face. "He called me and said he couldn't make it. But he's going to meet us later for dinner."

Grant nodded in understanding, but I continued to look at Maria, demanding more of an explanation.

Maria's smile deflated. "Karl isn't comfortable coming to the Meet. This is magician central. Wizards aren't really welcome here."

"Maria, they're about to start!" the voice belonged to a hippy-esque male I hadn't seen before. He had shouted the words at Maria as he jogged by, and was already gone before she could respond.

"Who was that?" Grant asked, curiosity mixed with disgust.

"It's Drew, he's with Magic First." Maria started to walk in the direction of the stage at the center of the Meet. "Come on guys, the rally's about to start."

The heart of the Meet was packed by the time we arrived. Through electronic or magical means, the Meet's residents had found themselves drawn there. I could feel a peculiar magical energy weaving throughout the place. It was different than the energy of the casinos, more wild and unpredictable.

The eyes of all those in the crowd were upon the empty wooden stage at the center of the Meet. A figure detached from the crowd and started to ascend the stairs. The crowd went wild, cheering as the figure reached the top.

Sorceress Corinna Windlass was wearing glasses. Although a full-fledged sorceress, she normally looked like she belonged in high school. With the glasses she could have passed for a college student. As she stood on the wooden stage her sorcerer's cloak shined, patterns appearing and disappearing as the cloak rustled in the wind. She looked approachable but also regal, in control.

"Who is that?" Grant asked.

"That's Sorceress Corinna Windlass," Maria said. "Out of the whole Guild, she's the only one who constantly criticizes the Branches and their crackdown on magicians. So even though she's technically part of the Guild, we all see her as one of us."

The cheering continued as Sorceress Windlass incanted a spell (I could see the slight movement of her hand as she cast it), then spoke out with a voice a hundred times louder than her own.

"Children of Magic!" she said. "Magic will be free!"

"Magic will be free!" the audience shouted back, gripped in the heat of the moment.

"The Branches are divided, they have been since the end of their Wizard War. Sometimes they call it the Great Wizard War, but the war wasn't great for us." Boos of anger all around. "No, not for us. The Branches drafted us, sorcerer and magician alike, and threw us like cannon fodder against each other. Then the war ended, and suddenly we were not allowed the freedom to practice magic as we wished, as we were promised."

Cries of injustice echoed throughout the audience.

"The Branches tell me I must pay the Tribute because I am a sorceress. I must give ten percent of everything I make to an evil entity who has never done anything to deserve it.

"And magicians, you are told you must have a Branch stamp if you want to practice magic. Even then, they can limit what type of magic you practice. Sure, you can dabble in trinkets or fortune telling, but if you practice the true magic, powerful magic, then they swoop down and kill you."

One person in the audience was actually wailing. I couldn't tell if the voice was male or female, if the wailing was caused by an especially vivid flashback or the memory of injustice towards a friend.

"But we will not stand for this. We cannot stand for this. Do you know why?"

"Why!" everyone yelled.

"Because the Branches do not come first, and the Guild does not come first, and we do not come first. The Magic comes first!"

"Magic First!" everyone yelled. "Magic First!"

The speech continued. Sorceress Corinna Windlass did not speak of magic, she spoke of Magic. She related stories about Magic like it was a close friend, a conscious creature with whom she could commune. When she spoke with a religious zeal of the need for Magic to be free, it didn't sound like a concept or movement, the way it sounds when an unSigned activist talks about free speech. Instead, her words painted an image of Magic as a bound winged creature, its wings tied with heavy rope, begging to be cut loose.

With a similar fervor, she talked about the need for everyone to come out the next day for the day of action on the Strip, the march right past the casinos that symbolized the Branches' power.

"They will see us from their casinos, from their towers of power," she said. "They will look out from their gambling dens and prostitution holes and they will quake in fear, for we are many and we are mighty!"

Sorceress Windlass ended the speech with a flourish. As the applause died down and the next speaker took to the stage, Sorceress Windlass walked through the crowd and stopped as she reached us.

"Maria, so happy you could make it," she said.

Maria looked star struck. She quickly touched the fingers of her right hand to her forehead while bowing slightly. "It is an honor to see you Sorceress Windlass," she said.

"Please, call me Corinna. And the honor as always is mine." She turned to look at me. I felt her magical sense sweeping over me, assessing my power and evaluating my abilities.

"Roy Nakamura, it is a pleasure to see you as well," she said.

She stuck out her hand and I accepted. Those around us looked on in awe that we *actually knew* the object of their adoration.

"I've been hearing a great deal about you," she continued. "Including how you are apprenticed to Sorceress Valentine, if rumors are to be believed."

"It's true," I said. "In fact, I will face the Trials tomorrow."

"I am glad to hear you found your path," she said. "Have you discovered yet why Magic brought you to Las Vegas?"

I laughed, unsure if she was joking, then stopped when I could see from her expression she was not.

"Magic didn't bring me here," I said. "I came here because I wanted to."

Sorceress Corinna Windlass adjusted her glasses without breaking her gaze. "You may think you came here of your own accord, but you are a magic user, which means Magic drew you here, even if you don't realize it." Staring into her eyes, for a moment I had the impression Corinna was far more ancient than she appeared, like she wore the body of a twenty-something magic activist as a disguise so her opponents would underestimate her. Then the moment passed and I was looking into the same eyes I had been looking at before.

A mousy man in a brown sports jacket ran up to us and whispered something into Corinna's ear.

"I must be going," she said. "I hope to see you all at the rally tomorrow. Especially you, Roy Nakamura."

I nodded, but there was no way I would be at that rally the next day. The next day, I was going to become a sorcerer.

For dinner, we met Wizard Karl Johnsen at Windmills, an upscale restaurant at the Spartacus casino. Windmills was the opposite of the Meet. Where the Meet thrived on disorganization, Windmills was a treatise in good order and discipline. Every table and chair was in its proper place. Silverware and napkins were lined up like soldiers to allow for maximum efficiency and aesthetic pleasure. Even the designs on the wall were sharp and angular, not flowing like the stalls of the Meet.

The clientele at Windmills was a mix of tourists with expensive tastes and businessmen taking a break from Branch business. The men all wore suits, with the exception of the wizards, who made up at least a quarter of the people there.

Naturally, Grant loved the place. "Now *this* is Las Vegas," he said to Karl. "We should have come here earlier."

"But of course. Nothing but Branch Merkasia's best for Mary's friends," Karl replied.

Karl was wearing his wizard uniform. We were still waiting for our main course to come, but I was already wondering if he would be able to keep his spotless white jacket clean. The waiter put out a plate of puffy white crisps resembling rice crackers. I was too skeptical to try one. Grant had no such reservation and grabbed two in one hand, popping them into his mouth one at a time.

"Very salty," he said.

"They are a traditional Atlantian appetizer," Karl explained.

"Interesting." Grant pointed at Karl's wrist. "By the way, nice watch."

Karl rotated his left wrist and eyed it, as if noticing it for the first time.

"It's a Rolex Explorer, right?"

Karl nodded. "You clearly know your watches."

"It's a hobby of mine." Grant stuck his own hand in the middle of the table for all five of us to see. "I figure after I've been working for a couple years I'll buy a Rolex. Right now I'm wearing a Citizen Quartz. Relatively inexpensive, but it's elegant and dependable. I also have a Casio for sports, but I wear this one for more formal occasions."

"Does one tell time better than the others?" Renée asked, in between two sips of a glass of wine. I hadn't seen her order it, and spent a second wondering where it had come from.

"I'll have you know, a watch tells a lot about a man," Grant said.

"Like whether he knows how to tell time?" Renée said.

"No, really." Grant was challenged, ready to argue his case. "Watches all tell the time, you're right about that. But that's what makes them so special. They are a pure luxury. If someone drives an expensive car, you wonder why he does it. Is it the leather interior, the smooth ride, the five star safety rating?"

Grant leaned forward. "But when you see an investment banker wear an expensive watch, you know there's only one reason why." Grant lifted his wrist. "Because he can. Cartier makes watches that cost a hundred thousand dollars. And do you know why they do it? Why people buy it? Because everyone else knows that it costs a hundred thousand dollars, and if a man can afford to spend a hundred thousand dollars on a watch, he must be a pretty important person."

Grant patted me on the back. "I keep trying to get this one to buy something other than a Timex, but he won't listen to me."

I instinctively touched my watch under the table. "What's wrong with a Timex?"

Grant shook his head. "We're not in college anymore Roy." He shivered. "Stop. Just, stop."

At this point our food chose to arrive. Karl ordered a traditional Atlantian dish consisting of meatballs in a creamy white sauce. Grant ordered a square piece of steak, which he started to saw through at once.

"Here, let me help you with that," Karl said to Grant. Karl lifted a finger (I could sense the magic flowing out of him as he chanted a quick spell), and Grant's steak cut itself into sixteen identical bite-sized pieces.

"I don't know exactly what to say Maria," Grant said. "But your boyfriend just cut my food for me, and I am absolutely okay with it." Grant high-fived Karl across the table.

I rolled my eyes. Renée, sitting to Karl's left, caught my gaze and gave a slight smile in agreement.

"Now Roy, why can't you learn useful magic like that?" Grant said.

Karl lowered his hand and put it around Maria's shoulders. Maria looked down at her own plate, which had its own piece of steak, then back up at Karl.

"As my boyfriend, I expect you to give me the same service you gave Grant," Maria said.

"Of course Mary." Karl flicked his wrist and half the steak divided into pieces.

Maria looked confused. "Did you run out of magic?" I was unsure whether she was serious.

"Not possible my dear." Upon seeing Maria's look of confusion, Karl added, "it reheats better if it is uncut. I mean, you were not going to eat the whole thing. You were going to take half of it home, right?"

I started to choke. Grant and Renée both turned to look at me, concerned, while I spit out a piece of food into a napkin and took a drink of water. By then the conversation had moved on.

"Where do you work that you know so much about watches?" Karl asked Grant.

"I work in finance." Grant put his fork down on his plate, allowing him to focus his full attention on telling us about his life. "I'm a junior financial analyst at Ravenwood Capital. I work in their Los Angeles office, it's on the fortieth floor of the Aqua Gulf Bank tower."

"Sounds interesting," Karl said. He sounded like he actually meant it.

"Yes, fascinating." Renée nodded, rolling her eyes, looking even more condescending than usual. I almost laughed at the gesture, but caught myself in time.

"I'm trying to transfer to the New York office," Grant was saying. "All the big deals happen in New York. But I just started a couple months ago, so for now it's important for me to just focus on having a real job and putting in the hours, you know what I mean?"

Karl nodded. "Absolutely. You just graduated from college, the important thing is to put in the hours now, even if it is in a job you do not like, so you can reap the rewards later. I keep telling Mary how she needs to leave this silly activism phase behind."

"Karl, not now," Maria mumbled.

"No, seriously," he said, spearing a helpless meatball off his plate and popping it into his mouth. He continued to speak as he chewed. "I could pick up the phone right now and get you a job working at any Merkasia hotel in five minutes flat. Then you could get a real paycheck and move out of that closet you live in. No offense Renée."

"None taken," Renée replied, examining her nails while taking another sip from her wine, which had refilled itself at some point.

"It's not about the money," Maria said. "You know that Karl. I moved out here to make a difference."

"Oh, that is so middle-class," Grant interjected.

Maria turned towards Grant. "What's that supposed to mean?"

"It's not about the money, it's about making a difference." Grant tried to mimic Maria's voice but did a terrible job. "It's just so clichéd. Of course money matters. None of us would be here, eating this meal, living in this city, unless we had money."

"Have you seen where I live?" Maria said. "I don't exactly have a lot of money right now."

"But you're poor because you can afford to be poor," Grant continued, now on a roll. "If you were really poor, if you were really worried about where your next paycheck was coming from, and didn't have mommy and daddy to fall back on, then you would be happy to take any job you could, like the one Karl offered."

Maria was silent. I thought about jumping to defend her, especially the part about her dad (Grant should have known better), but I stopped when the meaning of the words came to me. Grant hadn't been directing the comment at Maria, he had been directing it at me. When you know someone well, you also know how to hurt them.

"Oh please, you're the one being clichéd." It was Renée. She had put down the glass of wine and now seemed interested in the conversation. "You act like you're so much better than everyone else, Grant, but the truth of the matter is you drove here in a car that costs more than the average American salary for a year."

Grant shrugged and leaned back into his chair. "If it's a crime to sell out, then I'll sell out. I'm a realist, is that wrong?"

Renée shook her head. "I don't know where you came from, what your background is, or anything like that. But I do know you work in an office tower behind a desk, you drive a fancy car, and all this makes you a solid member of the middle class you so despise, if not richer."

Grant stared at Renée. At first I thought he had been offended, but then I realized the look I was seeing in his face was something else entirely. Admiration.

Karl broke the silence with a chuckle. "Renée, you and Mary are quite a pair. I cannot figure out which one of you is the bad influence on the other."

"What's that supposed to mean," I said.

Maria's big brown eyes shot me a look of death.

"I mean it," I said, looking straight at Karl. "What do you mean about them being a bad influence on each other? As far as I can tell, they bring out the best in each other."

Karl looked unbothered by my attempted verbal assault. "Calm down Roy, I only meant that maybe my idealistic paramour here would have left behind her failed attempted at activism if Renée, or you for that matter, were not constantly encouraging her."

"Failed attempt?" I said, ignoring Maria's signs to stop.

"Encouraging her?" Renée said, perplexed and offended. "I've never encouraged anyone in my life."

"She hasn't failed in her attempt," I said. "You should have seen her at the Meet this morning, she was like a minor celebrity. She was the only one who Sorceress Corinna Windlass made a point of talking to after giving a speech. And random people kept coming up to us and mentioning how they were looking forward to seeing her at the rally tomorrow."

Maria wasn't good at hiding emotions. From the look on her face, I could tell my comment was a mistake as soon as I made it.

Karl dropped his silverware onto his plate. The clang carried across the table. "My dear, what is Roy talking about?" He was still looking at me, not Maria, but it was clear where his question was directed. "Mary, you promised me you would stay away from the rally."

"Let's talk about this later," Maria whispered. It was just loud enough for me to hear.

I could see the discomfort on Maria's face, and normally I would worry more about how she was feeling than trying to prove myself right. But something about this wizard brought out the worst in me.

"Of course she's going to the rally," I said. "She's one of Magic First's premier activists, how could she miss it?"

Karl broke eye contact with me and spun to look at Maria, who was slowly shrinking away from him.

"Let's talk about this later," she said.

"But you told me…"

"I said, let's talk about this later."

Karl turned back to me. "Are you going to this rally too? Are you behind this?"

"I'm not behind anything," I said. "And of course I'm going to the rally. As soon as I finish the Trials at the Sorcerers Guild, I will be right over."

"The Trials?" Karl said in disgust. "This is perfect Mary. You have one friend encouraging you to throw your life away for Magic First, and another friend who is going to be a *sorcerer*," he said the word like it was an insult. "No wonder…" Karl said an Atlantian phrase I didn't know the meaning of. But Maria understood it. She seemed hurt.

Karl looked around the table, then fixed his eyes on me. "I have had enough of this assault on my honor. I invite you to a meal, to a nice restaurant in one of my Branch's finest casinos, and this is how you repay me." Karl got up to leave.

"Don't bother," I said, jumping up before he could fully stand. "You stay. I'll leave."

I turned and exited the restaurant.

The original plan had been for us to all go back to the hotel room to hang out after dinner. Grant, who exited the restaurant soon after I did, drove me back to our room at Merlin's Dream, mostly in silence.

Back at the room, Grant set to work making drinks. The ice I put in the sinks earlier had melted. I sat on the bed in my room, thinking, while Grant walked to the ice machine, trash can in hand, and filled the sinks back up with ice. There were a couple spells I could have used to help him, but I didn't bother. He had the ingredients back to a chill temperature by the time Maria and Renée arrived.

"Karl can't make it," Maria said. "He has to work tomorrow."

We both knew it wasn't true, but if it was the story Maria wanted to stick to, I wasn't going to contradict her.

Grant materialized from behind me with a glass.

"Drinks anyone?" he said.

Grant proceeded to make four Moscow Mules, one for each of us, while Renée produced a pair of small portable speakers which she plugged a digital music player into. By some unspoken decree, Grant's hotel room (well technically they were both his, but the one he was sleeping in) had become the party room.

The room had two queen beds separated by a dresser. Maria and I sat on one while Grant and Renée sat on the other. After the first Moscow Mule, Grant got up to make another.

"I thought you only drink wine," I said to Renée.

Renée arched an eyebrow. The thin white shirt she was wearing had a single strap, permitting the shooting star tattoo on her left shoulder to be revealed. The star almost seemed to sparkle in the hotel room light.

"I'll drink whatever I care to," she said.

Grant returned with a drink in each hand and gave one each to Maria and Renée. "Ladies first," he said to me.

Grant raced back to the sink to make two more as Maria started to sip hers.

"Something wrong?" I asked.

Maria looked down into her glass. "It could probably use a little more ice."

In the back of my mind, I could picture Sorceress Valentine exhorting me not to use physical magic outside of our training sessions. I pulled Maria's drink away from her and muttered a spell. I could feel the alcohol in my veins, and it took me longer than usual to summon the *aetas* in my mind, but a second later a series of small ice cubes formed inside Maria's glass.

She smiled. "Thank you very much, Sorcerer Roy Nakamura."

"I'd like to see Karl do that," I said.

On the bed across from us, Renée rolled her eyes. "Yeah, a wizard from one of the Greater Branches would never have the skill to form ice cubes in a glass. That's just crazy."

Grant sighed like a disappointed father. "You're doing it all wrong Roy." He grabbed Maria's drink out of her hands and inspected it for damage. "You need large ice cubes, not small ones. Small ones will melt and water down the drink."

Maria reached up and snatched the drink back from Grant. "I'm sure the drink will be just fine," she said. "Thank you again, Roy."

Grant got two more drinks, one for me and one for him, and sat down next to Renée. I couldn't help noticing he was sitting a little closer to her than he had before.

"How do you like the drink?" he asked.

Renée took a sip, swished it around in her mouth, then swallowed. "I've had better."

Grant laughed. "That's fair," he said, before taking a drink from his own glass. He put his glass down on the dresser, then reached over and grasped Renée's wrist. She started to jerk back her wrist, then relaxed and looked at Grant with her usual nonchalance.

"What does this mean?" he asked, looking at her tattoo. "L'art pour l'art?"

"It means 'art for art's sake.'" Renée looked bored at the prospect of a conversation with Grant. "It means some people look for the meaning behind beautiful things, instead of just appreciating that they're beautiful. And I don't."

Grant released Renee's wrist. "Well that's stupid."

"Come on Grant, even you can behave for one night," Maria said.

Grant picked his drink back off the dresser. "What, I can't be honest?"

"Well *I* think it sounds beautiful," Maria said. "*L'art pour l'art.*" She said it in a hysterical fake French accent, and I had to swallow to avoid choking on my drink.

"Take this song playing right now," Renée said, gesturing towards her portable speakers, which were playing Taliesin's *Remember*. "The modern audience feels the need to analyze each word, to understand who the singer is singing about, to find the meaning behind the meaning."

Remember me
When you're old and gray
There's not enough time
To make me stay

My precious love
Time's not my friend
I'll see you when
My journey ends

"But it's a beautiful song, and we should just be happy with that," I said.

Renée swiveled to face me. "Exactly! A truly beautiful song doesn't need any meaning behind it. It just *is*."

I was almost done with my second drink. The neon lights outside were dancing across Renée, creating a light show on her platinum blonde pixie cut and her pale bare skin. Renée's eyes looked even bluer than usual. Maybe it was the alcohol, but I felt like I would drown if I fell into them.

Renée broke eye contact with me and turned to Grant, planting a hand on his shoulder. "See, even he gets it. Why don't you?"

"I can't agree," said Maria. "Sure, a song might be beautiful, but if there's meaning behind it, like if it reminds you of an episode of your favorite TV show, or of a time you slow danced to it, then it becomes even more beautiful."

Grant finished his drink with a final gulp, then laughed as he put his arm around Renée. "You sure know how to make a party serious," he said. Renée cleared her throat, and Grant's arm retreated.

"Now who's up for another drink?" Grant asked.

I had another, as did Renée. Maria refrained. We continued like that for hours. The music got louder, as did our voices, and the open curtains allowed the neon lights outside to fill our room with color. At some point I remembered I had to face the Trials the next day, but only after four of Grant's patented Moscow Mules, and by then it didn't seem to matter.

Renée and Grant were competing for who could name the ugliest piece of modern art. Maria was telling me how excited she was about the next day's rally. Then a song came on that she liked, so she grabbed an empty Corona bottle out of my hand (I didn't remember getting it or drinking it, but I guess I must have), and jumped on the bed, pretending it was a microphone, while singing along. As always, she could only remember half the lyrics.

She kept singing, I kept laughing, Grant kept talking. Even Renée seemed in a good mood. For a moment, it was just like old times.

The sun woke me up, harsh rays piercing the blinds I had forgotten to close the night before. It felt like a knife was stabbing through my forehead and into my brain. I pressed my hand to my forehead, but my skull prevented me from making direct contact with the pain. If I could just reach through my skull and massage my brain directly, I could make the pain go away.

I tried to stand up, but my legs wouldn't cooperate and I collapsed back onto the bed. There was no way I was going to be able to make it to the Trials. Remembering a healing spell I had learned, I made the gesture, the words, and managed to fish the *aetas* out of the headache overwhelming all my other senses.

A soothing calm spread throughout my body. My headache was gone in an instant. I rose to a standing position, no longer off balance, and reveled in my suddenly alert body. Too late, I remembered Valentine's warning about using physical magic, like a healing spell, on one's self. The energy expended had to come from somewhere. Exhaustion overcame me, and I collapsed back on the bed.

The sun woke me up for the second time in one morning. This time there was no headache, or vertigo, so I sat up and checked my watch. It was later than I expected. Much later.

I jumped out of bed and noticed I wasn't wearing any pants. I scanned the room and saw them hanging on the dresser. I jumped into them and patted my pockets to verify that my wallet, keys, and phone were still inside.

"So how are we feeling this morning?" Grant asked, walking through the two doors, both open, dividing the two hotel rooms. He was holding a cup of coffee in his hand. "I figured you might need this. You were quite the life of the party last night."

"No time," I said. My pants were on, but my shoes were nowhere to be seen. I got down on all fours and checked under the bed. Not there.

"No time for coffee?" Grant said. "The Roy I knew always had time for coffee."

"I have to get to the Trials. I'm going to be late."

Could I just go without my shoes? My feet would probably get hurt running from Merlin's Dream up to Magic Hall. Would they let someone without shoes take the Trials?

"Tell me the truth," Grant said. "Is all this magic stuff really about Skylar dumping you?"

From the moment Grant arrived in Las Vegas, I knew we were going to have this conversation. It's a strange thing to see a best friend's visit as a chore rather than an occasion for excitement.

"I have to find my shoes," I said. "And what do you mean by 'this'?"

"You know, *this*," Grant said. He waved his arm in an all-encompassing gesture. "Abandoning law school, moving to Las Vegas, being a squire to some wizard."

"Apprentice," I said. "And I'm training under a sorceress, not a wizard."

"That's not the point. The point is you had everything together, your life was going in a great direction with a secure future, and you decide to throw it all away. So I'm trying to figure out what changed, and the only thing I can think of is that Skylar did a real number on you."

"This isn't about Skylar," I said, but I said it softly, almost to myself.

"I get it, I really do," Grant continued. "Skylar was fun, interesting, had a smoking hot body, and when she dumped you out of the blue you probably needed some time to get over her, so you came out here. But it's been two months now Roy. Two months! It's time to come back to Los Angeles and return to reality."

"Why do you care?" I said. "You never even thought I was good enough for her."

"That's not true. Why would you say that?"

"Because every time you saw us together, you hummed *Is She Really Going Out with Him* under your breath."

"That is ridiculous and completely untrue," Grant said. "It wasn't *Is She Really Going Out with Him*, it was *Somebody's Baby*."

"Whatever."

"Whatever? They're two completely different songs. How could you mix them up?"

"Either way, it shows what you really thought about me and Skylar."

"Fine, she's not the reason you're here, I'm sorry I brought it up. But give me a clue Roy, help me understand what you're doing out here."

"What was I supposed to do?" I said. "Stay in Los Angeles? Go to law school?"

"Yes!" Grant screamed. "That's exactly what you were supposed to do."

"That's my father's life, not mine."

"Oh please, stop acting like your life is some sort of tragedy."

"What is that supposed to mean?"

"You know what I mean," Grant said. "I'm Roy Nakamura, boo hoo. Look at poor old me. My girlfriend left me. I have to go to law school. You're acting like your life is a freaking tragedy, but you've never had a truly bad thing happen to you in your entire life."

A teacher once told me that in classical literature you could tell a tragedy from a comedy based on the ending. If it ends with a wedding, it's a comedy, but if it ends with a funeral, then it's a tragedy. I don't know why, but the lesson chose that moment to pop into my mind. If my life was a tragedy, whose funeral would it end with?

"Okay, maybe my life isn't a tragedy," I said. "But what are you doing out here? If you disapprove of my life so much, then why are you even here in the first place?"

"Because your dad asked me to!" Grant blurted out. He stopped, as did I. Finding my shoes didn't seem important anymore. I couldn't remember why I needed to find them. Grant shook his head, centering himself.

"Your dad asked me to," Grant said again, this time calm and controlled. "He came and saw me at my office a couple weeks ago."

Grant looked down at the floor, then at the ceiling, hesitant to meet my eyes. "He's really worried about you Roy. He's trying to figure out why you abandoned law school, especially after how hard he worked to get you in, and why you would then move to Las Vegas."

"So he sent you as what, an errand boy?" I sat down on my bed. "If my father wants to meddle in my life, he can do it himself."

"Come on Roy, is it that wrong for a man to be concerned about his son? I wish my father took half the interest in my life that yours does."

I finally found my shoes. They were under the other bed, probably kicked there while I was in the process of taking them off the night before. I slapped them on and stood, facing Grant.

Grant reached into his pocket and pulled out an envelope.

"Your dad called the Admissions Office at USC Law. I don't know what he told them, or what strings he pulled, but he convinced them your withdrawal was a mistake."

I grabbed the letter from Grant's outstretched hand. I held it tightly, the pristine white envelope starting to warp inside my fist.

"The letter says you are still admitted. As long as you're there by Tuesday, you can start along with the other first years."

The envelope continued to crumple in my grasp as I tried to process what Grant was telling me. My father had worked hard to get me into law school, that was true, but I had already decided three times to abandon that goal, once when I set-off for Las Vegas, once when I agreed to become Sorceress Valentine's apprentice, and a final time when I found out my apprenticeship had actually lasted only a day, and I could still choose again. Was the fourth time even a choice?

Besides, there was the matter of the OneSpell and the world, which according to Sorceress Valentine, only I could save.

Without even opening the letter, I dropped it to the ground and turned. The hotel room door opened in my hand, and I stepped out into the hallway.

"What are you doing?" Grant yelled after me.

"I have the Trials," I said. I didn't turn around.

"You're making a mistake!" Grant cried out. "Why can't you see you're making a mistake!"

I slammed the door behind me.

4 - Sorcerer

Like everything else in Las Vegas, Magic Hall, the home of the Sorcerers Guild, was a parody of itself. Passing by, one might think it was a Grecian themed casino, or perhaps a Roman themed night club, rather than the headquarters of the most powerful non-Branch entity in Las Vegas.

The hall was just north of Arabian Nights. It was technically on the Strip, but just barely (only Better Tomorrows, an old Shaskauer casino, was farther north). A large set of circular steps led from the street level up to the massive columns that dominated the front of the building. The entrance to the hall, set back from the columns, was perpetually shielded by the shadow of the overhang, concealed in just a little bit of mystery.

As Sorceress Valentine and I walked up the circular steps, we passed a large statue of a man on his knees, cowering before an unseen adversary. In front of the statue was a large box with a small slit at the top. The darkness within the box seethed forward, as if it were a tangible darkness and not just the absence of light. Sorceress Valentine pulled two five dollar chips out of nowhere and deposited them into the box.

"What's that?" I asked.

Valentine stopped mid-step. She looked at me, as always, as if I was so stupid I didn't even realize the stupidity of the question I had just asked.

"It is a statue of Adam the Defiant One, the first sorcerer and the founder of the Guild."

"Why does he look so scared?"

Valentine clenched her fists. "Because the statue is a representation of him during the moment before his head was chopped off by a wizard of Branch Shaskauer. Below it is the Tribute Box. It is a reminder that we, as sorcerers, exist only with the permission of the Branches. Each time a sorcerer enters Magic Hall, he or she must deposit ten dollars as Tribute."

"But the Branches are rich," I said. "Why would they need that money?"

Valentine kept walking up the steps. "It is not about the money," she muttered.

As we entered through the doors of Magic Hall and stepped into the large lobby, complete with dazzling marble floors, I could tell this was not going to go smoothly. The cavernous room, filled with dozens of men and women wearing sorcerer's cloaks, all of whom looked like they were doing something important or had somewhere important to be, fell silent. At first I thought they were all looking at me. Then I realized they were all doing their best to avoid looking at Sorceress Valentine.

Valentine paid them no attention. She strode through the crowd, which parted to allow her entrance, and made straight for a set of doors on the opposite side of the room.

The doors, large and inscribed with ancient runes, opened before her. I couldn't tell whether it was magic or technology. Behind the doors was a circular room that was a cross between a court of law and a classroom. Rows of seats curved downward until they stopped at a raised stage, on top of which was a long table with five seats, each of them occupied by a sorcerer. Although they varied in appearance, each of the five had the same demeanor. Bored.

The sorcerer in the center, an obese man with thinning gray hair brushed up in a pathetic attempt at a comb-over, was speaking. I recognized him from the interview on my first day in Las Vegas. It was Sorcerer Bastion Edwards, Chairman of the Guild Council.

"And since no one has come forward to face the Trials," he said. "I hereby decree a close to this month's…"

"Wait!"

The five sorcerers turned at Valentine's exclamation. Valentine was already walking down the rows of seats to approach the stage. I trailed a couple steps behind.

"Members of the council. I am here today because I have an apprentice who has come to face the Trials and become a sorcerer."

Sorcerer Edwards coughed. "That is why you are here Sorceress Valentine?" Venom dripped out of his mouth as he spat her name. "After all this time, you appear in this hall, in this chamber, and expect us to make your apprentice one of us?"

Valentine, as usual, did not look surprised at this resistance. "Any sorcerer may train an apprentice, and then sponsor that apprentice to face the Trials. That is our law. I see nothing wrong with my actions."

"Nothing wrong!" Sorcerer Edwards sputtered. His face started to turn red. "You have been a fugitive from this Council for almost eight years. You have not responded to any of our summons." Spittle came out of his mouth with each word. "I am in doubt that you can even still be considered a sorceress."

The sorceress to his immediate left, a middle-aged woman with small glasses and her hair in a bun (she looked like she belonged behind the desk at an elementary school library) nodded in agreement. "In violation of your oath as a sorceress, you have defied the Branches and this Council. We are still paying reparations for your massacre at the Shaskauer Archives five years ago, and our finances are slim enough as it is. Bastion is right, we should consider expelling you from the Guild."

Valentine gritted her teeth. She exhaled slowly. I couldn't remember the last time she had been this angry. "While you cower on your knees before the Branches, I stand. And for that, you wish to expel me from your ranks?"

The sorcerers at the table did not reply.

"Very well," Valentine said. "There is only one way to expel someone from the Guild. Combat, one on one." She released her clenched fists, then smiled and raised out her arms. "But in this case, let's make an exception. Let it be five on one. If all five of you can beat me, I will gladly withdraw from the Guild and forfeit the title of sorceress."

The sorcerer to the right of Sorcerer Edwards cleared his throat. Of the five council members, he was the youngest by at least a decade. He was large, but in a sturdy manner rather than a portly one. His carefully combed hair was completely white, either a sign of premature graying or the effects of a spell gone wrong.

Valentine pointed at the man. "Sorcerer Roland Tell. Is there something you wish to say to me?"

When he spoke, it was in a restrained manner, like a giant who has to whisper to avoid damaging the eardrums of the mortals around him. "It has been far too long Valentine," he said with a smile.

"As the current EndGame champion, I would be very curious to face you in one-on-one combat."

Valentine smiled in return, but there were cold calculations behind it. Valentine, having laid out her challenge, was now calculating whether or not she really could beat the entire council in a fight.

"However," Sorcerer Tell added, "I think a fight would be more than my fellow council members could handle. So I see no reason not to let the boy partake in the Trials and face the Token Master."

There was silence. Sorcerer Edwards started to say something, but then shook his head and remained quiet.

"If you will not expel me, then I am still a sorceress," Valentine said, speaking to the council but looking only at Sorcerer Edwards. "And as a sorceress, I demand that you let my apprentice face the Trials."

Sorcerer Edwards looked back up. "So be it," he hissed. "Show him to the Token Master."

"Welcome, Roy Nakamura. Are you ready to face your trial?"

The Token Master was younger than I expected. He wasn't young, he looked to be at least eighty years old. But it was a healthy eighty. He was not the wizened, hunched over, emaciated two hundred year old sorcerer I had expected.

He also had red eyes. Not pure red, like a monster in a comic book. His eyes were normal human eyes, except that instead of being brown or blue or green, the area around his pupil was a dull shade of red. I was reminded of what Valentine said, that he was not quite human.

He wore a plain brown robe as he sat cross-legged at one end of a dojo-like room, bamboo floor and surrounded on all sides with mirrors. To his right stood a tall object, about my height and maybe two feet across, draped with a black sheet. To his left sat a large wooden chest, the kind one would expect to see covered in sand and grime and buried beneath an "X" in a pirate movie.

"Well, are you?"

I had forgotten to answer. "What is my trial?" I asked.

The Token Master smiled the kind of smile Sorceress Valentine used to give when she was about to punish me for something. "For each applicant the trial is different, but at the same time, each trial is the same."

"I don't understand."

The Token Master stood, rather quickly for someone his age, and reached towards the mysterious object to his right. He took hold of the black sheet between his gnarled fingers.

"The trial tests one thing, and one thing only. Do you want to be a sorcerer?"

I wasn't sure whether this was a question or a statement, so I hesitated a second before replying. "Yes."

"So you say now. But think again. Deep down, truly, do you want to be a sorcerer?"

"Yes," I said, this time with more force, more determination.

The Token Master gripped the black sheet even more firmly. "Unfortunately I cannot just take your word for it. The trial will determine whether this is the truth, whether you truly want to become a sorcerer. If you wish to become a sorcerer, all you must do is defeat the thing underneath this sheet." The Token Master pulled the sheet, and revealed the object beneath.

It was a mirror. A large mirror, which reflected back an image of me. "This is some sort of joke, right?" I said, looking around. That was when I realized the Token Master was gone. I also realized that while the tall mirror was reflecting back an image of me, none of the mirrors on the walls were.

My heart beat faster. It was impossible. The mirrors around me were mirrors, how could they not reflect me? And why did the one large mirror reflect me? I took a slow breath. Think logically, what is the test here? What am I supposed to do?

And the image of me in the standing mirror was… different. I studied the image more closely. The image studied me back. It was a normal mirror, not a funhouse trick, but the image it sent back seemed a little taller, a little more muscular, a little… crueler.

I thought about the Token Master's assignment. He told me to defeat the "thing" beneath the black sheet. Maybe he meant I had to defeat myself, or some hippie mumbo jumbo like that. Or perhaps it was simpler than that. Perhaps, I just had to destroy the mirror.

I took a step back and conjured a simple fire ball. With a slight push of force, I sent it flying towards the mirror. I jumped out of the way just in time, as the fireball bounced off the mirror and headed back towards me. It hit the mirrored wall behind me, then bounced at an angle and hit another wall, diminishing each time until, in the span of a few seconds, the fireball was gone. A faint mist of magic hung in the air.

These weren't ordinary mirrors. They didn't just reflecting light, they reflected magic. Experimentally, I shot another fireball, this time being careful to step out of the way when the mirror fired it back. Once again, it ricocheted around the walls until it went out, but left a trace of magic in the air.

I walked around to the back of the mirror. On the back side there was nothing but brown paper, slightly crinkled, in the middle of a standard wooden frame. It looked like the back of any ordinary mirror. I raised my hand and shot a small stream of energy at the back. The back of the mirror shimmered, and the energy shot out the front of the mirror, hitting the mirrored wall and dissipating.

Returning to the front of the mirror, I was struck once again at the reflection in the mirror, the me that was not me. I was sure I looked worried, concerned, but the me in the mirror looked arrogant, satisfied, like it was laughing at me through a closed and emotionless mouth.

Something about that gaze started to bother me. This mirror reflected back magic, so the image inside it should be part of me. What part of me? Who did this arrogant part of me think he was to look at me so smugly while I was trying to beat the trial?

Before I knew it I summoned another fireball and threw it at the mirror, at this smug, bastard of a part of me. When there was no change, I threw another one, and another, but it had no effect. The figure in the mirror was now laughing, outright, at everything I did, at every futile effort I made to defeat him.

My mind was playing tricks on me, I knew it, but I kept throwing fireballs. And the image started to change. One moment it was an old version of me, arched over a desk. Another fireball, and it was me in a wizard uniform, head shaved and a Branch Mark on my neck. Another fireball and I saw my father standing there in the mirror, wearing his sorcerer's cloak, looking down on me.

I could barely stand. Physical magic required energy, and each spell I cast further exhausted me. I tried to take a deep breath and failed. The air was thick with the residue of my spells. A magic fog spun around the room, sucking the air out of my lungs.

I stared at the image of my father, the thick spell residue threatening to choke me. Suddenly it came to me. That part of me that I wanted to destroy, the part of me that was laughing at me, it was being protected by the mirror, sheltered by it. But if it was a part of me, then there was another way I could destroy it. If I couldn't destroy the reflection, I had to destroy the source.

I raised my right index finger and a beam of red light, just an inch long, appeared out of it. It was a trick I learned for simulating a knife when one couldn't be found. This was just such an occasion.

My arm turned inward, curling my hand until the red beam was pointing directly into my chest. The air around me pulsed thick with battle magic, and I sank to my knees. Steadily, I pushed the beam towards me, its deadly cutting point only inches from my chest, then less than an inch, then…

"Stop!" shouted a voice. My spell extinguished, and I looked up to see the Token Master standing above me.

"What are you doing?" he asked in a voice far more booming and authoritative than the one he had used minutes before.

"I am doing as you ordered," I gasped, trying to shout over the din of the magic but finding myself unable to do so. "I am defeating the part of me that is reflected in the mirror by cutting it out."

"You would cut out your heart just to beat this trial? Just to become a sorcerer?"

"Yes," I said.

"The part of you reflected in the mirror cannot be removed with a knife," the Token Master said.

"Then how do I remove it?"

"You cannot remove it, you must overcome it. But for now, there is one thing you must do, one question you must answer."

As the Token Master raised his voice, the magical residue around me thickened and spun around until it was a hurricane of magic. It seemed impossible for the Token Master to stand upright, unaffected, as this went on.

"What do you want?" the Token Master shouted, barely audible above the roar of the magical energy swirling around us. "What is your true desire, the one you will forsake before all others?"

"To be a sorcerer!" I shouted. "To be the best dueler the world has ever known."

The Token Master let his head fall back and he laughed at me, a deep, malevolent, mocking laugh. "That is not what you want young magician. That is not the desire of your heart. How dare you lie to me? How dare you lie to Magic!"

The magic flared as if alive. "It's true," I said. "I want to be a sorcerer. I want to be a dueler!"

The Token Master shook his head, and now his laugh faded as his visage took on a serious pose. "You are still lying!" he shouted, and the magical energy intensified as he yelled. "But if you want to be a sorcerer, so you shall be, if you swear that what you say is true."

I felt like the magic would pull me under. I tried to raise my hands to cast a counterspell, but my arms wouldn't move. I tried to think of a spell but my mind was empty. I couldn't harness the *aetas* of even the simplest spell. All I could focus on were the Token Master's words.

"Do you swear it Roy Nakamura? Do you swear that even though the words you say are not true, you will make them true? Do you swear you will pursue being a sorcerer, being the greatest sorcerer, with all your heart, and you will set aside all else in this pursuit?"

I gritted my teeth.

"I swear it!" I yelled. "I swear it!"

The Token Master smiled. "As you swear it, then so it shall be. Young sorcerer."

Everything stopped. The magical energies dissipated into the air, leaving a silence so profound it almost seemed loud in comparison.

"Congratulations," the Token Master said, walking towards me. He stopped. "It's okay to smile."

The Token Master reached into his robe, and pulled out a sorcerer's cloak. I couldn't understand how something so large could be hidden there, but somehow the Token Master pulled it, inch by inch, until the whole thing was before him, like one of the illusionists of old making a string of handkerchiefs appear out of his chest.

The Token Master held out the cloak.

"Rise, young sorcerer. Accept your chosen destiny."

I stood. My feet felt a little unsteady on the still ground. I reached out and grasped the cloak in my fingers, realizing as I did that I had never held one before. The material seemed thinner than I thought it would be, but at the same time it gave off a kind of warmth, like a blanket right out of the drier. One side was black, but as soon as I touched it, the other side, the one with the silver patterns, came to life.

"It recognizes you," the Token Master said. "Now it is yours, and the lights will dance only in your presence, only at your touch."

Slowly and deliberately, I opened the cloak and draped it over my shoulders. When I had seen sorcerers before, I always thought the cloak must be a burden, a bulky thing that was difficult to wear and got in the way. But it was lighter than air. Instead of pulling me down, standing straight and tall was easier with it supporting me.

The Token Master was searching through the large chest. The lid of the chest was blocking my view, but I could see the motions of the Token Master sifting through the contents of the chest, like a librarian looking for a certain book, until he found the right one. He pulled it out and stood to hand it to me.

"Here is your first token," the Token Master said, holding up a small gold medallion. "As you go on in life you will receive others, but this first one will always be special. It will always be at the core of your being."

I accepted the token from him and turned it over in my hand. It was an image of a cloud.

"I give you the cloud because there is a cloud over your mind," the Token Master said. "A cloud that hides your past from prying eyes."

I raised an eyebrow. This was not the congratulatory speech I had anticipated.

"The cloud also represents shelter," the Token Master said. "A cloud shelters those below it from the harsh rays of the sun. But it is a temporary shelter, and those who find shelter beneath it must eventually find shelter elsewhere, or learn to embrace the sun instead of being burned by it.

"Finally, the cloud represents the coming of rain, the coming of darkness." The Token Master looked almost sad at this next part. "I am sorry to tell you this Roy, but there are very dark days ahead for you."

Behind him, the lid of the chest closed by itself.

"Is there anything else?" he said to me. "Anything you wish to do before leaving this present trial and returning to the real world, and all the trials it has in store for you?"

I had prepared for this moment. "I have been told that since I have become a sorcerer, I can ask you one question."

"You have heard correctly. What is it you would seek to know?"

"I have heard you know of the OneSpell. I seek to know when it will appear."

The Token Master folded his hands. "Is that truly what you wish to know?"

"It is," I said. "When will the OneSpell appear?"

The Token Master sighed. "That is not what you really want to know, Sorcerer Roy Nakamura."

"Yes it is," I said.

"No it is not." The Token Master shook his head. "You can ask me anything you want Sorcerer Nakamura, and I will tell you the answer. I am confident there is something else you wish to ask me, something else you wish to know."

I felt my gut twist, my insides revolt against my body. My emotions had somehow, very briefly, seized control of my body. I shook my head, regaining control, and stared back at the Token Master with steel resolve.

"No," I said. "I wish to know when the OneSpell will appear. And because I have become a sorcerer on this day, I believe I am entitled to an answer."

Rather than react negatively to my tone, the Token Master smiled. It was a warm smile, like a grandfather might give a small child, a far cry from the artificial smiles most members of the magical community wore on their faces.

"The young are foolish above all else," the Token Master said. "Very well, I will answer your question." He paused, readjusting the hem on his robe, then looked me directly in the eye. "The OneSpell will appear at the stroke of midnight on December 31, 2000."

Sorceress Valentine's estimate hadn't been far off. December 31, 2000. That gave me less than three years to find the location where it would appear, and to become a powerful enough sorcerer to face the most powerful demon the world had ever known.

"That is all, Sorcerer Nakamura," the Token Master said. "I have to be getting to my other duties. And I assume, if you follow the traditions of sorcerers past, you are going to go out and celebrate."

Sorceress Valentine waited for me outside Magic Hall. She looked at my sorcerer's cloak waving behind me, and for a second an emotion flitted across her face. She looked proud.

"The token around your neck," she said. "Why did the Token Master give it to you? What does it mean?"

I looked down at the small golden medallion, bearing the image of a cloud, hanging around my neck. "The Token Master didn't tell me," I said. I wasn't sure why, but I felt the Token Master's words had been meant for me alone.

I looked at Sorceress Valentine's neck, at the two tokens, a sun and a unicorn, that she wore around it.

"More importantly, what did the Token Master say about the OneSpell?" Valentine asked.

I told her the Token Master's words about the date the spell would appear.

"That doesn't give us much time," she said. "We need you to start dueling right away, so we don't have objective time to train you."

"Objective time?"

"We need you ready to fight a duel as soon as possible, next weekend if we can. And you need time to train, I would say at least a year, before that happens. So I am going to train you the same way I did last time, in my suite, using subjective time."

I started to protest.

"It won't be like before," Valentine assured me. "You are not an apprentice anymore, so it will be one sorcerer teaching another."

"But, you said it was dangerous to practice physical magic inside your suite."

"You passed the Trials. I think you have the self-control to avoid setting my suite on fire a second time."

"And it's not just that," I said. "It's just, I can't imagine being away from my life for a whole year."

"You will not. To the rest of the world, no time will pass at all."

I thought about Maria's rally. "Do we have to do it right away?"

"It can wait until tomorrow," Valentine said, reading my mind. "Meet me in the lobby of the Last Emperor tomorrow at noon." She paused. I couldn't read minds, the way I was sure she could, but I could tell she was considering something, turning an idea over in her head again and again, deciding which fork of a river to pursue.

"I have some activities to which I must attend," she finally said. "But afterwards, later tonight, perhaps you can come by my suite and we can celebrate today's accomplishments. Not only did you bring us one step closer to getting the OneSpell, you also joined the ranks of sorcerers, which in itself is no small feat."

There was the Magic First rally to think about, but Valentine was right, this had been a big day for me. I deserved to have some fun.

"I would be honored, Sorceress," I said.

Sorceress Valentine nodded at my acceptance of her invitation. "Tonight, when you're ready, go to the lobby of the Last Emperor, and hit the space above the button for the highest floor. The elevator will obey you."

Her instructions complete, Valentine turned to leave.

"One last thing, Sorceress."

"Yes," she said, turning back.

"Are unicorns real?"

The words were out of my mouth before I realized how stupid they sounded. Sorceress Valentine stared at me.

"It's just that, the token around your neck," I said, still unable to form complete sentences when facing the most intimidating magic user I knew.

Valentine nodded in understanding. "A long time ago, in the old days of Atlantis, there were shapeshifters who could change their appearance into an animal of their choice. Some said they were powerful wizards who could turn into animals, and some said they were Signed animals who could turn into humans. Maybe they were so powerful they could change form, or maybe the fact they could change form made them powerful.

"Then there are tales from old Atlantis of lost travelers, often children, who would be rescued from danger or despair by a beautiful young woman, only to see her turn into a unicorn and gallop away. So was it a woman who could take the form of a unicorn, or a unicorn who could take the form of a woman? Maybe it was just a myth all together."

Valentine shrugged. "Regardless of whether unicorns are real, they remain a powerful symbol. Perhaps one day I will tell you what this token symbolizes, or how I received it."

Valentine checked her watch. "Now, I must be going. I'll see you later at my suite?"

"Of course Sorceress."

Valentine turned and departed. I made my way down the steps in front of Magic Hall and started to walk down the Strip.

Las Vegas seemed quieter than usual. The rally was taking place at the far end of the Strip, so I figured most tourists, frightened at the large gathering of magicians and their allies with picket signs, had gone home early. But it wasn't just that. The city was slumbering. Its neon lights had closed their eyes, pausing in their ceaseless watch, to let events transpire.

I checked my watch and realized that even if I hurried, I would never make it up to Better Tomorrows in time for the start of the rally. I quickly called Maria, and when she didn't pick up, left a message saying I wouldn't make it. I turned around and made my way south, towards the Last Emperor.

Walking into the Last Emperor while wearing my sorcerer's cloak for the first time was different than any other time I had entered a casino. I was a celebrity. As soon as I entered, a casino hostess greeted me and made polite small talk with a hint of flirting thrown in for good measure. I wasn't an idiot. I knew she was delaying me so the casino security apparatus could get my photo and compare it to their database of known sorcerers. Since I was a brand new sorcerer, and thus not in the database, they were no doubt adding me to it as the pretty hostess asked me what I thought about the weather.

Once I sat down at a blackjack table, another hostess arrived with a drink ("compliments of Branch Parthenia"). It was a vodka tonic, fairly standard for casino junkies. I knew if I were to order a different drink, which would probably be complimentary as well, the casino would add the order to my profile and have it waiting for me next time I entered. Being a sorcerer had just admitted me to the most exclusive players club in Las Vegas.

I knew the mere fact I was now a sorcerer didn't mean I was better at magic. I was the same person who had woken up that morning without a cloak. But something about the title, about the cloak on my back, made me feel more skilled than before. Each wave watching spell I cast seemed more powerful, each shield spell seemed sneakier. I decided to try my limits, and found myself able to cast a simple shield spell without hand movements or words, using my mind and the *aetas* alone to perform feats of magic.

I meant to play a couple hands, just enough so I would be on-time to Valentine's suite and not unfashionably early, but before I knew it I had spent three hours at the table, winning and then losing over a thousand dollars.

Wanting to stop before I lost any more money, I excused myself from the table and made my way to the elevators.

5 - Slow Dance

True to her word, I was able to take the elevator at the Last Emperor up to Valentine's suite. The room was empty (Valentine hadn't expected me to get there so soon), so I took a seat on one of the couches in the living room and waited.

I took a deck of cards off the shelf and placed it on the table in front of me. Taking the cards out of the sleeve, I started tossing them on the table one at a time, using a low level wave watching spell to count them as they flew by. I waited for over an hour, starting to wonder if I had misestimated what Valentine meant by "tonight," when Valentine arrived.

The elevator chimed, and I turned my head as Sorceress Valentine walked into her abode. She was drunk. The first sign I had was the way she treated her sorcerer's cloak. Rather than carefully transfer it from her back to the coat closet like she usually did, she allowed it to flop off (it took her two tries to extract her left arm from its embrace) and onto the floor. She bent to pick it up, then straightened (with some effort) and tossed it on the cushion beside me, on top of my own sorcerer's cloak which I had meticulously folded.

"Always practicing," she said. "Even after becoming a sorcerer. How impressive." She waved her right hand and the air around sizzled with magic. "*Explarian!*" The cards in front of me jumped up of their own accord and fell down, all facing the same direction, into their case.

Valentine continued, "I need a drink, and I'm not drinking alone." I refrained from asking any questions about who, in that case, she had been drinking with up until now. With an exaggerated sigh, she sat down on the large chair next to the couch where I was.

"Besides, we need to celebrate," she added. "You are no longer my apprentice, you are a sorcerer. Sorcerer Roy Nakamura!"

Valentine shook her head, as if to clear her mind, then stood up and lifted her left hand. Two of the wine glasses on the small bar came sailing over. Mid-way on their journey, Valentine stumbled, as if there had been a mini-earthquake that only she had felt. One glass maintained its position in the air while the other crashed against the carpet. I stood up from the table and started towards the mess.

"Sit down Roy. It's not a big deal." Valentine waved her hand again, and the shards flew back together into a wine glass, which joined its sister wine glass and continued its mid-air journey to where I was sitting. Sorceress Valentine took a seat herself, next to me on the couch, just as the glasses completed their harrowing journey.

Without touching them, and without being obvious, I examined the glasses. Both looked flawless. Try as I might, I couldn't tell which one had broken against the ground.

"So, what are we going to drink?" I asked.

Valentine closed her eyes, and I could feel them rolling in exasperation behind her eyelids. She leaned her head back to stretch her neck, and both glasses started to fill, from some unknown source, with a red liquid that I could only assume was wine. Valentine shook her head, then reached out and took a glass. I took the other. Valentine held out the glass before her face, and her next words seemed to be spoken to it more than to me. "To old lovers and new friends."

I raised my glass to clink it against hers, but she was already pulling it back and tilting it into her lips. I took a sip of mine and put it back on the table. It wasn't bad, especially for wine conjured out of the air. Furthermore, the glass had refilled the small amount I had drunk so it was once again full. I could tell this was going to be a long night.

"What do you mean about old lovers?" I asked.

Valentine took another sip. "Well Roy, today I am going to tell you something about my past, something that is not exactly standard for sorcerers to talk about to their apprentices," she corrected herself, "former apprentices." She picked up her glass again, this time taking a large gulp of it before placing it back on the table, the magic already refilling it as she did so.

"Today I saw something that reminded me of an old lover of mine."

I was going to interrupt, but I thought better of it.

"And so, I decided that tonight I should drink in his honor."

I wasn't sure if I was supposed to say something. Finally, I replied "Who was he?"

As if waiting for my prompt, Valentine continued. "He was the most amazing man I had ever met, the most amazing man there was. From the very first moment, it was as if we had always known each other, would always know each other, would always be together."

Valentine took another liberal drink of the magic wine. She put down her glass and paused in reflection. I felt the compulsion to continue the conversation.

"Did you break up with him or did he break up with you?"

"Neither," Valentine replied. "He died."

"I'm sorry to hear about that."

"Don't apologize. There was nothing you could have done to stop it. But he's dead. And it was not a glorious death, it was not a heroic death. He died a stupid, senseless, violent death. That is how I became who I am today actually."

"A sorceress?" I asked.

She nodded. "I was already studying magic, but when he died…" Valentine's face, as always, wore a mask, but I could see some inkling of what she was trying to hide. "The pain was always there, always present. I tried to forget, first with self-help books, then with magic." A bit of a smile came over her face. "I tried using a mirror to cast a memory shroud on myself one time. It did not work. As the caster you have to focus on the object, which means you have to hold it, and as soon as the spell is cast you look down and see the object, and the spell is undone."

She took another sip. "My research into memory, the nature of memory, introduced me to the concept of time travel. It's all about memory you see."

"So you really can travel in time?" I asked. "It's not just a rumor."

Valentine's throat gave off a short bitter laugh. "Of course I can travel in time. It is easier than you would think, actually. You just need the right motivation." She blinked back a tear. "And I had the motivation."

Valentine stood and walked over to the card table, to the black plaque with the line in golden script from *The Great Gatsby*. She read it aloud. "Can't change the past… Why of course you can!"

Valentine gestured at the plaque with her wine glass. "I got it made after he died. A constant reminder of my mission."

Valentine took a long drink from her glass, then walked towards me again. She sat next to me on the couch, this time only inches away.

"I made more trips than you can imagine, Roy." She sounded desperate, like she was trying to convince me of something. "I kept going back, time after time, to try to prevent him from dying. But it never worked. Instead, I just had to watch him die over and over again.

"That is how I learned that no matter how powerful you are, you cannot change the past. You can travel back in time over and over and see it play out, but you can never change it. It is like watching a movie over and over again, each time hoping the ending will be different."

"Why not?" I asked, "Why can't you change the past."

Valentine took another drink. "Have you ever heard of the Aladdin rule?"

I didn't remember exactly what it said, but I remembered hearing references to it in some of the books Valentine had me read.

"The Aladdin rule," Valentine explained, "is one of the most basic postulates of magic. It was discovered by the leading wizards of Atlantis that no matter how powerful their magic was, no matter how much they studied and casted, there were three things magic is unable to do. It cannot bring the dead back to life, it cannot give the Sign to those who were not born into it, and it cannot make someone fall in love."

My phone rang, the silent vibration waking me from the spell of Valentine's story. Valentine herself had paused to take a drink from her self-filling wineglass, so I took my phone from my pocket and risked a quick glance. It was Maria. I thought of answering, but didn't want to offend my former teacher. Hitting the silence button, I put the phone back in my pocket and continued to listen.

Valentine continued. "And if I could go back in time, if I could prevent his death, then the magic would be bringing him back to life. Which is impossible. Magic can't do that."

The sorceress sighed, lost in memory. She turned her gaze from the imaginary tableau in front of her to me. "You must have someone like that, someone you love?"

"There was someone I thought I loved," I said. "But now I'm not so sure. We broke up before I came here, to Las Vegas."

"Did you break up with her or did she break up with you?"

"We broke up with each other," I said. Valentine snorted at this, but I ignored her. "Her name was Skylar, but I used to call her 'Angel Eyes.'"

Valentine looked confused. "Why would you call her 'Angel Eyes?'"

"It was a line from our favorite song, the song that played the first time we slow danced in her dorm room."

"Slow dancing in a dorm room?" Valentine said. "This I have to hear."

So I told her.

It was our third date (if you count the night we met at *Ruby Red* as our first). Skylar and I watched *Reality Bites* at a rundown movie theater within walking distance of campus. I didn't pay much attention to the screen. Afterwards, we went back to her dorm room. I welcomed the opportunity to learn more about her, to see the part of her personality that was reflected off her bedroom walls and revealed by their contents. Once inside the room, I started to look at the pictures on her dresser to see what I could learn about her. As compared to the rooms of my other female friends, I noticed one thing missing.

"No prom picture?" I asked.

"I didn't go to prom," Skylar told me, sitting down on the bed. "School dances weren't really my thing."

I sat down next to her. "But don't you like dancing?"

"I like swing dancing, I like salsa dancing, but the stuff they do at high school dances isn't dancing."

"So you're not a slow dancer."

Skylar paused to consider. "I think I can confidently say I have never slow danced before."

I acted playfully shocked. "Well we have to change that then," I whispered. "Let me put on a song."

Skylar smiled, the coy playful smile girls can only get away with when a relationship is first beginning, as I reached around her and grabbed her laptop. I checked her playlist for some songs I had sent her a couple days before, then quickly selected one.

"My dad's really into Las Vegas, the history of magic, that sort of thing," I explained. "So when I was growing up, he would always play me a tape of this Atlantian rock band from the 80's called Taliesin."

I put the laptop down and stood up. Skylar stood as well. "What do I do now?" Skylar asked.

"Just put your arms around my neck," I replied. In true teenage fashion, I placed my arms around her waist, resting my palms on the small of her back. She reached up and draped her arms around my neck.

"Like that?" she asked.

"Just like that," I said. "And now you sway, just slightly, back and forth. That's not so hard, is it?" Skylar responded by smiling, and resting her head against my shoulder.

"It's not hard because it's not really dancing," Skylar said. "We're just hugging and swaying to the music."

"Well that's what a slow dance is." A phrase popped into my head, like something I had heard somewhere else, its source shrouded in memory. "The only difference between an embrace and a slow dance is the soundtrack."

The music started, power chords mixed with a synthesizer, melodies extracting themselves from Skylar's laptop. We started to move with it. A single voice started to sing, its mournful call trickling out of the speakers like blood from a seeping wound.

> *This is the story, morning glory,*
> *of what I learned in Vegas.*
> *You always hurt the ones you love —*
> *that's why love couldn't save us.*

"That doesn't make any sense," Skylar said. "Why would you hurt someone you love?"

> *You said that we were fated,*
> *that you heard it from above*
> *that a sacrifice isn't a sacrifice*
> *when it's for the one you love*
>
> *I told you from the start I'm not your type,*
> *So can't you see we're running out of time?*
> *To save us from these tears, both yours and mine,*
> *Baby you're the only one, my angel eyes.*

"So what do you think of slow dancing?" I asked.

"That's enough talking," Skylar replied. She lifted her head from my shoulder and pushed herself up into my waiting lips.

"And from then on," I told Sorceress Valentine, "I called her 'Angel Eyes,' because of the line in the chorus."

Valentine looked down at her glass, then back up at me. "You know Roy," she said, "It's been ages since I've danced."

She paused. I waited for her to continue, but she didn't.

"Did you... did you want to dance?" I stammered.

"I'm a traditional girl, Sorcerer Nakamura," she said. "I'm not going to ask the guy."

My phone rang again. I pulled it out and saw it was Maria. Again.

"Well?" asked Sorceress Valentine.

On any other night, I would have gone anywhere on a moment's notice if Maria had asked me. But Maria had Karl. Whatever it was she needed, I was sure he could handle it. I turned the phone completely off with the push of a button and placed it on the table.

I stood up, turned back to Valentine, and reached out my right hand. "Sorceress Valentine, would you do me the honor of this dance?"

Valentine reached out her own hand to accept mine. "I thought you'd never ask." She stood up and faced me, never letting go of my hand. She tilted her head to the left and whispered a spell.

Music began to play. It was *What I Learned in Vegas* by Taliesin, the very song I had been telling her about.

As the familiar lyrics washed over me (I hadn't listened to the song since the break-up, but I still knew every word by heart), we swayed in time to the music. For the first time since I met her, I had a bizarre revelation. Sorceress Valentine had a corporeal form. Her magic was certainly powerful, and that single feature had a way of defining her. But she was also a real flesh-and-blood human being. She had a height, she had a weight. When I held her in my arms, I felt her warmth. She even had a scent, a perfume with a hint of lilacs, which was quite nice. Valentine had always been attractive in a frightening, intimidating, imposing way. Now I realized she was also simply beautiful.

As if she could sense this realization, Valentine took her head off my shoulder and looked up into my eyes. She tilted her head up (or maybe I tilted mine down, I wasn't sure). We came so close to kissing, our faces separated by mere millimeters, that for a moment our lips might have grazed. But before anything could happen, I jerked my head back.

"I'm sorry, Skylar, I can't."

I had no time to react. The magic screamed out of Valentine's fingers like a hurricane, throwing me against the floor. All counterspells forgotten, I threw up my hands in front of my face, willing them to protect me, while Valentine raised her hand to throw another spell. With just moments left in my life, my final thought was a question. Was Valentine reacting to my attempt to kiss her, my refusal to kiss her, or the fact I had called her by my ex-girlfriend's name?

But no forbidden death spell came. Instead, Valentine lowered her hand. As if a sobriety spell had worked its way through her bloodstream (perhaps one had), she straightened, and her anger was replaced by her usual unreadable face.

"I drank too much, a fact for which I apologize. You can let yourself out, but be back by noon tomorrow."

Even after Valentine had turned and gone into her bedroom, I continued to lie on the ground, alternating thanks for my survival with questions about what had just happened. Finally, I picked myself up and went to the elevator.

6 - Duel

I returned to Grant's hotel room with a lot on my mind. It was late, the rally would have ended hours ago, so I wasn't surprised to see Maria, Renée, and Grant back at the room. But there were things I didn't know.

To this day, members of the magical community refer to Sunday, September 4, 1998, as "Black Sunday." As planned, the thousand plus protestors had gathered in front of the Better Tomorrows casino at the northern edge of the Strip, shutting down traffic in the process. At first the atmosphere was festive. Protestors seemed more like revelers. They laughed, sang songs, danced as they marched down the Strip, traffic stopping all around them. No rules could hold them anymore.

The protestors continued to march down the Strip, shouting their anti-Branch slogans as they went. They didn't count on how the city of Las Vegas, defiled by the invasion of those normally relegated to places like the Meet, would react.

As the protestors marched from their objective, they were met by over three hundred wizards and twice as many security personnel. Magic First managed to do something not done since before the Wizard War. They united the Branches of Magic behind a single cause.

Curious guests were whisked indoors by unSigned security guards, while wizards, without warning, shot out spell after spell into the masses. Protestors fell to the ground, fighting sensations of burning, unexplainable pain, or itching from all around. Others stood frozen in place, their minds possessed by images of their greatest fear or most shameful memory.

Some magicians cast counterspells against the first wave of magical assaults. These were singled out by teams of wizards and security personnel who ran from magician to magician, physically beating anyone who produced magical resistance while throwing up spells to shield anyone from seeing what they were doing.

Sorceress Corinna Windlass attempted to rally those around her. The only response was the groans of the tired and the defeated. With a dozen wizards closing in, Corinna sighed, as if she knew all along this would be the end to her crusade. She grabbed an amulet around her neck and vanished into the warm night air.

Once the Branches were done with their work, the Las Vegas Police stepped in and arrested the protestors for obstructing a public highway. The newspapers, all in the pockets of the Branches, would report that a peaceful protest by hotel workers for increased wages had turned violent when a small subset had set fire to a police car. The Branches would release a joint statement saying that, despite the violence, they would agree to pay hotel workers an additional dollar per hour. Hours later, under the guise of darkness, wizards found and attacked the remaining leaders of Magic First. Although it continued to fight for magic rights, the organization would not recover for some time.

That night the Meet burned. No one knew for sure who set the fire. Maybe it was one of the Branches. Maybe it was all of them. The stalls, the carts, the impromptu shops, were all consumed by flames, until even the platform at the Meet's center was engulfed in fire.

When I returned to the hotel room, I didn't know any of these things had happened. But I knew something was wrong as soon as I opened the door to Grant's room and saw Grant and Renée gathered around the figure of a sobbing Maria, who was sitting on one of the beds.

"Is everything okay?" It was a stupid question, but I didn't know what else to say.

Grant started to say something, but I blocked out his voice as soon as Maria looked up, revealing an ugly mark on the side of her face. Maria started to rise when she saw me.

"No Roy. Don't, stop. Let me explain."

I turned and ran out the door. I could hear Grant's voice behind me, and then his feet running to keep up.

I had seen this before. I knew exactly what had happened. Grant, trying to keep up with me as I ran, filled in the gaps.

Along with the other Magic First protestors, Maria was arrested during the rally. Stuck in a holding cell, she had tried calling me twice. She assumed I had passed the Trials, and figured that as a sorcerer I would have the authority to bail her out. When I didn't answer, she panicked and called Karl.

Karl, ever the gentleman, bailed her out. He then beat her, shouting at her that it was what she deserved for associating with magicians, and that he had tried to warn her not to. Afraid to return home because of the raids going on against Magic First leaders, Maria called Renée and went to Grant's hotel room, which is where I found them.

The Strip was far quieter than a routine Sunday night. The city had closed its eyes to permit the Branch crackdown on the protest, and now that the crackdown was over, the city was opening its eyes just a little, deciding whether it was safe to return to normal. The neon lights shined, but they shined for others. On the ground, maintenance workers emerged to clean up the physical trash, and sometimes bloody sidewalks, left by the Branches.

Karl sat at a cheap aluminum table on a patio just outside the Pirate Bay casino, taking a break from his clean-up duty. His uniform, normally spotless white, was streaked with blood and grime. He lounged next to two other wizards, both also from Branch Merkasia. While one was his age, the third was clearly older, and I took him to be in charge. The three were laughing, presumably telling war stories about the defenseless magicians they had just defeated.

Grant, who had been walking beside me for the last mile, constantly pleading with me to abandon what he considered a foolish endeavor, was suddenly several feet behind me. As I walked up to Karl, he pulled his sword from its scabbard and laid it across the table.

"Long time no see Roy," he smirked. He looked at my cloak. "I see you passed the Trials."

I didn't waste any time. "Wizard Karl Johnsen," I said in my best attempt to sound serious and menacing. "I challenge you to a duel." With my right hand, I fiddled with the fabric of my sorcerer's cloak.

Karl laughed. "You are not a wizard Roy, and I am under no obligation to accept a challenge from you."

"What's the matter?" I asked. "Afraid to face me?"

Karl snorted. "Do you even know any battle magic? Wizards duel with the magic arts, not with fists or knives or whatever it is you people are accustomed to."

In response I raised my right hand and cast a spell of object summoning, a basic physical spell allowing the caster to move an object with the mind. Mumbling the words to the spell I acquired the sword Karl had put on the table. I envisioned the sword flying majestically into my hand as I pulled at it with my mind. But something was wrong. The spell was replaced by a sudden pain that shot through my right arm. I released the spell and my arm returned to normal.

Karl's fellow wizard, the younger one, smirked. "A wizard's sword is a charmed object. Only a complete imbecile would seek to use magical arts to turn a wizard's sword against its owner."

Pretending I knew what that meant, I did my best to snarl back at him.

"Now if you would not mind," Karl said, "My friends and I have better things to do than watch you fail." Karl reached for his sword. The third wizard, the older one, reached out his hand and stopped him.

"Wizard Johnsen," the older wizard said. "I fail to see the harm in indulging this young man in a bit of magical combat." He removed his hand and looked at me. "What is your name?"

I squared myself and tried to stand tall. "Roy Nakamura," I replied.

"And what is your quarrel with Wizard Johnsen, Sorcerer Nakamura?"

"He hit my friend. In the face."

The wizard looked at Grant's muscular six foot frame and shaved head. "Your friend looks like he can take care of himself."

I shook my head. "He's not the friend I'm talking about. Maria, my friend who Karl hit, is back at my hotel room. And until now, she was his girlfriend."

Something passed across the wizard's eyes, something fleeting that was gone before I could analyze it with natural or magical means.

"Here are the terms," the older wizard said. "If Wizard Johnsen wins, you will leave Las Vegas at once and never return. If you win, Wizard Johnsen will never again bother you or your friend. Are these terms acceptable?"

It took me a second to understand he was waiting for a response. I decided to gamble. It was Vegas after all.

"Unacceptable," I said, leading to a single raised eyebrow on the part of the elder wizard. "He hurt her. He can't just agree not to do it again. If I win, he has to do something to make amends."

The wizard nodded in agreement. "If Sorcerer Nakamura wins, Wizard Johnsen will owe him one favor, to be performed at any time in the future. This obligation will pass down to each of their heirs until such a time as the favor is performed."

"Unacceptable!" Karl cried out. "If I owe him a favor he could ask for anything! I shouldn't have to do this just because Mary wants to slum it with magicians."

The elder wizard turned to him. "That is enough Wizard Johnsen."

"But I was the one challenged, I can set the terms."

"You did not accept the challenge, Wizard Johnsen, so I accepted it on your behalf. That gives me the right to set the terms."

Karl stood up and grabbed his sword off the table. The clang of metal on metal rang out in the night air. "The terms are irrelevant. I will not be defeated by some sorcerer." He stepped away from the table and looked me in the eye. He pulled his handgun out of his holster, then bent down and put both his gun and his sword on the ground next to him.

"I won't need them for you," he said.

I thought I heard Grant yelling at me to back out, but my attention was now fully focused on the task before me. I shifted my legs and arms into a fighter's pose, the position sorcerers hold at the start of a duel.

"Your move, wizard," I said.

Karl left his hands at his sides. Both palms began to faintly glow. A single yellow flame licked up his right hand. Anticipating his attack, I threw up a simple counterspell effective against all forms of fire. Karl pulled his hand back, then threw a fully formed fireball at me. I tried to think of an offensive move. My counterspell was decent, but would never survive more than a few of his attacks.

I was wrong about even that. The fireball cut through my defense in an instant, and the impact threw me to the ground. I smelled a faint burning scent that was likely my own hair. The fireball had been a small one. Its purpose hadn't been to kill me, it had been to show me Karl could get through my defenses with ease.

Jumping to my feet, I threw a hail of ice shards. Karl shrugged them off and threw a second fireball at me. Rather than attempt another counterspell, I physically dodged the fireball, letting it crash against a patio table behind me.

I saw a large planter, an artificial palm tree rising up from its real dirt, and jumped behind it before Karl could throw another spell. Safely behind the planter, I wasted a moment trying to think. Karl started to walk around the planter to face me. He was distracted by the rustling of something in the leaves of the tree. Seizing the opportunity, I jumped from behind the planter and hit him with a nausea spell. Karl fell to his knees and vomited the contents of his stomach.

I stood back as he rose from his knees. Now he was angry. He took a step forward. The area between us filled with mist, a spell I learned from Valentine. It did nothing to impede Karl. A second later magic hit my knees. I felt both break, heard the bones crunch, and I fell down.

Rolling over to avoid a follow-up strike, I found I could still move my legs. The spell had just been an illusion, though a painful one. I staggered up and jumped aside in time to dodge another spell. I indulged my pain for a moment. The decision cost me as Karl used the chance to hit me with something that caused my vision to become blurry for the few seconds it took me to remember a counterspell.

"Can we hurry this up?" Karl yelled. "After I beat you, I plan to call on Mary again. Right about now she is probably realizing how much she misses me."

My vision darkened. My muscles contracted. My despair turned to rage. My anger welled up in me, like a physical force, like an animal rattling its cage, begging to be let out. I took the rage, aimed it at Karl, and a fireball crashed towards him. He easily deflected it.

We went back and forth for another minute, my spells failing to affect him while his always barely hit me, not enough to disable me but enough to wear me down. Finally, I dodged a bit too late, and a spell punched into my gut with the force of several fists. I blacked out for a second as I collapsed to the ground.

I was against the planter, barely able to stand. For the first time I was thankful Valentine resorted to physical punishment so often. It had caused me to build up a much higher tolerance for pain than before my apprenticeship. I managed to stand up.

"That's it huh?" Karl yelled. Like all wizards, Karl usually spoke in a formal, aloof tone. But now in the heat of the moment he was losing his usual affectations. "You know what, I feel bad. Let me tell you what. Take a shot. You can use any spell you like and I won't block it. Hell, punch me if you want, I can take it." Karl held his arms out to his sides. "Well, what's it going to be?"

My previous spells barely did any damage. This was nothing like my training against Valentine. Where her spells were slow and controlled, Karl was a brawler, using any magical weapon at his disposal in a random merry go round of hurt.

And then I had an idea. I put my arms out to my sides, then brought my hands together. Holding my palms in a praying pose, I concentrated for a moment, then spoke in a firm even tone, just loud enough for Karl to hear.

"I summon… Merlin's lance."

Karl crossed his arms. "Seriously? There's no such thing. And even if there was, a half-rate sorcerer like you wouldn't know the first thing about…" Karl stopped.

In front of me a translucent golden ball was forming. A second later it started to stretch. It spun along its axis, and with each spin it got a little longer, a little more solid. After another second it was a foot long, thin like a pole, and aimed directly at Karl's heart.

Karl stared, mesmerized by the golden object, frozen in place. Finally he managed to whisper. "No way."

I looked up at him and could see the slightest hint of fear, of uncertainty, in his eyes. I yelled, *"MERLIN'S LANCE!"* The golden pole flew through the air towards him.

Karl raised up both arms and, making two fists, brought his forearms together in front of his face. *"Deux ex machina!"* he yelled. Blue flames engulfed him. Just as the golden pole reached him, he collapsed to the ground. The blue flames extinguished. The planter that had hit him in the back of the head fell to the ground with a crash. Before he could recover I crossed the distance between us, and grabbing the sword off the ground where Karl had dropped it, I leveled it at his throat.

"Yield or die," I gasped, for a moment ignoring my own injuries, in the most intimidating voice I could muster.

Karl blinked back a few tears. I couldn't tell whether they were from pain or rage. "I yield."

Stepping back, I dropped the sword on the ground. The younger of Karl's fellow wizards came over and helped him up. The two of them wandered off. The third, the leader, came up to me. The vicious smile on his face reminded me of the way Valentine looked whenever I got a lesson right.

"Merlin's Lance," he said. "Very impressive, Sorcerer. I will have to remember that one."

"You could," I said. "But it will probably only work once."

"That it will. Wizard Johnsen will not bother you or your friends again. You have his word, and you also have mine. But if I were you, I would come up with a plan for next time you cross one of us. The whole of Branch Merkasia was not bound by that oath, and we tend to bear grudges." With that, he turned and left.

Grant looked at me. "What was that?" he asked. "What's Merlin's Lance?"

"Merlin's Lance is a lost spell," I told him. "Merlin had a lance, a weapon of pure magical energy, that was buried with him when he died. It had the property of targeting the opponent's magic, supposedly destroying his ability to do magic while leaving a body intact. Later, some powerful magicians created a spell they called 'Merlin's Lance.' It summons the weapon from his tomb, uses it to defeat the caster's opponent, then teleports it back to the same tomb."

"And you know it?"

"No, no one knows it. It's a lost spell, so no one has known it for years."

"Then what did you do?"

I started to walk away, back towards the hotel. "I created a simple illusion. The hands, the words, the golden rod, were all theatrics designed to make Karl think I knew the spell. From the looks of it he didn't think I knew it, but just in case he cast Glory Shield."

Grant's blank look necessitated an explanation. I had to remember I was no longer around people well versed in the magic arts. "Glory Shield is a very powerful counterspell. Only great sorcerers and trained wizards know it. It is an effective shield against most spells, so if I really had known Merlin's Lance, it would have been the only counterspell that might have saved him.

"Unfortunately for Karl, one of the downsides of Glory Shield is that while it's effective against magical weapons like Merlin's Lance, it provides no protection at all against physical objects."

"So while Karl was concentrating on the counterspell," Grant said, finally understanding.

"I used a simple spell of object summoning to pick up the planter and crash it into the back of his head."

Grant smiled in appreciation. "Remind me not to piss you off."

I was only dimly aware of Grant's compliment. Not only that, I was no longer totally fixated on defending Maria's honor, or consumed with anger at Karl for his actions. Instead, one thing drew in my thoughts above all others. I had used magic to fight a duel, and I had won. It was just like Valentine said, I was a natural. I was the one.

Picture this. I turn away from Grant and start to walk away from the scene of the battle. POD's "Southtown" plays in the background. I walk in time to its booming beat. Slow motion, of course. Around me tourists point, snap pictures, and gape in awe. They are too scared to ask for my autograph, afraid I may strike them down simply for talking to me. No longer half anything, I am a full blown sorcerer, a force to be reckoned with. No one can stop me now.

When I arrived back at the hotel room, Maria was still crying, Renée at her side. Grant got there a few minutes before me, and was standing off to other side awkwardly. Sadly, from past experience, I knew Maria's tears were as much a result of my actions as Karl's. Maria looked up when I entered and she blinked twice.

"What did you do Roy?"

"What did I do?" I said. "I made sure Karl will never bother you again!"

"He's *my* boyfriend Roy. He's *my* business. What part of that can't you understand?"

The room started to get fuzzy. My gaze was focused only on Maria's face. "Well excuse me Maria," I said. "Excuse me for trying to save you from a guy like Karl."

"Save me?" Maria clenched her fists. "I don't need someone to save me Roy."

Maria stood and faced me eye to eye. "Don't you get it Roy? Karl was the one. And thanks to you, I'm never going to see him again."

"Well good," I said.

"Good? After all this time, I finally found someone who got me, who accepted my faults."

"Are you serious!" I screamed. I knew I was letting my anger get the better of me, I could feel that force, the one that defeated Karl, rising inside me, but I didn't care. "Accepted your faults? You shouldn't be with a guy who accepts your faults, you should be with a guy who loves you for them!"

Maria stopped mid-tear. She sniffed once and looked at me. And I could tell by the look that she wasn't going to back down. I could tell I hurt her, and she was thinking as hard as she could, reaching back through all our shared experiences together, to think of something she could say that would hurt me back just as much, that would make me feel just as bad as her. The closeness that gave me the ability to comfort her allowed her to hurt me as well.

"No wonder Skylar left you," Maria said. She didn't wait for a response. The door slammed behind her.

I knew she wouldn't be back that night. She would go cool off, would call up Karl and find some way to apologize to him for my actions, however twisted that might seem. Hopefully my victory over him in the duel, and the promise he would leave her alone, meant he would refuse to talk to her. Then the next day she would come and apologize to me as well, and we would act like nothing had happened.

But something had happened, just as it always did. And even though each time I told myself nothing had changed, I knew that one of these times it wouldn't be true.

The saddest thing, at least for me, was that for her she would be angry at me for a night, but thanks to my training scheduled for the next day, in my timeline it would be a year before I saw her again.

Grant coughed. "I better go after her, make sure she's okay."

I nodded in approval, and Grant left the room, shutting the door behind him with significantly less force than Maria had used.

Renée and I were alone now. An awkward moment made its way across the room. I sat down on the bed across from the one where she was sitting. We faced each other for a moment. She crossed her arms. Her eyes appeared to consider something. She stood up, walked the two steps between the beds, and sat down next to me.

With her sitting beside me, I could smell a lingering scent of bitter vanilla, evidence of the clove cigarette she had smoked at some point in the last hour. I turned to look at her. Her short blonde hair was just inches from my face. The cut of her tank top allowed me to see the shooting star that graced the back of her left shoulder.

Her right hand detached itself from her body and patted me gently on the back.

"Don't worry Roy," she said. "She'll forgive you." There was a pause. "She always does."

She left her hand on my back. I turned my head to face her. "In all the time I've known you, Renée, I think that's the first nice thing I've ever heard you say."

Renée smiled. "Nobody's perfect."

I laughed. Renée did too. I realized I was staring at her, at Renée. Staring into the bluest eyes I had ever seen. I could feel myself drowning in them.

I leaned forward to kiss her. She pulled back.

"Roy, I don't think this is a good idea."

Renée stood up. I did as well.

"Renée, I'm sorry."

"Don't worry," she said. "I get it. It was no big deal."

Renée looked at the room around her. "Maria was my ride, so I'm going to lie down in the other hotel room. If that's okay." Renée turned and walked towards the doors separating the two rooms.

I didn't think about what I was doing, or why I was doing it. All I knew was that I didn't want to be alone that night. I cleared my mind in anticipation for the love spell Sorceress Valentine once taught me. A millisecond later my right hand, acting of its own accord, leapt from my side where it had been limply hanging and formed the proper gesture. Pointing my hand at Renée, I whispered "*Eros erat, faskul kanaytoo. Indak Roy.*" I felt the spell in my hand, like a tangible object, and flung it at Renée's receding figure.

Renée stopped mid-step and turned back around to face me. My hand dropped back to its previous position, no indication of the journey on which it had travelled.

"Did you say something?" she asked.

"No," I said. "Just mumbling to myself."

Renée raised an eyebrow, then shrugged. She turned back and walked through to the other hotel room. The door on her side slowly closed, the hinges whining the entire way until it shut. The spell didn't work after all. Probably for the best. Valentine had warned me not to use it lightly.

Getting up from the bed, I walked to the door on my side and shut it as well. I sat back down on the bed. The television remote was just an arm's reach away, but I didn't want to watch TV, not really. I waited for a moment, thinking, then stood back up and stepped over to the door. I gently opened the door on my side with my left hand, my right hand already raised, poised to knock on the second door.

It never fulfilled its purpose.

When my door opened, I found Renée standing there, her door already open, her left hand raised in preparation for a knock. We stood there, just like that, for a brief second, before she used that left hand to grab my waist and pull me into the inky nothingness behind her.

Part III: EndGame

Memorial Day, 1999

1 - The Way We Were

July 8, 1998

It was a scorching Friday night, six days (in objective time) after I first arrived in Las Vegas. To me, over a year had passed while training in Sorceress Valentine's suite. Maria had invited me to a Magic First fundraiser at Hopmeister, a craft beer bar near her apartment. I protested, insisting I wasn't interested in meeting any of Maria's friends. There was also the fact that after a year of isolation with Sorceress Valentine, I was still wary of being around other people, especially magical people who might be able to sense my burgeoning magical talent. Or smell on me the stink of the demon Valentine and I had fought. But Maria always got what she wanted, and so I found myself sitting by myself at the bar, staring at a list of unfamiliar brands and trying to pick one that wouldn't make me look like an idiot.

It was a Friday night in Vegas, and I was about to meet Renée Winters for the first time.

"Las Vegas is the only city on earth where people get less interesting when they drink."

I jumped for a second. Every time I heard a noise, I was convinced it was a demon come to get me. But I regained my composure, turned away from the poster I was studying (a pictorial history of which beers would have been preferred by which Branches), and into the eyes of a girl. She was short, barely five feet, with one hand on her hip while the other hand held a wine glass just inches from her lips. She managed to exude a carefully crafted air of indifference.

"Where did you get wine?" I asked. "I thought they only served beer."

The girl shrugged, bringing the glass to her lips and tilting it back to take a sip. "I'm not a beer person."

The beer in my own hand now seemed uncultured. I stuck out a hand.

"I'm Roy."

The girl stared at my outstretched hand until I withdrew it.

"I'm Renée."

Renée, of course. "You're Maria's roommate."

"Yes." She took another sip of wine.

"I'm Maria's friend from college. And high school."

"I know."

Staring at Renée's glass of wine, I noticed a tattoo on the forearm leading to it. It was writing, a phrase in delicate script. I turned my head sideways to read it. "L'art pour l'art."

"It means 'art for art's sake,'" Renée said before I could ask.

"What does that mean?"

"It means some people look for the meaning behind beautiful things, instead of just appreciating that they're beautiful. And I don't." She took a final sip, emptying her glass.

"I don't suppose you know a spell to refill a wineglass?" she said.

I shook my head. "I haven't gotten to that spell yet. I think we cover it in Sorcerer 201."

"Then I don't suppose you know a time travel spell, so I can travel back in time and get a bottle of wine instead of just a glass."

I smiled. "Time travel spells are also part of Sorcerer 201."

Renée snorted. "Time travel spells. That would certainly be something."

I thought back to Sorceress Valentine, to her claim of being able to travel in time. "Well I for one believe that someday they'll invent time travel."

Renée looked at me quizzically while playing with her wineglass, slowly spinning it over and over in her hand. "You actually believe in time travel?"

"Of course," I said. "You see, time doesn't just flow in one direction, relativity proves that. Someday, through a combination of tunneling, or closed timelike curves, they'll discover a way to let people travel in time."

"Remind me to brush up on my ancient Latin in case I get stuck back in ancient Pompeii," Renée said. There was just a hint of sarcasm, enough to make me feel inadequate without making her seem cruel.

I continued. "The thing is, in order to prevent a paradox, people will have to obey two rules. The first is they can't travel forward. After all, if someone knew what was going to happen, they could do something to change it. Then, what they thought was going to happen wouldn't happen, and all sorts of things would get messed up."

Renée pulled a cigarette case out of the air and withdrew a single cigarette, which she lit. It smelled like bitter vanilla. A moment later, a bar employee, short and overweight, walked by us.

"I'm sorry Miss," he said. "You can't smoke cloves in here."

Renée inhaled a deep drag and blew it out into the air. "What if I do anyways?"

The bar employee opened his mouth to protest, then shut it and walked away.

Renée turned back to me. "What's the second rule?" While smoking, she continued to spin her empty wineglass in her other hand.

"The second rule," I said. "Is that if you travel back in time, you can't change anything. It's the same reason really. If you change something in the past, then when you get back to the present you wouldn't have a reason to go back in the first place, and you'd create a paradox."

"Then what's the point? Why travel at all?"

"Nostalgia," I said. "People would still travel in time for nostalgia, to be able to repeat things from their past. It would be like reading a diary, but one that shows how things were instead of how you remember them. If you like, you could go back in time and watch yourself make the same mistakes over and over again."

Renée reached up with one hand and brushed a stray strand of short blonde hair behind her ear. "Sounds depressing," she said.

"Not when you think about it." Maybe I was thinking of Skylar as I continued. "Time and memory are inexorably linked, because the only thing that can heal memory is time. In fact nostalgia, normal nostalgia, is a form of time travel. When the fire burns out, when even the embers die, the memories are all you have to keep you warm."

Memorial Day Weekend, 1999

The tradition of EndGame started around the same time the Sorcerers Guild was first forced to swear fealty to the Branches. Some said (and still say) the purpose of the tournament was to scare off the Branches, to show our might in battle. But given the timing of its establishment, I've always believed the opposite to be true. EndGame is a chance for the best and brightest sorcerers to take their aggression out on each other and leave the Branches alone.

As an EndGame quarter finalist, I was given three complimentary rooms at Pirate Bay, a Branch Merkasia casino that was EndGame 1999's official sponsor. Reserving one room for myself, I had offered one to Maria and Renée so they could walk to the tournament, and enjoy a nice weekend on the Strip.

A couple months earlier Maria obtained a job working as a receptionist at Versailles, a Branch Parthenia hotel on the Strip. She spent the months immediately after Black Sunday isolated in her apartment, refusing to see anyone. Her savings ran out (she was fired by the coffee shop for her Magic First connection), so she got the receptionist job as a way to make ends meet. Maria took on more and more hours at Versailles, until she and Renée were able to afford a bigger apartment that allowed each to have their own room. Maria dated a guy named Drew, a fellow Magic First activist, for a couple months, but they broke up a week before EndGame for some reason I never fully knew. At that point I was too focused on training to pay attention to the reasons for her relationship's demise.

I was reluctant to invite Renée, afraid it might send her the wrong message, but Maria convinced me that since they were still roommates, it would be rude not to. Renée cut ties with Magic First all together. She spent most of her time as a fixture at various Las Vegas art galleries, presumably trying to put her Art History degree to use. According to Maria, she would have left months ago for some more cultured city if it hadn't been for me.

My third complimentary room was offered to Grant. I hadn't spoken to him much in the previous year, and I figured that inviting him would be a nice olive branch. From what I heard in our brief phone conversations and e-mails, Grant was a rising star at the Ravenwood Capital Los Angeles office. There were even rumors he might be able to transfer to a coveted space at the New York office.

Grant asked to bring his co-worker Derek along, which I said would be fine.

Pirate Bay, as the name would suggest, was a pirate themed casino. The reception desk was shaped like the hull of a ship, so even when I was standing right up against it, there was an uncharacteristically large distance between me and the receptionists, all of whom were dressed in comical pirate outfits.

After dropping the luggage off in our rooms, Grant, Maria, Renée, and I (Derek had driven separately from Grant, and had yet to arrive) went to the lobby to grab food. I wanted to check out the blackjack table, but I figured I would need to eat sooner or later. We only made it ten yards out of the elevator.

"Roy. Roy. Roy!" I turned towards the direction of the voice. Standing before me was a tall, slim figure, a couple years older than me, with prominent Atlantian features. Behind him stood a stocky middle-aged man, also Atlantian, weighed down with four pieces of luggage.

"Roy? It is you! I didn't know you were going to be here," the tall figure said. He reached me and stuck out a hand. "Long time no see!"

"Yeah, it's been a while, Jayden," I said.

According to every girl I knew, including Skylar back when we were dating, Jayden was a profoundly handsome man. Jayden had been in a couple of my classes back at USC, but I didn't remember him from class. I remembered him because in a school filled with perpetual partiers, he turned having fun into a profession, almost an art. He had a massive apartment just a block from campus at which he threw at least one party a month, always themed, and always open to the public. Despite the open invites, he managed to maintain an air of exclusivity and high society. He also made an appearance at every party I went to for the duration of my college experience, and seemed to know every person at every one of those parties (often better than I did, even if they were my friends). The fact he appeared at every party with enough alcohol for him and those around him, as well as several attractive women, did not hurt his popularity on the party circuit.

Throughout all those parties, I had managed to develop with Jayden what passed for a friendship. Of course I had lived in Las Vegas since graduation, so I hadn't seen him in the past year.

I quickly introduced everyone to Jayden, who for his part nodded and promptly forgot each name as he heard it.

"So what brings you here?" Jayden asked.

"EndGame," I said. "Tomorrow is the quarterfinals."

"EndGame?" Jayden said, confused. "I thought you had to be a sorcerer." Jayden cocked his head to his left, noticing for the first time I was wearing a sorcerer's cloak. "And you are a sorcerer! Congratulations!"

"How about you, what are you doing here?" I asked.

"Visiting family," he said. "For EndGame as well. We have this family tradition where we all attend the final match together. It's a dirty job, visiting family. Often times involves a crapload of drama, but it makes for interesting stories later."

I was about to say I didn't know he had family in Las Vegas, but based on his Atlantian features, it made sense he was from here. During our previous talks, serious topics like family rarely came up.

"So who's the guy behind you?" I asked, gesturing towards the stocky man surrounded by suitcases.

Jayden turned and took a moment to figure out what I was talking about. "Oh, that's my bodyguard. Whenever I'm in town, my family always thinks I'll misbehave, so they have him look after me. His name is T-Lock."

"T-Lock?" Maria asked with a hint of disbelief.

Jayden seemed startled that someone else was speaking, then looked around and remembered that Maria, along with Renée and Grant, were standing there.

"His real name is something in Atlantian," Jayden said. "I always forget how to pronounce it. Atraneyu? Atreneeus?"

"Atareenar," the man identified as T-Lock said.

Jayden shook his head. "No, that's not it. Ateenarus? Anyways, literally translated it is a combination of the word for 'tea' and the word for 'lock,' so I call him 'T-Lock.'"

"*Reenar* doesn't mean 'lock,' it means 'key,'" said T-Lock.

"Whatever." Jayden waved his hand, shooing him away. He directed his attention back at me. "Hey, are you still with that girl Sharon? The hot Chinese one?"

I thought for a moment. "You mean Skylar?"

"Skylar, right," Jayden said. "How's she doing? She dump you for someone better looking yet?"

Maria started to say something, but I beat her to it. "Actually, we broke up about a year ago. And she wasn't that hot."

"What are you talking about she was totally hot," Jayden said. "I mean, umm, a year ago? Oh. Umm, I'm sorry Roy, I didn't mean to… but wait, that means you broke up right after college?"

"That's right," I said. "We broke up during the summer after senior year."

Jayden looked confused. "But I saw her at parties during that summer, and she was with you."

I shook my head. "Maybe it was a guy who looked like me?"

"But I swear it was you. Did you go to parties the summer after senior year with a girl who looked like Shannon?"

I shook my head again. "I didn't go to very many parties that summer."

"Oh." Jayden looked to the side, at Grant, then to Renée, then to me. "Well, this is *aw-k-ward*," he said, turning the word into three syllables. "But nothing that can't be cured by drinking." His face brightened. "What are you doing Monday night?"

I looked to Grant, who shrugged.

"Monday night?" I said. "If I make it to the final round, that's on Monday. But I should be free Monday night."

"Cool cool," Jayden said. "I'm having an EndGame after-party at Club Heartbreak, it's this night club at the Giza hotel. You should come! We can catch up, and we can celebrate what I'm sure will be your victory in EndGame." He looked around. "And bring your friends, of course."

"Of course," I said.

Jayden leaned in to whisper. "These three. They're with you, right?"

I nodded.

"Then definitely bring them," Jayden said, pulling back from me. "All are welcome."

Jayden paused, as if trying to remember whether he was supposed to tip us or not. "Well, I better be off. There's money to be spent, women to be seduced, family to disappoint, all the usual." Jayden bowed his head slightly towards each of us, then turned and walked off.

"I think I remember him," Grant said, staring after the form of T-Lock trying to walk with Jayden's luggage. "Is he the one who tried to jump off the roof of our apartment building into the pool that one time junior year?"

"If we can get into Club Heartbreak for free, that would be awesome," Maria said, her eyes lighting up. "They're practically one of the best clubs in the city. They throw these End of the World parties every New Year's Eve that are legendary. Besides, there's normally a cover to get in, if you can even get in. If we're there for Jayden's party, do you think the cover is waived?"

Renée looked around at us. "You guys know him?"

"Yeah, that's Jayden," I said. "We used to party with him back in college."

Renée shook her head in disbelief. "That's Jayden Parthenia."

Yes, that was it. I knew he had an Atlantian last name, but I could never remember what it was.

"Yeah, Jayden Parthenia," I said. "How do you know him?"

"Because he's Jayden Parthenia, as in Branch Parthenia."

I shrugged. "So, he's a member of Branch Parthenia?"

"He's not just a member of Branch Parthenia, he *is* Branch Parthenia. His dad is Ricardo Parthenia, the Lord of Branch Parthenia, the famous leader of the Alliance during the Wizard War. His older brother Marcos is next in line to the Wolverine throne. He's Atlantian royalty!"

"Are you sure?" I asked. "He never mentioned anything about it before." And given how much he bragged about everything, it seemed unlikely he would have been royalty and failed to mention it.

"Yes I'm sure," Renée said. "He's the famous bad boy of Atlantian society. He was supposed to become a wizard, like all members of the Branch, but instead he rejected his heritage and moved to Los Angeles, which made quite a splash among the Branches. Atlantians are still pretty traditional, they obsess about the 'old ways,' and tradition says that sons of a Branch Lord don't just run-off and do whatever they want."

"If you say so," I said. After the initial shock had worn off, the fact Jayden was Vegas royalty didn't really surprise me as much as it should have. It certainly explained where he got all his money.

"I didn't realize you had such influential friends Roy."

I looked down. At some point during the conversation Renée had maneuvered herself so she was standing next to me, and while making this latest comment, she had placed her hand on my arm.

I observed her hand for a moment. Renée looked up at me. Beneath her blonde pixie cut, her eyes blinked. I gingerly stepped back.

"I think I'm going to go gamble," I said to no one in particular.

"But what about dinner?" Maria said.

"You guys go without me. I'll grab something later."

"You know what, I may join you," said Renée, stepping towards me. She nodded at Grant. "I'm pretty sure this one is going to start talking about emerging financial markets again, which makes even blackjack seem entertaining."

Grant clutched his chest, pretending to be hurt.

"I don't think so," I said. "I need to gamble alone. Easier to concentrate that way."

Renée shrugged. "Whatever. Blackjack is so 1998 anyways." She meandered over to where Grant was standing.

"Good luck," said Grant. "Once Derek gets here, I'll call you so we can all meet up for drinks."

"Sounds good," I said, already turning to walk away.

"Roy, wait a minute," said Maria. She turned to Grant. "You guys start walking, I'll chase after you."

As Grant and Renée walked away, Maria looked at me and scowled.

"What do you think you're doing Roy?" she asked, eyes shooting accusatory rays that no counterspell could repel. "Are you trying to lead her on?"

"Lead her on? I am not leading her on."

"I told you she was interested in you, and you said the feeling was not mutual. So the least you can do is stop flirting with her every time you open your mouth."

"She's Renée, she's incapable of being interested in anything other than herself," I said. "And I am not flirting with her."

"What about the hand on the arm just now?"

"That was her hand on my arm." I held up my arm for emphasis. "Her hand! And I moved it off as soon as I felt it."

"Well what about inviting her to EndGame?" Maria said. "It totally gave her the wrong idea. The last month she's been talking about how much fun you guys are going to have together, staying at the same hotel this weekend, it's practically all she's talked about."

"I'm pretty sure you were the one who demanded I invite her," I said.

Maria shook her head. "Look, the point is she obviously has a crush on you. And while having my roommate date my best friend might sound like a good idea, I'm pretty sure it's not. So deal with it. I'm sick of hearing her talk about how great you are all the time."

"Renée talks about how great I am all the time?"

Maria spun around and stalked off towards Grant and Renée's receding figures in the distance.

I never told Maria what happened the night of Black Sunday, after she left my hotel room. Renée and I never talked about it either. When Valentine taught me the love spell, she didn't tell me the parameters, so I assumed it only lasted one night. Sure, I had seen plenty of Renée since then, and Maria had made occasional references to her burgeoning interest in me, but I never thought anything of it. Until now.

If Maria was right, was there a possibility the love spell had longer lasting effects than I anticipated? I made a mental note to look into the reversal of love spells before this got any worse. Next time I saw her, I could ask Sorceress Valentine whether there was anything I could do. But for now, all I could do was take my mind off it.

I knew I should go back to my room to prepare for my first duel. I had bags to unpack, spellbooks to review. At the very least, I could lay down and rest. I had barely slept all week from nervousness about EndGame. But I could hear the song of the casinos emanating from the gaming room, feel the energy from the city's neon lights empowering me, super charging me for the spells I was about to cast.

So I gambled.

The dealer was showing a jack, and I had a queen and a seven. The hundred dollars I started with had become two hundred dollars, and at the urging of my spells (which told me the probability waves were in my favor) I had fifty dollars in the betting circle. But a dealer jack did not appear to be "in my favor."

"Don't worry," the spells told me. "All will be well."

I stood. The dealer's hole card was a four. The total was fourteen. As long as the next card was a seven or higher, I would win.

"See, we told you," the spells said. "Have faith in us."

Where did Maria get off telling me about Renée? If there was one person in the world unqualified to give relationship advice it was her. Even Skylar was more stable when it came to the men in her life.

Skylar. If there was one person who was responsible for all this, it was her. If she hadn't broken up with me for no reason, if she hadn't compelled me to go to Las Vegas, none of this would have happened.

The dealer dealt himself another card. It was an ace. I breathed in sharply. The total was fifteen, but I worried at the prospect of a cascade of small cards. The dealer dealt himself another card.

Two. Total of seventeen. Push. The dealer rapped his knuckles in the air above my fifty dollar pile of chips, signaling to the cameras above that it was a tie. While I wouldn't win anything, at least I could keep my money.

I hadn't talked to Skylar since the break-up. I had avoided asking about her. I had no idea where she lived these days or where she worked, but for the first time in a year I started to wonder.

My luck for the day was clearly at its capacity. Not that I believed in luck. At least not most of the time.

I was supposed to deactivate my spells one at a time, making sure the shield spell stayed in place until the very end and gently removing the shield to avoid a spike of magical energy, but I felt reckless. I had only won a hundred dollars after all, hardly enough to draw the casino's attention. If a wizard or magician had been monitoring the floor, they would have noticed a slight shimmer when I deactivated the spells simultaneously. But if they did, and if they went a step further to look for the culprit, all they would have seen was me taking my chips to the cashier, getting back two crisp hundred dollar bills, and making my way out of the casino.

2 – Quarter Finals

Duelers were a diverse crowd and lived varied lifestyles. Many lived outside of Las Vegas, toiling away their days as stockbrokers or fast food workers, saving up all their money to make weekend trips to Vegas during which they dueled to provide a purpose, and excitement, to their otherwise quietly desperate lives.

Other duelers stayed in Las Vegas, getting magical or mundane jobs while dueling in their free time, hoping to do well enough to break into the professional circuit. Or, perhaps, get a job in the magical studies department at some community college teaching parlor tricks to bored Vegas housewives.

Then there were the elite few, an exclusive club that now included me, who actually made a living by dueling. Duelers who took part in official matches earned a percentage of the pool of money bet on the duel (this was carefully regulated to ensure sorcerers didn't accept money in exchange for losing). There were also occasional sponsorships from magic shops, or even the Branches (if one were good enough, and willing to take the money). And of course, there was EndGame.

Although they had varied lifestyles, every dueler in Las Vegas had the same dream. To participate in, and win, EndGame. The invitation-only Tournament, held each year on Memorial Day weekend, featured the best of the best, a pantheon of dueling greats. The winner received a prize of $100,000, more than a year's salary for even the highest paid dueler. Even more important than the money was the pride, the prestige. The reigning EndGame champion for the previous five years, Sorcerer Roland Tell, had a seat on the Sorcerers Guild Council specifically because of his repeated victories at the tournament.

Each April, thirty-three sorcerers were invited to participate in that year's EndGame. Thirty-two of the participants were chosen by the Sorcerers Guild Council, and the thirty-third was the previous year's Champion. There were some eyebrows raised when I was chosen after less than a year on the dueling scene. But I had made quite an impact in that year, starting with my defeat of Wizard Karl Johnsen (albeit in an unsanctioned duel), so most saw my invitation as an attempt to make EndGame relevant to the younger generation (and sell more tickets) by featuring the hot new sorcerer in at least one match.

The tournament started the weekend before Memorial Day. Through single elimination, the thirty-two invitees were whittled down to sixteen, then eight, then four. On the Saturday of Memorial Day weekend the quarter finals were held, narrowing the four to two. On Sunday the semi-final was held, and on Memorial Day itself, the winner of the semi-final faced off against the previous year's Champion. When I made it from the field of thirty-two to the field of four, winning my first three matches without a hitch, the voices that questioned my invitation to the tournament were silenced.

The first weekend of EndGame took place in venues across the city, but during the second weekend all matches took place at a special arena adjacent to Magic Hall, established specifically for this purpose.

The dueling floor of the arena was a large oval, paved with small white tiles except for two black X's where the duelers stood when the match began. The tiles were in sections that could be easily replaced, a concession to the violent nature of magical duels which often scarred large areas of the floor. Surrounding the floor was a seamless seven foot high white wall (the entrances were carefully hidden), with a glass barrier extending another seven feet above that. Duelers tried to be careful, but nobody wanted a spectator to be fried by an errant fireball.

The arena had seating for ten thousand spectators, including a raised dais (I called it the "skybox") which provided the best view for the Council and their chosen VIPs. In recent years it had been rare for a match, even the final championship, to sell out.

I thought of all this as I stood on the tournament floor, on my black X, while the spectators took their seats. There were no more than a few hundred, low even by EndGame standards. My friends had probably been able to move up to better seats. Maria and Grant, and Renée, were somewhere up in those stands. If Grant's friend Derek had arrived, he'd be up there too. No doubt Maria had made some sort of sign showing her support for me, and Grant was probably on his cellphone, dealing with some business issue going on back in Los Angeles. I scoured the seats for any sign of them, but could barely make out any faces over the harsh lights flooding the arena.

As far as I could tell, Sorceress Valentine had not shown up. Part of me expected her to appear, like a proud soccer mom, at each of my duels. Beyond the need for affirmation, there were things we needed to discuss. But the time-traveling sorceress had been absent from all my duels the previous weekend, and with minutes left, it looked like she would be absent from this round as well.

Up in the skybox, a middle aged woman with her hair in a bun (I recognized her as a member of the council but could not remember her name), stood up and cleared her throat. Magic, either her own or an assistant's, carried her voice throughout the sparsely populated arena.

"Children of magic," she said. "Welcome to EndGame."

There was polite applause and a few cheers.

"Before we begin," she continued. "Let us pledge allegiance to those who provide order and justice to our city." She nodded to her left, towards a wizard who had remained sitting in his chair. From the floor I couldn't see his Mark, so I didn't know which Branch he belonged to, but even from a distance I could tell that he was not pleased to be there.

"All members of the Guild, please rise."

Half the audience shuffled to a standing position. From the floor I placed my hand over my heart, as did my opponent, and faced a banner at the back of the arena that featured the Marks of all the Branches (minus Primm, of course).

"I pledge my loyalty to the Sorcerers Guild, and to the Branches of Las Vegas," the elderly Sorceress began, various Guild members repeating it under their breath.

"Death to the Branches!" came a voice from the stands.

"Magic will be free!" shouted another.

The sorceress in the skybox looked shaken, but she continued, raising her voice in the process. "I will obey the orders of those sorcerers appointed above me, and the directives of the Guild."

There were more scattered shouts of opposition, and I could sense security personnel moving to intercept them and throw them out of the match.

A year ago this wouldn't have happened. Opposition to the Branches existed of course, but those who felt that way were smart enough, or scared enough, to stay silent. Black Sunday changed everything. The initial response had been an immediate stop to all outward discontent, and the virtual end of Magic First. But after the fires died out, and injured magicians had time to lick their wounds, opposition returned stronger than ever. Magicians, and some from the sorcerer ranks, now voiced open contempt for the Branches of magic, and for the first time, for the Guild that supported their rule.

The pledge complete, the sorceress shakily started to sit, then quickly stood up and mumbled before sitting down all the way. "Let the duel begin."

My opponent and I turned to face each other.

"I suppose we should get this over with," he said. "I have lunch plans."

This was not the first time I had been in the presence of Sorcerer Arnold Davidson, although it was likely he didn't remember me. Almost a year ago, when I first came to Las Vegas, I saw Sorcerer Davidson wave watching in a casino, a sight that propelled me to try wave watching myself.

When I first saw him, I had mentally referred to him as "the frat boy sorcerer," a title I thought even more appropriate now than before. His hair lay so perfectly coifed that he must have used magic to keep it in place. His square jaw would have looked equally at home on a college recruiting ad or a wanted poster.

"Did you hear what I said?" he repeated, looking almost hurt that I hadn't responded to his taunt.

"I heard what you said." I fell back into a crouch and shot a fireball at his torso.

Rather than dodge it, Arnold reached out a hand, which turned sparkly blue, and caught it like a baseball. Grunting, he absorbed the fireball into his glowing blue hand.

"That the best you got?" he laughed.

The fireball opening was a technique Valentine suggested to me. It expended only a small amount of magic, and an opponent's reaction to it revealed a great deal about said opponent's style.

Here is what I learned. Arnold was flashy. He could have stepped to the side and let the fireball crash into the wall. Instead, he absorbed the energy, even though he had to expend energy himself to do so.

Arnold was already readying his first spell. Waving his hands theatrically and chanting with a loud flourish, he spun energy in front of him until an illusion appeared.

It was a dragon. My blood went cold. I froze in place. The voices of the audience faded as I looked at the dragon in front of me. The dragon soared towards me, roaring fire as it flew. I shook my head and took a breath. It was just an illusion. It wasn't a demon, it was just a parlor trick.

I raised my hands as if to cast a counterspell, then dropped to a knee and thrust my hand into the air. Chanting a spell, my hand turned to steel, cutting the dragon in two as it continued to fly in the direction it was sent. Severed in half, the illusion dispersed into air.

Still kneeling, I fired a volley of three fireballs at Arnold and jumped up. Arnold crossed his arms. A wall of ice shot up from the floor. The fireballs crashed against it. The wall caught all three, but also hid my movements for a precious second. Most sorcerers would have used an invisible wall of dense air (simpler to cast and far less draining), but the audience wouldn't have been able to see the wall, and I was counting on the fact Arnold, above all else, pandered to his fans.

As the third fireball hit, I ran diagonally to the right. While Arnold turned to face me, I was already pushing a column of air into him. It wasn't powerful enough to hurt him, but it knocked him to the ground.

Jumping up, Arnold incanted. A gray cloud formed in the air above his head. It rolled violently, small sparks of lightning dancing from one part of the cloud to the other. I had seen this spell before. If I tried to shoot or throw anything at Arnold, lightning from the cloud would intercept it.

I continued to run as Arnold cast the cloud spell. By the time the spell finished I was behind him. I chanted another spell (it was mental magic, so it took longer to cast, but I had the time). Arnold was possessed by an intense itching sensation. The cloud lightning could stop physical objects, but it couldn't stop pure magic. Arnold was professional enough to dispose of the itching with a counterspell, but wasted a precious three seconds during which he wasn't casting a spell at me. By the time he recovered, I was running from behind him to his right side. I chanted again. The illusion of a snake appeared at Arnold's ankles.

Arnold actually jumped back at the sight of the snake. It must have been a phobia of his. It only took a second for him to realize it was an illusion, and I hadn't summoned an actual snake, but then he wasted another second destroying it instead of letting the harmless illusion continue to exist.

By now I had almost run a complete circle around Arnold, and was feet away from the "X" on the ground where I started the duel. At this point Arnold probably realized what I was doing, but it was too late. He reached out his hands and spelled my feet. I could feel them freeze, useless, but I was so close to my "X" that I simply let my body flop, the momentum carrying me like a runner sliding into home.

Walls of flame shot up from the entire path I had just run. The Circle of Fire is a complicated spell that requires the caster to make a complete circuit, returning to his starting position, without the opponent crossing the line once. It is rarely successful in a duel, especially at this level, and for that reason was also rarely attempted. But I had seen Arnold's flashy sense of style, and the wave watching spell I cast moments before the match began had told me that, in this rare circumstance, a Circle of Fire would work.

Sorcerer Arnold Davidson gulped at the circle of fire surrounding him, and I could hear cheers and shouts from the audience. The wall shrank inward. Arnold tried to freeze the air around him into ice crystals, but the fire was too intense.

"I yield, I yield," he cried out with the flames just inches away from consuming him. I relaxed my hand, and the flames fell away.

Arnold was on his knees, gasping for breath. He was obviously faking, a final performance for the crowd. Rather than help him up, I turned to the skybox and raised a fist into the air.

The elderly sorceress stood up. "I declare this duel to be over, the victor is," she glanced down at a notecard, then back up, "Sorcerer Roy Nakamura."

The crowd erupted in applause.

3 - The Archmage and Me

For lunch we went to Little John's, an Italian restaurant at Pirate Bay. It was supposed to be one of the nicer Italian restaurants in Las Vegas, and the fact that as guests of Pirate Bay we got a ten percent discount didn't hurt. The wait for a table of five was thirty minutes (I tried telling them I was an EndGame semi-finalist, and was told, in that case, the wait was thirty minutes), so I had plenty of time to get to know Grant's friend and co-worker Derek Hastings.

"What did you think of the match?" I asked.

Derek shrugged. "It was exciting, I guess. Kind of short."

"Well next time I promise to defeat my opponent slower," I said. "Whatever my fans demand."

Maria nudged me. "Come on Roy, there's no need to be defensive."

After exactly thirty-three minutes, we were shown to a table at the back just barely large enough for the five of us. Somehow I ended up between Renée and Derek. Normally I wouldn't have given a second thought to sitting next to Renée (we certainly hung out enough thanks to Maria), but after Maria's warning the day before I was over-thinking her decision to sit next to me.

"That was quite a decisive victory," Renée said, putting her hand on my arm.

Maria shot me a look. I rolled my shoulder, shrugging Renée's hand off of my arm in the process, and I scooted closer to Derek.

Derek Hastings, the allegedly personable co-worker about whom Grant frequently spoke, was a few inches taller than I was. He was Grant's height, six feet or close to it. He wasn't as muscular as Grant, but he possessed a somewhat athletic build, like he played sports in college but only intramural. He was white, of course, but not just normal white. He was a sort of pale white that made me wonder how quickly he would burn if he went to the beach without sunscreen. His hair was nondescript brown, and he had a five o'clock shadow, likely deliberate, that seemed to frame his otherwise unremarkable face.

He was wearing a long sleeve striped shirt with the sleeves rolled-up and shirt tucked into his khakis. He had clearly spent several minutes getting the rolled-up sleeves just right so it looked like no effort had been put into it. Tying together the whole outfit was a black watch that, I'm sure, cost more than I made in a year.

"So, what do you do?" I asked Derek.

"I'm in consulting," he said. "I'm a senior consultant at Ravenwood Capital, where Grant works."

"What does a consultant do?" Maria asked.

"My guess would be consult," Renée said before taking a sip of her wine. I hadn't even seen a wine menu, much less seen Renée order, but somehow she always managed to find a glass.

"It's pretty complicated," Derek said. "It involves quantifying our areas of expertise, which in my case has to do with systems management, and then applying it to benefit the business of the client."

I looked around to see whether anyone else was buying this.

"There's a lot of crowd-sourcing involved as well," Derek added, as if this would cause his vocation to sound like a real one.

I already disliked Derek, but I was one hundred percent sure "crowd-sourcing" wasn't a real word.

"What do you do?" Derek asked me.

I took a gulp of my water. It was going to be a long meal.

"Roy's a famous dueler," Maria said.

"Well, I get that," Derek said. "But what do you actually do? Like, for a living?"

"I'm a dueler," I said. I wanted to brag to him that I was also secretly a wave watcher, and used blackjack to make most of my money. Even more so, I wanted to tell him the wave watching was just to finance my real job, which was to train as hard as I could so I could someday defeat an evil all-powerful demon, and thus save the precious lives of him and all his co-workers at Ravenwood Capital.

"Oh," Derek said. He scrunched up his face (it took me a moment to realize this must be his "thinking face"), then he shrugged. "I didn't know you could make money doing that."

"You'd be surprised," Grant said. "Between commissions, sponsorships, and betting percentages, dueling can be a lucrative business for those at the top of their game."

Grant loved to criticize my vocational choices. It was apparent I was losing the argument, badly, if Grant was actually jumping to my rescue. I started to defend myself, but the conversation had already moved on.

"How about you Maria," Derek was saying. "What do you do?"

Maria brushed her hair behind her ear. She wore it shorter these days, so it didn't get in the way of her eyes like it used to, but she still made the gesture out of habit. "I work at Versailles. It's a casino here on the Strip."

Renée leaned in and whispered into my ear. "So how long do you think it took Derek to get his hair to look like that?"

I turned to Renée and raised an eyebrow.

"It has so much gel in it, it looks like it's solid," she said. "I kind of want to touch it."

A chuckle managed to escape from my lips, but I turned back to see how Maria was faring against Derek.

"Do you work in, like, the finance department or something?" Derek asked. Derek assumed since we were friends with Grant, we must all be corporate sell-outs just like him.

"I'm a receptionist," Maria said. "I work the front desk."

"Oh," Derek said, again making his scrunched up thinking face. "If you wanted to be a receptionist, why didn't you just stay in Los Angeles?"

Grant, Renée, and I all cringed at the question. Maria didn't seem fazed.

"I came to be an activist, to work for Magic First. But since that didn't pay the bills, I settled for the receptionist job as a way to make money."

Derek pursed his lips. "That's too bad," he said. "You shouldn't have to settle."

I almost choked on my food at the comment.

"Well, thank you," Maria said, looking a little surprised at the comment. "But fighting for magician rights is my dream, so I don't really see my life here as settling."

Maria looked down at her plate. While answering Derek's question, she had been trying to cut through a roll with a butter knife.

"Let me get that for you," I said.

"That's okay," Maria started to say, but I was already chanting a spell.

Maria's roll split into four perfectly equal pieces.

"I said it was okay."

"A simple 'thank you' would have sufficed," I mumbled under my breath.

We continued eating.

The girls planned to spend the rest of the day at Pirate Bay's complementary spa, and Grant wanted to take Derek on a private tour of Las Vegas (I assumed this was code for going to a strip club). I told everyone I would see them the next day at the EndGame semi-final. I intended to go back to my room to spend the afternoon resting, but instead I found myself wandering down the Strip, seeking out a place to gamble.

Even an amateur wave watcher will warn you not to wave watch in the casino where you are staying. That way, if you get discovered and kicked out of the casino, you won't also get kicked out of your hotel. I take it a step further. I never wave watch in a casino owned by the same Branch as the hotel where I'm staying. I was staying in Pirate Bay, owned by Branch Merkasia, so I set out to find a non-Merkasia casino.

After a half hour of wandering, I ended up in front of the Los Angeles casino, a Branch Parthenia establishment. I went inside and quickly found an open seat at a blackjack table.

The conversation from lunch still played in my mind. I cast my spells and started to play, but the usual rush I got from each dealt card failed to appear. I tried doubling my bet, ignoring the shrieks of my spells, but no matter how much I gambled, the conversation from lunch kept returning, unbidden, to the forefront of my mind.

"You shouldn't have to settle." What was Derek trying to get at? Maria believed in Magician rights, pursuing her passion. Where did he get off claiming she had settled?

My spells started to fail me. I was thinking about the conversation from lunch, and my spells, jealous at being ignored and disobeyed, decided to leave me before I could leave them. After losing four hundred dollars in a single hand, I took a break.

I stepped out of the Los Angeles casino onto the sidewalk of the Strip. It was still day, so many of the neon lights hadn't come on yet. It occurred to me that if my wave watching spell had failed so badly, there might be deficiencies in my shield spell as well. Had it been a bad enough mistake? Had I been discovered?

Then again, if I had been discovered back in the casino, no one pursued me. Perhaps this was false confidence. Perhaps the casino was daring me to come back and try to wave watch with larger amounts of money, at which point security would descend on me from places unknown, and some wizard would break my legs and cast a spell that would give me nightmares for the rest of my life. Of course, I was a skilled dueler now. I wouldn't go down without a fight.

I crossed the street at a light, then turned back to look back at the casino. The Los Angeles casino was designed to look like the Los Angeles skyline, or at least an artist's rendition of it. In reality most of Los Angeles' skyscrapers are far enough apart from each other that, seen from afar, it looks not so much like a unified skyline as a collection of independent buildings. Like the top of an almost bald man's head, a hair here and a hair there, but no cohesive plan. Here in Las Vegas, the architect had smashed all the buildings right next to each other to create a continuous façade, one building fading into the next.

Just then the sun finally set behind the mock Los Angeles skyline, and the last rays of sun streamed over the mock skyscrapers. It's strange how fake things, like the fake Los Angeles skyline in silhouette, can appear more beautiful, even more realistic, than the real thing. The reflection looked more real than the original.

I was so busy looking at the mock skyline, marveling at its beauty, that I didn't notice the black van pulling up next to me on the Strip. I didn't hear its wheels squeak, and I didn't notice the two figures emerging from it. I didn't notice the two wizards until they were right in front of me. One reached out a hand. I brought my arms in front of me, crossing them and starting to mutter a counterspell, but it was too late.

Darkness fell over my vision like a curtain, blotting out the Strip (whose buildings were now coming to life with neon light) and robbing me of a final view of the sunlight streaming behind the fake Los Angeles skyline.

One of the two wizard kidnappers undid the blindness spell as the black van came to a stop. Just prior to this I felt the van bump a few times, heard the grating of metal against metal, and concluded we were in a parking garage.

When the van stopped and I, once again able to see, was pulled out of it, I found myself at a small underground loading dock. It looked like the kind of place buried in a casino's bowels where deliveries are made. In this case, the delivery was of a wave watcher who was apparently not as good as he thought.

A wizard, along with a man in a conservative black business suit who could have been a lawyer, an accountant, or a waiter, were standing on the loading dock in front of a service elevator.

"Is that him?" asked the wizard, eyeing me carefully, as my two kidnappers dragged me in front of him.

"It should be," said one of the kidnappers. "Isn't that why you're here?"

The man in the suit took out a folder. Opening it, he studied an item inside, then studied my face, then looked back down at the folder.

"It's him," said the man in the suit. "Take him upstairs."

The elevator only went up one floor, and even "upstairs" I still felt like I was underground. It was a feeling of artificiality, like being in a casino that's lit up to look like it's day when you know outside it's actually night.

The hallway I found myself in looked like any other basement hallway. Concrete and dusty, various areas to the side marked off with chain link fencing, a place where visitors didn't tread. This place to which I had been brought was for function, not for show, with the exception (of course) of the massive mahogany door at the end of the hallway.

One wizard detached himself from me and pounded on the door, twice, then opened the door while the other wizard pulled me in. I heard the door close behind me.

The single wizard now escorting me stepped away as we entered the room. Letting go of my arm, he dropped to his left knee and touched the fingers of his right hand to his forehead.

"Ark'Telga," he said, head still bowed. "We have the sorcerer you were looking for."

"Very good, you may go now."

The wizard left. I heard the massive door open and shut behind me.

The windowless office in which I was now standing wasn't large, but it had the aura of power, the type of office where a CEO might sit, or maybe even a president.

Nothing in the office came from a catalogue, none of the furniture had been mass produced. The desk, which dominated my vision and extended almost the entire width of the room, was mahogany, the same shade and build as the door. The surface of it was flat. The large legs that supported it were etched with patterns that at first appeared to be abstract designs, but on closer examination were people, most of them battling each other with various forms of ancient weapons. The bookshelves lining the walls on either side were some sort of lighter wood, but were large and solid enough to be equally imposing.

Behind the desk, hanging on the wall, hung a large map of the city of Las Vegas. When I moved my head slightly I saw that it, also made out of wood, was three dimensional. Someone had chiseled each street into the wood so the entire map had depth.

Sitting still behind the desk, as if he were a part of the office, was a man in his mid to late fifties wearing a white leather wizard's jacket. His sword, still in its scabbard, was lying on his desk. A gold chain wrapped around his neck, whatever emblem it held hid beneath the folds of his jacket.

The man was both professional and terrifying. The wrinkles of his face looked like battle scars, and the magic user in me could sense the magnitude of his magical ability. Although he was not casting a spell at the moment, I could see his potential to do so emanating like steam rising from asphalt on a hot summer day.

"Sit," he said.

I immediately sat in the small wooden chair in front of the desk, the only piece of furniture in the office that did not appear alive and menacing.

"I am Archmage Artimus Cantor," he said. "Do you know why you are here, Sorcerer Roy Nakamura?"

I looked around, as if the answer might be written on one of the bookshelves. It was not. I swallowed. "I… I think I know, sir."

The man raised an eyebrow. "Is that so? Then tell me, why are you here?"

"Because…" I stopped myself as I looked at the Branch mark on Artimus Cantor's neck. Suddenly I remembered the marks on the necks of the wizards who brought me here, the emblems on their jackets.

"I thought I knew why I'm here, but this doesn't make any sense. The Branch Mark on the side of your neck means you're a wizard of Branch Shaskauer."

"I am not *a wizard* of Branch Shaskauer," Artimus said. "I am the Archmage of Branch Shaskauer. What about that is so surprising?"

"But if you're from Branch Shaskauer," I hesitated to say the words, worried what would happen, "then why did you kidnap me for wave watching in a Branch Parthenia casino?"

Artimus stared. He opened his mouth to speak, then closed it. He scrunched his lips together, unable or unwilling to talk. His ancient, powerful eyes looked as if they might be starting to cry. It took a moment for me to comprehend the gesture, and then it came to me. Artimus Cantor, the Archmage of Branch Shaskauer, was trying not to laugh.

His body triumphed over his mind, and he let out a small squeak. "Wave watching?" he said. "You think we brought you here because you were wave watching?" Artimus stood up, causing me to jump in my chair. He reached out his arms to his sides. "I am an Archmage, not a security guard. I do not care if you were wave watching, and I certainly do not care if you were doing it in a casino owned by our greatest enemy."

He sat back down. "No, young sorcerer. I am here, or should I say I brought you here, because of your close relationship with someone I have been trying to track down for a long time."

"Sorceress Valentine?" I could have denied knowing her, but something told me it was useless to try lying to an Archmage.

Artimus nodded.

I swallowed. "What's your interest in Sorceress Valentine?"

Artimus folded his hands on the desk and leaned back in his chair. He acted as if he were considering whether or not to reveal a secret to me, though I was sure he had already planned out his next several moves. "Five years ago, Sorceress Valentine approached Johannes Pendragon, my predecessor. She wanted access to the Branch Shaskauer Archives to assist her in some of her research.

"Naturally, her request was denied. She was not a member of our Branch, nor could she tell us any reason why allowing her access to them would benefit us."

"So you only let people look at your archives if it will somehow help you," I said. "How generous."

Artimus was unfazed by my insult. "The Branch Shaskauer Archives contain priceless information, and they are our most precious asset. No one outside our Branch has accessed them in over a hundred years. Indeed, even those within our Branch rarely have access. It is said by some that the information contained in them, the fact we could destroy them in an instant, and along with them irreplaceable information about pre-Fall Atlantis, is the only reason Branch Parthenia declined to destroy us at the end of the Wizard War.

"No, we were not about to let some, *sorceress*, with no good reason, look at the most dangerous magic books in existence. When we denied her request, she seemed calm, as if she could see the future and had known she would be turned down."

Artimus paused. If he wore glasses, he would have taken them off and wiped the lenses for emphasis. Instead, he settled for clenching his hands, still folded, then releasing them.

"She attacked later that night. We were prepared for an attack. The guard at the Archives is always prepared. Nevertheless, she got through fifteen of our wizards before the remaining ones managed to turn her back."

Artimus paused again, caught up in the reliving of his memories. "She killed seven of us, more wizards than died in the line of duty since the end of the war. One of those who died was Archmage Johannes Pendragon. In his absence, I was promoted to Archmage, and assigned the task of figuring out who this Sorceress Valentine was, how she had managed to kill so many of us, and most importantly, why she was so desperate to gain access to the Archives."

"It seems pretty obvious," I said. "You said yourself they contain priceless information."

"Someone as powerful as Sorceress Valentine has no need for money. And it didn't seem as if she bore any animosity towards the Branch that would make her want to destroy us.

"No, there had to be another reason, some specific piece of information she needed to obtain, and after studying her for the last several years, I think I know what it is."

Artimus stood up, forcing his chair back against the wall. Unsure whether I was also supposed to stand, I continued to sit.

"Valentine wears three tokens around her neck. A dolphin, a sun, and a unicorn. The problem with tokens is that unlike Branch marks," Artimus pointed to the right side of his neck, where the square and two diagonal lines of Branch Shaskauer were prominently featured, "they have multiple meanings, so it is hard to tell in a specific instance what it represents.

"After some research I determined that the sun token is used by those who pursue research into memory or time travel. This confirmed what we had been told about her. That she was 'the time travelling sorceress.' That she could, in fact, travel in time."

My lips remained shut, unwilling (and unable) to confirm or deny whether she could simply stop time, or if she could actually travel in it.

"Every branch has a symbol, an animal from which it takes its name," Artimus said. "The unicorn is the symbol of Branch Shaskauer. Just as 'Parthenia' means 'children of the wolverine' and 'Merkasia' means 'children of the bear,' 'Shaskauer' means 'children of the unicorn' in Atlantian. The Lord Shaskauer is said to 'sit on the unicorn throne.' Thus, the unicorn token particularly interested me. I already knew, from personal experience, that some sorcerers wear a unicorn token to demonstrate their affinity for Branch Shaskauer, showing they supported us during the war, or perhaps that we had helped them at some time.

"Obviously, this could not be why Valentine wore it, so I dug deeper. Tokens often portray the wearer's interests, or obsessions. I found, in addition to being the symbol of Branch Shaskauer, the unicorn was affiliated with a very specific obsession. The unicorn token is worn by sorcerers who are dedicated to the study of the OneSpell."

I tried not to look shocked, but the effort backfired. I sat too still, too calm. If I had been taking a polygraph, my readings would have fluctuated wildly, the instrument proclaiming that anything I was about to say was a lie. I knew Artimus's magical abilities far outpaced any mechanical test, and wondered what, if anything, my rapidly beating heart had just revealed.

One look from Artimus both convicted and reassured me. One look from Artimus, now standing over me, told me I had revealed nothing, because he already knew about the OneSpell, already knew why Valentine had chosen me as her apprentice.

Artimus sat back down, once again folding his hands on the desk and leaning back in his chair. "Normally at this point I would tell you what the OneSpell is, but I hate games. I know that you know what it is. I know you are somehow part of Valentine's plan to acquire it, and so I am confident she has given you a sufficient overview of it. However, I will tell you something about the spell that your master most likely did not."

In spite of myself, I could feel my body leaning slightly closer to the desk, my ears straining to hear what was next.

"The OneSpell belongs to us," Artimus said. "It is our property, our birthright, our destiny. Let me tell you a little story, one Valentine likely neglected to tell you. A thousand years ago, the two greatest wizards of that time came together to create a spell which would allow them to correct the wrongs they saw around them by controlling the very essence of magic itself. Those wizards were Trannanir Shaskauer and Mianna Panashka. After years of research and study they succeeded, and the result was the OneSpell. Trannanir wanted to use the spell to improve the island kingdom, like they promised they would, but Mianna wanted to save the spell for herself. There was a fight, and during the struggle Mianna sent the spell a thousand years into the future, denying Trannanir access to it.

"Trannanir Shaskauer is, obviously, one of our line, a member of our Branch. Branch Panashka no longer exists, which leaves Branch Shaskauer as the sole rightful claimant. Mianna's treachery does not negate our claim."

Artimus leaned back. "So now the question is, what do we do with you?"

I had been bracing myself for this moment. I was a better fighter than I had been when I faced off against Karl. But this was not just any wizard, this was the Archmage of Branch Shaskauer. From what I knew of Branch politics, he was likely the Branch's most skilled magical warrior.

There was also the voice in the back of my head pointing out that if Artimus Cantor wanted me dead, I would be dead by now.

"I'm not going to hurt you," Artimus said, as if reading my mind. "But know that our Branch will be watching you from now on. More importantly, remember that the OneSpell is ours. If there comes a day when you somehow acquire it, or acquire knowledge of its

219

whereabouts, and try to hide it from us," Artimus clenched his fists, "I will kill you myself."

I did not doubt he was serious.

I wasn't surprised, not even a little, to find Sorceress Valentine waiting for me in the lobby of Pirate Bay. My kidnappers were polite enough to drop me off back at my hotel, although they instituted the blindness spell once again when I got in the van and didn't remove it until we arrived at our destination. They didn't want me to know the location of the Archmage's secret bat cave.

"Sorcerer Roy Nakamura," Valentine said, standing up from a lounge chair near the reception desk. "It has been too long."

I took her hand and shook it, bending my head down near her ear.

"We don't have time for this Sorceress," I whispered. "Branch Shaskauer is looking for you. They're probably watching us right now."

I pulled my head back just in time to see Sorceress Valentine shrug her shoulders.

"Please Roy. Branch Shaskauer has been hunting me for the last five years."

"But, they just kidnapped me!"

Valentine sighed. "You used to be my apprentice. It was bound to happen sooner or later."

"So what are you going to do about it?"

"Nothing. At least nothing new."

Valentine studied the back of one of her hands, then the other. "I have constantly running illusion spells to mask me from those, like Artimus Canter, who wish me harm. Illusions are one of the simplest spells to cast. The art of illusion has been practiced by so-called magicians, most of them not even Signed, for hundreds if not thousands of years."

Valentine turned the palms of her hands up towards me, then held them out from her body. "It's all about making people look at one thing," she extended her right hand, "while you're doing something somewhere else," she extended her left.

"So what if someone discovers you?"

"Then they would immediately discover something even more interesting, just in another place," Valentine said. "A place where I am not."

"But what about me? The Archmage of Branch Shaskauer had me kidnapped right in the middle of the street. He could have killed me!"

Valentine thought for a moment. "Did you eat anything at his office?"

"What?" Why wasn't she taking this seriously? Why didn't she understand the magnitude of this?

"When he kidnapped you, I assume he took you to his office," she said.

I nodded in response.

"And not the fake office he keeps in Branch Shaskauer headquarters, but the real office, the underground one?"

Again, I nodded.

"Well, did you eat anything? Did he offer you any food and did you eat any of it?"

After thinking for a moment, I shook my head. "No, he didn't offer me anything."

"Then you're fine," Valentine said. "Besides, he's not going to kill you."

"Why not?" I asked.

"Because he knows it would make me angry," she said without a hint of humor. "Now, if you are finished being worried that we are going to be discovered, let's go to the bar. We need to talk."

At the bar I ordered a rum and cola, my standard, while Valentine ordered a vodka on the rocks. She offered to pay, which I would normally think generous, except that a minute later she handed the bartender a one dollar bill and told him to "keep the change." Based on the way he thanked her profusely, I can only imagine what he thought he was being handed.

"Where have you been?" I asked. "I was starting to worry you'd forgotten about me. About our plan."

"I've been busy." Valentine sipped on her vodka. "Don't forget, I'm trying to save the world. I may be able to stop time, and travel through time, but certain tasks still require time to be completed."

She studied me. "Hopefully your mind is capable of understanding that distinction."

My drink was already half empty. I made a mental note to slow down. "I'm not your apprentice anymore. You can stop pretending you have the ability to travel in time."

"Except that I do," Valentine said, taking another sip from her vodka on the rocks. "Someday you'll realize that." She looked into her glass. "Someday I'll show you."

I put my drink down on the bar and stretched out my arms. "There's no time like the present. Why don't you go ahead and take me back in time to before Archmage Cantor kidnapped me."

Valentine rubbed her right temple with her free hand. "I can travel in time, but I can't take others with me. The very idea is ridiculous."

"Then at least use your knowledge," I said, trying to poke at Valentine's inconsistencies. "Go forward in time, then come back here and tell me what spells Sorcerer Hofstead is going to use in the semi-final tomorrow."

Valentine shook her head. "It doesn't work that way. I can't tell you the future, or else I risk changing it. I have to be very careful to make sure everything happens exactly the way it is supposed to."

"Can't change things? What about your supposed journeys back in time to save the guy you loved?"

Valentine shot me a look of death. "Not now Roy. I know you meant it as a joke, but not now."

I finished my drink in one gulp. I had faced an Archmage one on one, and Valentine didn't seem to care. I had another duel to fight the next day, according to Valentine, if I failed the world would be in danger.

Six months earlier, Valentine and I had finished with the day's training when she told me I was going to enter EndGame. It had been my life's dream, so I was beyond excited. But it was Valentine, which meant there was a catch.

"Why do you want me to enter?" I said. "Shouldn't we focus on the OneSpell?"

"The current EndGame champion is Sorcerer Roland Tell," Valentine said. "That means after all the other competitors are eliminated one by one, he duels the winner in order to retain his title as champion."

I knew of Roland. I first saw the famous white-haired sorcerer in Magic Hall when I went to take the Trials. Since then I had heard of his renown as a powerful orator, a skilled politician, a ruthless dueler, and of course, reigning EndGame champion.

"Roland knows where the OneSpell is going to appear," Valentine said. "And facing him in EndGame is the only way to get the information from him."

That was it. There was the catch. The significance of the tournament now made sense.

"Roland was in the service of Branch Merkasia during the Wizard War," Valentine said. "Somehow, that experience gave him an interest in the OneSpell, at least for a while. When he faced the Token Master during his Trials, he asked a question, just as you did, but rather than ask 'when' the spell would appear, he asked 'where.'"

"I don't suppose he would give us the information if we just asked nicely," I said.

Valentine shook her head. "There is only one way to get it from him."

Which is how I found myself in a bar with Sorceress Valentine, the quarter finals completed, making sure my entry in EndGame would not be in vain.

"Have you prepared the spell for the final round?" I asked.

"It will be ready on time," Valentine said.

"You're not done with it?" I hissed. A stare from Valentine's eyes reminded me to change my tone. I continued. "This isn't messing around Valentine. If you don't have it ready in time, there's no way I can get the information we need from Sorcerer Tell."

"I said it will be ready it in time. That means it will be ready in time." Sorceress Valentine's tone was firm. "Your job is to win the next match. If you cannot beat Colin Hofstead, nothing I do will matter."

Valentine raised her glass and finished the last of her drink. She got up to leave.

"Wait, Sorceress, there's something I need to know."

"I thought you wanted me to go work on the spell."

I swallowed. "How do I reverse a love spell?"

"A love spell?" she asked, looking slightly confused.

"Yes, a love spell. Remember the love spell you taught me during my training?"

Valentine nodded.

"Well, I cast it, or at least I think I cast it. And now I need to undo it."

Valentine took a step closer to me.

"Listen very carefully," she said. "On whom did you cast the love spell?"

"My friend Renée." I figured there was no use in trying to hide the details.

"You cast the love spell I taught you on Renée?" There was disbelief in her voice. Her eyes looked to the side. Then she nodded. "Of course, that makes sense."

"Makes sense?"

Valentine sighed. "A love spell is serious business Roy. You should not be casting one lightly."

"I know, I know," I said. "But I wasn't thinking. And I didn't think they lasted this long."

"Love spells are derived from love, and love, even when unrequited, can last a long time." Valentine stroked her chin. "I will look into it and let you know if I find anything. But we are not dealing with this issue, and are not going to mention it again, until after you face Roland in the final round of EndGame. That is our priority."

With that she turned and left. I waited a moment for her to exit the bar, then I ordered another drink.

3 – Counterspell

The semi-final was better attended than the previous round, but I wasn't the reason. Almost half the seats were full, which might seem pathetic for a sporting event, but was more attendees than had seen a match in some time. Those in attendance were also rowdier, more excited, than those at my duel with Sorcerer Arnold Davidson the day before. Several were holding signs. A couple had my name on them, but far more consisted of a large number "1."

The previous evening I learned that the other quarter-final match had been an upset. Instead of facing Sorcerer Colin Hofstead, a balding man whose strategy I had meticulously studied in order to beat him in our anticipated match, I would be facing off with none other than Sorceress Corinna Windlass, the unofficial spokesperson (and rumored leader) of Magic First.

Like most members of Magic First, Corinna disappeared in the aftermath of Black Sunday. Many of the leaders had been abducted by the Branches, held and tortured. Some died. But after a couple months had gone by, the movement began to re-emerge. People were no longer scared by the crackdown, now they were angry about it. Into that anger stepped Corinna.

Corinna was the leader the movement had been looking for. Seeing a lack of momentum, she started organizing them, daring them to go farther and harder than they had before. At least that was the rumor. I didn't associate with Magic First, and although Maria was still a member, she did her best not to tell me about their activities. At the end of the day I was a sorcerer, which meant I was loyal to the Guild, which meant, according to Magic First rhetoric, I was on the side of the Branches.

Magic First devotees had taken to putting posters of Corinna up on walls throughout Las Vegas. They were more common in the rundown areas, like the burned out stalls and alleys that used to be the Meet, but they were occasionally placed in casinos on the Strip (although they were quickly ripped down by Branch security).

Corinna's invitation to EndGame had been a surprise to many in the magic community. Her advancement into the quarter-finals, and now the semi-final, was even more shocking. I was surprised as well. Despite my admiration for her passion, and her impressive demeanor when I had met her at the Meet the year before, I always figured her obsession with magician rights had been an indicator that she herself was not very talented.

I scanned the crowd but could not see any of my friends. Maria, as a member of Magic First, would probably be conflicted about who to cheer for. I started thinking about the party Jayden had invited me to that would take place the next night. Hopefully it would be a celebration.

This duel was important. I needed to win in order to face Roland the next day, and the results of that duel would give me access to the OneSpell, helping me to save the world. Saying it in my head made me feel crazy. Save the world. No matter how many times I said it in my mind it still didn't seem real.

According to Valentine, and according to the images she had show me, I had to save the world. But all I wanted was for this to be over so I could go to a fashionable club and hang out with my friends.

Focus! I looked over to the other "X" where Corinna stood.

"You seem to have done okay, Corinna 'win-less,'" I said snidely.

Sorceress Corinna Windlass stared back. Behind her eyes a judging mind carefully evaluated what had been said, considered the evidence, and delivered a verdict.

"That's the stupidest thing I've ever heard," she said.

I planted my feet on the ground. "You're all about doing what the Magic tells you. So, what's it telling you?"

Corinna rolled her shoulders and flexed her back. "Magic is telling me to destroy you."

I turned to the dais, where the same elderly Sorceress from the day before was standing up.

"People of Las Vegas," she began. "Welcome to the semi-final round of EndGame."

Cheers and shouts followed, then died quickly as she cleared her throat again.

"Before we begin, we will pledge allegiance to the people to whom we owe our loyalty."

"NO!" cried out a voice. It took me a moment to realize it had come from next to me.

"NO!" Corinna said again. "I will not pledge allegiance to the Guild, or to the Branches, but only to Magic itself!"

Shouts of agreement rang out from the stands.

"Corinna! Corinna!" the chant rang out. It wasn't just a few rogue magicians like the day before, it was half the stadium calling out my opponent's name.

Corinna cast a spell. At the back of the arena, the flag featuring the marks of the Branches burst into flames. The cheers and chanting increased.

"CORINNA! CORINNA!"

Corinna cast another spell, her lips mumbling and fingers waving, and on the other side of the arena another flag unfurled, featuring a giant "1" with a dolphin underneath. The symbol of Magic First.

The elderly sorceress was yelling, magnifying her voice a hundred fold in order to restore order, but she was drowned out by five thousand screaming voices.

"CORINNA! CORINNA!"

I saw the Branch representative in the skybox stand up. Two other wizards were behind him. One touched his shoulder. The three of them turned and left. I couldn't blame them. If I were in an arena with five thousand people who hated sorcerers, I would have done the same thing.

I turned to face Corinna, who was smiling.

"Are you ready to start?" she asked

"I think it's tradition for the mistress of ceremonies to declare a start to the match." I motioned towards the elderly sorceress, who was still screaming for order, tears coming out of her eyes as she used more and more powerful magic to amplify her voice.

"I don't think that's going to happen," Corinna said, still flashing an infuriating smile.

She lifted a hand to her face, a glow surrounding her fingers, then her hand, then her entire arm.

"*En garde!*" she shouted, rapidly punching the air in my direction. Her arm was fully extended. The flames surrounding her arm detached and flew towards me.

I spelled the air in front of me. The fist of fire deflected off of me and hit the wall to my side. But I lost my balance. I stumbled, barely catching myself. The crowd exploded in cheers.

I was losing. I was losing, and people were cheering at the fact that I was losing. Corinna was fast. My dueling strategy was to fire the first fireball and gauge my opponent's reaction. I couldn't remember the last time in a duel that my opponent had gotten off the first shot.

Steadying myself, I took a few moments to cast a mental spell, one that created a field of instability, and shot it towards Corinna. But Corinna was already running towards me. She sensed the instability spell (her reflexes were amazing) and jumped over it, shooting fire at me as it passed harmlessly under her.

I used an ice shield to burn up the fire, and almost collided with Corinna as she ran towards me. I spun, using the remnants of the ice shield to push her as she ran by. I jumped over the path she made, just in case she was going to use a fire circle spell like I used in my last match, and hit her with a dizziness spell.

Corinna was caught defenseless and vomited everything she had eaten in the last day. I was backing up, trying to get some distance between us, while shooting a column of wind at her.

But she was already ten feet away, shooting more fire at me as my wind column hit her pool of vomit, scattering it across the tile.

The fire hit me straight on. An unSigned person would have been killed, or severely burned, but all duelers have low level protection spells active at all times for situations like this.

Instead of dead or burned, I found myself on the ground. I opened my eyes (I had blacked out for a second) to see Corinna running full speed towards me.

Sorceress Corinna Windlass was fast, relentless. The vomiting spell had done some damage, I could see a look of pain on her face, but she was still standing.

I was lying on the ground. Corinna chanted as she ran. The spell complete, she raised her hands and shot a beam of ice straight towards me.

It was now or never.

I raised both arms in front of my face and cast the most potent counterspell I could muster. With my magic senses I could see the spell appear as a physical shield in front of me. Corinna's beam of ice crashed into it, and was reflected back into the sorceress who cast it, surrounding and freezing her entire body.

Corinna was spent magically and had no time to cast her own counterspell. I shifted to the side, letting a frozen Corinna spin past me and crash into one of the walls. The encasement of ice shattered, parts of it falling off and other pieces clinging to her clothing and exposed skin.

I jumped up and turned to where Corinna was sprawled on the floor. For the first time in the match, the audience was silent.

"Do you yield?" I asked, but it came out as more of a gasp than a shout. I cleared my throat. "Do you yield!" I said, louder.

Corinna raised her right hand. It was holding a small metallic object. I took a step back.

Magic exploded out of Corinna's hand, knocking me onto the ground. Again. This time, before I could get up, Corinna was on top of me. My torso was locked between her legs, her hand with the object hovered above my face.

"Yield or die!" she shouted.

The object in her hand was an amulet, a physical object into which a spell had been bound. She had been too exhausted to cast another spell of physical magic, but she was still able to use the amulet to knock me down.

"What will it be Sorcerer Roy Nakamura!" Corinna shouted. "What will it be? Yield or die!"

"Halt!" shouted a voice above me.

I looked up. The elderly sorceress, as well as four other sorcerers, had floated down from the skybox and were standing above Corinna.

"I said, halt!"

Corinna turned from me, murder in her eyes. I think Corinna would have actually killed the mistress of ceremonies if it hadn't been for the other sorcerers. All four of them were rapidly incanting, preparing to fire spells at Corinna if she did not comply.

"You have used an amulet," the elderly sorceress said. "That is a violation of EndGame rules. You have forfeited the match."

"But, but…"

"There is no but!" the elderly sorceress said. "I declare this duel to be at an end. I declare Sorcerer Roy Nakamura the victor." This time she didn't need a notecard to remember my name.

There was a murmur of discontent in the stands. Sorceress Corinna Windlass jumped off of me. I pushed myself into a sitting position. After another second I was able to stand.

The murmur of discontent continued, until someone shouted "Roy!" It had come from the stands, though I couldn't see exactly where. Then another followed it. "Roy!"

They were chanting now, they were chanting my name.

"Roy! Roy!"

I stepped back so I was in the center of the arena.

"ROY! ROY!"

More people were joining in now. Corinna sat down. I wasn't sure if I had somehow injured her, or if it was just from exhaustion.

"ROY! ROY!"

It might have been the melting ice on her face, but it looked to me like Corinna was crying as five thousand people chanted my name.

4 – From a Lover to a Friend

It was Monday morning, and my body still ached from facing Corinna the day before. In a few short hours I would face Sorcerer Roland Tell in the final round of EndGame. I felt uncharacteristically calm. I had avoided gambling for the previous day, trying to save my magical strength for the final duel ahead of me. I supposed it would have been possible for me to gamble and not use magic, but I lacked that kind of self-control.

Ever since the day Sorceress Valentine told me I would have to make it to the final round of EndGame, or else the world might end, I had been nervous. But now that I was at the final round, it seemed everything was going according to plan.

My encounter with Archmage Cantor had scared me, and I worried the love spell I cast on Renée was still in effect, but other than that life was turning out exactly as planned. Once this duel was done, I would be able to spend the night relaxing with Grant and Jayden, and then take a few weeks off of training (surely Valentine couldn't begrudge me that).

All these optimistic thoughts were going through my head as I opened the door from my hotel room to the hallway. Maria was standing in the hallway waiting for me. There was something about her big brown eyes, either a lack of make-up or too much make-up, that gave an uncomfortable edge to her look. She was standing with her arms crossed, just inches away from my door. At first I thought she had been about to knock, but something in her posture told me she had been there for some time, waiting for me to open the door.

"Did you sleep with Renée?" She said the phrase in a jumble, like it was a single word she spewed out with a single thought, not bothering to preface it with a perfunctory introduction. I had to take a moment to unjumble the phrase in my mind, comprehend its meaning, and prepare a response.

"Yes," I said. Maria wouldn't have asked the question if she didn't already know the answer.

Maria sighed. At first I thought she was going to yell at me. But this, this sigh of disappointment, was far worse.

"Come on Roy," Maria said softly, more to herself than to me. "How could you?"

I swallowed, my hand still on the door knob. "I don't think it's any business of yours who I sleep with."

"You knew she was into you Roy, you knew it," Maria said. "You said you didn't like her, and I get that, but then you sleep with her? You had to know the type of message that would send her."

I took a step forward. "It was over a year ago. It was the night of…"

"Of Black Sunday," Maria said. "Why not? On the same day I got arrested, thrown in jail, and beaten up by my boyfriend, you decided to SLEEP WITH MY BEST FRIEND!"

"Renée isn't your…"

Maria was looking up at the ceiling now. "Of all the people you could have slept with, of all the girls in Las Vegas, it HAD TO BE HER." She dropped her gaze to make eye contact with me. "Did you do it to hurt me?"

"No, of course not," I said. "That doesn't even make any sense. Why would I want to hurt you? Why would sleeping with Renée…"

"Then why Roy? Why? Help me to understand. Why on earth did you do it?"

I had nothing to say. There was nothing I could say. Apparently that was the wrong answer.

Maria turned and walked away. I checked my watch. It was ten o'clock on the dot. I had two hours to make it to the Arena. Cursing Maria, I chased after her down the hall.

I caught up to Maria at the bank of elevators just as the elevator doors opened. She didn't make eye contact as I followed her figure into the elevator.

"Maria," I said as the elevator doors closed.

Maria took out her phone and tried to call someone.

"Look, you can't just… let's talk about it." Somehow I couldn't put my thoughts into words. All I knew was that facing Sorcerer Roland Tell was going to be the toughest duel of my life, and there was no way I could do what I had to if I spent the whole time thinking about how angry I had made Maria.

Maria continued to press buttons on her phone.

I pointed at her phone. "Would you just put that thing down for one second and look at me."

Maria hit a final button, dropped her hands to her sides, and looked up into my eyes.

"Well?" she said.

The elevator chose that moment to scream to a halt.

An hour later, Maria and I were still trapped in the elevator. The emergency lighting had come on, bathing us in an otherworldly red light. I stood, pacing from the emergency phone to the adjacent corner, while Maria sat on the opposite side. At times she used her phone as a hacky sack, throwing it up in the air and catching it over and over again.

I reached for the emergency phone.

"Give it a rest," Maria said from where she was sitting. "They said help was on the way."

"I only have an hour," I snapped, looking at my watch. The tone was harsher than I intended, and even in the low light, I could see its effect on Maria. But I was angry, and regretted it less than I ordinarily would have.

"I understand," Maria said.

"I don't think you do. I have," I checked my watch. "Fifty-nine minutes before the most important duel of my life begins, and some half-wit hotel worker can't be bothered to get me out of here!" I yelled the last part, looking up at the ceiling, at the hidden camera I imagined was there.

"Most important duel of your life? Listen to yourself. When did duels become the most important thing in your life?"

"It's not just about the duel," I said. "It's about... it's about winning." I had almost said it was about the OneSpell. If Maria knew about the OneSpell, about the importance of what I was doing, then it would all make sense to her. But Valentine's warning about the Dragon, and what it would do to the ones I loved, reverberated in the back of my head.

"It's about winning?" Maria said, giving a cruel half-laugh. "This is great Roy. You really have changed."

I shook my head. "Screw this. I'm a sorcerer."

I reached out with magic and grasped the elevator carriage. Sensing the rails on which we hung, and the wheels that held us there, I slowly spun the wheel, and we started to move down.

We hit something. The shriek of metal against metal filled the air. Maria clapped her hands over her ears as the entire carriage shook.

"Stop it Roy!" Maria screamed over the din of the shaking. "You're going to get us killed."

Reluctantly, I withdrew my spell and let go of the carriage, just as I had the previous two times I tried, and failed, to use magic to get us out.

"You're going to get us killed over a duel."

I sat down and faced Maria. It was a small elevator, we couldn't have been more than six feet apart, but it felt like there was a chasm between us.

"What do you mean?" I made eye contact as best as I could in the limited light.

"You're not an elevator expert, so if you use magic to rip us free but don't know how to catch us…"

"No, not that," I said. "What did you mean about me changing?"

Maria looked up at the ceiling, as if searching for answers, then dropped her eyes to stare directly into mine. "Why did you come to Las Vegas?"

"To become a famous sorcerer, and then to win EndGame, just like…"

"*Call me Sorcerer*," Maria and I both said at the same time.

"So here you are," she said. "You became a sorcerer, you entered EndGame, you made it to the final round. It's everything you ever dreamed of. But you don't seem that happy about it. In fact, you seem pretty miserable."

"I've been busy," I said. "I still train with Sorceress Valentine, and she's not easy to work for."

"It's not just that Roy," Maria said. "Maybe it's just growing up, not seeing each other at school every day anymore, but you're different." She paused. "Did you know that today is exactly one month since I broke up with Drew, and you haven't even asked me how I am?"

"Please, you can't still be hung up on Drew," I said. "His name wasn't even in the present tense."

Maria gave a slight laugh. Then it turned into a frown. "In the old days you would have shown up at my apartment with a DVD and some sort of food item. Then you would have threatened to go beat up Drew for me, as if that might make me feel better."

"So you're upset I don't pay more attention to you?"

"That's just it!" Maria exclaimed. "It used to be I wouldn't have to tell you, you just would. But you're so consumed with being a sorcerer, with following Sorceress Valentine, with winning EndGame, you're practically not you anymore."

"I'm a sorcerer now," I said, wishing again I could tell her about the OneSpell. "I have responsibilities."

"Well I liked you just fine before you were a sorcerer. And I'm not the only one who feels this way. I was talking to Grant. Is it true you haven't talked to him in a month?"

I shrugged. "So what?"

"So what? He's your best friend!" Maria said. "When someone is your best friend, and you live in a different city, and ignore them, after not too long they stop being your best friend."

"Look, maybe it's different for girls, but guys don't need to talk on the phone all the time in order to keep in touch. Especially when there's an important tournament at stake."

Maria threw up her hands. "And now we're talking about the tournament again."

"Are you freaking kidding me?" I screamed. "Yes we're talking about the tournament again."

"Don't yell at me!" Maria cried out. She snorted once. "We've known each other for twelve years Roy, you don't get to yell at me!"

We sat in silence. Another five minutes ticked by.

"You know, I'm planning on going back with Grant to Los Angeles," Maria said. "I haven't seen my parents since Christmas, I figure I can ride with Grant, visit them, fly back."

"That sounds fun," I said, voice devoid of any emotion. Magic hadn't worked the last time I tried to dislodge the elevator, but maybe there was a way around.

"You didn't go back for Christmas last year, did you?" she said.

I shook my head. "I had some duels."

"I think it would be good for you to go back for a visit. There's something about this city. Maybe it's the magic, or the gambling and the drinking, or even the neon lights, but there's something about this city that eats you up alive. You need to get out every once in a while or else you adapt too well, and then you can never leave."

"I'll think about," I said.

"I know your dad would be happy to see you."

"I said I'd think about it."

"EndGame is really that important to you, huh?"

I thought about the OneSpell and the Dragon. I thought about my encounter with lesser demons, with pure evil, and what it could do if it got the type of power Valentine described the OneSpell as having. I thought about the year before when I crested the hill, saw Las Vegas before me, and everything seemed so wonderful. I had every opportunity in the world ahead of me and nothing to hold me back.

But all I said was this. "Yes, it's really that important to me."

Maria stood up and walked over to the elevator control panel. She removed a key from around her neck. Magic emanated from it.

"Sometimes guests use magic to stop the elevators so they can make out," Maria said. "So they issue these to all of us who work the front desk."

Maria took the spelled key and placed it flush against the panel. There was a flash of magical energy and the elevator jolted, causing Maria to stumble. I caught her. We both steadied ourselves as the lights came on, and the elevator started to move downward.

We were both silent.

"Thank you Maria," I finally said. My voice was choked up, but only a little.

"You're welcome Roy."

5 - Roland

The noise in the arena was deafening. Every seat was taken. There were people standing in the aisles, having used some magical trick to get past the entrance without a ticket. People were screaming, crying, arguing, laughing, all the activities they would carry on in the outside world. But here they were confined to a finite space where every sound bounced back and forth, building like a wave until it became a physical construct I could reach out and touch. Football games last well over three hours, but these fans had paid good money for the chance to watch a duel that might last fifteen minutes at the most. They had paid good money for the chance to watch me.

Security was also tripled, probably quadrupled, from the previous match. Even if Corinna wasn't competing, the Guild was not taking any chances.

The skybox was more crowded than before. It had seats for four members of the Council (there was no seat for Sorcerer Roland, since he was my opponent), as well as six chairs for six wizards, one from each Branch. At first I thought one of the wizards was Jayden, but upon closer examination the man occupying the Branch Parthenia seat was older, gaunter. It was Jayden's father, the famous Ricardo Parthenia, leader of the Alliance during the Wizard War, and current Lord of Branch Parthenia.

This time the duel was presided over by Sorcerer Bastion Edwards, the chairman of the Sorcerers Guild Council. There was applause as he stood and cast a spell to magnify his voice.

"On behalf of the Guild, and the Branches that protect us, welcome to the final round of EndGame."

More applause and screaming. Throughout the arena, security guards used physical and magical observation to probe for any signs of protest.

"Sorcerer Roland Tell," my opponent raised his hand, "and Sorcerer Roy Nakamura," I raised mine, "begin!"

I paused in confusion. There had been no pledge to the Guild or the Branches. I risked a quick look up at the skybox. The wizard representatives, one from each Branch, were talking with each other. The conversation complete, the six wizards, along with assorted aides and advisors, stood and walked off of the dais.

Sorcerer Bastion Edwards had a smile on his face. I couldn't imagine what sort of behind the scenes magical intrigue I had witnessed, but I knew this was no time to focus on it.

I turned to Sorcerer Tell, who looked as confused as I, but quickly shed his confusion to concentrate on the duel before him.

"Don't expect me to take it easy on you because you are young," he said.

"Don't expect me to take it easy on you because you are old."

He pointed a finger at me. "You are *definitely* Valentine's apprentice." A spell sprouted from his fingertips, and before I could register what happened, it was barreling towards me.

I didn't recognize the spell, but did my best to dodge it, jumping several paces to the side. The spell, a miniature black cloud complete with lightning crackling from one side of it to the other, followed my feint. The cloud honed in on me like a missile. It slammed into me and pushed me to the ground. The cloud evaporated.

I jumped to my feet, throwing up a shield spell and awaiting the next attack, but nothing came. Instead Roland stood on his X, watching me. It had been a test, just like I usually did at the beginning of duels. Roland wanted to see how I would react to a spell like that.

Smiling, Roland began to incant and move his hands. The air between us shimmered. I shook my head. It had to be my imagination, like seeing stars after a fall. But the shimmering continued. Then I discerned a pattern in the shimmering. I took a step back.

The air in the space between us started to rotate. Roland was spinning the air around the center of the room, and the shimmer I saw was light reflecting off the dust particles caught in the artificial wind's grasp. The rotation quickened, pulling the air around me into its maw. Physical magic on this scale shouldn't be possible.

By the time I snapped out of it, there was a bona fide tornado, forty feet high, at the center of the arena. Roland gave a push, and the tornado stalked towards me.

I threw a fireball, which was absorbed by the tornado, then another which was absorbed just as easily. Streaks of magical fire now spun around inside the tornado, giving it an eerie red tinge.

Roland stood back calmly, watching his creation do its work. I took slow and deliberate steps backward. I let the tornado almost back me against a wall. Then I took off running to one side.

While the tornado tried to change directions to pursue me, I threw a series of four air darts at Roland. He blocked three, but the fourth knocked him to the ground. The tornado began to wobble.

I continued running toward Roland, but was forced to slow down. My feet were dragging, like running through sand. I risked a quick glance down. The floor was moving, waving, like it was the floor of a bouncy house.

Roland mumbled a spell while pointing at the floor in front of me. The floor became even spongier, grabbing my feet like a tentacle. I threw up my arms in front of my face in a counterspell, and felt the ground release me. Free of any encumbrances, I threw myself at Roland.

He put his hands up, mumbling a counterspell of his own, but I wasn't planning a magical attack. The crowd gasped as my body slammed into Roland, knocking him again to the ground. Physical contact between duelers was not forbidden, but was generally frowned upon in polite magical society.

Roland and I both pushed ourselves to our feet. Roland raised his hands to cast a spell, then spun around when he saw my smirk. Roland was now standing between me and the tornado, and since it was following me, that meant it was now bearing down on him.

With a scream, Roland incanted a spell. The tornado dissolved before it could hit him. The wispy remnants shot out in every direction, making Roland a silhouette as he turned to face me. The duel continued.

Roland fired a spell, and I fired one back. We continued, tit for tat, as the audience cheered louder and louder.

I was holding my own, but all magic came at a price, and I was getting weaker with each spell. I was also getting sloppy, and I let a fireball get past my defenses, singeing me slightly and throwing me off guard. Roland noticed my mistake and hammered me with a volley of fireballs I just barely fended off. He was sweating though, and panting as well. Sorcerer Roland was winning, but like me he was also tiring. He hadn't planned on my being able to beat his tornado, and his fall had knocked the wind out of him.

This was enough to set our plan in motion. In the stands, Valentine started chanting rapidly. If it hadn't been for the excitement of the match, someone around her probably would have noticed. I dodged another fireball. Valentine's chanting got louder.

A stream of five fireballs, patterned to make dodging almost impossible, came my way. Time slowed down, as I tried to think of a way to fight the fireball pattern.

Magic exploded out of Sorceress Valentine like a shockwave. Everything froze. The audience, the fireballs, everything. Almost everything.

Roland looked around.

"Impressive spell Roy," he said. "Almost impossibly impressive. But isn't the idea to freeze me, not to freeze everyone in the room *except* me?"

"That's not quite the purpose of the spell," said Sorceress Valentine from behind the barrier. She couldn't move without breaking the spell, but now that the audience was silenced, it was easy for us to hear her.

"Now this makes more sense." Roland turned to address Valentine. "I should have recognized the scent of your magic."

He looked around.

"So is this the plan?" he said. "Freeze the world, then gang up on me in order to win?"

"Like the sorceress said, not quite," I replied. I allowed myself to smile, if only to confuse Roland a little bit more.

Two months earlier, Sorceress Valentine had approached me about entering EndGame in order to learn Roland's information about the location where the OneSpell would appear. But she had a specific way we had to do it.

"There is no way you can beat him," she said. "Even if you could, beating him wouldn't force him to reveal to you his information about the OneSpell. Instead, you will offer to surrender."

"You want me to get all the way to the finals, then surrender? You want me to lose?"

Valentine shook her head. "You cannot just lose. If you lose, we learn nothing. You have to make Roland think you have a chance of winning. Roland will never give something away for nothing, and right now we don't have anything to offer him. You have to create something to offer him.

"If you face him in the final duel, and you do well enough to make him think you might win, then you can offer to throw the duel in exchange for him telling you where the OneSpell will appear. Roland values his role as EndGame champion more than anything else in the world. If you offer to let him keep that, he will trade."

I nodded in agreement. I understood what was at stake. Winning EndGame would be the chance of a lifetime, but finding the OneSpell before the Dragon did was infinitely more important.

"So that's the deal," I said to Roland. "You tell me where the OneSpell will appear, and in return, I let you win."

Sorcerer Roland Tell raised an eyebrow. "You, Roy Nakamura, the rising star of the sorcerer world, are going to throw a duel."

"I go home with information about the OneSpell, you remain EndGame champion and retain your seat on the council. Everybody wins."

Roland rubbed the back of his neck. He was a proud man, Valentine told me that much, but was he also smart enough to take a sure thing over the possibility of losing?

His answer was interrupted by an unexpected voice.

"How precious!"

Sorcerer Roland, Sorceress Valentine, and I turned as one and looked in the direction of the skybox. A man I didn't recognize, wearing a red ruffled jacket that looked like something a glam rocker might keep in his closet for special occasions, was standing and slowly clapping as he looked at us. He was tall and thin, as if someone had taken Roland's mass and stretched it a foot taller. He had high cheekbones and a pronounced chin, a combination that gave him a gaunt appearance. He was mostly bald, but a few stray white hairs stood up from the middle of his scalp.

"There is nothing more heartwarming than two opponents putting aside arms and coming together," the tall man said, bringing his hands together for a few more seconds of earnest clapping.

I looked to Valentine. "Why didn't the spell work?"

"It did work. It just didn't work on him." Valentine narrowed her eyes. "Something is wrong."

The tall man leapt from the skybox and soared through the air, landing on his feet in the arena. He strode towards me and Roland.

"And how does this play into the plan?" Roland said. "If I do not agree to let you throw the match, does this man fight me?"

"Who are you?" I asked the tall man. "Are you here to fight us?"

The tall man's gaze whipped across the room and found me.

"Why Roy," he said with a wicked smile. "I'm not here to fight you, I'm here to kill you."

With a high pitched shriek, the tall man stretched out his arms, and his entire body was immersed in fire.

Valentine tore her eyes away from the burning man-shaped image and looked at me.

"Demon!" she cried. "Run!"

I raised my hand and threw a fireball at the tall man. Halfway between us, the fireball started to slow, and by the time it reached the man engulfed in flames it stopped. "Foolish sorcerer," the man said. "My master, the Dragon, has given me power over fire, and yet you try to use fire to defeat me?"

The man cackled, and the fireball raced back towards me. I dove to the ground as it soared over my head. I pushed myself up from the surface, my vision swimming, and threw up a wall of ice in front of me. I heard several satisfying smacks as my shield absorbed whatever fire the demon had thrown.

Now on my feet, I chanted a spell and the ice wall shattered into knives of ice that hung in the air for a moment, then rotated and sped towards the demon. The demon put his hands together, closed his eyes, and a sword of flame sprouted from his hand. Eyes still closed, the demon waved the flaming sword and obliterated each piece of ice that got too close. The task done, he plodded towards me, eyes now open, flaming sword still in his hand.

"Is that the best you have?" I said, trying to catch my breath. "You'll never get the OneSpell."

"Oh, you speak of the OneSpell." The demon cackled. "It is not I, but it is my master the Dragon who seeks the OneSpell. The Dragon is mightier than I. I am not worthy to clean the footprints he leaves in the dust. He is mightier than I, and you are so weak you will not live long enough to face him."

I looked to my left, to the stands, where Valentine was using all her energy to keep the time freezing spell in place. There was no chance she would be able to help me.

"Use a spell of destruction!" Roland yelled at me. He was on the other side of the floor. We had separated after the demon's first volley.

"What?" I screamed back.

"The demon's weakness is its physical body!" Roland yelled. "If you destroy the body, it can no longer remain coherent and it will dissipate."

I focused on the demon's body, the body of the man the demon had once been, and using a particularly nasty spell that would never be tolerated in a duel, I tried to rip it in half. Instead, I modified my wave watching spell.

A precious second went by. The demon walked towards me. I tried to figure out what just happened. I had already been using a wave watching spell to fight Roland, but now the spell was changing, evolving. I didn't always have complete control over my magic, no sorcerer or wizard did, and it was not uncommon to mess up a spell. But I had tried to cast a spell of destruction and instead an entirely different spell had been modified.

The demon was just seconds away. Fire had been ineffective. I concentrated on my hands and watched as a sword of ice emerged from them.

I glanced up at the demon, just an arm's reach away, and threw up my sword of ice to block the demon's flaming sword. There was a crash and hiss of steam as the swords collided. My blade held. The demon backed off a step.

The demon roared. "Fire and ice. How nice." The demon lunged forward, raising his sword again to strike.

But I could see where he was going to strike. In my mind, I could see the path of the demon's blade, and I raised mine to meet it. It was the wave watching spell! Instead of showing me what cards would be played next, it was showing me the actions of my opponent.

We went back and forth as I parried each strike from the demon. Strike, block, strike, block, strike, block. I couldn't keep it up forever though. A burst of magic caught my eye. Roland had cast a spell and sent it in my direction. When it hit me, it felt like a giant gust of wind.

The flames around the demon went out. In that exact instant, I raised my blade of ice and slammed it into the demon. Rather than bleed, the demon shuttered once, and then dissolved into ash.

I stood there panting as Roland walked over. He looked down at the ashes at my feet. "You killed a demon," Roland said, eyes still focused on the pile of ash.

"We both did," I said.

"But it was mostly you," he continued. "I have never seen someone move that way. It was like you could see the demon's moves before it took them."

He pushed at the pile of ashes with his foot, causing them to dissipate. "Maybe that's why she made you learn wave watching," he said to himself.

"What was that?" I said.

Roland made a gesture with his hand, and the pile of ash was scattered into the air. This done, he turned his face up and looked at me.

"New deal," he said. "If you beat me, fair and square, I will tell you what you want to know about the OneSpell."

I felt a sudden change in the atmosphere around me as Sorceress Valentine, exhausted beyond what even she could bear, collapsed, causing her spell to come apart. All around the arena, people came to life, cheering and hooting at the duel.

Some must have been puzzled, watching the two duelers suddenly appear in different parts of the arena, but most seemed so caught up in the emotion of the match that they just kept cheering.

I turned to where Valentine had been standing, casting the spell, but she was nowhere to be seen. She must have transported out before everyone unfroze.

A wave of wind slammed into me, knocking me to the arena floor. I rolled, then jumped into a crouching position and fired a volley of fire towards the place where Roland had been standing moments before. But he had already run to a different part of the arena, and shot another wall of wind, high enough that it mostly passed over my still crouched figure.

I shot fire, ice, wind, as Sorcerer Roland did the same, trying to best each other with the basest of elements. The audience was going wild. This was the fight they had come to see.

I was distracted for a moment and allowed one of Roland's spells to get through. My left arm was turned to ice. I tried to warm it up, but my spell was useless. I could sense Roland casting another spell, so I threw up my right arm, intending to cast a shield spell, and watched as it turned to ice as well.

My arms were frozen at my side, hanging useless. I thought of conjuring a fireball, or an ice wall, but without the use of my hands I had no way to throw them or direct their power.

Sorcerer Roland Tell stalked towards me, closing the gap between us, and there was only one thing I could do. The key to magic is the *aetas*. A spell requires the words, the gesture, and the *aetas*, but the *aetas* is what truly matters. A powerful enough sorcerer can cast spells without the words, and without the gestures, using only his mind.

I reached out with the magic, focusing on the *aetas* of a spell to move objects. But rather than grab an object near Roland, I grabbed Roland himself. I pushed with all my might, and I kept pushing. Roland went airborne and flew towards the wall behind him.

With my magical senses, I could see Roland use magic to grab the wall he was flying towards and push against it with all the energy he had left. It was the wrong move. If I had pushed him with a burst of air, a standard dueling move, then pushing against the wall would have reversed his direction, or at the least cushioned his fall. But I hadn't used air to push him a single time, instead I had used magic to grab him with an invisible fist and thus was continuing to push him.

So while Roland pushed against the wall with all his might, which was a great deal of force given his magical prowess, I pushed against him with all my might in the opposite direction.

Sorcerer Roland Tell, the reigning EndGame champion for five years, was crushed by two opposing forces. I heard a physical crunch as he was suspended for a moment in mid-air, then came crashing down.

The crowd cheered my name without reservation. I looked down at Roland's fallen figure.

A day later, I was on the front cover of Sorcerer's Weekly as the new EndGame champion. Reporters hounded me, and my friends, for weeks afterwards to get the inside scoop on my rise from obscurity, my connection to the perpetual tabloid fodder that was Sorceress Valentine, and my rumored past affiliations with Magic First.

A month later I received offers to teach, or guest teach, classes on battle magic at Vegas' most prestigious schools of magic. There were whispers that one of the Branches might try to recruit me for their security apparatus.

Before EndGame I worked to scrounge up a duel each weekend. After the tournament, I had to turn down offers of combat. Every sorcerer in the city wanted to face me, and I beat all of them.

But for now, I was a sorcerer, a dueler, staring at the still body of an honored opponent and silently praying he would get up again. Standing there, I realized the crowd had fallen silent as well. There were quiet murmurs just within my range of hearing, speculations that someone should call a magical healer, or perhaps a mundane ambulance.

There was a stir, and Roland coughed, then slowly pushed himself up to a sitting position. There was polite applause from the crowd and sighs of relief. I walked over, ready to help him up, but he shook his head so I stopped. He rose to a standing position.

I stuck out my hand. We shook.

"Ladies and Gentlemen," shouted Sorcerer Bastion Edwards from the dais. "May I present this year's EndGame Champion, Sorcerer Roy Nakamura."

I caught up with Roland just outside the arena. We were surrounded by well wishers and reporters, and had to constantly stop to pose for a photograph, answer a quick question, or provide an autograph. Somehow, we still managed to carry on a conversation, with hushed tones, in between the distractions.

"Are you going to give me the information you promised?" I asked.

"How about a counter-proposal," Sorcerer Roland said. "Instead of telling you the location where the OneSpell will appear, I will provide you with a beautiful girl a night, every night for a month. I'm a famous sorcerer, I have no shortage of beautiful women who would do anything for me."

I wasn't sure if he was joking, but it made no difference. "How about what you promised."

"Ah, the follies of the young," Roland said. "Very well, I will answer your question." He paused, readjusting the hem on his sorcerer's cloak. "The OneSpell will appear at the end of the world."

My face darkened. "I already know *when* it will appear, I need to know *where* it will appear."

"I had the same reaction, young champion, when the Token Master gave me that answer so many years ago." Roland was almost as condescending as Sorceress Valentine. "I responded the same way you did, so the Token Master repeated it. 'The time when the OneSpell will appear, that is information I will give to another,' he told me. 'But the location where it will appear is the end of the world.'"

I realized I wasn't going to get anything else from him.

"One final thing, Sorcerer Tell," I said. "At the end of the match, when I slammed you against the wall and you used your magic to push back against the wall, the difference in forces smashed you between them."

"I am quite aware of this." Roland rubbed his mid-section. "I think one of my ribs may be broken."

"But why not just pull against me instead?" I asked. "You would have neutralized my force instead of introducing another force into the equation. Or why not cast a cushioning spell against the wall? Or simply crash against the wall and then cast a spell of alertness?

"It seems like you, the greatest dueler in Vegas, responded to my spell with the one spell that would cause the most damage to you."

"What are you trying to say Roy?"

"Did you throw the match? Did you let me win? Are you trying to help me find the OneSpell?"

"The OneSpell is not what you think," Roland said. "I've tried to tell Valentine, but she won't listen. Even if the Dragon gets a hold of it, it will not be able to use it. Not without paying a price that is far too high for the Dragon to ever pay."

The questions spilled out of me like water from a bursting dam. "Then why throw the match? Why do you care about the OneSpell? Why did you use your one question from the Token Master to find out its location?"

Roland continued to smile. "I did it for her."

I followed his gaze and saw the receding figure of Sorceress Valentine departing the arena. I was unsure how much of our conversation she had heard, but I was confident she knew exactly what had transpired during EndGame's final match.

According to the history books, I won EndGame 1999, but I would never consider myself the EndGame champion. That position was, and always would be, occupied in my mind by Sorcerer Roland Tell.

6 – Heartbreak

As planned, my friends and I met up with Jayden at Club Heartbreak. Jayden had been right. It had turned out to be a celebration.

Maria looked beautiful without even trying. She wore a simple skirt and a fashionable blouse, her hair held back in a pony tail. She wore almost no makeup, allowing her natural light brown skin to glisten in the neon lights. I thought things between us would be awkward after the incident in the elevator, but when I called her after the match with Roland to remind her about the party at Club Heartbreak, she sounded excited to go, even happy to talk to me.

Renée, in contrast, looked like she was trying too hard. She wore a tight and revealing silver dress, so shiny it hurt to stare at it, that had been ripped from the pages of a fashion magazine's high school prom issue. In the time I had known her, it seemed like she didn't care about anything at all, but now she was suddenly making an effort. Sadly, I knew what had changed.

It was my first time in public since winning EndGame, and everything was different. Casino and club staff looked at me as if I were one of them, like they didn't have to tell me which line to stand in because I was a powerful sorcerer, an EndGame champion. I already knew which line I was supposed to stand in, and if I wasn't standing in it there was probably a very good reason.

Not only that, girls looked at me differently. A college co-ed in a comically small tank top holding a yard-long margarita, the kind of girl who never would have glanced at me in the past, made generous eye contact as I walked by.

Club Heartbreak was located towards the top of the Giza Casino. In front of the club's entrance was a palatial set of stairs, covered in blood red carpet, that started off a hundred feet wide, but narrowed as one ascended the thirty three steps leading to the doors of the club. The bouncer, a uniformed wizard with the mark of Branch Shaskauer on his neck, stood halfway up the stairs.

There was no need for a velvet rope. Due to some clever spell, those who were not admitted to the club found themselves unable to ascend past the first few stairs. I was powerful enough to break the spell, but I didn't have to. As my group ascended the stairs, the bouncer made eye contact with me. Due to Jayden's placement of us on the guest list, or possibly my new found celebrity, we were allowed to pass.

The entrance to the Club Heartbreak was marked by two giant wooden doors with a large Shaskauer emblem over them. Rather than simply leave them open, as would make the most sense, two doormen (dressed in traditional Atlantian warrior garb) opened and closed the doors each time the bouncer let a group of people past the velvet rope.

Picture this. Warren G's "Regulate" plays as I walk into the club. Even though we're indoors, wind causes my sorcerer's cloak to billow out behind me. People marvel at me as I walk by. Girls want me, guys want to be me. A cocktail waitress, dressed in a skin tight shirt with strategic shapes cut out, offers me a complimentary glass of champagne. I drink it in one gulp, and using magic, refill it before I place it back onto her tray.

Just past the doors was a mirror image of the entrance. A set of stairs started narrow at the top and widened at the bottom after thirty three steps. At the bottom sat an enormous oval shaped dance floor. The center of the dance floor was a large circular bar where dozens of bartenders darted from point to point, mixing wild concoctions with bright colors I had never seen in a beverage.

Branching off from the stairway down to the dance floor were three raised rings each surrounding the dance floor. It resembled the arena I had been dueling in earlier that day. The rings were composed of several luxury areas, half-moon tables and accompanying booths that looked out over the dance floor. It was to one of these tables that my friends and I were led by a waitress in a sexualized version of a traditional Atlantian servant's garb.

Jayden was waiting for us at the table. It was large enough to easily accommodate me, Maria, Renée, Grant, and Derek. We made small talk for a while. Maria dragged Renée onto the dance floor, and Grant and Derek followed, hoping the vision of them leaving a luxury box would lead others to believe they were some kind of celebrities.

After a couple drinks, I thought back to the events of the day and turned to Jayden for guidance.

"What do you know about demons?" I asked.

"You mean like that girl Skylar you used to date?" Jayden gently elbowed me in the side. He lowered his head. "You guys broke up, right?"

I nodded.

"So, like, we don't like her anymore, right?" he whispered.

I nodded again.

Jayden raised his head. "Well in that case, demons like that girl Skylar you used to date?"

I shook my head, smiling. "No, real demons."

"Like the one who seeks the OneSpell?"

The hair on my arms stood up. "How do you know about the OneSpell?"

Jayden gave a little laugh. "It's the OneSpell, Roy, everyone knows about it. Among Atlantians it's like the Loch Ness monster, or Big Foot. Everyone's heard of it. And, the most famous demon, the one known as the Dragon, is the one who supposedly seeks it. It's what Atlantian moms use to get their kids to go to bed." Jayden cocked his head to the right. "That and sleep spells."

"And people also know about the Dragon?" I asked.

"Yeah, of course we…" Jayden paused mid-sentence, as if he had just remembered something very important.

"I just remembered something very important," he said. "We need to do more shots."

It took only a minute for him to procure two more shots of a drink called Ambrosia. Club Heartbreak had several waitresses ready to run at Jayden's call, and eager to get close to the new EndGame champion. Shots in hand, Jayden continued.

"Legend says the OneSpell was created by two powerful wizards, Trannanir Shaskauer and Mianna Panashka, who wished to unite all the Kingdoms of Atlantis. Once they created it, and they saw how powerful it was, Trannanir wanted to use it as planned, but Mianna saw it was too powerful to be controlled and wanted to destroy it. They had a duel, and Trannanir was killed. However his ghost became a demon, the one called the Dragon, and has hunted for the OneSpell ever since."

"What do you mean his ghost became a demon?" I asked. "I thought demons came from anger, from when several people are all angry at the same time."

Jayden motioned a waitress over with a finger. "Well, that's not entirely correct. I mean, demons are pretty rare, so the details on them are a bit sketchy, but virtually all academics agree on where they come from. A demon is born of anger, but from one person's, not a bunch of people's."

The waitress (like all the girls who worked there, painfully out of my league), calmly waited for Jayden to finish. He looked surprised at her presence, as if he had forgotten he called her over.

"Are you an actress?" he asked.

The waitress shook her head demurely.

"Because you look like an actress. Anyways, enough flirting. Two shots of Ambrosia please." He looked at me. "And two more for my friend as well."

The waitress nodded and ducked away, but not before looking at me furtively, mischief in her eyes.

Jayden turned to me and continued. "You see, certain wizards are so powerful that the magic they contain takes on a life of its own, with its own abilities and its own desires. When a normal person dies, their magic just kind of dissipates. But those powerful wizards I mentioned, the ones whose magic takes on a life of its own, it tends to stick together instead of falling apart.

"If the wizard is angry enough, if there is enough hate in his heart, then the magic within him becomes a demon while he is alive, a creature of magic solely consisting of his anger. When he dies, the demon is released. It can then possess people at will, cause general problems, and so on and so forth."

What Jayden was telling me seemed difficult to reconcile with the explanation Valentine had given me. She had no reason to lie to me. Then again, neither did Jayden. And his explanation fit better with the history of the OneSpell Archmage Artimus Cantor had told me.

"So the Dragon, the demon that hunts the OneSpell, it has nothing to do with Branch Primm being exiled from Las Vegas?" I asked.

Jayden snorted. "Branch Primm being exiled? No, no, no, the demon has been around since the OneSpell was created. At least that's what most of the myths say. And Branch Primm, none of them are powerful enough to generate a demon." Jayden gestured with his drink. "They're just so, you know, *Primm*."

Jayden looked around. "Do you want to dance? I think I want to dance."

I must have looked at him strangely, because he added, "I don't mean I want to dance *with you*, I just mean we should go find some girls, and dance."

"If the two of you wanted to talk to each other all night, you should have stayed at the hotel."

Jayden and I both looked up at the voice. It was Renée. "We were just waiting for you," Jayden said, scooting in. "Please, take a seat."

"Thank you." Renée carefully sat down at the seat across from me.

"Let me call someone over." Jayden raised a finger, again sending a waitress scurrying over. "Order whatever you like. My treat."

As Renée turned to talk to the waitress, Jayden looked at me and mouthed "SHE IS HOT" in the instant before Renée turned back.

The music continued, the indescribable siren call of Las Vegas, translated into sighs and whistles and set to a beat, now pumping through the speakers.

I happened to look out at the dance floor and saw Maria standing there. This should have been my first clue. Maria was the life of the party. She didn't *stand* on the dance floor, she *danced* on the dance floor. But there she was, standing still, watching the party unfold around her. I excused myself and walked out towards her.

Due to the magic augmented sound system, the music in the luxury booths had been quiet. Down on the dance floor it was overpowering. The music didn't flow into my ears, it was somehow generated from inside my body, taking over my entire being and causing my heart to beat along with the music.

I approached Maria's statue still figure from behind. I called her name, but she didn't answer, so I gently tapped her on the shoulder. Maria spun around, her brown hair framing her perfect face, and I could tell that she had been crying.

"What's wrong?" I shouted.

Maria blinked, then shook her head and pointed at her ear. I bent down, putting a hand on Maria's shoulder as I said it again. "What's wrong?"

Maria gestured towards a couple, a guy and a girl, dancing a dozen yards away. The girl was short, blonde, gyrating while barely covered in a short black dress. Grinding up against her was a man with a goatee in his late twenties, a little overweight, wearing a sports jacket that didn't fit quite right.

I looked back at Maria and made a shrugging motion. Maria said something back, but the music was so loud I couldn't hear it. I cast a spell enhancing my senses, while dialing down the music, and focused all my attention on Maria's lips.

"That's Drew," she said.

I shrugged again. Maria responded with a shocked look, almost offended. "That's Drew."

Of course, Drew. It all came back. I had met him before at Maria's place while they were dating. I had never been particularly impressed by him, but as far as I could tell he treated Maria well, so I didn't complain. When they broke up after dating for a few months, I didn't pay much attention.

Now here he was, rubbing his body over a girl who looked barely old enough to drive.

Maria shook her head. My senses were still on overdrive, so I was able to hear her.

"I'm sorry Roy, I can't stay here," she said, then turned around and started towards the club entrance.

I thought about running after her. There was a time I would have chased her without even thinking. But then I thought about the year before, the last time I tried to help her. I thought about Wizard Karl Johnsen. Then I turned around and went back to the table. Maybe Maria was right. Maybe I had changed.

Back at the table, Jayden was chatting up a waitress. Renée was nowhere to be seen. As soon as he saw me, Jayden shooed the waitress away and we started talking again.

"So you're from Las Vegas," I said.

"Guilty as charged." Jayden took another shot, which had miraculously appeared in front of him.

"How did you end up in Los Angeles?"

Jayden looked confused. "Umm, I went there because Los Angeles is awesome?"

"But you're Vegas royalty," I said. "Aren't you expected to become a wizard, that sort of thing?"

"Ahh, I see what you want to know." Jayden stirred a drink, then looked up at me. "It's kind of a sad story, but I'm getting drunk, so there's no better time to tell it." He stopped stirring, took a large gulp, then put the drink down.

"Have you heard of the Wizard War?"

"Of course," I said. "One of my favorite books is *Born into Magic*."

"Well, the war officially ended in 1989, but there's still bad blood between Branch Parthenia, we were in the Alliance, and Branch Shaskauer, they were in the Pact. They hate us for defeating them, and we hate them because they're a reminder that we had the power to beat them, but never had the power to destroy them completely.

"Anyways, when I was in high school, I met this girl named Genevieve. Genevieve Shaskauer. There's this school called Valhalla Academy where all the important people in Vegas, including the Branch Lords, send their children, so it's not uncommon for children of rival Branches to meet and become friends. Or even lovers."

Jayden paused to take a shot. He took the empty shot glass and spun it around on the table, watching it slowly come to a halt.

"And Genevieve and I, we were in love, at least as close as high school students could come to love. At first she wanted nothing to do with me, but eventually I won her over, and from then on I was hers and she was mine."

"What did you do?" I asked. "Cast a love spell?"

Jayden looked at me strangely. "Yes," he said, in a tone I think was an attempt at sarcasm. "I cast a... love spell."

Jayden took another drink. "Anyways, we were together, inseparable, sweethearts, whatever you want to call it. Then senior year came along, and my father, Lord Ricardo Parthenia, the great hero of the Wizard War who killed Lord Edgar Shaskauer in one-on-one combat at the Battle of the Steeple." Jayden paused. Another drink. "Sorry, I digress. My father sat me down and told me to break-up with Genevieve.

"You see, it's fine if a member of one Branch dates a member of another, or even sleeps with one, but my father was starting to worry our relationship might last past high school, that it might lead to marriage. And marriage between our Branches would be a very serious matter. Marriages are sacred to Atlantians. During the Wizard War, Branch Merkasia joined the Pact mostly because Lord Edgar

Shaskauer was married to Lady Lillian Merkasia, the Lord Merkasia's daughter.

"My father didn't want our Branch being forced to make nice with *Shaskauer*. So he told me to end it."

"What did you do?" I asked.

Jayden looked out into the distance. For the first time since we arrived at Club Heartbreak, he went a solid minute without sipping from a drink. "I broke up with her. You don't understand what it's like." He got defensive before I could even attack him. "My father isn't just my father, he's a Branch Lord. He's like my father, and the president of the country I live in, and my boss at work, all rolled up into one. Besides, I was only in high school at the time."

Jayden leaned back in his seat. He smiled and shook his head. "But Genevieve, she didn't take it well. Even after I told her it was over, she kept calling me. It happened so often my parents took away my separate phone line. She would be at my locker at school every day, begging me to take her back. She even started showing up at the gates to our family compound, begging to be let in.

"My father sat me down again, told me to make her stop, told me it was an embarrassment to our Branch. But no matter how much I told her not to, how much I pleaded with her, Genevieve would not leave me alone.

"Then one day, I showed up to school and everyone was crying. I found one of my friends who broke the news to me. Genevieve had died the day before, in a... car accident."

The way he said the words made it sound like he meant something more. "What do you mean a car accident?"

"I sometimes forget you didn't grow up here," Jayden said. "Cars are large contraptions with all sorts of moving parts. It is very easy for a wizard to stand at the side of a road, watch a car go by, and make the slightest of changes. Move this piston there or change this brake cable like that. Once the deed is done, there is no way for even the most skilled investigator to tell if magic was involved.

"I left school immediately, went to my father, and asked him if he had ordered Genevieve to be killed. He looked me in the eye, and I'll never forget this as long as I live, he looked me in the eye and said 'Son.' He said 'Son, I love you, but I love our Branch more.'

"I left the next day and went to Los Angeles, where I stayed with friends until the next year, when I started as a freshman at USC."

I looked down at my drink. I didn't know what to say.

A hand grabbed my shoulder. "So that's where you've been hiding."

It was Renée, and she was drunk. I didn't know how many drinks she had while I had been talking to Jayden, but she could barely manage to stand up. Jayden rose, and reached out an arm to try to steady her, but she shrugged it off and reached a hand down to where I was seated.

"Come on Roy, let's dance," she said.

"Not now Renée."

"I insist." She grabbed my arm and pulled me up so I was standing next to her. A whiff of vanilla filled my nostrils. She wobbled and almost fell backwards, but I caught her. She dragged me out of the ring of tables and down a dozen stairs onto the dance floor.

It was a slow dance kind of song, and Renée (the alcohol on her breath was so strong I was surprised she was still standing), wrapped her arms around my neck and began to sway to the music.

"What happened to us Roy?" she asked. She sounded curious, like her voice was emerging from a haze. "How come we're not together?"

"We're just friends." It was the wrong thing to say, and I knew it, but I didn't know what else I could do.

Renée flashed a coy smile. "But haven't you ever wondered what it would be like if we were more than that?"

She leaned in close and spoke in my ear. "That one night was magic, and I know you know it. I haven't been able to get it out of my head."

I sighed. "Renée, that's just the spell talking."

"The what?" Renée looked confused.

I sighed again. "You're drunk Renée."

"Think about it Roy," she said. "Think about us. Just think about giving it a chance."

I took a step back and extricated myself from her arms. It took a moment for Renée to discover I had stepped away. When she realized it, she crossed her arms and looked at me.

"I'm going to be a sorceress," she said.

"Okay." The music continued to play. "You're going to be a sorceress."

The light in the club cast dark shadows on Renée's blue eyes, giving them a gaunt, almost creepy appearance. The same light played tricks with her hair. Each flashing of a strobe turned her short blonde hair into menacing peaks and valleys.

"I'm serious," she said, slightly louder, as if declaring it to the room. "I got into a school here, a magic school. I was waiting until the perfect moment to tell you. But since that's not going to happen," Renée stumbled a little and gestured at the club around her. "I thought you'd be happy for me. I thought you'd congratulate me."

I didn't wait to see how her rant would end. I turned and walked, practically ran, to the bar. Grant was there, sipping some dark drink out of a tumbler.

"Something wrong?" he asked.

"Renée is being Renée," I said.

Grant set his jaw. He put down his drink and clenched his fist.

"What?" I asked.

"Nothing," Grant picked his drink back up.

"No, tell me," I said. "If you have something to tell me, then tell me."

I didn't mean to use magic to grab Grant's shoulder, but I did. Somehow the emotions I directed at him caused me to cast a spell without even meaning to. Grant felt it and slammed down his glass, spilling alcohol onto the bar.

"You ruined her," Grant said.

"I'm sorry, what?"

"You ruined her," Grant said again. "Don't you get that? She was the perfect girl, and you ruined her."

"Are you talking about Renée?"

"Of course I'm talking about Renée," he snapped. "There are guys out there who would do anything for her, anything to be with her. Then there you are, just toying with her emotions until she's ruined. Until she has created an image of you in her mind so perfect no one else could ever live up to it."

I felt unsteady on my feet. "I'm sorry Grant, I never meant to…"

"Exactly, you never meant to," Grant said. "That's always the way it is with you Roy. You don't mean to do the things you do. You didn't mean to be a pathetic excuse of a boyfriend to Skylar, you didn't mean to be overprotective of Maria, you didn't mean to screw up Renée, but you just do it anyways."

"I didn't know you felt that way about Renée," I said.

"Of course you didn't." Grant sighed. "And that's the worst part. You didn't know, and I can't even be angry, because it is so *you* that by now I shouldn't be surprised."

The music in Club Heartbreak was still blaring, but the silence between Grant and I overpowered it, cancelling it out.

Grant spoke first. "Have you ever had a song stuck in your head that was so loud you couldn't concentrate? And you keep telling yourself that if you could just hear the song one more time, hear it with your own ears, then it would be enough, then you'd be able to move on. But the more you try to ignore it, the louder it gets, until the song is just screaming, over and over, in your mind, and you can't do anything about it."

Grant turned and walked away. In my mind I tried to yell at him to stop, but my pleas had no effect. So I said nothing and let my best friend walk out of the club.

Maria was waiting for me in my hotel room, sitting on my bed and facing the entrance. I didn't ask her how she got in. Her position in the hospitality industry had its benefits.

"Sorry about Club Heartbreak," she said. "I know it was supposed to be a celebration of your victory and all. I was just in a weird mood."

"Don't worry about it." I shut the door behind me. I took the sorcerer's cloak off of my back and draped it over the chair seated behind the tiny hotel desk.

"I'm going back to Los Angeles," Maria said.

I nodded. "I know, you told me. I might go back tomorrow as well."

Maria shook her head. "You don't get it Roy. I'm not just going to Los Angeles, I'm going back to Los Angeles. I'm leaving Las Vegas. For good."

She said it softly, as if she didn't want the neon lights to hear her, as if she were afraid that, given the chance, the magical city would continue its siren's call and find the right words to make her stay. Meanwhile, I did the same thing. I tried to find the words to make Maria stay where she belonged.

"You don't have to go," I said. "I know things didn't turn out the way you thought they would."

"I can't do it Roy," Maria said, tears springing unbidden from her eyes. "I just can't do it."

I sat down next to her on the bed and tentatively reached out a hand to pat her back. I thought back to college, to the way Maria looked when she failed her organic chemistry exam, back when she was pre-Med at USC. The setting was different, and the lock of blue hair was gone, but it was the same Maria.

"Is this about EndGame?" I asked. "Is it about what I said in the elevator?"

Maria shook her head. She used a hand to brush away her tears and sniffed gently. "It's not you Roy," she said. "If anything, you're the reason I stayed as long as I did."

Maria sniffed again, and regaining her composure, sat up straight. "With or without you though, I have to face the facts. I came here to fight for magician rights, to make a difference, and that's never going to happen. The Branches are just too powerful."

"Is there anything I can say?"

"You can come with me," Maria said.

"I already told you I was thinking of visiting…"

"To stay, like me," Maria interrupted. "Come back to Los Angeles with me Roy, there's nothing for us here anymore."

I looked over to my sorcerer's cloak lying on the chair next to the desk. Maria noticed my gaze and shook her head.

"I get it, you're a sorcerer now, you won EndGame, but is that what you really want? Are you happy now?"

I tried to talk, but Maria kept going.

"You said you wanted to become a famous sorcerer and win EndGame, and you did. So what's keeping you here?"

Screw Valentine and her secrets. I wanted to tell Maria about the OneSpell. I wanted to tell her the reason I was here, the reason I missed the Magic First rally on Black Sunday, the reason I had insisted on winning EndGame and had cancelled at the last minute so many lunches and hangouts. But instead all I said was this.

"I would do anything else for you Maria, anything, but I can't go back to Los Angeles."

Maria nodded. I think she knew deep down it was what I was going to say. "In that case, will you let me stay here tonight?"

I think I might have raised an eyebrow, because Maria gave a slight chuckle. "Not like that Roy. It's just... I just don't want to be alone right now."

It was late, and sleep was beckoning. I let Maria have the bed and placed an extra pillow and blanket on the armchair in the corner of the room. I was tired enough that I would be able to sleep anywhere. Reaching out with magic, I turned off the lamp on the nightstand. I lay back on the armchair in the silent darkness, with only my thoughts to keep me company, until I heard Maria whisper.

"Are you asleep Roy?"

"Not yet," I said.

In the darkness, I could hear Maria shift on the bed. "I just wanted to make sure you were still there."

"I'm not going anywhere," I said.

We both drifted off to sleep.

Part IV: OneSpell

New Year's Eve, 2000

1 - New Friends, Old Enemies

December 30, 2000

The sharp knock on the door of my apartment startled me out of my daydreaming. I walked towards the door with a mix of dread and anticipation, the same way I was approaching the next day. In one day it would be New Year's Eve 2000. I had spent two and a half years focused on that day. The day the OneSpell would appear.

That time had been spent training, gambling, or dueling, honing myself like a weapon for the single fight that would determine (if Valentine was right) the future of the world. Sometimes during the day I would avoid thinking about it. But then night would come, and demons and mushroom clouds would haunt me until morning.

The Sorcerer's Weekly rankings, used by bookies to handicap duels between sorcerers, now placed me as the third most powerful sorcerer in Las Vegas. I shot to first after I won EndGame, but a few months later I lost a heavily advertised (and widely televised) re-match against Sorcerer Roland Tell, leading to a drop to second. When I refused to enter the 2000 EndGame, allowing Roland to once again become EndGame champion and causing a small scandal in the dueling community, I lost my chance to regain the number one spot. Thanks to a new upstart from New York who had made an impressive showing at EndGame, the rankings now placed me as third. Of course neither Valentine nor the Token Master were ranked, so I thought of myself as fifth.

I didn't care about the rankings. I didn't train every day because I wanted to be famous. I did it for a single, fast approaching duel to save the world.

Then in November, I received news that Maria was going to visit. For the first time in over a year, she was returning to the magical city of neon lights. And of all the times she could choose, she was coming for New Year's. She and her friends would spend the weekend in a hotel on the Strip, and she had invited me to stay with them. The fate of the world depended on my fighting abilities that weekend. I wasn't going to spend my last free days rehashing old drama. But an oddly insistent Valentine (who had never before been interested in my personal life) advised me to take Maria up on her offer.

Before opening my apartment door, I cast a quick scanning spell to ensure there was no demon on the other side. Since EndGame 1999, I had fought six more of the Dragon's minions, and you couldn't be too careful. The spell returned back a response. One human female, no demon signature. I waved my hand and disabled the half dozen charms on the door that made it impervious to most demonic attacks.

The task complete, I undid the three physical bolt locks and cautiously opened the door. Rather than announce Maria's smiling face, the door revealed the face of a friend of hers who Maria said she'd bring along. It was the one person who I still had trouble believing had managed to spend the last year and a half re-entering Maria's social circle. Maria's friend paused, hand on the door, staring at me through switchblade eyes.

"Roy," she said, after a particularly pregnant pause. "How nice to see you."

I was standing face to face with none other than my ex-girlfriend, and Maria's new bestie, Skylar Trope.

Skylar was dressed completely in black. Her black boots went up halfway to her knees. Above her knees, a black skirt took over, which almost reached her sleeveless black blouse. Her face was framed by perfectly straight black hair, not a strand out of place. The only marks of color other than her tan skin were her red lipstick and a silver cross that hung around her neck.

I pointed at the cross.

"I see you've finally managed to wear one without it burning you. Congratulations."

Skylar stuck her nose up in the air. "Why yes, I'd love to come in."

It occurred to me I had not actually seen her, in person, since the night we broke up. Sure I had thought about her, talked about her, spent countless nights fantasizing about what I would do to her if I had the chance, but this was the first time since the break-up we had actually stood face to face. And for a moment, as I stared at her flawlessly beautiful face framed by her perfect black hair, my heart stopped.

The moment passed.

"Well are you going to come in?" I asked. "Or do I have to explicitly invite you so you don't burst into flames?"

Before she could answer, Skylar was interrupted by another voice.

"Roy, what's up man!"

Skylar and I both stepped aside to allow Jayden Parthenia, dragging a suitcase behind him, access to my apartment.

Jayden stopped for a second, putting down the heavy suitcase and stretching his arms. "Cool place. Maybe we should just stay here, right?" He lightly elbowed me in the ribs. "Wait, since we're not, why do I have my stuff?" He looked around, as if expecting an answer. Behind him, his bodyguard T-Lock was carrying two other suitcases.

"T-Lock, back to the car!" Jayden said with a royal flourish, and walked back out of my apartment to the parking lot.

I was completely perplexed by Jayden Parthenia's presence. I vaguely remembered Maria talking to Renée who talked to him, or something like that. Then again, if Skylar and I were going to be stuck together for three days and two nights, why shouldn't Jayden join us? There was also the fact he had arranged for our lodging, no small factor. Although he claimed he was still estranged from his family, and would be until he agreed to enter wizard training, somehow that family had found out about his trip to the magic city. As a result, we would all be staying at Parthenia, the newest and fanciest of Branch Parthenia's casinos. As the commercials put it, it was the only casino so majestic the Branch had agreed to adorn it with its own name.

"I love what you've done with the place," Skylar said, stepping into the apartment and looking around my living room. Walking into the apartment uninvited did not cause her to burst into flames.

She dragged a finger against a side table, leaving a trail in the dust. "You do realize the fact you didn't explicitly invite me in reveals how much you actually wanted to invite me in."

Back in college Skylar had been a psychology major, which she often used as justification for analyzing me. From what I heard, she was now almost done with her master's in educational counseling, her stepping stone to becoming a school therapist.

Skylar planted herself just inside the doorway and surveyed the room around her. She was putting her newest psychology degree to use, using my apartment to analyze me.

My living room had seen better days. Or at least cleaner ones. Every surface was covered with magic books and manuscripts I spent my free time studying, hoping to find some overlooked clue of how to beat the Dragon. The walls were filled with hand-drawn charts (I had given up on getting my deposit back) showing spells I was trying to create or study.

"This is definitely more worthwhile than law school." Skylar's gaze lingered on the three bolt locks on my door. "And it doesn't look even remotely serial killery."

She looked at me. "That was sarcasm." She continued to look around. "By the way, your father is worried about you."

"What?"

Skylar sighed, and spoke louder and slower. "I said, your father is worried about you. I had lunch with him downtown the other day, and he said you hadn't called in a while."

"I heard you," I said. "I just don't understand. Why would you have lunch with my father?"

Skylar shrugged. "Your parents liked me when we were together. Just because we broke up, doesn't mean all your friends stop being my friends."

"But these aren't my friends, they're my parents!"

"Roy!" I turned back to the door to see Maria step in. She looked around the apartment, and as soon as her eyes met mine she smiled.

Before I could say anything, she had danced into the room and thrown her arms around my neck. "Sorry I haven't visited," she said. "Things were just so busy."

I couldn't help smiling myself, a gesture I stopped as soon as I tilted my head up and saw Skylar staring at me. Clearing my throat, I stepped out of my Maria's arms.

"I'll grab my bag," I said. "I don't want to keep the others waiting."

Just outside my apartment waited a black limousine. A circle with two vertical lines, the mark of Branch Parthenia, was proudly featured on the side of the door. Jayden was enthusiastically shoving his suitcase back into the trunk, T-Lock at his side.

The windows were tinted, but I already knew that waiting inside were Renée, who had been picked up before me, and two other guests.

Maria's stated reason for this trip was to visit Renée and bring her back to Los Angeles for her winter break. Renée was halfway done with her Master of Science program in Practical Magic at the University of Las Vegas. Unlike Sorceress Valentine, who forbid me from using any magic until I was fully ready, Renée's program encouraged them to use spells irresponsibly. And Renée never missed a chance to show off.

It was weird having another magic user in my little group of friends. I ignored any insinuations on Maria's part that I was the reason for Renée's obsession with magic.

True to form, as I entered the limousine, Renée waved her hand and caused a spattering of stars to appear in the air and sparkle before dying out. It was a simple enough illusion, but everyone looked impressed. Even Maria.

There were rumors Magic First had scheduled a rally for New Year's Eve. The premiere magic rights organization had taken a slight dive after I defeated Sorceress Corinna Windlass at EndGame, but it resurged after and was now stronger than ever. When Maria told me she was coming for New Year's, I worried she was coming for the rally, but she assured me she was no longer in contact with Magic First or its famous leader.

In addition to Jayden and Skylar, there were two other members of our group.

The first new member was Grant's co-worker Derek Hastings, who had accompanied him to watch me compete in EndGame the previous year. When Maria left Vegas to move back to Los Angeles, she caught a ride with Grant and Derek. During the long car ride Maria and Derek bonded. This led to coffee, which led to almost a year of dating, which in turn led to an epic meltdown of a break-up. They could still barely manage to be in the same room for more than five minutes at a time. So having us all share a hotel suite for a weekend was clearly a good idea.

The second new member, also through romantic association, was Skylar's boyfriend Rico. I never got the full story of how they met. One person told me they went to high school together, another told me they worked together, and someone else told me he had been set-up on a blind date with one of Skylar's sisters, who made the mistake of bringing him home to meet the family after their first date.

Sitting in the limo, it was hard to tell whether Rico was taller than me. He was certainly more muscular than I was, a fact I normally wouldn't have noticed except that he was wearing nothing over his black t-shirt, which was at least one size too tight.

"Hey bro, nice to meet you," he said, sticking out a hand. "I'm Rico."

We shook. His grip seemed enough to kill me, but I managed to avoid a grimace. Rico was a police officer. He was originally scheduled to work New Year's Eve, which would have prevented him from coming on this trip, but at the last minute he managed to trade New Year's Eve for New Year's Day. This meant he would have to fly back the morning of New Year's Day, arriving back in LA just in time for his afternoon shift, but he would still be able to party with us for the next two nights. Joy.

Thanks to Valentine's insistence, I would be spending the day before the OneSpell appeared with my best friend and her ex-boyfriend, my ex-girlfriend and her boyfriend, a one night stand who was currently stalking me, and the biggest party animal in Atlantian society. No magic could save this situation.

After putting Jayden's luggage back into the trunk, T-Lock circled around to get in the driver's seat. And like that, we were off.

The Strip looks different when viewed from a limousine. I drove down the Strip almost every day, but I had never viewed it like this. It was a movie montage come to life.

T-Lock took the scenic route to our destination. There were other, shorter ways to get to the hotel, but he ensured we drove down the Strip in its entirety. The magical city stared out at me from its immortal eyes, examining me, determining whether I was worthy to remain. It was day, so the neon lights weren't shining, but I could still sense their presence. They were watching me, wondering what luck had befallen me that I was now riding in a limousine, judging my choice in company.

We passed a billboard being covered up by a shampoo ad. The old image featured a defiant face, carefully photoshopped hair, striking eyes staring out into the world. The face was mine. Below it read "Sorcerer Roy Nakamura, 1999 EndGame Champion."

I felt Maria's hand on my knee.

"It must be tough, watching them tear it down."

I shrugged. "It's been half a year since EndGame 2000. I'm surprised they waited this long."

"It was such a disappointment when you failed to enter EndGame this year," Derek said.

Most of the limousine turned to look at him.

"I didn't know you cared," I said.

Derek smiled. I had never liked Derek. I mistrusted him when I first met him in Las Vegas, when he started going out with Maria, and after they broke up. But now, something seemed even more untrustworthy than usual.

"Why didn't you enter the tournament?" he asked. I tried looking into Derek's eyes, the so-called windows to the soul, but I couldn't see anything recognizable as a soul behind them.

"I had other things on my mind," I said.

"Other things you were training for, perhaps?" Derek responded.

Maybe the bottom line was this. Derek was still Derek. I hadn't talked to Grant in over a year, but as far as I knew Derek still worked with him at Ravenwood Capital, doing consulting or crowd-funding, or whatever it was he did for a living. After enduring a year of Maria calling me every time she and Derek got in a fight, and a month of talking to her constantly after their relationship melted down, Derek had managed to fall to the bottom of the list of people with whom I wanted to spend a weekend. Almost the bottom. There was still Skylar.

"Something like that," I said.

A minute later, the limousine ended its meandering journey down the Strip and pulled up in front of the Parthenia Hotel and Casino. I stepped out into the sunlight.

I first saw the Parthenia Casino in a commercial that ran throughout the country beginning three months before it opened. The commercial starts with an image of a mosaic depicting a battle between two warring Branches in the old days of Atlantis. It was a re-creation of course, all the authentic Atlantian mosaics had been destroyed when the Island Kingdom sank, but it had been deliberately cracked and dirtied until it truly looked like something one might find magically preserved and relatively unmolested if one could journey underneath the dark waves that hide the ancient continent's ruins.

Majestic music starts to play, and a narrator (I think it was Morgan Freeman) extols, briefly, the meritorious history of Branch Parthenia. Then Lord Ricardo Parthenia (it was still weird to think of him as Jayden's dad) steps in front of the mosaic wearing a black and white tuxedo, the top third of his Branch Mark peeking out from the collar like a tantalizing reminder of his past.

"And now for the first time in my Branch's history," he says, looking straight into the camera and directly at the viewer with the unwavering gaze befitting a famously skilled wizard and ruthless businessman, "we have created a casino and world class resort so mighty, so impressive, it is worthy to bear our Branch's very name."

The camera zooms out and we see the mosaic is mounted in a giant atrium, the hotel's lobby. The camera zooms out more, somehow passing through the exterior wall of the lobby and to the outside, where we see the building laid out in all its splendor, a massive silver tower, shaped like a sword, rising out of the Las Vegas Strip, taller than any other building for miles around.

The commercial ends with the word "Parthenia" scrawled across the screen, the Branch's circle with two vertical lines below it, as the chorus of *Don't Stop Believin'* plays in the background.

In person, the tower was even more impressive. We were staying in one of the four penthouse suites ("Jayden, I thought you were estranged from your family." "I am. If my brother's friends were visiting they would get to use all four."). The room came with its own elevator, which reminded me more than a little of Sorceress Valentine's residence.

As we exited the elevator, everyone gasped. I think even Jayden was a little impressed. The ceiling of our penthouse soared far above us, as if we were inside an auditorium instead of a hotel suite. The floor in front of us was a giant living area featuring a dozen couches, some of which faced giant windows overlooking the Strip. To our right and left were curling stairways that led up to a second floor, a balcony looking over the area where we were, and eight doors that led to sleeping rooms for each of us.

But it was the view of the city that drew me in the most, more so than the full bar to the right side of the main room, or the absurdly giant flat screen TV on the left. Any person who stayed in this room couldn't help but be reminded of where he was. With the city stretched in front of me, it felt like the window was not so much for us to observe as it was for the giant that was the city of Las Vegas to look in on us and see what we were doing.

My reverence for the hotel penthouse was tempered by the voice of a bellboy behind me, who had remained after the other two bellboys deposited our luggage into our rooms.

"Excuse me mister, I mean Sorcerer, Nakamura, these came for you." The bellboy looked almost embarrassed, like a waiter telling a customer his credit card had been declined.

I looked at the two pieces of paper. The first one was a simple note telling me to meet the note's author at the Last Emperor Casino the next day. As always, Sorceress Valentine had not bothered to sign her name.

The second one was titled "Official Summons," and bore a stamp showing it had been approved by the Sorcerers Guild. I had been summoned to appear before none other than the Archmage of Branch Shaskauer, Artimus Cantor.

It felt strange to go willingly into the lion's den. Unlike my previous visit, this time there was no blindness spell, no wizard escorting me. Artimus Cantor's official office (I assumed the one I had been to before was the real one and this was just for show) was located in the Branch Shaskauer compound just outside Las Vegas city limits. Each Branch maintained its own carefully guarded compound outside the city. The Branches had offices on the Strip as well of course, but the compound is where the high up officials and their families lived, where the Branch could retreat in times of trouble. In the case of Branch Shaskauer it was the location of their most precious possession. The Branch Shaskauer Archives.

The office was, with one notable exception, identical to the one I had visited before. That one exception was a large window that took the place of the map of the city I had seen before. The view revealed better scenery, and I was sure far fewer secrets, than the map in the Archmage's true office.

I was thoroughly searched by two unSigned security guards, overseen by a wizard, before being allowed into the office. I found this process humorous. My ability to potentially hurt the Archmage had nothing to do with anything I might be carrying on my body.

"Good morning sorcerer," Artimus said as I entered, standing to acknowledge my presence. "Thank you for agreeing to come on such short notice."

I sat down in the chair across from his desk as he sat down in his own. "Agreement has nothing to do with it, Archmage," I said. "By Guild rules, I am obligated to cooperate with a summons from any Branch authority when that summons is approved by the Guild leadership."

"But you have never been one for following the rules, have you Sorcerer Nakamura? I remember reading a report about a duel you had some years back with a wizard from Branch Merkasia, something I am sure was not sanctioned by the Guild."

I was unsure what he was trying to get at. "We all make mistakes from time to time."

"And what of your continued association with Sorceress Valentine?" Artimus asked. "I hear the Guild no longer respects her, no longer wants anything to do with her. Your support of her must cause some friction with your fellow sorcerers."

I did my best to meet his gaze. "I don't care about the opinion of my fellow sorcerers. Besides, Valentine's pull was strong enough to sponsor me when I became a sorcerer."

"Do not confuse fear with respect, Sorcerer Nakamura. Just because the others in the Guild fear her, it does not mean they like her, or would follow her. Or would protect her."

"What do you want, Archmage?" I only had one day before the OneSpell was supposed to emerge back into the world. "The rules say I must obey your summons in order to provide for cooperation between the Guild and the Branches. They don't say I have to be badgered about my personal life."

"So be it." The Archmage folded his hands. He looked down at some of the papers on his desk, then back up. "There are rumors of a rally tomorrow evening, what do you know of it?"

"I've heard the rumors. Same as you. But I don't associate with Magic First."

The Archmage continued to stare at me. "We have intelligence that the OneSpell is scheduled to return tomorrow night, New Year's Eve. Don't bother denying it. You and Valentine may be powerful sorcerers, but I have the resources of a whole Branch at my disposal. I won't give you the same lecture I gave last time, about how the

OneSpell is ours and you should let us have it. Instead, I'll tell you something you don't know."

Artimus leaned forward. "Last time you were before me, we took a sample of your DNA. During the last year, we ran some tests on it and came to a very interesting conclusion. You're Atlantian."

Despite my best efforts, my face betrayed my surprise. "That's impossible."

"Your mother is Atlantian," Artimus continued. "At least part Atlantian, probably a quarter."

"She doesn't look Atlantian at all," I said. "Besides, how can she be part Atlantian? Atlantians don't intermarry."

"Not usually," Artimus said. "But it has been known to happen. She is also part Celtic, but I will get to that later. Even more surprising than your Atlantian heritage was our discovery about your heritage on your father's side."

"I'm Japanese on my father's side," I said. "I already knew that."

"Not just any Japanese. Your father is part Ainu, did you know that?"

I answered with a blank stare.

Artimus continued, as if he were a history teacher giving a lecture. It almost reminded me of my father. "The Ainu are a people group in Northern Japan. Although many have been absorbed into the greater Japanese population, they are still a distinct ethnic group. What most people don't know is that they were one of the three original ethnic groups to use magic."

Now I was totally lost. "Three ethnic groups?"

"Yes, three ethnic groups," Artimus said, impatiently. His tone reminded me of Sorceress Valentine's constant condescension back when she first trained me. "Magic is most commonly associated with Atlantians. However in the old days, before the fall of Atlantis, magic still worked everywhere. Just as the people of Atlantis discovered magic, there were two other ethnic groups who, through a combination of a large Signed population and a little luck, developed magic in parallel. Those two groups were the Celts in what is now Wales, and the Ainu in Northern Japan.

"Neither the Celts nor the Ainu were as competent as the Atlantians, but they nevertheless developed a stable practice of magic. At least it was stable until superstitions and the like drove both people to slaughter all their magic users."

"What does all this have to do with me?" I asked.

"The magic of the Atlantians, the Celts, and the Ainu was all different," Artimus said. "Different strengths, different weaknesses. You are the first person we have ever come across, in the history of the Branches, who is descended from all three lines of magic. This may explain your abilities.

"Roy, you are one of the most powerful sorcerers in the city, and you don't even try. Just think what you could become if you actually applied yourself."

"Are you trying to give me a lecture?" I asked. "Are you moonlighting as a high school guidance counselor?"

"No. I'm offering you a job."

This part didn't surprise me as much as it probably should have.

"A job?"

"Come join us," Artimus said. "Become a wizard."

I didn't know what to say. And the fact I was stunned into silence, rather than immediately responding "*no*," probably revealed more than I wanted it to.

"But I'm a sorcerer," I said. "And I'm not Atlantian."

"Half of all wizards are not Atlantian," Artimus said. "I'm certainly not. And as we just went over you are, in fact, part Atlantian.

"Think about it Roy. You've been playing in a sandbox, and I'm offering you a palace. As a wizard of Branch Shaskauer you would have access to the latest magic research, to expert teachers, to the Archives. It would be hard work, make no mistake, but you could thrive. You could become powerful beyond your wildest dreams."

We sat in silence for a moment. I was lost in my own thoughts. Ever since I first read *Call Me Sorcerer*, I had wanted to be a sorcerer, wanted to win EndGame. And I had. The idea of being a wizard had never crossed my mind, but now that I actually thought about it, I couldn't help feel like it made sense. It felt right.

Artimus reached under his desk and took out a bowl of small brightly colored rectangles.

"Here, have a candy."

It seemed weird for the Archmage of a Branch to offer me candy, but it also seemed rude to decline. I took one candy out of the bowl, gently unwrapped it, and popped it in my mouth. It had a slight sour taste, but I had eaten worse.

"My offer will remain open," Artimus said. "Anytime you want, come find me and your life as a wizard of Branch Shaskauer will begin. But until that day, you are still my enemy. And if you stand between me and the OneSpell, I will kill you myself."

There was nothing in Artimus Cantor's tone or demeanor that led me to believe he was saying anything other than the truth.

2 – When You Were Young

Skylar was angry because Renée wasn't wearing jeans. Since Jayden had declared himself in charge of our trip (both the lodging and the entertainment), he decreed we would go to Club Heartbreak to celebrate the night before New Year's Eve. I tried to protest, remembering the previous time we went to the club over a year before (and how well that turned out), but I was overruled. I was surprised Maria and Renée were willing to go back to Club Heartbreak after their previous experience, but apparently their memories of the night had faded faster than mine.

Renée, Maria, and Skylar were wearing identical sleeveless black shirts, cut at an angle, that went down to their knees. However, Maria and Skylar were wearing jeans underneath their shirts, and apparently this made their outfits less formal. Skylar was angry because she felt Renée, by not wearing jeans, was trying to outdo her two female companions.

Of course Skylar couldn't simply say this. That would have been too easy. Instead she dropped subtle hints, insinuating how cute it would look if all three of them matched, and how cold the weather might be. Renée offered to put on pants, or to make them magically appear (I doubted she was powerful enough, but didn't say anything), but Skylar insisted this wasn't necessary, while also insinuating it absolutely was necessary.

All this, and probably more, took place as we stood in our suite, waiting for the elevator to reach us. Normally I wouldn't notice these kind of things, but all this talk of clothes made me realize Rico and I were wearing identical shirts, and for all I could tell, identical pants as well. For a moment I doubted the wisdom of my earlier decision to leave my sorcerer's cloak in my room and wondered if I had time to go back and get it. At least my two tokens were still securely around my neck, providing a visual cue as to my identity.

We were all standing in front of the elevator, all within a step or two of its doors, but Maria had managed to seat herself against the wall as far as physically possible from her ex-boyfriend Derek. Derek in turn was deep in conversation with Rico. They had spent the last hour discussing Derek's religious worship of the free market, and right now were likely discussing the pros and cons of mandatory euthanasia for the homeless and the elderly. Watching Derek and Rico, it was impossible not to notice Maria, physically removed as she was, was also watching them.

It was one of those gazes that was impossible to decipher, not even worth trying to interpret. Anger? Jealousy? Regret? Maria looked away, and I couldn't help feeling like she knew the moment Derek looked back and met her eyes, she would have no choice but to throw herself at him all over again. And Maria wasn't the only watcher. There was at least two more.

Jayden was watching Renée, planning his next move, figuring out how he could turn Skylar's distress over Renée's dress into an opportunity to get inside Renée's pants. Then there was Skylar, who was watching Rico with pure adoration. Reflected in her switchblade eyes you could see all the things he meant to her. Something about that gaze caused my anger at Skylar, which I had done my best to repress for the last couple hours, to simmer to the surface.

Like I said, all this and more took place as we waited for the elevator to reach our suite.

Cut to an hour later. Thanks to Jayden's royal status and the tokens around my neck, we were able to walk right in to Club Heartbreak, still one of Las Vegas' hottest nightclubs, without a reservation. Our entrance was straight out of a movie.

Picture this. We enter in layers, allowing the camera to focus on one of us at a time as we stroll in. It's in slow motion of course, with Rush's "Limelight" playing over the background. Highlights of the montage include Derek masterfully pulling sunglasses out of his pocket and throwing them over his eyes, Maria looking wistfully off into the distance, Rico putting his arm protectively slash jealously around Skylar's bare shoulder, and me playing with my shirt cuff, feeling like it's the first day of school, wondering if I'm in the right classroom.

A minute later the montage ended, and Jayden and I were standing at the bar. "What do you want?" Jayden asked me with a broad smile, looking more like a kid who broke into his dad's liquor cabinet than a member of Vegas royalty. "First drink is on me. And the second.

And the third. Actually, my Branch is paying for all the drinks, so, yeah, just order whatever."

Two seconds later I was on the dance floor, a rum and cola in my hand. I was doing my best to stay away from Renée while Jayden was doing his best to get close to her. It put me in an awkward position I had been in with Renée a dozen times in the last dozen months.

Ever since Renée's confession of love for me the night I won EndGame, I had done my best to avoid her. However the magical community was a small one, and even with Maria not in the picture, Renée and I kept running into each other. Each time she told me again how much she wanted me, how we belonged together. I started flat out ignoring the emails she sent me saying we needed to talk, or asking what she had done to deserve my scorn.

I had done my best to reverse the love spell I cast, putting up with questionable glances and derision from the top dozen experts in the city. Valentine warned me that spells could be powerful, could have second and third order effects. I wished Valentine really could travel in time, so I could travel back to that night and never cast that cursed spell.

On the dance floor, Renée was everywhere I turned. She dodged in and out of my vision to the beat, never quite dancing with me, but always making her presence known. It was like she was dancing parallel to me. She wanted to be the hunted, not the hunter, but I refused to pursue her.

Meanwhile, as some song by Mariah Carey segued into Mandy Moore's *Candy*, Skylar did her usual strut on the catwalk. Back when we were a couple, Skylar was reserved when it came to public displays of affection, and she disdained any form of over-sexualized dancing. All that apparently changed when we broke up.

Skylar grabbed a hold of Rico's collar and dragged him towards her, then expertly spun around and grinded her backside against his front. It was hard to believe this was the same girl who taught me to swing dance to 80's music at *Ruby Red*.

I walked off the dance floor, up the short set of stairs to a VIP table where Jayden had set-up shop. I sat down beside him. Jayden was staring at Skylar.

"Was she that sexy when you were with her?"

I shook my head.

"So, in other words, after you guys broke up, she got hotter?"

I shrugged my shoulders. "Something like that."

"Wow," Jayden said. "You have the worst luck Roy. The worst luck."

"So how are we all doing tonight gentlemen?"

It was Derek. With a swagger, he collapsed down onto the seat next to me, then sat up straight and looked me in the eye.

"Anyone score yet?" When I shook my head, he quickly turned his head towards Jayden, then back to me.

"Of course not," he said. "Maria always told me what a nice guy you were. You're not the type for one night stands. But you Jayden, I figured you'd be off in the corner with someone by now. That's your reputation, right?"

Derek patted me on the back, something that in his world was probably a mark of affection.

"Roy, you see that girl?"

Derek pointed to a short girl, long and wavy blonde hair, who was wearing a black tank-top and a short pink skirt that left nothing to the imagination. She was on the dance floor, near the circular bar at the center, dancing by herself to the music.

"I've been talking to her all night, and she is a junior at Arizona State. Just turned twenty-one. Looking to party."

Derek licked his lips. "She's also a yoga instructor. I mean, she told me she was. I have significant doubts that it's true. But the fact a girl would lie to me and tell me she is. Well, that tells you what she's down for.

"She also has daddy issues. At least I assume she does. I'm not a hundred percent sure yet, you never can be, but girls like her are just so easy to read."

I tried to figure out what it was Maria had ever seen in him. I also noticed the blonde from Arizona State had stopped dancing and was looking in the direction of our table.

Derek nodded at her. "She asked if I was famous, so I told her I was the personal financial advisor to both the infamous Jayden Parthenia, and a former EndGame champion. Now that I've proved the truth of those statements, I'll be going."

With a pat on my back, Derek jumped out of his seat and practically ran back to the blonde girl.

"Wow, he's kind of a jerk," Jayden said. "Was he always a jerk? I think I met him last year, but I think he was less of a jerk back then."

A waitress had arrived, unbidden, and dropped off drinks for me and Jayden. I took a large sip, draining almost half of the glass in one gulp.

"He's definitely more of a jerk now," I said.

Another full drink appeared on my table to replace the one I had half-finished. Either Club Heartbreak used magic to provide refills, or the waitresses were quicker than I thought. Jayden and I continued to drink until we could think of another topic of conversation.

"What do you think of Rico?" I asked.

Jayden pinched his face as if he had just sucked a lemon. "That's a pretty random question Roy. Is this your way of telling me you want me to ask you what you think of Rico?"

Rico and Skylar were still dancing on the dance floor. Kind of. Skylar was clearly dancing, and was trying to pull Rico into it, but he looked somewhat uncomfortable at the prospect of a dance that intimate in public.

"I just think he and Skylar are sort of weird together," I said.

"So that would be a yes," Jayden said to his drink.

"He seems like a nice guy and all," I said. "I mean, he's a police officer, he puts others first, saves people, that sort of thing. But then you have Skylar, the aspiring psychologist. She's career driven, analytical, has no heart. I just don't know what she sees in him."

Jayden cocked his head to one side. "You mean you don't know what he sees in her."

I took a sip of my drink. "Yeah, exactly."

Jayden put down his glass and looked up at the ceiling, deep in thought. "Well it's like they say," he finally said. "Relationships look different from the inside."

I put my own glass on the table and ran a hand through my hair. "That's actually pretty deep."

Jayden shrugged. "I think I got it from a cartoon."

"Hey Roy." It was Renée, shyly walking up to us.

"Hey gorgeous," Jayden exclaimed. He jumped up, allowing her access to the inside of the table. She remained standing, however.

"Imagine running into a girl like you at a club like this," Jayden continued.

Renée ran a hand through her short blonde hair as her eyes lit up at the compliment. She smiled, and I realized it had been a while since I saw her smile.

"Now what can I do for you?" Jayden asked.

"I just came to see if the 1999 EndGame champion wanted to dance," Renée said, turning to face me. "Or if he's too scared."

I scooted out of my seat, exiting on the other side of the table, and stood up.

"Well?" Renée said. "How about it?"

Standing just behind Renée, Jayden looked at me and slowly shook his head back and forth.

"Normally I'd love to," I said, sensing someone walking up behind me. "But I already said I would dance with her." Without looking, I pointed a thumb to the figure behind me, and spun around to grab her (whoever she was) and drag her down to the dance floor.

My hand made contact with another hand. I looked up. The hand was connected to an arm, which led to a body, which was topped by a face. That face belonged to Skylar.

"Well this is… interesting," Skylar said.

"Of course I'll dance with you for old time's sake," I said loudly enough for Renée and Jayden to hear, then pulled Skylar down the stairs and onto the dance floor.

I can't remember what song was playing, but somehow we started dancing to it with a minimum of awkwardness.

"So, this is unexpected," Skylar said. "I didn't realize wizards were allowed to dance."

"I'm not a wizard, I'm a sorcerer," I said. I tried to avoid stepping on Skylar's feet. I didn't want to give her the satisfaction of seeing how bad a dancer I still was.

Skylar rolled her eyes. "Whatever."

"So how have you been?" I asked. Skylar spun around, almost knocking over both members of another dancing couple.

"Just fine thank you," she said. "I'm almost finished with my degree in educational psychology. You were in graduate school at one point, right?"

I lost my beat. "Not again with…"

"Oh, that's right. You got in, but you didn't go because you wanted to go to Las Vegas and become a wizard instead. How's that working out for you?"

"Just fine thank you," I said. "And I'm not a wizard, I'm a sorcerer."

I glanced over to where Renée and Jayden were standing, still talking. Skylar followed my gaze.

"I can't believe the way Jayden is flirting with Renée," Skylar said. "It's just so obvious, so uninhibited, so…"

"Innocent?" I suggested.

"Disgustingly so," Skylar nodded.

"Come on Angel Eyes," I said. "Remember when we were that young?"

Skylar stopped mid-step, causing me to stumble and almost fall. "One, don't call me Angel Eyes, that's just weird." She gave a shudder. "And two, come on Roy." Her gaze softened. "We were never that young."

Skylar started dancing again, and I followed. "I'm pretty sure we were that young," I said, not sure what I was trying to prove or what trap I was walking into. "I still remember sitting with you on the roof of the parking structure next to your dorm."

For three years I rehearsed all the things I'd say to her if I ever got the chance. But now that I had the chance, all the memories came back.

"I think that was where I first realized I loved you."

If Skylar was surprised, she didn't show it. "On the roof of the parking structure? The first time we kissed?"

"No, the other time," I said. "The first time I saw you cry."

This caused Skylar to raise an eyebrow. "You enjoyed seeing me cry?"

"No, I enjoyed seeing *you*. It was as if all your walls, all your masks, came down. I saw you, the real you, for the first time. And I couldn't help falling in love with that person."

Again Skylar stopped mid-step. She gave me one of her patented indecipherable looks, the ones she had always expected me to understand when we were together. Then we started to dance again.

"So you and Rico seem to be a nice couple," I said.

Skylar glared. "Do whatever you want, but don't make fun of Rico."

"I'm not making fun of you. What, I'm not allowed to be happy for an ex-girlfriend who finally found love?"

"Whatever," Skylar said.

"I'm serious," I said. "He seems down to earth, he has a good job. He literally fights bad guys for a living."

Skylar sighed. "He's a real angel all right."

"You say that like it's a bad thing."

Skylar looked off into the distance, at some imagined future she would never be able to fulfill. "He's an angel, and demons don't belong with angels, Roy, they belong with other demons."

We continued to dance in silence. Off to the side I could see Derek, who had been off talking with Rico, grab the blonde from Arizona State and start to dance with her. Looking farther, I could see Maria had taken note of this. She was leaning against the wall surrounding the dance floor, separating it from the raised VIP tables. She was staring, no emotion on her face, as Derek continued to dance with the girl, who was writhing in seemingly unearthly pleasure.

"I can't believe he does that to her," I said.

"Who does what to whom?" Skylar asked.

"Derek." I gestured in his direction with my head. "Hitting on a girl like that right in front of Maria."

"Yes, that's terrible," Skylar said. "How dare a guy hit on a girl in front of another girl who he is not even going out with. That's just terrible and evil and disgusting. It's definitely something you've never done. Especially not five minutes ago to Renée."

"That's different," I said. "Maria and Derek used to be together."

"And now they're not."

Skylar and I were gradually making a circle around the bar at the center of the dance floor. We had progressed far enough that Derek, along with his conquest for the night, was hidden from view.

"I just can't stand Derek," I said. "The whole 'I'm cool because I make lots of money' attitude. The yuppiness. The way he treats women."

Skylar sighed. "Face it Roy, the fact you don't approve of Derek Hastings has nothing to do with him and everything to do with the fact you're in love with Maria."

"Again with Maria," I said. "It's like you're obsessed with her. How is it that we've been broken up for years and we're still having the same fight we used to?"

"Maybe it's because you're in love with Maria," Skylar said.

"It's not like that. Maria's one of my best friends."

"Fine." Skylar removed her hands from me and crossed her arms in a challenge. "Look me directly in the eye, and tell me you don't have romantic feelings for Maria."

I tilted my head, and without blinking, looked Skylar directly in the eye. "I don't have romantic feelings for Maria."

Skylar's glare turned into a smirk. "I knew it," she said, turning around and starting to walk back towards Rico.

"What, I said it!"

"We were together for four years Roy," Skylar shouted without turning around. "I know you better than that."

I found Maria just outside Club Heartbreak, sitting by herself at the very bottom of the steps leading to the club entrance. Even from behind, I could tell it was her, and I could tell she had been crying. Without saying a word, I sat down beside her.

The music in the club was loud (the DJ was playing a mash-up of Jennifer Lopez and Marvin Gaye), but in the lobby it sounded more like background music, like wallpaper, instead of music that is supposed to overwhelm all other senses until it pumps through your body like blood.

I didn't say anything to Maria at first, I just sat beside her. I knew she knew I was there. I knew when she was ready, she would talk. After a few minutes she sniffed and finally looked over to me.

"What are you doing?" she said. "I thought you and Jayden were having fun in there."

"I just wanted to make sure you were okay," I said. I smiled at her. "I wanted to be sure you were still you."

Maria smiled back, and for a second she looked like her old self, like the girl who was the center of every party, of everyone's attention. She looked ready to run back through the doors of the club, past the two bouncers, and make the dance floor hers.

Finally she spoke. "If this was a movie, if this was *Pretty in Pink* or something, then this is the part where Derek would walk out of the club, down those stairs, and sweep me up in his arms."

Maria's smile, a sweet smile of nostalgia, turned into a sob. "Why didn't we work out, Roy? I don't get it. I did everything for him. Why wasn't it enough?"

Maybe it was the alcohol, or maybe it was just me being me, but I started talking without thinking. Listening to Maria talk, all I could think of was standing in a hotel room almost three years ago and telling Maria what I thought about Karl.

"You're beautiful," I said. "Don't you get that? You're beautiful. And I don't just mean the way you look, but the way you act, the way you carry yourself. Guys like Derek aren't worth crying over."

She didn't say anything, so I continued. "Come on Maria, it's not like you were happy when you were with him."

"Happy?" Maria's head jerked up.

"I mean, you're complaining about how bad things are now, but when you were with him, when you and Derek were a couple, you were constantly fighting, you were constantly unhappy…"

"Well I'd rather be unhappy than alone!"

Silence.

"I didn't mean that," Maria lied.

"I know you didn't," I said.

The music continued to play. The DJ started a remix of *Boys of Summer*. Outside the building the neon lights of Las Vegas, brightening and dimming like a rapidly beating pulse, proclaimed that despite Maria's distress the city breathed on.

Maria had stopped crying. Now she was staring off into empty space.

"You know what love is?" She didn't wait for a response. "It's wondering every night if he'll be there when you wake up." She leaned back and looked up at the ceiling, her gaze tracing the constellations of imaginary stars above us. "My mom taught me that."

I couldn't think of anything to say, so I didn't say anything. I just joined Maria in looking up at the ceiling, at the imaginary stars. There were real stars outside of course, beyond the ceiling. Even with the Vegas lights, you could still see a few. I wanted to see them for a moment through the ceiling, just to get a taste, but even magic has its limits.

Maria dropped her gaze and looked at me. She stared at me in silence for a solid minute. I had the sense she was carrying on an entire internal monologue, and at the end of it, even if it was out of context, she would reveal the conclusion at which she had arrived.

"Sometimes I worry I'm addicted to you," she finally said, devoid of any emotion, then looked back up at the ceiling.

I emulated her gesture. It was then I noticed the banner above us, the one that had been there this whole time. I started to laugh.

"It's Club Heartbreak," I said. "This whole time, it's been Club Heartbreak."

"What are you talking about?" Maria said. I ignored her.

Boys of Summer continued to play, blaring out of the speakers like a ritual chant. In dark red letters on a black background, the banner read "Club Heartbreak, New Year's Eve Party TOMORROW. Come celebrate THE END OF THE WORLD."

3 - The Watcher

Las Vegas is alive. It breathes, it waits, and it watches those who scurry along its face for a brief season. To the immortal city of Las Vegas, we are fireflies that soar, flare, and burn out in a single day. But it would be a mistake to think this means we escape the city's notice, or that anything we do is without its implicit permission.

The sun had been up for several hours by the time I pulled myself out of bed and walked through the doors of the Last Emperor casino with a single thought on my mind. Wave watching. The freshness of the new day was tainted by the musty sweat of the gamblers around me, most of whom had been playing all night. The electronic whir and clang of slot machines jarred me awake. At least semi-awake. Hungover and half asleep, I was the most alert person in the cavern the gaming tables called home. The hangover was possibly my imagination, my mind telling my body what it should be feeling. I was in all likelihood not hungover at all, but in fact still drunk from the night before.

Even though I was inside, sheltered from the view of the harsh neon lights that clothe the city, I could still feel their gaze on me. I could feel the city watch me, passing judgment on my actions from the night before and the actions I was contemplating for the night ahead.

The path before me was abruptly blocked by two unSigned security guards. Between them stood a casino hostess (blonde hair, blue eyes, a red qipao tightly hugging her slim figure). She stopped a few feet away from me, just out of reach, and bowed her head while tapping the fingers of her right hand to her forehead in the traditional Atlantian gesture of submission.

"Sorcerer Roy Nakamura," she began, "on behalf of Branch Parthenia, I would like to welcome you to the Last Emperor. We hope you enjoy your time here." She looked down for a second at the two tokens around my neck, which because I left my sorcerer's cloak in my hotel room were the only sign of my office. "We would like to take this *opportunity*," she pronounced the word slowly, emphasizing each syllable, "to remind you that the use of magic to affect the outcome of a game of chance is strictly prohibited by Branch Parthenia rules, as well as Las Vegas Municipal Code Title 6, Section 40, Sub-section 230, and will result in immediate expulsion." She tilted her head to the left, towards the larger of the two guards.

It was all I could do to stop myself from laughing at the threat. I was a famous dueler, a magical warrior skilled in the art of one-on-one combat. Depending on who was consulted, I was likely the fifth most powerful sorcerer in Las Vegas. Even if wizards were thrown into the mix, I was still one of the top twenty magic users in the city. I could dispose of two unSigned rent-a-cops with a gesture, probably even a thought.

And the idea of me not using magic to play games was absurd. Of course I would use magic. The Branches knew it, the pit bosses knew it, and this hostess knew it. However as long as I didn't win too much, and as long as the presence of a famous dueler, of a *real sorcerer gambling*, drew curious onlookers to the tables, thus providing even more business for the casino, I would be tolerated.

With a nod I dismissed the hostess, who was all too happy to escape from my gaze, and walked forward. I blinked away the crust from my eyes and scanned my surroundings. Most of the tables were empty. A single blackjack table popped into my peripheral vision, its dealer methodically distributing cards with slightly less emotion than a slot machine. The table, a ten dollar minimum, was occupied by two people, both of them sweaty monstrosities kept alive by pure adrenaline. Well past small talk, they pointed and grunted to signify their intent, not even bothering to register pleasure or pain at their wins or losses.

They were pathological gamblers of some yet to be discovered kind. They were not action gamblers or escape gamblers, they didn't gamble for excitement, or to forget about the real world, but because they simply had nothing else. Like crying out of boredom.

I sat down at the table, nodding to the dealer as I withdrew three crisp hundred-dollar bills from my pocket. The dealer started to ask for my ID, but he glanced at the two tokens around my neck and reconsidered.

The dealer took twelve green twenty-five dollar chips out of his caddy and put them before me. I picked the chips up in my fingers and dropped them back onto the table, considering how much to bet on my first hand. Behind me I could sense a person, most likely a tourist eager to watch a *real sorcerer* play a game of chance, hoping that this was a *real wave watcher* just like they feature in the half dozen police procedurals about this magical city. I turned as the presence sat down to my right. It was definitely not a tourist.

Sorceress Valentine was dressed in a blue blouse, conservative black pants, and a black sorcerer's cloak, the silver patterns on it defiantly glittering in the non-existent sunlight. She pulled a hundred dollar bill out of the air and laid it on the table in front of the dealer. Without looking up, she greeted me. "Roy."

I turned to acknowledge her and nodded my head in greeting. "Sorceress." Although I was no longer her apprentice, the drive for me to use her title rather than her first name was slow to die.

Sorceress Valentine, likely the most powerful magic user in the world (sorcerer or wizard), was an attractive woman of Asian descent somewhere in her late-thirties. This morning however she looked older than usual, frailer.

"Roy," she whispered under her breath, "when I told you to meet me here, it was not to gamble."

"And yet here I am, gambling." A slight smile crossed my face. I made up my mind and pushed two green chips into the betting circle. Valentine, who now had four green chips of her own, pushed a chip into her circle as well.

The dealer dealt the cards. "There is something we need to discuss," Valentine said. "The OneSpell will appear tonight. Have you determined where it will appear?"

"Sorcerer Roland revealed its location to me over a year ago, you know this." Valentine's habit of taking forever to get to her point used to make her intimidating. Now that I was also a sorcerer, I found it annoying.

"But have you deciphered his message? Do you know the actual physical location?"

I checked the cards, noting the way the dealer dealt them. "Yes."

"Now that we have that out of the way, we need to talk. Away from this table. Alone. If you are to defeat the Dragon, there is something you must know."

This was enough talk. I was here to gamble. Ignoring Sorceress Valentine, I focused on the cards in front of me.

The shield spell I quietly cast the moment I sat down was obscuring any attempts, technological or magical, to observe my actions. Valentine was probably powerful enough to see through it, but she didn't care. The wave watching spell I cast soon after was returning a steady stream of information on the outcome of the game before me. With my magical senses I could see the probability waves manifested in front of me, tying all the actions of all the parties at the table together and showing me the chances of which card would be played next.

"Roy," Valentine said, but my thoughts were somewhere else.

Sometimes I like to imagine my life is a movie. Picture this. "Fascination Street" by The Cure is playing over the background. Instead of being surrounded by half-dead gambling addicts, there are three men in tuxedos seated at the table with me. Each of us has two or three adoring women on our arms. The chandelier high above gives off a crystal infused light which bounces off the silver threads on my sorcerer's cloak (the one that in this movie I didn't leave back in my hotel room), and into the wide-open eyes of one of the adoring women. The camera zooms in on the table and cuts between images (a card falling to the table with an exaggerated thud, my fingers picking up a chip and throwing it into the betting circle), all in slow motion.

But back in the real world, things weren't quite as magical as they were in my imagination. There were no chandeliers, no adoring women, my sorcerer's cloak was still in my hotel room, and when I tried to concentrate on the cards, all I could think about was what Maria had said.

"I'd rather be unhappy than alone," Maria Perez told me the night before while drunk and crying on the steps leading up to Club Heartbreak, the hottest nightclub in Vegas.

It had frightened me because even though she had been drunk, I had known she meant it. In fact, it had been her attitude towards life for as long as I had known her, which was a very long time.

FOCUS!

Two nines to a dealer six. Waving my hand to signify I was standing, I watched as the dealer drew a queen and a six, busting. I won another hand, and then another, the cards flying by so quickly that if it were not for the spells, I would never have been able to keep track of them all.

Out of the corner of my eye I glanced at Valentine. She didn't respond. She seemed to have, at least for the time being, given up on her goal of luring me away from the betting table.

Two more hands went by. Thinking for a moment, I pushed my entire pile, five hundred and seventy-five dollars, into the betting circle. I kept my hand on the chips. The dealer raised an eyebrow. I turned to Sorceress Valentine.

"If you're really a time traveler," I said. "Answer me this. Am I going to win this hand?"

Valentine shook her head, and something about her entire demeanor bothered me. It wasn't just how she looked older and more tired than usual. She looked somehow different, changed. "You know it doesn't work that way Roy. I can't reveal the future or else I risk changing it."

I smirked. "I knew it. You may be able to *stop* time, but you're no time traveler." I pulled the pile back out of the betting circle and placed two twenty-five dollar chips instead. The dealer dealt the cards.

My cards were a three and a seven and the dealer had a five. Every blackjack guide in existence said a player should double down, but the spells I cast were warning me not to. I generally listened to the spells in my head (I created and cast them after all), but I also loved to double down. I loved the excitement of knowing the stakes were now twice what they were a moment before.

There is a thing some wave watchers do called "going native." It's what happens when a wave watcher likes to gamble a little too much and starts ignoring the spells in his head, making wild bets in an effort to catch that high they got the first time they tried to gamble.

Some say this is the real reason casinos let sorcerers gamble, let people like me who may be wave watchers play games of chance. It wasn't the business we drew, or the way we added to the magical mystique of even the dingiest gaming establishment in the city. No, it was because no matter how good we were, no matter how impressive the spells we cast, none of us could resist the impulse to go against them. And that's why in the long run, no matter how good we were, we always lost.

I decided to give in to those impulses and added two more twenty-five dollar chips to the pile. For a moment my hangover disappeared, and I felt like myself again. I felt better than myself! I turned to Valentine who was now looking straight at me, not even pretending to pay attention to her own cards. I realized what it was about her demeanor that had bothered me before, as I finally identified the strange look on her face. It was fear.

For the first time in all the years I had known her, Sorceress Valentine, the most powerful magic user in the world, looked scared.

The spell had been right and I had been wrong. After doubling down on my ten I got a five and the dealer revealed a five underneath his six. His next card was a jack, and just like that I was down fifty dollars. I turned to Valentine who slowly rose. I shook my head in response.

"One more hand," I said, "I need to win back my money."

Eyes narrowed, Valentine sat back down. I didn't have time to marvel over the fact that back when I was her apprentice, any attempt to disagree with her would have brought on immediate retribution.

I placed fifty dollars in the betting circle, ignoring the probability waves that were warning me my chances of winning this round were low. My spell told me my first card would be a five, so when the dealer gave me an ace I could barely contain my elation. The dealer dealt himself an ace as well, a somewhat alarming development that had been predicted by my wave watching spell, but the king I then received demonstrated how wave watching spells do not always work.

I waited to receive my payout. "Even money?" the dealer asked. I paused for a moment like a novice, not comprehending. Then I remembered. The dealer had an ace, so there was a possibility he had twenty-one like I did. Rather than give me an immediate three to two payout as was customary for players who got a blackjack, he was offering me even money before checking his own hand. If he checked his hand, and had less than twenty-one, I would get my full pay-out. But if he did have twenty-one, I got nothing.

I shook my head, not even bothering to consult the probability waves, which by now had likely abandoned me for a player who cared. The dealer twisted his hole card into the corner mirror embedded into the table. He turned it over. It was a king.

Dealer blackjack. I got nothing. As the dealer reached forward to take my chips, I felt an icy grip on my shoulder. "Now Roy," Sorceress Valentine said in a threatening whisper.

"Or what?" I said.

"Or else!" she hissed.

Gathering up my remaining chips I followed her as she walked towards a lounge area at the edge of the gaming floor. I could feel the cameras following us, hear the security monitors, as well as the wizard or two they had probably called over by now. They were wondering why two of the most powerful sorcerers in Las Vegas were hanging out together, speculating about what we could be planning.

We sat at a small metal table, more decorative than functional, and Valentine shooed off a cocktail waitress. As usual, she was all business.

"Tonight you face the Dragon," she said. "It is what you have spent the last several years preparing to do."

I nodded. I had heard this exhortation before.

"In order to defeat the Dragon you will need to watch, and use, the probability waves better than he can. Just as when you faced the Token Master during the trials, you will need to take into account not just everything about your opponent, but everything about yourself."

Valentine reached into her shirt, and I was once again struck by the fact she looked scared. The apprehension in me rose up like a wave. What could possibly frighten someone as powerful as her?

"There is something you do not know about yourself." Valentine pulled an object out of her shirt, connected to a chain that went around her neck. "Something you used to know, but has since been hidden."

She lifted the chain off of her neck, continuing to clutch the object it held. I looked at her, at the power oozing out of her skin even while her face portrayed fear and vulnerability. The scent of magic followed wherever she was present, and it filled my nostrils like a field of flowers.

"You lied to me about the Dragon's origins," I said.

Valentine stopped.

"When you first told me about the Dragon, you told me it was the anger and despair of Branch Primm. You said all that rage somehow coalesced into a living creature, which was a demon."

"I remember," Valentine said.

"But a year ago I was talking to Jayden, Jayden Parthenia, and he told me something different. He said the Dragon is the spirit of

Trannanir, the wizard who created the OneSpell. He said when Trannanir died, his anger became a demon, became the Dragon, and ever since it has been hunting the OneSpell."

Valentine clenched her fist, the one holding the object which had been around her neck.

"Everything I do has a purpose Roy," she said. "If I misled you, it was not without reason."

"And what was the reason?" I said.

"It was like the illusionists of old," Valentine said. "You remember them, right? They wanted you to look at one hand," she held out an empty palm, "when they were really doing something with the other," her other hand, the one holding the object connected to a string, opened.

Inside it was a token. It wasn't one of the two she normally wore, it was a third. She shifted her hand so it held the chain, letting the token hang free in front of my eyes.

I stared at the token. Of all the devastating and life changing secrets I had anticipated, this had not been one of them. It wasn't some magical bomb or incriminating letter, it was a token.

A very familiar looking token.

I looked at it more closely, let the focal point of my vision hone in on it like a hawk hunting prey.

The token was engraved with a dolphin. Inside the engraving was one word, three letters. "SKY." A nonexistent wind picked up the token, rotating it, and a fraction of a second later the other side of the token came into view.

My heart stopped. On the other side of the token was another word, also three letters.

"ROY."

The world shattered.

Everything happens at once. All the memories come back to me.

It is the first day of my apprenticeship. I am sitting in Sorceress Valentine's suite, sitting at the table we used for my training. She just used a Queen of Hearts to cast a memory shroud on me. She puts away the Queen of Hearts and pulls out the dolphin token. "And as long as you're under," she says to me, "we're going to cast a second memory shroud.

"Arcane knowledge lost in time,
hide his past from prying eyes,
bind it up upon this sign,
take his pain and make it mine."

It is freshman year of college. Skylar and I are on our third date. I have brought her back to my high school for Homecoming, and we have time to kill so we stop at Magic Haven, a bookstore I used to go to back in high school.

I didn't go there with Maria the day of Homecoming, I went there with Skylar!

I look at a manuscript featuring a knight riding towards a dragon, a lance in his hand and a long explanation in Atlantian script. Meanwhile, Skylar finds a machine that sells personalized tokens. Stamped on each token is the dolphin, the symbol of Magic Haven, but on either side we have our names engraved, at least the portion which will fit.

Once again it is freshman year. I just told Skylar I never went to my senior prom, so Skylar insists we slow dance right then and there in her dorm room. For my first slow dance, Skylar puts on her favorite song, a love ballad by Taliesin.

"I don't know how to slow dance," I say, somewhat sheepishly, hoping the admission won't kill our blossoming relationship.

"Slow dancing is easy," Skylar tells me. "It's just like a hug." She pauses, as if remembering something she had once heard or read. "The only difference between an embrace and a slow dance is the soundtrack."

I listen to the lyrics.

This is the story, morning glory
of what I learned in Vegas.
You always hurt the ones you love –
that's why love couldn't save us.

"That doesn't make any sense," I say to Skylar. "Why would you hurt someone you love?"

You said that we were fated
That you heard it from above
That a sacrifice isn't a sacrifice
When it's for the one you love.

As the notes fill her tiny dorm room, musical phrases bringing to life images I have of what our perfect life together will be like, it occurs to me that a line from this song would make a perfect nickname for Skylar, for my new girlfriend.

> *I told you from the start I'm not your type,*
> *So can't you see we're running out of time?*
> *To save us from these tears, both yours and mine,*
> *Baby you're the only one my valentine.*

The line in the song, the end of the chorus of "What I Learned in Vegas," it wasn't "my angel eyes," it was "my valentine." And that means my nickname for Skylar, the one I called her for the four years we were together, it wasn't "Angel Eyes" either.

I was back in the present. There were tears, only a few but still noticeable, falling out of the pair of switchblade eyes staring back at me.

"Skylar?" I asked.

Sorceress Valentine smiled. "It's been a long time since you've called me that."

I thought back to that night in her penthouse suite, the night we danced to her favorite song. "No." I shook my head. "If you think about it, it really hasn't been."

The memory shroud had been a complex one. Unlike the other memory shroud she cast on me, it didn't just change my memory of the lyrics of a song. Instead, it changed everything the song implied, it changed countless memories of our time together. It managed to conceal any similarity (eyes, hair, demeanor), anything that might connect Skylar and Valentine in my mind.

"So, you really are from the future," I said.

Valentine nodded. She closed her eyes briefly, then opened them and the tears were gone. "Now you're ready," she said. "Now that you have all your memories back, now that you know the truth, you're ready to face the Dragon."

4 - Things Fall Apart

With the revelation of Valentine's identity, and the knowledge the last several years of my life had been partially a lie, I should have gone back to my apartment. I needed to prepare for that night, for the arrival of the OneSpell, and as impressive as Jayden's hospitality was, a penthouse suite was not the place to do that.

But I was not in a logical frame of mind, so I went back to the suite at the Parthenia. It was empty, the others were either out gambling or eating, so I settled on one of the large couches by the windows overlooking the city.

The view was incredible. It felt like I wasn't actually in Las Vegas, but was looking at a postcard of it, or seeing the feed from a video camera. I was up above it, God's perspective, looking down.

A strange feeling welled up in me, a desire to talk to someone. It was like I had been keeping a secret for a long time, and suddenly realized there was no need to because the information couldn't hurt anyone anyways. I pulled out my cell phone and dialed a number that appeared in my mind.

"What is your status?" the voice on the other end asked.

"The OneSpell will appear tonight at midnight, at Club Heartbreak at Giza."

"Thank you for your cooperation." I heard the line go dead as Archmage Artimus Cantor hung up on his end.

The strange feeling disappeared. I stared at my phone. What had just happened? What had I just done?

With my magic sense I detected a presence behind me. I jumped up from the couch, spinning around. It was just T-Lock.

The middle-aged bodyguard looked at me with a smile, and my magical sense started to tingle again.

A voice came out of him that didn't sound quite like his own. "Club Heartbreak at midnight," he said. "My master will be most pleased to learn of this. But first, I must take care of you."

He cackled as his skin began to shimmer.

There was a bang, and his head exploded. His body was suspended in the air for a moment before it too keeled over onto the ground.

Standing behind where T-Lock had been was Jayden, holding a raised handgun.

"I never studied advanced magic," he said, "so this seemed like a quicker option."

He looked down at the body, which was bleeding all over a very expensive carpet.

"That's going to leave a stain," Jayden said.

Jayden arranged for the two of us to meet with Sorceress Valentine in a conference room at the Parthenia, just a couple floors below the suite. I had thought it strange when Jayden told me he would call Valentine (how did he have her number?), but I was still in shock at seeing my friend's bodyguard killed before my eyes. Besides, I had a feeling there was a lot I didn't know.

The conference room had a large table, built for twelve or more people, that seemed wasted with only three of us in there. There were floor to ceiling windows on one side that gave an amazing view, at least they would have except something had been done to the window to black them out, likely a temporary spell enacted during important meetings to prevent intrusions. To one side of the room was a large flatscreen TV, allowing for video conferencing with any Branch agents who happened to find themselves outside of Las Vegas. Inscribed on the table was an oversized branch mark, a circle with two vertical lines, and at the center a teleconference device. Better than any textbook, this room summed up the contradiction of the Branches, the mixture of the "old ways" with the modern society they depended on.

Valentine spoke first. "Let me guess. You ate something Artimus gave you."

Before I could respond, Jayden spoke. "First things first." Jayden dismissed the two guards (both actual wizards) with a gesture. "It's time for me to tell you the real reason I came on this trip."

"I know I promised an end to secrets," Valentine added. "Unfortunately it is time for me to reveal one more. I had hoped to keep Jayden's role in all this a secret, but now that Artimus Cantor knows when and where the OneSpell will appear, we must take action."

Valentine turned to Jayden. "You said your Branch had not been compromised by the Dragon."

"And you said your charms would allow me to detect the Dragon's minions," Jayden said. "It looks like we were both wrong."

Jayden turned back to face me. "If you feel I insinuated myself into this trip, it's because I did. Two months ago I received word from my Branch's leadership. They told me of the rumors that the OneSpell would appear soon. They also told me about your involvement in it.

"They knew you were a sorcerer, that you would be reluctant to discuss sensitive matters such as these with a wizard, so they thought I would be a compromise. Loyal enough to Branch Parthenia to report to them, but enough of an outcast that you would be able to identify with me. Of course, the fact we knew each other didn't hurt.

"If legend is to be believed, the OneSpell gives the person who wields it control over all creation. Obviously, Branch Parthenia has a vested interest in preventing that power from falling into Branch Shaskauer's hands."

In retrospect it made sense. Jayden's presence on this trip had seemed a little weird, and his supposedly estranged father letting us use a penthouse suite suddenly seemed more logical.

"So you want me to help Branch Parthenia get the OneSpell." Before he could respond, I added, "How is that any better than Branch Shaskauer getting a hold of it?"

For a moment I saw the old Jayden, the perpetual party-goer Jayden, beneath the exterior of the Branch Jayden to whom I was now talking. "Come on Roy," the old Jayden said. "Would you rather give it to some stuffy old Branch, or to me?"

"I may know you," I said. "And I know Sorceress Valentine has bad history with Branch Shaskauer. But this magic is too dangerous for any one person, or Branch, to control."

Jayden smiled. "You really are a sorcerer, aren't you?" He shook his head. "I won't bother trying to appeal to your self-interest, so I'll appeal to your interest in the fate of all of your kind.

"I have been authorized to offer you the following deal. If you give us the OneSpell, we will end the Tribute and the requirement that the Guild swear fealty to the Branches. Sorcerers will, in effect, be independent from the power structure of the Branches."

"And what about magicians?" I asked. "What about those who aren't even sorcerers?"

Jayden shook his head. "Magic is power, and we have to restrict that power. It is one thing for sorcerers to be independent of the Branches, but magicians are another thing entirely."

I thought back to when I first came to Vegas, to when Maria had worked so hard to try to get equal rights for magicians. Back then I could have cared less. Now here I was, years later, an inadvertent symbol of the anti-Branch elements of the Guild. And now Maria had a life of her own.

"I'll do it," I said. I looked around the table. "Now how is this going to work? Artimus knows where the OneSpell will appear. There's no way he'll let me anywhere near Giza."

"Simple," Jayden said. "Branch Parthenia, along with Sorceress Valentine, will stage a diversion. This will give you a chance to get into the club so that when the OneSpell appears at midnight, you can grab it."

Valentine cleared her throat.

"The Dragon will be drawn to the OneSpell, so as soon as it appears, he will appear as well, and you will have to face him. Facing him will be challenging enough. We do not want you to have to face Branch Shaskauer wizards at the same time."

"What type of diversion are we talking?" I asked.

Jayden spoke first. "I will take thirteen of my Branch's wizards, that's the most I can commit without violating the treaty that ended the Wizard War, and stage an attack on Giza."

"Meanwhile," Valentine said. "I will target the one thing just as important as the OneSpell. I will attack the Branch Shaskauer Archives."

"The Archives aren't even in the city," I said. "How will attacking them help us get control of Giza?"

Valentine explained. "As Archmage, and thus head of Shaskauer's security apparatus, Artimus will reduce the guards at any other location, including the Archives, to a bare minimum in order to secure Giza. In addition to normal security guards, he will probably have a hundred wizards at Giza tonight."

"Against which my wizards won't be able to do anything," Jayden said. "Not even cause a distraction."

"But, the Archives are his Branch's most precious resource," Valentine continued. "If Artimus receives word they are under attack, especially if he learns they are under attack by me, he will have no choice but to send some of his forces to defend them."

"Which will allow us to have a fighting chance," Jayden added.

"Even if your plan works," I said. "Will Jayden and his wizards be able to break through?"

"We'll be able to break through," Jayden said. "Parthenia beat Shaskauer during the war. Shouldn't be hard to do it again."

I took a deep breath. "So let me get this straight. Sorceress Valentine will attack the Branch Shaskauer Archives."

"I will do it at eleven thirty," Valentine said to Jayden. "It needs to be soon enough for Roy to get in before midnight, but not so soon they can deal with me, then return to Giza before then."

Jayden nodded in agreement.

"So Valentine will go out to the Shaskauer Compound and attack the Archives at eleven thirty. Back at Giza, Jayden and thirteen wizards will wait until we can see that Shaskauer forces are leaving the hotel to get to the Archives, and then they will attack."

"Don't call it an attack," Jayden said. "An attack would be a violation of the treaty. We're just going to escort you into a hotel." Jayden smiled. "If we happen to be attacked while escorting you, we will naturally have to defend ourselves."

"And while this is going on, I'm supposed to sneak into the hotel, go to Club Heartbreak, and somehow get everyone to leave the club. At that point the OneSpell will appear, and once it does, I have to fight an ancient demon who has been hunting the OneSpell for a thousand years and managed to infiltrate the entire magical community."

Jayden and Valentine looked at each other, then looked back at me.

"Defeat," Jayden said. "You have to *defeat* the demon."

"Well if that's all," I said. "What could possibly go wrong?"

As I left the meeting I turned my phone back on. I trusted Valentine and Jayden, to some extent, but I needed back-up just in case. So there was a phone call I had to make. I had a favor to call in, though it wasn't one I was ready to share with Valentine and Jayden. If the phone call worked, there was a possibility I might come out of the night victorious.

Before I could make the call, I noticed my phone showed eight missed calls, all of them from Skylar.

Rather than call Skylar back, I went straight to the suite a couple floors up. When the elevator doors opened, I found Skylar sitting on the couch in the living area, her arms circling her knees, which were curled up in front of her body. The room was in disarray, the cushions and decorative blankets littered across the floor.

As soon as she saw me, Skylar jumped up and ran over. "Where the hell have you been Roy?" she demanded. She looked as if she might punch me depending on my answer, so I chose my words carefully.

"I was in a meeting…"

Skylar cut off any further explanation. "Rico's gone."

"What do you mean he's gone?"

"He's gone, I can't find him." Skylar ran a hand through her hair and exhaled. "He said he was going downstairs to get a drink, and that was hours ago. I've been calling around and no one's seen him."

A thought occurred to me. This was the first time I had seen Skylar since Valentine's revelation about her identity earlier in the day. When Skylar dumped me, I had to reconcile the idea of someone I loved hurting me. Now I had to reconcile the idea of someone I loved hurting me, and then years in the future coming back in time and training me to be a sorcerer. They didn't make self-help books that addressed issues like this.

"So have you seen him?" Skylar asked, snapping me out of my nostalgia.

"No. I haven't seen him since Club Heartbreak last night."

Skylar crossed her arms. "If you don't like him, you can just say it," she said.

"What are you talking about?"

Skylar responded with an exaggerated sigh. "Why can't you just be happy for me Roy?"

"I am happy for you."

"You know, he's twice the boyfriend you ever were."

"What do you want me to say Skylar?"

Skylar stared me down. "I want you to admit you were a bad boyfriend, that you never showed me you loved me, and that you all around didn't deserve me."

"Maybe I never showed you I loved you because I never actually loved you. Did you ever consider that?"

"No!" she shouted. She was usually in control, usually too sarcastic to show pain, but now her emotions were ruling her. "No! You don't get to do that to me. You don't get to do that! You can't pretend what we had wasn't real."

"What does it matter to you?" I shouted back. "You're the one who broke us up."

Skylar's eyes went wide. She took a step closer, then another, until she was only inches away from me. "I'm the one who broke us up? I'm the one? Think about why we broke up."

"We broke up because you cheated on me."

Skylar tilted her head to the side, like she was examining an ancient artifact, trying to understand its significance.

"Is that really what you've been telling people Roy?" Skylar said. "Is that what you've been telling yourself? Think about our relationship, really think about it."

So I did. The whole time we were together I never did what Skylar told me to, but now that we had been apart for so long, I did it. I thought about us. Maybe it was the fact Valentine had removed the memory shroud, but everything about my time with Skylar suddenly seemed clearer, and I remembered us as we had actually been.

Memories still fresh in my mind, I stepped forward. I reached out my right arm and grabbed Skylar by the small of her back. I pulled her in while tilting my head down and kissed her. Skylar seemed startled at first, but then she kissed me back, pressing her body against me.

The kiss was short, it couldn't have lasted more than a second. But in that second there was an entire lifetime.

Skylar pulled away. She looked up into my eyes for a moment. Then she slapped me. Hard. I had never been slapped before, and it hurt more than I thought it would. The entire side of my face was on fire.

At that moment my phone chose to ring.

"Hello?" I answered. It hurt to open my mouth at first, but as I talked the pain faded.

"It's me." Maria didn't say her name. She didn't have to.

"What's wrong?" I asked. I could hear the terror in her voice.

"It's Derek," she said. "I can't find him anywhere."

"Can't find him?"

"He never came back to the hotel last night," she cried. "At least I don't think he did. I'm worried he might be passed out drunk somewhere."

If only we should be so lucky.

"Please Roy, could you help me look for him?" she said.

"Of course," I said. I hung up the phone.

I took a moment to compose myself. Skylar looked like she had calmed down, at least a little. She was standing off to the side, arms crossed again. She didn't look like she was planning another slap.

"I have to go," I said. "Maria can't find Derek."

"Derek?" Skylar screamed. "Maria's not with Derek. I'm with Rico. The fact I can't find Rico is alarming. The fact Maria can't find Derek is because he's just not that into her."

"Look. For all we know Derek and Rico are together, so if I find Derek I'll find him. Now, I'm going."

I turned and walked to the elevator. Skylar inhaled deeply. "You know what Roy?" she yelled after me. "The reason you can't get a girl is that no girl will ever live up to the image of Maria you have in your mind. And even if you find one, even if you get the wife, the job, the minivan, and the two point five kids, you will drop it all at a moment's notice to rescue Maria from whatever problem she wanders into."

The elevator door opened. I walked inside.

Unfortunately, Renée was waiting in the lobby as soon as the elevator doors opened.

"Roy," she said. "We need to talk about us."

"There is no us." It was a little more curt, a little more blunt, than I usually was (even with Renée). But I was in a hurry.

"We need to talk about last night, about what happened."

"Nothing happened," I said, exasperated.

Renée shook her head. "You can't deny that the two of us…"

"I cast a love spell on you."

It was a secret I had never meant to reveal, not to anyone and especially not to Renée. But somehow it just came out.

"What do you…"

"That night, the one we spent together," I said. "The only reason you slept with me was because I cast a love spell on you. And that's the only reason you've wanted me ever since."

Renée swallowed. Her eyes went wide. She spoke carefully, pausing between each word of her reply.

"You… cast… a… love… spell… on… me."

"Yes," I said. "I did."

There was a pause, all too brief.

"ARE YOU FREAKING SERIOUS!" Renée screamed. "THERE IS NO SUCH THING AS A LOVE SPELL!"

Some of the guests in the lobby stopped and turned at the sound of her outburst, but most kept walking. Emotional outbursts in the lobby were not noteworthy in Las Vegas.

I wasn't sure how to respond. "I understand this must be hard for you to accept."

"It's not hard for me to accept, it's impossible!" Renée sniffed, a snort that transformed into a bitter laugh. A tear came out. The laugh continued. "Come on Roy, you're…" she waved a hand at the length of my cloak, "you're a sorcerer for crying out loud, how can you not know the Aladdin rule?"

I thought for a moment. The Aladdin rule. It sounded familiar, but I couldn't think of what it was.

"The Aladdin rule?" I asked.

"Yes, the Aladdin rule!" Renée yelled. "If you had gotten a real degree in magic, you would have learned it on the first freaking day."

Renée looked up to the ceiling, as if it contained a textbook from which she could read. "The Aladdin rule, the only inviolable postulate of magic. No matter how powerful the magician, no matter how powerful the spell, there are three things magic cannot do, three boundaries that cannot be crossed.

"It cannot bring the dead back to life, it cannot give the Sign to those who were not born into it, and it cannot make someone fall in love. And that is why there is NO SUCH THING as a love spell!"

Renée stopped. I was silent. Part of me wondered how Valentine could have not realized the spell she taught me wasn't real. Another part of me knew Valentine's hand was, as always, in everything. The oversight on her part was likely intentional.

Renée sniffed again. "When I invited you into my hotel room Roy," she repressed another sob, "it wasn't because of a spell, it was because I love you."

I gulped. Renée waited for me to respond, but when I didn't, she continued talking.

"But that wouldn't matter to you Roy, would it?" she said. "You just do what you want."

"That's not fair." I regretted it the moment those three words leapt from my lips.

"Not fair?" Renée said. "It's completely fair." Renée was on a roll now, truth after truth spilling out of her mouth. "You act like you're so much better than everyone else, like you're the nice guy while every other guy out there is a jerk. But the truth is that you're a jerk too Roy Nakamura.

"Everything you do is about you. You want to be a sorcerer, you become a sorcerer. You want Maria to get hurt by a guy and come running to you, and it happens. You want to sleep with me, use me so you can have a warm body for one night, then cast me away the next, and it happens."

"Well what does that say about you Renée?" I said, cutting her off before she could cut me anymore. "If I'm such a jerk, then what does it say about you that you still want me?"

Renée sniffed. "I used to think beautiful things were simply beautiful, that they didn't have to have a meaning behind them to be appreciated. After a while, I started to believe there was no deeper meaning, that beauty is all there was.

"But you showed me I was wrong Roy. From the first time I met you, from the night we spent together after Black Sunday, you made me feel like life has meaning. You made me feel like the life I've lived has a purpose, like the love songs on the radio have a deeper meaning and aren't just empty words. You made me feel whole."

Renée raised a hand to her mouth, putting two fingers to her lips. She kissed them, in the process casting some minor illusion so I could visually see the imprint of the kiss, stuck there on her finger tips. Then she reached her fingers out, brushing them across my right cheek, and I could feel it, the kiss, stick there when she pulled her fingers away.

She shook her head. "And if only a jerk like you can make me feel whole, then yeah. I must be pretty pathetic, huh?"

Renée turned around and walked away.

5 – The End of the World

I spent the four hours before I had to meet Jayden looking everywhere for any sign of Derek or Rico. I should have been preparing for a duel with the fate of the world at stake, but instead I went from casino to casino, reaching out with magic for any sign of the two. I was sure Derek was shacked up in the hotel room of the ASU girl from the night before, and I didn't care where Rico was, but I tried my best anyways.

Eventually I was forced to admit defeat. I called Maria to tell her I hadn't been able to find Derek, but all I got was a busy tone. I didn't leave a message. There didn't seem to be a point.

I was so distracted, I didn't notice the phone calls, emails, and good old fashioned letters, along with more subtle magical forms of communication, that spread like wildfire across the denizens of Vegas' magical underground.

Throughout the city, a call went out for magicians, those true servants of magic who had refused to ally with wizards or sorcerers, to gather for a march down the Strip. It would be a rally to end all rallies, a protest that would outdo even the events of Black Sunday. The message said Sorceress Corinna Windlass had returned, and she was ready to lead her magical children to victory.

When I arrived at the parking structure of Merlin's Dream, located strategically across the street from Giza, Jayden was already there with an assortment of wizards. Instead of their normal white leather jackets and pants, they had form fitting black jackets barely visible at night. Branch marks blended into their necks in the dim lighting of the structure.

They looked like a SWAT team, or more precisely I realized, this is what wizards looked like before carrying out a night raid. But this time they wouldn't be raiding the home of a defenseless magician, they would be fighting fellow wizards.

I looked out over the edge of the parking structure to the front of Giza. To the untrained observer, it looked like Branch Shaskauer had beefed up security, slightly, for the New Year's Eve festivities. With my magic trained eyes, I could see a ring of wizards arrayed around the entrances to the casino. They were casting a glamour so most party-goers couldn't see them (not that they would care in their intoxicated state). There were at least a hundred, almost every wizard loyal to Branch Shaskauer. They were augmented by scores of unSigned security.

I fingered a token around my neck, a new one Valentine gave me earlier that day before I departed the meeting with her and Jayden. Similar to one of the three around her neck, it bore the image of a unicorn. "You are preparing to face the Dragon in an effort to guard the OneSpell from evil," Valentine had told me. "It is time you wore the token of those who do the same."

"You ready?" It was Jayden. I nodded, and he made a gesture towards the Parthenia wizards.

We all climbed up and stood, in a line, at the edge of the parking structure.

"You know how to do a long jump, right?" asked Jayden.

"Please." I tried to inject a little humor into a deadly serious situation. "I'm an EndGame champion. Wizards aren't the only ones with magic."

Jayden's watch beeped. Eleven thirty. It was time. Down below, nothing changed.

"Sorceress Valentine should be starting her assault," Jayden said.

We continued to wait. One minute, then two minutes went by.

"What do we do Roy?" Jayden asked. "Something should be happening by now."

It was eleven thirty-five. Only twenty-five minutes remained until the OneSpell would appear.

"Why are you asking me?" I said.

"You're the one who knows Sorceress Valentine."

I shook my head. "No one knows Sorceress Valentine."

The seconds kept ticking.

"We're going to have to abort," Jayden said. "Find another way into the casino."

"One more minute," I said. "Valentine may be many things, but if she said she'd come through, she'll come through."

As if on cue, there was a commotion on the street below us. Wizards started talking to each other, momentarily de-glamouring so they could run towards each other and speak in terse whispers. There was a debate of some kind. A convoy of black SUVs pulled up to the curb. I watched as ten, then twenty, then thirty wizards jumped into the vehicles.

As they drove away into the densely packed New Year's Eve traffic on the Strip, I looked at Jayden. "Valentine did her job."

Jayden shook his head. "Not well enough. There are still at least fifty wizards down there, not to mention the security. That's way more than we can handle."

"We don't have a choice, this is the best chance we'll get," I hissed. "Valentine won't be able to fight them at the Archives for long, and as soon as she leaves, they'll come back here. It's now or never."

Jayden was right. There was no way our attack would be successful. But we had to try. I stood tall, took a step towards the edge, and prepared to jump.

Then I heard another noise coming from down the street.

"Do you hear that?" Jayden asked.

The noise resolved itself into voices, hundreds, thousands of voices, marching down the Strip, towards Giza. They were chanting slogans, waving banners, casting magical fireworks into the chill air.

At the head of the march, at least ten yards in front of the pack, strode the defiant figure of Sorceress Corinna Windlass.

The guards outside Giza grew nervous. They had been anticipating an attack from me, maybe even from Branch Parthenia, but they were not prepared for a thousand angry magicians.

Calling out orders, they deployed across the Strip, stopping traffic and preparing to block the path of the marchers. Corinna summoned a colossal amount of magic. I could sense it all the way from my perch on the roof of the parking structure across the street. She reached out her hand.

A single wizard approached Corinna. "In the name of Branch Shaskauer, stop your…"

Magic flew out of Corinna's hand and blasted the wizard into the pavement. She readied another blast and hurled it at the mass of wizards and security guards.

Several of them fell over, while several others unhitched swords or handguns from their belts. With a bellow, the mass of protestors began to run, and collided with the front ranks of the Shaskauer security apparatus.

"I take it back," I said in awe, staring at the raging chaos below us. "*This* is the best chance we'll get."

Jayden nodded in agreement. As one, we all jumped off the ten story parking structure and plummeted towards the sidewalk below. The wind whistled loudly, and I experienced a moment of primal fear from the sensation of falling. A dozen feet from the ground, our magic kicked in and we decelerated until we landed firmly on the sidewalk.

Despite the chaos around us, the Shaskauer wizards noticed the arrival of new magical forces to the battle. Even as we landed I sensed Shaskauer wizards converging on our position.

Jayden and the thirteen Parthenia wizards fanned out, forming a wedge around me as I ran towards the entrance to the casino. Those Shaskauer wizards not involved in quelling the rally-turned-riot started to attack us, but the Parthenia wizards shielded me.

We were a loose group, separating each time we ran through a group of battling protestors and security guards, then coalescing together once we were through. Attacks by security guards were quickly fought off, but each time a wizard attacked us we were forced to leave one of our own behind to guard our rear.

The group got smaller. There were just two wizards still running with me. I didn't know what had happened to Jayden. A dozen yards from the giant glass doors at the entrance to the casino, both wizards peeled off and shot fire to the rear, guarding my exit.

I made it two more steps before a large mass slammed into my side. I landed rough on the concrete. My left shoulder felt like it had been crushed in a vice. I tried to stand up, but immediately felt a body holding me down.

Looking up I saw a wizard, not much older than me, with the symbol of Branch Shaskauer on his neck. My arms were both pinned behind me. I started to whisper a spell, hoping that if I could properly master the *aetas*, then I'd be able to cast it even without the use of my hands.

"Die sorcerer scum," he said, raising his right hand to cast a spell.

A massive gust of wind hit him from the side. He fell to the ground, passed out.

I pushed myself up to a sitting position. Standing just a few feet away was Renée Winters. Instead of her usual fashionable threads, she wore practical jeans and a hooded sweatshirt. She was indistinguishable from any of the other protestors. Her arm was still upraised, as if the force of casting the wind spell had frozen her in place. I stood up, only a little wobbly, and nodded at her in thanks.

"Run!" she screamed, before twirling around and shooting another gust of wind at an approaching security guard.

Turning, I sprinted the last couple feet before the glass doors at the entrance to the casino. With a push, I was through and into the building.

I ran through the lobby. Two security guards came at me from the right, each carrying fierce looking firearms. With a quick spell, both guards fell to the ground. As I cast a spell causing both guns' barrels to melt closed, I noted these were not standard issue weapons for casino security guards. Artimus was ready for me.

People in the lobby, most of them panicked at the riot unfolding outside, stared at me as I ran through. Then a large explosion sounded from outside the casino, and I became just another headless chicken in the chaos that was the hotel lobby.

I was almost across the lobby, in view of the staircase that would take me up to Club Heartbreak. Just ahead of me, a wizard stepped in front of the staircase and cast a barrier in front of me. Mentally conjuring up a counterspell, I wordlessly ran through the barrier and threw a ball of fire at the wizard. He jumped out of the way of the fire and I was on the stairs.

A couple steps up, I took a moment to turn and look back. The wizard had gotten to his feet and seemed to be preparing another spell. I hit him with a blast of magic that would freeze him for at least a couple minutes, then put a barrier of my own at the bottom of the stairs to prevent anyone from following me. The sound of the battle outside the casino escalated.

The usual guards at the entrance to Club Heartbreak were gone, deployed to join the fight outside. The doors were wide open and unattended. Above the entrance hung the same sign as the night before, inviting me in to celebrate the End of the World. I ran through unimpeded, my sorcerer's cloak billowing in the nonexistent wind.

Inside the club, it was just another New Year's Eve. Patrons danced, drank, and flirted, as Outkast's *B.O.B.* drowned out any noise from the battle.

I walked down the stairs and onto the dance floor, annoying those trying to dance when I pushed them aside. I ignored them, closed my eyes, and focused on the room around me. My mind searching it like a pair of search lights, I found what I was looking for and cast a spell.

Simultaneously and without warning, every single piece of electrical equipment in the club died. The music cut off mid-note. People were silent at first, then started to talk in confusion. Red emergency lights came on and the panicked club-goers began to exit the club.

I checked my watch as the last of the revelers departed. It was eleven fifty, still ten minutes until the OneSpell would appear. The club was empty, all except for a solitary figure leaning against a railing on the other side of the room.

I walked towards the figure, navigating my way around the bar at the center of the dance floor, as he straightened up. I stopped when I was still several feet away, because in the dim light of Club Heartbreak's emergency flashers, I could see the figure's face.

Standing in front of me was none other than Derek Hastings.

"Surprised?" he asked, in a voice at once deeper and more forceful than the one I was used to. As much of a jerk as Derek had acted before, I could tell the creature before me was much, much worse.

"Not really," I replied.

"You lie," laughed the demon known as the Dragon. "I can smell the fear pouring out of you, just as I can hear your heart beating faster."

"How long have you possessed him?" I asked.

"This, thing?" said the Dragon. "I found him over a year ago. He was in this exact club, in fact. His body was strong, and his mind was weak." The demon grinned. "The perfect combination."

The way the Dragon was standing was also different than Derek. The real Derek gave off the perpetual air of an investor appraising livestock, upright and aloof. This creature was in a slight crouch, a warrior's pose. He looked at ease, but I knew he was ready to strike at any moment.

"Besides," said the Dragon. "I have heard of you Sorcerer Roy Nakamura. I have been waiting for you. Sorceress Valentine thought she was so clever, thought she could hide you, that I wouldn't know she was training you to fight me. But I knew. I have always known.

"So when I needed to find a new body, I was sure to find one close to you. Besides, I could not pass up the opportunity to make you fight the body of your friend."

It was my turn to smile. "You are wrong demon, that body you possess is no friend of mine."

The Dragon shrugged. "Is that so? Well what about this one?" The Dragon reached down and grasped what at first looked like a sack of laundry. On closer inspection it was a body curled at his feet. He picked it up by its hair and raised it a couple feet, allowing me to see the face, before letting it drop to the floor.

It was Rico. Rather than fear, or any related emotion, my immediate reaction was contempt for Skylar. I had been right after all. Rico was with Derek.

"I was going to use this other one as a shield." The Dragon gestured at Rico's slumped over body. "But instead, I'll turn this into a game. Or should I say a promise."

The Dragon grinned, a wicked grin that revealed, once and for all, that Derek was being inhabited by a soul even more evil than himself. "After I kill you, I will dispose of this body too."

I squared off and used a quick calming spell to stop the tingling at the ends of my nerves. I thought back to my first duel ever, the one with Karl. I had been confused then, scared, unsure. Now, despite years of training, part of me was still all those things.

I reached back my hand, and let out a stream of darts that flew towards the Dragon. I was concerned, for just a second, that the only way to kill the Dragon might be to kill the body it was possessing. But the fate of the world was at stake. If a single not-so-innocent life was the price of saving the world, so be it.

The spell I cast was Dante's Dart, designed to shred the flesh of all but the most skilled shield caster. I had never used it in a duel. It was frowned upon to permanently injure an opponent, and this spell would have killed most.

The Dragon didn't run, or dodge, or cast a counter-spell. Instead, he just stood there. When they were inches from his face, the darts froze, like flies caught in a web. The darts stayed there, frozen in the air, for a moment, before clattering to the ground.

The Dragon laughed. "Now it's my turn." A mighty wind swept in through the entrance of Club Heartbreak and surrounded the Dragon's body. I could sense magic greater than any I had ever encountered as Derek's body began to contort and change.

The magical energies being exerted literally knocked me to the ground. I scooted back until I hit the bar, and pushed myself up to a standing position.

Crouched in front of me, where Derek had been standing, was a dragon. In the past, the lesser demons I fought had always referred to their master as "the Dragon." I had assumed it was a title, or a nickname, or a metaphor. I was wrong.

The Dragon before me was definitely not a metaphor. It was gigantic, everything storybooks had taught me to expect, but far more terrifying. A massive tyrannosaurus-like body was connected to two giant wings, folded in to avoid striking the walls of the suddenly cramped club. Its scales were a pure black that sucked in the scant light around it. There were immense muscles hidden underneath the scales, rippling each time the Dragon moved.

A fearsome head at the end of the long neck twisted towards me, and with a rush of magic, it breathed fire.

I was already running. The column of flame slammed into the wall of the bar behind me. I had dealt with magic fire my entire time as a sorcerer, but this was something different. It was natural, real, as if flames could become solid and thrown in a single direction.

I pivoted and cast a series of my own fireballs before turning and continuing to run. I cut right and ran up a short series of steps into the ring of VIP tables. Behind me my fireballs bounced harmlessly off of the Dragon.

There was a loud creak and a groan as the Dragon took gigantic deliberate steps towards my side of the club. Dante's Dart had been useless against the Dragon's human body, so there was no way it would work on the monstrosity now in front of me. There was only one way to know what spell to cast. Ask the magic itself.

Mumbling words, I reached out with my magic and cast the wave watching spell I had been working on, the one that would help me predict not the actions of cards, but the fighting style of the Dragon. Probability waves streamed from the world around me into my mind.

The Dragon could sense magic. There was no other explanation for why, as soon as I cast the wave watching spell, it tilted its head in a confused manner.

Without knowing why, I reached out my magic and cast an ice wall to my right. That moment a column of fire erupted in that direction. The Dragon had jumped to the other side and breathed fire at me. The ice wall was destroyed, but it had slowed down the fire enough to save me.

I cast a confusion spell, filling the club with flashing white light. I took off running down the row of VIP tables, depending on the light to cover my tracks. The wave watching spell told me to suddenly stop, which I did, just as dragon fire demolished the area into which I was about to run.

I jumped off the VIP area back onto the club dance floor, spinning around to fire a flight of metal darts directly at the Dragon's face. They bounced off of the scales surrounding his blood red eyes.

I took a running jump and sailed over the bar. Fire consumed the area where I had been. I stood up behind the bar and turned to face my enemy. The Dragon was now up in the ring of VIP tables, crushing chairs and couches beneath its feet, turning its head towards me.

I picked up a bottle of liquor and threw it at the Dragon, using magic to ignite it as it sailed across the distance between us. The bottle exploded when it crashed against the Dragon's face. There was a flicker of pain. I grabbed more bottles and threw one after another, igniting each one.

Shaking off its head, the Dragon roared and breathed fire at me. Quickly I ducked behind the bar for cover. When I peaked above the bar wall, I saw the Dragon readying another salvo of flame.

I threw up an ice wall connecting the bar to the far wall of the dance floor and started to run away from the bar, using the wall as cover. I turned around just as I reached the wall. The Dragon breathed fire at the bar, at where I had been seconds before, and it exploded.

Overhead, every single sprinkler on the ceiling went off. The red emergency lights cast eerie shadows through the falling water that I might have considered beautiful in other circumstances. The Dragon bellowed with rage as the falling water put out the miniature fires throughout the club.

Taking advantage of the distraction, I ran back onto the dance floor. Reaching out with magic, I attempted to acquire the Dragon to see if I could lift him up and smash him against the floor.

The Dragon noticed my magical attempt and shot fire in my direction. Even with the water coming down, the fire burned bright and I had to run to avoid being burned.

We went back and forth, spell after spell. The wave watching spell kept me alive, kept me one step ahead of the Dragon, but nothing I could do affected him. Every spell bounced off him, every magical trick I had picked up in my years of dueling had little or no effect on this magical creature from beyond my worst nightmare.

Meanwhile, I was getting tired. Every physical spell left me more and more drained. The Dragon didn't seem to be weakening, and I knew I couldn't keep this up for long.

The water from the fire sprinklers trickled to a stop, whatever reservoir that filled them finally out of water. I leaned against the wall of the dance floor, panting and soaking wet. The Dragon stopped and looked at me with two flaming red eyes.

"Foolish little sorcerer," the Dragon yelled. "You cannot destroy me, you cannot win! Even if you destroy this body, I will simply possess another. Maybe I will even possess you!"

The Dragon reared itself on two hind legs, barely able to stand without hitting the ceiling of the club, and stared down at me. Its serpentine tongue darted out of its mouth and hissed.

"It is almost midnight little sorcerer," the Dragon bellowed. "So before then, I will give you a final chance, I will let you try a final time to defeat me."

I was out of ideas. The world's most powerful spells, which I had spent years memorizing and perfecting, were useless. And the Dragon was right. Even if I managed to destroy its body, I could not kill its magical essence.

How could you kill an entity of pure magic? With that question, memories flooded unbidden into my mind.

I thought back to the time I had gone to Magic Haven with Maria when I went back to my high school for Homecoming during my freshman year of college. Except it hadn't been Maria, it had been Skylar. And we looked at old manuscripts, and one of them featured the image of a knight with a blue lance fighting a dragon.

That was it. That was what Valentine had been trying to teach me. The words, the gestures, all they did was put the caster into the right frame of mind. The true essence of magic was the *aetas*, the correct mental state. You didn't need to know the right words, or the right gesture. True magic envisioned the spell, then used the magic to cast it.

Holding my palms together, I concentrated for a moment, then spoke in a firm even tone, just loud enough for the Dragon to hear. "I summon… Merlin's Lance."

The Dragon laughed. "Foolish little sorcerer, I have been following you, tracking you, spying on you, ever since you first came to Las Vegas. Did you really think I would not have heard of your battle against Wizard Karl Johnsen and how you beat him?"

In front of me a ball of blue flame appeared. A second later it started to stretch. It was spinning along its axis, and with each spin it got a little longer, a little more solid. After another second it was a foot long, thin like a pole, and aimed directly at the Dragon.

"Do you expect to hit me with a table?" said the Dragon. "Do you think to win with the same trick twice?"

I looked up at the Dragon, and in its eyes I saw nothing but hate. I yelled. "MERLIN'S LANCE!"

Blue fire exploded out of the pole. In the split second before it hit him, the Dragon breathed out fire towards it. The blue fire of the spell and the red fire of the Dragon met halfway, consuming each other. I pushed harder with Merlin's Lance, and the Dragon breathed out more fire, until the two colors consumed the room.

I started to give way, my physical limitations finally catching up to me, and the Dragon's fire came closer to the source of my own. I tried reaching within me for strength, but there was none left. I thought of the world I had to save, I thought of my friends, thought of those back in Los Angeles. With each second, the border between the blue fire and the Dragon's fire got closer to me.

I thought of Independence Day, 1998, when I drove Maria out into the desert to see the fireworks. I had driven over ninety miles an hour while Maria sang along to the radio.

From deep inside me, I pushed one final time. There was no strength left, but somehow I pushed, and pushed, and pushed. In that instant, the blue fire from Merlin's Lance overwhelmed the Dragon's fire, surrounding him in a bright blue light.

The Dragon tilted back its head and roared an unearthly and unholy scream. With my magic, I could see the body of the Dragon was not being harmed, but the magical creature within was trying to fight off the one spell in the world that could do it harm.

The Dragon made a last effort to remain intact, but it failed. One moment the creature was there, the next it was ripped apart by the pure blue fire. As the body of the Dragon continued to scream, energy exploded throughout the room.

All alone, away from the adorations of his minions and the spoils of his Atlantian kingdom, the demon who had once been Trannanir Shaskauer screamed and died. Merlin's Lance, the lost spell that only affected magic, had destroyed him while leaving the physical body he inhabited intact.

The body of a dragon lay on the ground, and as the last vestiges of the demon inside it died, the body started to shrink, change, until it was once again Derek Hastings.

The clock struck midnight. Everywhere else, people were celebrating the New Year. And against all odds, I had lived to see it.

I was pulled out of these melancholy thoughts by a bright light that appeared in front of me. There was no warning (in retrospect I don't know what I expected), just a bright light hanging in the middle of the room. The light dimmed as I walked closer. It was an amulet, just as the legends said it was, suspended in the air.

The amulet started to move away from me. I followed the amulet as it floated through the burnt out husk of Club Heartbreak, past the giant door now open and abandoned. It went into a utility staircase, and I had to run to keep up with it as it floated up two flights of stairs and out a door.

It was a couple yards ahead of me by the time I exited the door and found myself on the roof of the Giza casino. The New Year was only a couple minutes old. There were still thousands, hundreds of thousands, of revelers out in the streets, not to mention echoes of a massive battle still going on below, the fight between Shaskauer security and Magic First still permeating the air with magic.

The amulet hung there, floating four feet in the air, the majestic city of Las Vegas laid out behind it. I stepped towards it and reached out my hand.

"If you would not mind, Sorcerer Roy Nakamura, please refrain from taking any additional steps towards the amulet."

I turned towards the voice. I had expected a horde of Shaskauer wizards to descend on me, and was frankly surprised they hadn't done so already. Instead of a horde there was just one. It was Archmage Artimus Cantor, looking more violent than usual in his wizard's jacket.

The handgun in his right hand was pointed directly at me, and I had no doubt he would use it.

6 - OneSpell

There were no birds this high up, but for a moment I thought I could hear them.

"Have you ever wondered why wizards carry guns?" Artimus asked. He pulled back the hammer with his thumb.

"We magic users always emphasize how powerful magic is. But half the time, good old swords and guns work just as well. During the war, just as many wizards were killed with bullets as with spells. And I am betting that whatever spell you are thinking of right now is not fast enough to take effect during the time between my pulling the trigger and a metal slug embedding itself in your chest. Not even you, Roy, are that fast."

My eyes were drawn to a shiny piece of metal around Artimus' neck. If it hadn't been on a wizard, I would have thought it to be a token. Artimus was just close enough for me to see the image of a dragon engraved onto the metal.

Artimus noticed my gaze. "I know you defeated my master," he said. "I felt the loss of power when he was destroyed. No matter, I have all the power now."

"You were working for the Dragon all along," I said. "You spelled me to find out where the OneSpell would appear, and then you passed it on to him."

"You would be surprised how many wizards swore their allegiance to him," Artimus said. "Come tomorrow morning, there will be a great deal of soul searching within the Branches. But it is of no matter. I have what I came for."

The sound that I thought was birds grew louder, sharper. It wasn't birds, it was a helicopter.

"Why is it you want the OneSpell so badly?" I asked.

"It gives the user power over everything," Artimus said. "It is the birthright of Branch Shaskauer, of my Branch. Why would I not want it?"

"I don't think that's it," I said. I looked at the amulet, floating inches from my grasp. "I think it's something else."

"Stop trying to stall," Artimus said. He placed his left hand under his right one, steadying the handgun and continuing to point it at me. "Back away from the amulet."

"You just want to fit in." The sound of the helicopter grew louder. "But you're never going to. Because you're not Atlantian, and without that Atlantian blood, those who follow the old ways will never let you become one of them. They may fear you, but they'll never respect you."

The helicopters were almost deafening now, drowning out my thoughts.

"Your stalling is pointless." Artimus' voice was full of contempt. "I can take that amulet out of your dead hands just as easily."

Four intense beams of light caught the two of us in their cross hairs.

"Put down the weapon," yelled a magically enhanced voice. A dozen wizards, fully decked out in battle gear and bearing the mark of Branch Merkasia on their necks, jumped down onto the roof.

Archmage Artimus Cantor bent down and laid his handgun on the ground. Somehow, he managed to make even that gesture of defeat seem regal.

While eleven of the wizards formed a circle around Artimus, hands raised, ready to fire spells at him, one wizard walked over to me.

"I was wondering when you were going to show up," I said to Wizard Karl Johnsen.

"I said we would show up, and we showed up," he said. He was still the same jerk I had dueled years ago. "I fail to see what the problem is."

"No problem," I said. "And I guess we're even now."

"Even?" Karl said in surprise. "I was obligated to perform a favor. I saved you from an Archmage, I think that makes us even. Now, it's time for me to take what is mine."

A dozen wizards fixed their magical gaze on me, preparing spells of combat.

The glittering object was still floating in front of me. There was no time to cast a shield spell, no time to think about my actions.

I reached out and grasped the floating amulet.

Everything was white. Everything. Whiteness surrounded me. It was like a white room, but there was no floor, or ceiling, or walls, just pure whiteness everywhere. My first thought was that I must be dead. I tried reaching out with my magical sense, trying to see where I was, what had become of the OneSpell.

Magic was everywhere. The whiteness was magic. The whiteness was the OneSpell. It was all so confusing I had to stop to process it. I reached out with my magical ability again.

I was inside the OneSpell. I had touched the amulet, absorbed the spell into me (or the spell had absorbed me into it), and I was frozen in the act of casting the spell. This new reality was my brain's way of trying to understand it. And there was more. Sorceress Corinna Windlass always preached that Magic had a consciousness, an awareness. She had been right, and that awareness was somehow tied up in the OneSpell. The OneSpell didn't just give the user control over magic, somehow it *was* magic.

The lack of a ground, or walls, was disconcerting. My mind grasped for a frame of reference. The whiteness around me coalesced into shapes. The area below me became a floor of gray tiled stones while the area above became blue sky. A forest of pillars sprouted up around me, then buildings formed beyond the pillars. Within moments (figuratively speaking, time was meaningless here), I was standing in the courtyard of an ancient Atlantian villa. I had never seen one of course, no one living had, but the knowledge of the OneSpell enabled me to see it for what it was.

The floor was a mosaic made up of different shades of gray. It was more complex than any I had seen before, yet somehow I had created it. At the center of the courtyard was a large pool of water with a fountain in the center. There were buildings to one side. I knew they were empty, just husks of buildings created for my visual enjoyment, but I also knew that if I wanted I could fill those buildings with anything I could dream of, so boundless were the limits of the OneSpell.

"Interesting choice."

The source of the voice was a figure winding its way towards me through the pillars. The figure emerged from the pillars so I could see her clearly.

"I see you made it," said the figure with a smile.

It was Valentine. Sorceress Valentine was standing there, waiting for me, inside the OneSpell. No matter what happened, she never stopped surprising me.

"Valentine?" I asked. "Or Skylar?"

"No," she said. "I am just a shade of the woman you know, or knew, or will know. Anyone who touches the OneSpell also becomes part of the OneSpell. And so here I am."

I looked around again at my surroundings. It was deathly quiet, and I thought it should have the sound of birds to be more realistic. No sooner did I think it, then I was able to hear birds around me.

"Did I do that?" I asked the shade of Valentine.

"You did all of this." She gestured at the forest of columns and the buildings beyond them. "You pulled this place out of your memory, out of the memories the OneSpell gave you, when your mind was trying to create a safe place for you where you could process the OneSpell."

I reached out magically. The shade was right, the OneSpell was still there. Just as when I was in the plane of pure whiteness, the spell was all around, except now it took the form of an ancient Atlantian villa.

Experimentally, I reached out to touch the spell around me. It was like pushing against a brick wall to see how solid it was, placing a hand against one brick at a time to see how securely they were placed. Then, I pushed against a brick that moved.

I am looking down at two wizards dragging a large bundle between them. They throw the bundle down onto the cold marble floor. It moves. It pushes itself to a sitting position, and I see that it is wearing a sorcerer's cloak.

"Ark'Telga," the first wizard says. "We brought the one you were looking for."

They are talking to me! I am sitting on a throne, high up, looking down at the two wizards and a frail sorcerer between them. I raise a hand and make a downward chopping motion.

The words are in a deeper, older, voice, but they scream out of my mouth. "Death to all enemies of the Branch!"

I was back in the villa. My head was reeling from what I had just seen. I tried to focus, to understand it, but suddenly…

I am sitting at a blackjack table. It is late at night, or early morning, the casino floor is almost deserted. I reach out a frail hand and place a single red chip into the betting circle.

"Are you sure about that old timer?" the dealer asks. "That's your last one."

"I have a good feeling about it," I say.

Once again I was jolted back into the folds of the OneSpell, the shade of Valentine staring at me.

"What was that?" I asked.

"You know what it was," she said. "The answers are already inside you. I am only here to help you put them into words."

Reaching out with magic, I studied the spell more carefully, taking caution not to push too hard lest I trigger another flash.

The structure of the spell, the core of the OneSpell's essence, was a wave watching spell. It was so complicated, so powerful, that at first glance it bore no resemblance to the spells I cast while playing blackjack, or used to fight the Dragon. But at its root, its core, the same basic structure was there.

Someone without training in wave watching might not have noticed the similarity, might not have been able to understand and thus wield the spell, but that was not the case with me. I felt the explanation for the spell's existence washing over me, like it was a page from a history book being read by an old professor.

The OneSpell was the ultimate wave watching spell. Instead of seeing probability waves for which card would land next, or seeing which move an opponent would throw in a duel, I could see the probability waves for everything. *Everything!*

"Those visions I keep having," I said. "Those are the future."

"Possible futures," said Valentine's shade.

"Well which one is the actual future, the one that will come true?"

"The OneSpell has two functions," she replied. "The first is to let you see possible futures, see the ramifications of your actions. Before you leave you can choose a future, and when you leave, you step into that future."

I focused on the shade again. "What did you mean when you said you were here because you had touched the OneSpell before?"

"She never told you?" Valentine said. She looked at me, and I instinctually knew this shade, this manifestation that was part of the OneSpell and also my own subconscious, was scanning my memories.

The task complete, she explained. "In my timeline, we didn't break up after college, we broke up after your first year of law school during summer break."

"So I went to law school?" I asked.

Valentine nodded. "You were a great student, but you felt life as a lawyer wasn't for you, so you decided to go to Las Vegas to become a wizard. You broke up with me and moved to Las Vegas. At first you couldn't get admitted to any of the wizard training programs, but then you reconnected with Jayden, an old friend from college, and he got you a position as an apprentice to Branch Parthenia."

Even with all the knowledge of the OneSpell, this seemed implausible.

"I was a wizard?" I said.

The shade of Valentine nodded. "You were the greatest. Your magical ability was off the charts, and you quickly rose through the ranks to become Archmage of Branch Parthenia." The shade of Valentine tightened her mouth. "You married Maria."

"I did?"

Valentine nodded again. "You don't understand though Roy. You got everything you ever wanted. You became a wizard, then Archmage, but it destroyed you. You became an alcoholic, a gambling addict. Your children hated you."

"We had children?"

"You used your power as Archmage to start a second Wizard War, and even though you won, thousands died in the process. Meanwhile, I went to Las Vegas. I had always been fascinated with the city, and after we broke up, I thought... why not. I became an apprentice, then a sorceress, and in my timeline I was the one groomed to fight the Dragon and take control of the OneSpell."

"And did you?"

"I did," Valentine said. "But just like with you, getting that dream wasn't enough. As leader of the Branches, you cracked down on sorcerers and magicians, grinding them into the dust far worse than anything you've seen in your timeline. The Sorcerers Guild knew about my powers, so they sent me back in time."

"To convince me to join your side?"

She shook her head. "I was sent back in time to kill you Roy. To prevent the second Wizard War and the purge that followed. I went to the Arabian Nights casino, to the blackjack table where I knew you would be. But when I saw you, it all came back. So I came up with another plan. I decided to groom you, instead of me, to be the one to take the OneSpell."

"Why?" I asked.

"Because of what the OneSpell showed me back when I touched it."

The shade of Valentine reached out and grabbed my arm.

I am standing on a raised stage. It is the main chamber room at Magic Hall. The chamber room itself is filled with sorcerers cheering my name. I look to my left and see Valentine, or is it Skylar, standing there holding my hand.

"Sorcerers!" I call out. "Today we celebrate the end of the reign of terror of the Branches!"

More cheering. Skylar squeezes my hand, and I'm struck by how beautiful her smile is, how majestic

Gesturing behind me, I continue to speak. "Behold the source of your terror, brought to his knees by the might of the Sorcerers Guild."

Behind me is Jayden Parthenia, tied to a stake, bleeding profusely from a hundred cuts on his body.

"Now watch, as the last wizard dies," I say, casting a ball of magical fire at Jayden's bleeding figure. His screams are drowned out by the cheers around me.

"Another possible future?" I asked.

"It's the future you could have," she said. "A future with me."

"But it's a future where I killed all the wizards," I said. "How is that any better than your timeline. And Jayden? What did he ever do?"

"He is a wizard, of the Branches," the shade of Valentine insisted. "His death is unfortunate, but it is a necessity. If any member of a Branch survived, they would eventually challenge you, and war would continue."

"There has to be another way," I said.

"There is not," the shade said. "Wizards and sorcerers cannot exist in the same future. From the very moment that Atlantis sank and Atlantians made their way into the rest of the world, teaching non-Atlantians magic in the process, they were destined to destroy one another. And with you in the mix, a magic user with almost unlimited power, there can be no neutrality. Whichever side you choose will prosper over the other."

I kept looking, kept examining possible future after possible future, ignoring the shade's insistence.

"It is time for you to choose, Roy. A life as a wizard, or a life as a sorcerer? A life with Maria, or a life with me?"

I looked at all my possible futures, one by one. The shade was right, most fell into those two camps. Wizard or sorcerer. Maria or Skylar. The only exceptions were a few that ended with me prematurely dead or in jail. And even those ended in war and tragedy for all those I loved.

Then I found it. There was another future. A way for there to be peace, a way for everyone to win. Everyone but me.

Reaching out with my magic, I was aware of the frozen reality outside the OneSpell. Using some effort, I could sense the entirety of Las Vegas, of the world, outside this fake villa I had created. There were thousands of minds out there close enough that they could be swayed or influenced.

"You told me the OneSpell has two functions," I said. "The first is to view possible futures and pick one. What is the second?"

"You already know the answer to that," the shade of Valentine said.

I did. "The second function is far more powerful," I said. "It lets me influence the minds of magic users, all magic users, and create a new future instead of simply choosing one."

"Anyone who is Signed, anyone who is within the reach of magic, can be changed," said the shade of Valentine. "But there is a price for using this second function."

"I know," I replied.

And I did. As soon as she said the words, I could see it, the failsafe Mianna had sewn into the essence of the OneSpell. It was one thing to use the spell to view possible futures, or to fling it a thousand years in the future. But actually casting it, actually using it to influence the world, would require something very specific.

"Are you sure you can pay that price?" Valentine asked.

Ignoring her, I planned my path carefully. I used the wave watching abilities granted to me to plan the way to cast the OneSpell just right so it would accomplish my aims in the present, would touch a thousand people in a thousand subtle ways, then fling itself into the future to where someone more deserving than I was destined to find it.

This task required all my concentration. It would have taken me a hundred years to do the mental calculations, but here in the OneSpell time was meaningless. As I immersed myself in the task, I lost focus on the artificial world I had created around me. Everything began to shake. The conjured pillars toppled over and crumbled. In the distance, one of the fake buildings exploded into dust. Even the tiled floor below me cracked and splintered.

The shade of Valentine lost her physical form, fading away as the buildings crumbled into dust. But I could still sense her presence, and I could still hear her voice.

"You will regret this, you know you will!"

Hovering in the air, I pulled the crumbling world into me. I inhaled the magic, the OneSpell, into my body. There was so much magic, so much power, I thought I would burst, but even more came.

Finally I was done. The entirety of the OneSpell was inside me. My mind was focused on the path I had planned out to the future I would create.

I could still hear the shade of Valentine, although it was now a disembodied voice originating from somewhere inside me.

"This will take all your magic," the shade of Valentine cried faintly. "If you cast the OneSpell, if you create a new future, you will become unSigned. You will sacrifice your ability to do magic."

I smiled.

"It's not a sacrifice."

I cast the OneSpell.

It was night. I stood on the roof of the Giza casino. My eyes looked around. Wizard Karl Johnsen stood with his arm raised, looking at me.

"Where did it go?" he asked, pointing towards my empty hand. For him, only a second had gone by since I grabbed the amulet.

I smiled. "To the future of course. That's where it belongs. That's where, a hundred years from now, it's actually needed."

It was the truth, it was needed in the future, although without the OneSpell the knowledge of why was already fading from my mind.

Karl did not look amused. With a reluctant sigh, he lowered his arm, pulled a handgun out of his holster, and aimed it at me. Some of the other wizards did the same.

"Without the OneSpell, my Branch Lord will be greatly disappointed," he said. "I have to go back with something."

I raised a hand to summon a fireball. Nothing happened. The events of a second ago came back to me. I had given up my magic. I was now unSigned. There was nothing I could do anymore except wait for the inevitable end to come.

Far below me, the sounds of fighting between Magic First and Branch Shaskauer died down. If I had done my work right while casting the OneSpell, each of them had suddenly realized that there was nothing to be gained by continuing to fight. Each human being was suddenly, if temporarily, filled with empathy for his fellow man. They wouldn't be completely changed, at least not overnight, but perhaps over time they would be able to achieve a separate peace.

Closing my eyes, I comforted myself with the thought that, before I died, I had been able to see part of the future I had created. There was a burning sensation against my chest. I raised my right hand to my throat and grabbed the source, the unicorn token around my neck, the one Valentine had given me just hours before.

The world around me shimmered, swam, like looking at fish through the glass of an aquarium. Then it dispersed into a field of white.

And suddenly I was somewhere else.

I blinked my eyes and looked around. I was sitting on a couch in a familiar looking hotel room. Trying to stand, I was overcome by a wave of nausea and collapsed back down onto the couch.

It was Sorceress Valentine's suite. Valentine herself was sitting on the other couch, looking at me with relief. She jumped up and ran over to me, embracing me with an uncharacteristic level of emotion.

"You did it," she said, head buried into my chest. "I knew you could."

Sitting on the couch, next to where Valentine had been moments before, was Sorceress Corinna Windlass. She looked different than she usually did, calmer and more at peace.

Valentine extracted herself from me.

"You were there," I said, still slightly nauseous from the teleportation spell. "In the OneSpell, you were there."

Valentine nodded. "I thought that might happen. You cannot touch something like the OneSpell without it affecting you, and you affecting it."

"So it was all true then?" I asked. "Everything that version of you said about the timeline you came from?"

Valentine thought for a second. "Possibly. When magic is involved, it is always hard to tell where truth begins and ends."

"What of the Dragon?" asked Corinna. "What of Trannanir?"

I shook my head. "I killed him. There was no other way."

Corinna looked sad, but nodded in agreement. "You are correct, Sorcerer Roy Nakamura. There was no other way."

"I was worried the token would not work," Valentine said, cutting in. "That is, the spell I cast on the token to get you here if anything went wrong. If you lost your magic."

I shook my head knowingly. "You didn't cast that spell, Valentine." I pointed at Corinna. "She did."

The look on Valentine's face was the confirmation I needed. My time with the OneSpell had given me knowledge, clarity, and although it was rapidly fading, there were still some things I remembered.

"You're Mianna, aren't you?" I said to Corinna. She nodded in response. "You and Trannanir were both shapeshifters. When Trannanir tried to use the OneSpell, you did your best to kill him, but he was so powerful that even without his body, his magical self continued to exist as a demon, and retained its ability to turn into a dragon.

"You knew the OneSpell would return, so after your physical body died, you used your shapeshifter ability to possess others. You bided your time for a thousand years, waiting to confront Trannanir again. You realized the Branches would be compromised by Trannanir, so you ingratiated yourself among the sorcerers, and then when they were compromised, among the magicians. You created Magic First, then possessed Corinna Windlass to be their leader."

"Corinna is strong-willed, so I could not possess her at all times, but I could when it counted," she said. "Please know I gained no pleasure from deceiving you. I merely intended that you should figure out for yourself the way of things."

The ancient being possessing Corinna's body stood up to address me and Valentine. "Now that the threat of the OneSpell is over, I must be going." She smiled at me. "I have spent longer than I intended in this body, and it is time for me to return to my true form."

I stood up, wobbly on my feet, and walked over to Corinna. I bowed slightly and tapped the fingers of my right hand against my forehead. "Great Mianna," I said. "I can never repay you for what you did. But I must ask you for two final favors."

"You may ask," she said.

"First, I need the ability to cast a spell."

"You gave up the ability to do magic," Corinna said. "That was the price of casting the OneSpell, the sacrifice that had to be made. It was the defense mechanism I built in to make sure no one misused it."

My legs were still unsteady and started to give way, but I balanced myself with a hand on the couch and managed to stay upright. "But the magic, the ability to cast one final spell, it's not for me."

The spirit of Mianna looked at me through Corinna's eyes, piercing through me. Whatever she saw satisfied her. "Of course," she said. "Now I see. In that case, your wish is granted. Now what of your second request?"

Conscious that Valentine might try to listen, I leaned into Corinna's ear and whispered. When I pulled back, the look on Corinna's face was as close to puzzlement as I ever expected to see on the face of an ancient, all powerful magical creature.

"Are you sure?" Corinna asked. "When you were inside the OneSpell, did you see what the ramifications would be?"

"I did," I said.

"Very well," said the being who possessed Corinna. "It is a fitting reward for the one who fought Trannanir, and lived."

Something emerged from Corinna. A bright white light emanated from her, filling the suite until it was bright as day. The light vanished, but not before Valentine and I received a momentary glimpse of Mianna's true form.

"I always suspected," said Valentine. "I was never completely sure, and she never confirmed or denied it, but I always suspected."

The body of Corinna remained on the couch, peacefully sleeping.

"She is going to sleep for a while," Valentine said. "And when she wakes up, there is a lot I am going to have to explain to her."

I sat back down on the couch. The danger of the Dragon and the rooftop was past, so adrenaline was no longer coursing through my veins. I became aware of how tired I felt, how dull everything seemed without magic to give me energy or heighten my senses.

I looked over to the wall, to where Valentine had hung a plaque with a quote from *The Great Gatsby*. I had seen it before, but the events of the night caused me to examine it more carefully.

"The quote's wrong." I pointed at the plaque. "The original quote, the one in the book, it's not 'can't *change* the past,' it's 'can't *repeat* the past.'"

Valentine nodded. "As I recall, it was one of your favorite books. Yet the whole time you trained here, you never noticed."

"There was a lot I didn't notice," I said.

All around the city, former servants of the Dragon were waking up, as if from a nightmare. Their power gone, some were frightened they would be hunted down by those they had hurt while in the Dragon's service. Others looked at their actions with fresh eyes, no longer blinded by the tempting lies of the Dragon, and were horrified at what they had done in his name.

Several other key people were waking up as well, refreshed by visions I had given them while in possession of the OneSpell. They were key members of the magic community, especially the Branches, who suddenly felt that equality for sorcerers and magicians was not something to be feared. The differences were subtle, and would take some time, but seeds had been planted throughout the city's magical elite that would someday blossom into something different and wonderful.

The OneSpell was no longer in my grasp, and I had given up my magic, so I could no longer see every event unfolding in the city of Las Vegas. Thus, I wasn't able to observe it, but I later found this out to be true.

At the exact moment I sent the OneSpell a hundred years into the future, the Tribute box outside Magic Hall split into two halves, spilling a day's worth of five dollar chips all over the giant marble steps leading to the statue of Adam the Defiant One. It was never repaired.

7 - Denouement

According to news reports, the city of Las Vegas escaped relatively unscathed from a routine New Year's Eve. Over two hundred celebrants had been arrested by the police, and an equal number had been detained by the security apparatuses of various Branches, but this was about average for a holiday focused on intoxication.

The news further reported there had been a fire at the Giza casino, completely unrelated to a peaceful rally by a magic rights activist group that took place nearby. Guests and gamblers alike were calmly evacuated by hotel staff. According to a spokesman for Branch Shaskauer, wizards from Branch Parthenia and Branch Merkasia were in the area at the time of the fire and assisted with the evacuation.

I arrived back at our suite at Parthenia around six in the morning. Jayden, who arrived at Valentine's place by unknown means an hour after I did, arranged for Branch Parthenia security to drop off Rico and Derek (their passed out bodies were discovered in the remnants of Club Heartbreak) at the suite. He thought it would be too suspicious if all four of us arrived together. Against all odds, the biggest party animal I knew was turning into a decent covert operative.

When I got there, the suite was quiet. I made my way across the massive living room, and up the stairs that led to the balcony and its set of bedrooms.

Skylar and Rico were sitting at the top of the stairs, propped up against the wall next to the door to their room. Rico, fast asleep, had his head leaned against Skylar's shoulder. His eyes were closed, but he looked as if he had been crying. Skylar had her hand snaked across his shoulder and patted his head gently.

She looked up at me as I passed and mouthed "thank you" before putting her head back down to be close to his. I ducked into my room, quickly dropping my sorcerer's cloak on my bed. I wouldn't need it again.

Leaving my room, I climbed down the stairs that led to the main part of the suite, walked gingerly across the carpet to avoid making too much noise, and plopped myself on one of the couches seated next to the giant wall-sized window. Night still reigned in the city. The neon lights of the Strip were still shining at full volume. But it was almost dawn. A new day, a new year, was about to begin.

There was a shuffle, and I looked up to see Skylar following in my footsteps. She sat beside me without speaking. We enjoyed the silence for a moment, both looking out over the city.

"I'm not stupid," Skylar said. "I know I was a jerk to you sometimes."

"I don't know what you're talking about," I said with a smile.

"My biggest fear was always that you would fall back in love with me," Skylar said. "I knew you hated me for breaking up with you, and in a weird way, I was okay with that. I was okay with you hating me, because it meant you didn't love me. And the idea of you still loving me, well I just couldn't handle that."

"I thought about what you said," I whispered. "And you were right. The breakup was my fault too."

I folded my hands in front of me. "In the end, we didn't work."

Skylar leaned her head back. "Give us some credit. We worked until we didn't."

We enjoyed another moment of silence. From far, far away, I could see the faintest glint of the sun starting to rise.

"I'm sorry," I said.

"It doesn't work like that." Skylar was being playful, mostly, but there was a serious edge to her words. "You have to say what it is you're sorry for."

"I'm sorry," I said, "that I didn't make you feel special. I'm sorry that actions speak louder than words, but that words are pretty important too." I looked at Skylar's switchblade eyes, the ones that had taken me in so many times, that I always knew would someday be the death of me. "I should have told you I loved you. Every day, every minute, every second, I should have told you how I felt." I swallowed. "I should have told you that you meant everything to me."

Skylar closed her eyes. "Thank you," she said. "I think I needed to hear that."

The sun was on its way up now, nothing could stop it. And the neon lights of the Strip, one by one, turned off. Those magnificent lights, which featured so prominently in that billboard of my youth, which appeared to overpower everything around them, shut off in anticipation of being overpowered by the sun, the one thing infinitely bigger and brighter.

Skylar and I sat there, in silence but at peace, as the sun rose over Las Vegas.

We all drove to the airport to see Rico off. With the exception of Jayden, none of my friends knew the full magnitude of what had happened the night before. Nevertheless, we all had the feeling we had been through something together. Like old battle buddies who had been through a deployment, we all wanted to be there to see one of our own fly off to his destination.

We parked in the cell phone lot and each said our good-byes to Rico. While this was going on, Jayden asked me, under some pretext, to step to the side. We walked away, not far enough to be obvious but far enough that no one would ask questions.

Jayden started to open his mouth, and I felt a faint breeze. Sorceress Valentine appeared, standing beside us. I was far past the point of her being able to surprise me.

"Sorcerer," she said in greeting.

"Sorceress," I replied.

I gestured towards the car, where Valentine's younger self was standing with Rico, staring into his eyes. "They're a cute couple, aren't they?" I said.

"I suppose," Valentine said. "But she does not really love him. Not the way she loves you."

I grinned. "Are you sure?"

Valentine frowned, then pursed her lips as she cast her magical sight on the couple. She recoiled.

"She loves him!" she said. "But that is impossible, how could…" She paused and smiled. "I knew the OneSpell was powerful, but I had no idea." Valentine had a foreign look on her face, and it took a moment for me to recognize it for what it was. Awe. Sorceress Valentine was in awe of me, of what I had done.

She finally spoke. "You did it, you actually did it. You broke the Aladdin rule. You changed the past."

I shook my head, smiling with the satisfaction of a student who had finally outdone the teacher. "I didn't change the past, I changed the future."

Valentine kept pressing. "But you also broke it by making someone fall in love."

I shook my head again. "I didn't create love. It was always there. I think it just took some prodding."

Jayden cleared his throat, and we both turned towards him. Ignoring Valentine, he began to talk to me. "You kept your end of the bargain, so Branch Parthenia will keep its end."

"Bargain?" Valentine asked.

"Yes, the deal we made yesterday," Jayden said. "Roy would fight the Dragon, take the OneSpell, and send it into the future where it can't hurt anyone. In exchange, we would end the Tribute and the requirement for the Guild to swear fealty to the Branches, as well as allow magicians to practice magic, even without a Branch Stamp."

Valentine's confused look caused Jayden to look confused as well. "Weren't you there when we made the deal?" he asked.

"Of course I was." She looked at me. "I suppose I just didn't remember Branch Parthenia being so... generous."

Jayden continued. "Naturally the Branches reserve the right to intervene in the event of especially dangerous magic."

I nodded in agreement. After the embarrassment suffered by Branch Shaskauer the previous night, Branch Parthenia was once again firmly in control of Las Vegas. What they said was law, and with his pronouncement, Jayden had in one second accomplished what Magic First had worked at for years.

"If you boys are done," Valentine said. "I have to be going. But before I do, there is business that needs to be attended to."

Valentine removed one of the tokens from her neck. She held it out to me. It was the one that featured a unicorn, the emblem of those who pursued the OneSpell.

"You already gave me a unicorn token," I said.

"I am not giving this one to you," Valentine explained, "I am giving it back to the person I got it from." She considered her words carefully. "When the moment comes, you will know what to do with it."

Valentine looked around, as if taking in the world for a final time before departing on a long journey. "And with that, if there are no further questions, I must be going."

I raised a finger. "Not so fast. There's one thing that's still bothering me."

"Yes?" Valentine replied nonchalantly.

"Branch Shaskauer knew where the OneSpell was going to appear, so they left their Archives almost unguarded and sent the bulk of their forces to Giza."

Valentine nodded. Jayden looked curious, wondering where I was going.

"When you attacked the Archives, when you breached its defenses, that caused a number of wizards to leave Giza and rush to protect them. You were gone by the time they arrived, but it still reduced their forces at Giza enough that the wizards from Branch Parthenia, and the people from Magic First, could fight the rest, allowing me to enter Club Heartbreak."

"Yes," Valentine said. "And, you are welcome."

"What bothers me is that if it hadn't been for the OneSpell appearing at Giza, if it hadn't been for the fact that Archmage Artimus Cantor wanted to intercept it and sent most of the Archive guards to Giza, then as powerful as you are, you still wouldn't have been able to breach the Archive defenses in the first place, just as you weren't able to years ago when you tried the first time."

Jayden looked uninterested, but a flash of understanding crossed Valentine's face.

"During my training, Sorceress Valentine, you told me about sleight of hand artists, how the key to their profession was convincing people to look in one direction," I held out my right hand, "while they were doing something in the other," I held out my left.

"In your timeline, you defeated the Dragon and took control of the OneSpell. If your concern was really for the OneSpell, you could have done it again. Instead you insisted I be the one to do it. Even if the Dragon had managed to get a hold of the OneSpell, would he have been able to use it? The OneSpell lets anyone who accesses it see possible futures, and choose one accordingly. But the only way the Dragon could have obtained true power and created his own future is by casting it, which would have required a sacrifice he wouldn't have been willing to make. It was a defense Mianna built into the spell, and if it came down to it, it would have done its job.

"So it begs the question, was your attack on the Archives really a diversion to enable me to retrieve the OneSpell? Or were our efforts to get the OneSpell, and everything I've done over the years to prepare for the battle with the Dragon, was it all a diversion to enable you to do the only thing you were never able to do on your own? Gain access to the Branch Shaskauer Archives."

Valentine smiled. "You must think quite highly of me, Sorcerer Roy Nakamura, to think I could do anything of value in the mere three minutes during which I had access to the Archives."

"Knowing you Valentine, that's all you would need. You are, both now and in the past, the most brilliant manipulator I know."

Valentine took it as a compliment. "If I'm a master manipulator, Ark'Telga, it is only because I learned from the best."

She took a step closer and whispered in my ear so Jayden would not be able to hear. "The future is not written in stone," she said. "Take it from someone who has been there."

Sorceress Valentine dropped her head slightly and touched the fingers of her right hand to her forehead. There was a slight shimmer in the air around her, like a blast of hot air confined to the immediate space around her. And as suddenly as she had appeared in my life, Sorceress Valentine, the most powerful magic user in the world, disappeared.

I turned to my left, to where Skylar, the now-Skylar, was saying goodbye to her boyfriend.

Rico turned as if to leave, then turned back, leaned down, and kissed Skylar. It wasn't dramatic or romantic, at least not in the classic Hollywood sense, but in a way it was the most beautiful kiss I have ever seen. They, the two of them, were at the center of the universe. All the other cars and passengers, the planes in the air, even the city of Las Vegas, were all rotating around them, caught by their gravity well and coerced into rotating around them.

That wasn't the last time I saw Skylar, not by a long shot, but that's how I like to remember her. Head tilted up, lips on her beloved's, eyes closed, looking only at the present.

That was also the moment I decided to leave Las Vegas. I always thought that someday Las Vegas would make me leave, that it would spit me out, used and dried up, just as it had once welcomed me into its embrace. But in the end it wasn't like that at all. Instead, I just no longer had anything keeping me there. I had done everything I set out to. I became a dueler, won EndGame, fought the Dragon, and sent the OneSpell into the future.

Everything I thought would make me happy had been accomplished. And sure, in a way I was. I had a sense of satisfaction, of accomplishment, of having fulfilled my destiny. I saved the world after all, not many people can say that. But it just wasn't me anymore. I was no longer Signed, which was admittedly a big part, but it was more than that. It was like the magically enhanced senses I had been using for so long had overwhelmed something deeper, a longing to go back home to Los Angeles where I belonged. I felt like Nick in *The Great Gatsby*, who after seeing everything the big city had to offer wanted to return to his home. And so I did.

Everything I owned, or at least that I wanted to keep, was packed into two suitcases which fit easily into the trunk of my car. I left a note on my kitchen table addressed to my landlord, apologizing for not moving the rest of my stuff out. I told him he could keep it, or sell it and keep the money, it no longer made a difference to me. I did mention that the sorcerer's cloak I left in my closet belonged to a former EndGame champion, and thus might fetch some money at an auction. I thought about taking the cloak with me, but ever since I lost my magic on the roof of Giza, it had stubbornly refused to sparkle for me. I was just another unSigned human now, and it was just a piece of fabric.

I looked around at the apartment a final time before closing the door. It had been my residence for most of my time in Las Vegas, so I expected to feel a pang of regret, but none came. The truth is that even in my three years of life as a magic user (five years if you count subjective time), that apartment was never really my home. It was just where I slept at night. My home, my true home, was the Strip. The lights glittering all around me, reflecting off of every surface. The sound of the clink of glasses, and the electronic music of the slot machines, and the soft thud of cards against the green felt, harmonized by cries of victory and defeat. The Strip, the neon lights, the magic. That was my home.

I left Las Vegas around noon. Jayden and Renée rode with me. Without T-Lock, Jayden no longer had someone to drive his limo. Renée wanted to be with me for obvious reasons. Maria and Derek rode back with Skylar. After the events of the previous night, I knew they probably had a lot to talk about. Jayden insisted Renée ride up front with me. I tried to argue, but as always he was convincing.

From my apartment I could have gotten directly onto the freeway and avoided the Strip, but instead I entered the Strip at the very top, by Better Tomorrows, and drove south. I rolled down the top of my white LeBaron Convertible so I could breathe in the Vegas air one last time. Jayden complained briefly about the effect the wind would have on his hair, but I was already ignoring him.

It was afternoon, but most tourists were still in bed, sleeping off hangovers from the night before. In relative silence I drove past Magic Hall, just next to Arabian Nights, as well as smaller casinos I had gambled at from time to time. Then I hit the core of the Strip. There was Parthenia, where I had been hours before, then Pirate Bay, where I had stayed when I competed in EndGame. The Last Emperor, the site of many gambling adventures.

The neon lights of Las Vegas were off, but I could still feel them watch me as I drove by Spartacus, Hyperion, Versailles, even Los Angeles, the casino that attempted to recreate my home town in a one block area.

There was Merlin's Dream, where Renée and I had had our one night stand, an event it turned out had not been caused by magic after all. Renée might have winced as we drove by, or it might have been my imagination. And then there was Giza, the home of Club Heartbreak, the site of an event that could have caused the end of the world.

Each casino I drove by, each miniature world, contained hundreds of memories for me. As I drove by, each one took those memories back so by the time I reached the end of the Strip, I was naked and new. The baggage I accumulated while in the city, the burdens I had incurred, had fallen away.

Unbridled by the past, I merged onto the freeway and pointed my car towards home.

It was almost midnight when we arrived back in Los Angeles. I pulled into the street outside Maria and Skylar's apartment. It was where Renée would be staying for the duration of her winter vacation and where Jayden had left his car. Jayden got out first and shook my hand through the driver's side window.

"Good luck with everything," he said.

"You too." I popped the trunk and could hear him go around back to retrieve his baggage.

Renée opened her door.

"Wait," I said. "I need to ask you about something."

Renée froze. Her blue eyes wide, she looked down and to the left to where my hand was on her shoulder.

It was just me and Renée in the car now. I withdrew my hand from her shoulder and put it in my lap. I had practiced what I was about to say for most of the drive, but I was still unsure how to start.

"Renée," I swallowed. "I've been thinking about what you said. About how there's no such thing as a love spell."

Renée nodded.

"And I couldn't figure it out. If there isn't, how is it you still have feelings for me?"

"Because I do," Renée said. There was a look of resignation on her face as she spoke. "Because I choose to."

"That's the thing. Anyone else would have given up after two years of unrequited feelings, would have chosen someone else."

Renée's eyes narrowed. She could tell this wasn't going to go the way she wanted.

"But that's where your feelings are different than most, because they're not completely unrequited. For one night, that night in Vegas after I passed the Trials and fought Karl, they were quite requited. And that's why you can't move on. You have a memory of one night of us together, and it gives you hope we could have a future together."

Renée looked like she would cry. "It's like I keep telling you Roy, I don't care if I get hurt, I don't care if I'm doomed to a lifetime of unrequited love, I don't regret anything I've done."

"Still, if there was a way…"

"There is no way to take back that night," Renée cut me off. "Are you going to try a time travel spell now? You can't change the past."

"No," I admitted. "But you can change the future, and you can change the future impression of the past. If nostalgia, if dwelling on memories, is our way of travelling back in time and reliving them, then taking away that ability is the way to change it."

While this conversation was going on, I slowly reached my left hand down into my left pocket and pulled out a deck of cards I had stashed there. While Renée was concentrating all her energy on me, willing me to give her a chance, I had taken the cards out of the deck and drawn one at random. I turned to look down. It was the Queen of Hearts. Of course. I held the card up so Renée could see it.

In the minutes since I asked her to stay in the car, Renée had been trying to figure out where this was all going. I had debated whether or not to give her an explanation at all, afraid she would figure out my intentions and jump out of the car before I could do what I had to. And afraid the spell wouldn't work after all, that the small sliver of magic Mianna had given me wouldn't be enough to cast this one final spell. But I felt like I owed her an explanation, even if she wouldn't remember it. And as soon as I held up the card, she figured out what was going on.

Her eyes, the ones I had seen cry so many times, the ones that hid an unexplainable desire for me that scared me more than any demon, went wide. Her lips were frozen, but her eyes screamed at me to stop. I ignored her pleas and began.

"Arcane knowledge lost in time…"

In the cramped confines of the car Renée threw out her hands and brought her two forearms together vertically in front of her, fists clenched, lips mumbling words.

"Hide her past from prying eyes…"

The meaning of the gesture came to me. It was a counterspell. Renée was trying to cast a counterspell. But counterspells didn't work this far away from Las Vegas, no magic did. No magic except for the one spell I was casting.

"Bind it up upon this sign…"

Renée's arms dropped. She must have remembered her magic was useless in Los Angeles. The tears were falling in rivers across her face as fast as her eyes could give birth to them. All she could do was make a final plea.

"Roy, please, I…"

"Take her pain, and make it…

"I LOVE YOU!"

"MINE!"

344

When Sorceress Valentine told me memory shrouds continued to work outside Las Vegas, I started to wonder whether they could also be cast outside Las Vegas. Magic only exists in Las Vegas, but in the case of memory shrouds, memory wasn't linked to the casting of the spell, otherwise the spell would cease once the person left the city. Instead, it must be that magic was linked to the event being shrouded. So, as long as the memory being shrouded had some connection to Las Vegas, it would be possible to cast the memory shroud outside the city.

As I said the final word to the spell, I learned my theory was correct.

Time froze. Paused. Held its breath. Then time started running again, but this time in reverse. I had never cast a memory shroud before, wasn't even sure I'd be able to. I knew theoretically what came next, but descriptions didn't do it justice.

I was inside Renée's mind, her memories were before me like a filmstrip, like a scrapbook, like cells in an infinitely large spreadsheet. The words of the spell were right. I truly had made her pain mine. I felt what she felt, the pain, the longing, and not just about me. I felt every pinprick from every insult anyone had ever thrown her way.

And I could see me. But this wasn't looking at me the way I appear in the mirror, instead I saw myself the way Renée saw me. It was beautiful. All my imperfections were stripped away, all my sins were forgiven. And there was, just as I suspected, the pervasive hope that since we had been together once, we would be together again. The background, the hope, that made her choose to love me.

Relationships look different from the inside, and so do unrequited crushes.

With care and precision, I ripped the memory out of her head. And with it came all the other memories, the memories of remembering it. Time was going forward again from that moment, and every memory connected, in a web, was slowly exorcised. It ended with the conversation we had just had. All stored up in that single playing card, which I palmed into my hand and slipped back into my pocket.

I was back in the car, and Renée was looking at me quizzically. "Well?"

"Well, what?"

"Why did you want me to wait?"

The conversation never happened. At least not in her memory.

"I just wanted to thank you for riding in my car," I finally managed to say. "I hope you enjoyed it."

"Any time Roy," Renée replied. It was playful, easygoing, the kind of tone you would expect from a girl with the smallest of crushes. She reached her hand up to her face and felt the wetness beneath her eyes. She paused, as if maybe there was an echo of a memory my spell had failed to find.

"Was I crying?" she asked.

"Not that I know of," I replied. "It's probably just from the wind on the highway."

"Of course." She opened the door and stood up.

"See you later Roy!"

I smiled.

"Later Renée!"

I waited until Renée had walked up the driveway to her building, until I could see her waving from the entrance, before turning the car back on. Renée had her whole life in front of her now, a chance to find love with someone who would love her back.

As for me, when I found a place to live I would put the playing card at the bottom of a big box, somewhere Renée would never find it. But I wouldn't throw it away. I would keep it, take it out and look at it from time to time, as a reminder of the person I had once been. That person had departed for now, but could always come back if I wasn't careful.

I put my white LeBaron Convertible into drive and eased my foot off the brake. The road in front of me dominated my vision. I didn't know where it led, but I was ready to go there.

Renée once told me I was selfish, and the OneSpell showed me I was. Seeing every possible future, even the bad ones, made me see the monster I had the potential to become. I wanted to think the actions I took, including shrouding Renée's memory so she would be able to move on, were for her. But maybe it was for me, to assuage my own guilt.

The future spread out before me. The city of neon lights and demons was behind me, and the city of angels, the home of my birth, beckoned. The knowledge of the OneSpell was gone from my head, so I no longer knew exactly what my chosen future held in store, but I did know one thing.

I was finally home.

Epilogue: 3 Endings

---

1 - The Wedding

A teacher once told me that in classical literature you could tell a tragedy from a comedy based on the ending. If it ends in a wedding, it's a comedy, but if it ends with a funeral, then it's a tragedy. When all is said and done, I'm not sure whether my story is a comedy or a tragedy, but it ends with a wedding.

It was two in the afternoon on the last Saturday before Christmas. A single piano played Pachelbel's Canon in D. Despite the chill in the air (at least by Los Angeles standards), I was sweating in my suit. I didn't know what to do with my hands. I tried putting them in my pockets, which made me feel too informal, then I tried putting them behind my back which felt awkward as well.

Everyone in attendance looked cool and comfortable sitting in the pews, while I stood at the steps in front of the altar, facing the entrance to the sanctuary.

"Are you okay Roy?" asked Grant, standing to my left.

I exhaled deliberately, trying to slow my breath. "A little nervous I guess."

"Why are *you* nervous?"

"I'm not good at standing still, and this could take a while."

"Don't worry," Grant said. He smiled. "No one's here to see you."

As if on cue, the two doors at the front of the sanctuary screeched open and the piano changed its tune. In time with the processional song, those in the pews stood and turned to face the entrance.

I risked a quick glance at Grant, whose face was contorted in a look of displeasure. "I think I know that song. Where do I know that song from?"

Everyone in attendance was standing now, facing the back.

"Is that the song from the final scene in *The Closest Exit?*"

I shook my head and put a finger to my lips. The song continued to play.

"That *is* the song from *The Closest Exit*," Grant hissed. "Why on earth would she want to walk down the aisle to…"

"Shut up," I whispered. "It's a beautiful song." I was loud enough that those in the front row might have heard me, but they didn't, because the eyes of every person in the room were fixated on a single point of white.

Skylar Trope stepped into the sanctuary, her white dress glowing in the soft light of the church. Her father walked next to her, taking measured steps to keep pace with her.

My heart stopped. My fidgeting body froze. All other noises, even the piano solo that Grant identified as the song from *The Closest Exit*, faded into the background as I watched Skylar walking down the aisle.

Unbidden, my mind raced back to years before, to the roof of a parking structure, to the time when Skylar first told me she loved me. It was just a single moment from our life together, but it replayed over and over in my mind as she took step after step, pacing herself to avoid tripping. Like everything else in life, she made it look easy.

To my right I could hear Rico clear his throat. "You've got the rings Roy, right?"

I patted my pocket. "Of course."

Skylar arrived at the bottom of the steps that led up to the altar. Skylar embraced her father, who held back a tear. Then Rico jumped down the two steps from his spot standing to my right to meet Skylar's father, who shook his hand. As the older man sat down, Rico took Skylar's hand in his own. Together, the two of them ascended the stairs and walked towards the altar.

In 2004, a couple years after the Branches officially repealed the practices of the Tribute and the Branch Stamp, the Las Vegas tourism commission sponsored a series of billboards across the nation that featured the smiling faces of a dozen people involved in various forms of magical activity, carefully selected to reflect a balance of gender and racial diversity (and none of them Atlantian), accompanied in the lower right hand corner by a simple three word phrase. "Vegas is Changing." In those three years, my friends and I changed as well.

Renée completed her Master of Science in practical magic, but decided the world of theory was really more her style. After being admitted to a magical studies PhD program at Havenshire, a small liberal arts college in New York City, she left the world of Las Vegas behind. She is currently a professor there.

Skylar completed her graduate degree in educational counseling and became a school therapist at the same high school she graduated from years before.

The evening of her graduation, Rico proposed to Skylar outside the coffee shop where they first met. At that point Rico had become fully integrated into our group of friends, so I helped him plan the proposal. Skylar accepted. She and Rico were married on a Saturday afternoon at the church where she grew up.

A year later, Rico got a job with the Clark County Sheriff's Department, allowing him to join Skylar, who for reasons not particularly clear to anyone, left her job as a therapist and took a position as a sorcerer's apprentice in Las Vegas.

Shortly after Skylar's wedding, Grant's dream came true and he was able to transfer to his firm's New York office. He continued to work in the finance field for a couple years, but eventually left to work in the non-profit world. He is currently the Director of Development for an organization that teaches music to inner city children.

While sitting in a trendy coffee shop, he ran into Renée for the first time since his trip to Vegas to see EndGame. Rumor is they are now dating.

The experience of dealing with the OneSpell gave Jayden something he never had before, a sense of the importance of his role in his Branch, and the role of the Branch in safeguarding dangerous magic. Shortly after the New Year's trip, Jayden quit his job in Los Angeles and returned to Las Vegas to start training as a wizard. As with everything in life, Jayden completed his training in record time and at the top of his class. It was rumored he also threw some legendary parties for his fellow apprentices.

In a break from tradition, rather than being Marked in a ceremony at the family compound, he held the ceremony on the roof of the Parthenia Casino. He said he liked being able to look out over the city during big moments in his life.

Shortly after Jayden was Marked, his father and older brother were killed in a freak climbing accident while on vacation in Colorado. As the next person in line, Jayden ascended the Wolverine throne and became the new Lord Parthenia. His first act as Branch Lord was to contact the US Attorney for the District of Nevada and tell her that Branch Parthenia would fully cooperate with any re-opened investigation into the death of Genevieve Shaskauer.

A month after I moved back to Los Angeles, Maria moved away. She spent a year teaching English in Japan, then taught community organizing skills to migrant workers in New Mexico. Eventually she settled in Northern Virginia, where she used her skills from her time as a hotel receptionist to get a job in the hospitality industry. From what I heard however, she still took part in the occasional protest.

While in Virginia, she agreed to go on a blind-date arranged by a co-worker and was surprised to find herself sitting face to face with Derek Hastings, now an associate at a DC-based consulting firm. Maria and Derek are currently married and live in the DC area, along with their three year old daughter Saffron.

When Maria told me about her date with Derek, I was suspicious, but there was more to the story. With the demon exorcised from his body, Derek changed back to a different person, perhaps the person he originally was. And Maria didn't go running back into his arms. He had to pursue her, at least from what I heard, and he had to work at the relationship (in a way I suppose they both did).

After they got engaged, I asked Maria whether or not she was really happy with Derek, whether she was settling for being unhappy because it meant she wouldn't be alone.

"Roy," she told me, looking at me in a way that only she could. "When I first dated Derek, I was afraid of being alone. Now I'm not afraid at all. I just want to be with him."

As for me, well that's a long story. But there is one particular day that stands out. It was about a month after I moved back to Los Angeles. Even after such a short time, my life in Las Vegas was starting to fade, to seem unreal.

I was walking through downtown Los Angeles on the way to my father's office to have lunch with him. We hadn't seen each other since I got back, and somehow his office seemed closer to neutral territory than his house. It was a cold February day, well at least as cold as it gets in Los Angeles, and I was trying to make my way down Figueroa as quickly as possible when I heard someone shout "Roy! Roy!" behind me.

I stopped to turn and saw a man (average height, average build, perfectly ordinary hair), waving at me from inside an oversized JC Penny winter coat. I waited while the figure caught up with me.

"What are you doing here in Los Angeles?" he asked, slightly out of breath.

"I live here," I replied, still not sure who he was.

"Oh right, you probably don't recognize me without the sorcerer's cloak. It's me, Arnold Davidson. Sorcerer Arnold Davidson."

It took me a moment to remember him from the quarter-finals of EndGame, and even earlier, from the first time I saw someone wave watch in person.

"I live here now," I said again.

"Yeah, I heard you left the circuit," Arnold said. "When I found out that you didn't even compete in EndGame last year, I was so pissed off, I was like 'you beat me, and now you're not even going to compete.' Argh. You know?"

I slowly nodded my head.

"So what are you doing here?" I said, hoping the conversation wouldn't last too long.

"Same as you I'm sure," Arnold said. "Just got too old for it all, you know? I mean, being a sorcerer was glamorous and all, but it's just not *real*, know what I mean?"

In a way, I did. We exchanged pleasantries for a couple more seconds, then I found an excuse to leave and we parted ways.

My father's office was meticulously neat and tidy. Every piece of paper, every paperclip, every pen, was in its proper place. He looked up at me as I walked in, his eyes peering over the top of a large report that he quickly put down on his desk. The report, sitting diagonally across the desk's surface, looked almost profane in the way it broke the desk's perfect symmetry.

"Sorry I'm late," I said.

My father checked the clock. "It's okay Richard. It's just by a minute."

"I ran into an old rival," I said, without even thinking.

"Rival?"

I hesitated, sensing I was about to cross a boundary. But I plunged ahead. "From when I lived in Las Vegas."

"I see."

I thought about what to say, how to make him see. Because suddenly it seemed very important that my father understand what I had done, that he know what I had gone through.

"You see, I used to be a sorcerer." My dad's eyes grew wide at this comment. "But not anymore."

My dad looked back down at the report, then up at me, as something glistened in his eye. "It's okay, Richard," he said. "I understand. We don't have to talk about this if you don't want to." He paused. "But also, we could talk about this. If that's what you want."

I looked up at him, into his eyes, as a shared understanding borne from shared experience crossed the gulf between our normally unyielding countenances. I had no idea where this conversation would lead, but I had the feeling it was time for us to have it.

My father was a history major in college. His dream was to be a museum docent, to light up the faces of tourists and school children with stories of ancient battles and mighty heroes, ensuring their deeds would not be forgotten. He later shelved this calling in favor of the more practical vocation of being an actuary.

In a way, I always judged him for that, subconsciously criticized him for taking the safe route instead of following his dream. But sitting there in his office, I wondered about the choices he had made. He had never touched the OneSpell, I would have been able to sense it if he had, but I had the unmistakable impression he had touched magic, and that magic had shown him what the future could hold. Just like me, my father had been forced to choose from a host of possible futures (I suppose in a way everyone does). And even though this future might seem like selling out to me, maybe it was far better than the alternative. Maybe he made his own sacrifices for me, for my mother and brothers, for the ones he loved.

"So what are you going to do now Richard?" he asked.

I tried to come up with the words, but what could I say? How could I explain what I was thinking or feeling when I could barely understand it myself? How could I tell him I had been to a distant country and back (and I didn't regret any of it – it made me who I was), but in the end, there was only one path I wanted to follow?

"I think I'm going to go back to school," I finally said. "I think I'm going to become an actuary."

My father didn't say anything, and his reaction to the news was unreadable. He leaned back in his chair, and started to hum a tune. It seemed abstract at first, like he was just trying to moisten his lips and somehow a sound came out, but the abstract sound coalesced into something deeper, something more coherent. Something that made me take notice.

You see, the tune my father hummed was unmistakable, unforgettable. And even though he didn't sing the lyrics, they sang away anyways in my head.

This is the story, morning glory
of what I learned in Vegas.
You always hurt the ones you love –
that's why love couldn't save us.

I never returned to Las Vegas.

2 – A Letter to a Friend

Julius,

Hope all is well. Enclosed please find the latest (and hopefully final) draft of my autobiographical manuscript. As you can see from the first page, I have changed the title from *Life in a Distant Country* to *What I Learned in Vegas*. I will probably have to change the epigraph as well, but we can get to that later.

The most significant change is that I condensed the book into four parts rather than five. I had to take a bit of artistic license in regards to which events took place when (and who was staying at what hotel, that sort of thing), but I don't think it's anything severe enough to get me sued for libel. After all this isn't a strict autobiography, it's "based on a true story."

As you can tell, I took most of the advice from the letter you sent me about the previous draft. I got rid of the character of Derek's brother (although now it doesn't makes sense why Skylar had her own car to drive back after New Year's Eve). Gary and Jonas have been combined into one character, Grant, and in order to protect the identity of the person she is based on, Skylar is now stated to have been adopted from Korea. There were, however, three suggestions I took issue with.

First, regarding the character of Roy (and I realize I sound schizophrenic talking about myself as a character), I disagree with your assertion that Roy is an "unreliable narrator" (your words, not mine). Sure, Roy describes the world as he sees it, lends his own implicit bias to every description of characters and events. But doesn't everyone?

Once again, this isn't a strict autobiography. If a researcher or detective were to look into it, maybe everything didn't happen to me exactly the way I describe it, but I never claimed this story was meant to be a hundred percent true.

Second, I disagree that Maria had a depressing ending in which she "never gets over her addiction to love." Maria wasn't addicted to love. Her greatest flaw was that she needed to be wanted. And I needed to be needed. We worked well in a fashion, her always chasing after some uncaring guy, me always there to save her, but in the end we both had to grow up. When I cast the OneSpell, I thought it meant I would have to give up magic to save Maria. But in the end, I had to give up Maria to save Maria. Her real, true need was to learn to live on her own, without a man supporting her. And that included me.

Third, as you can see, I wrote a new ending. I took your suggestion and created mini-epilogues that would create, as you put it, "closure for both the characters and the reader." However, after writing it, I feel like it provides no closure at all.

Do you remember when I first started working on this book? We met for drinks at that hipster coffee shop on La Brea. You had just read my first draft and told me something I'll never forget.

"Roy, this story shows a lot of promise, but no one wants to read a book about relationships."

I must have looked a little hurt, because you added, "Roy, you're a famous sorcerer. People want to read about *magic*."

To that end, I started to write about magic. I added in stories about duels and fights, wrote page after page detailing my battle with the Dragon and elaborating on how close I came to instigating a second Wizard War.

And I admit, the book got better. Ultimately I agree with your assessment. No one wants to read a love story about a guy who's not a particularly good lover, but everyone wants to read the story of how an average guy from the Valley rose to become the most talked about sorcerer in Las Vegas, and just as quickly faded into obscurity.

However, somewhere in all those revisions, I feel like my original idea, the soul of the story, got lost, hidden, to the point where now a reader would have to search carefully in order to reveal the strands that made up the reason I wrote this book in the first place. I feel like the old story, the story I wanted to tell at first, has stuck around like a forgotten childhood friend. And even though we've grown apart, it still wants to be part of my life.

The new title comes from the song by *Taliesin* (tell me if you think this will cause any copyright issues), but its significance is more than just that. I got the idea to use it from something else you told me.

When I asked you what the mark of a good ending is, asked why the "mini-epilogues" were so essential, you told me the ending shouldn't be about what I did in Las Vegas, it's about what I learned, about how after my time in the city I left it a different person than when I arrived. Thus, I needed mini-epilogues to show how learning magic changed me, how it changed all of us.

Here is the thing though. There were many things I learned in Las Vegas, but magic wasn't one of them. Magic, as I've said again and again, just came naturally to me. What I learned, what I truly took away from that magical city, was something about me not necessarily specific to Vegas. It was something I could have learned anywhere, except I didn't. I learned it, a simple lesson, against the backdrop of world changing events that seemed to impact everyone except for me.

And so, although I value your input and can never thank you enough for the help you've given me over the years, I'm going to use my original ending (*What I Learned in Vegas*). I may use the ending with the mini-epilogues as well, but I feel a need to include the story about my run-in with Maria at Skylar's wedding. I'm not doing it for me, I'm doing it as a favor to the little novel that was, a favor to the original story I showed you in that hipster coffee shop on that December afternoon, which you told me showed so much promise.

Sincerely, Roy Nakamura

PS – One last thing. The other day I went back to my parents' house and looked in the closet where they keep all my old stuff in an effort to find my dog-eared copy of *Call Me Sorcerer*, the book I read as an eight year old that started my whole obsession with the city of Las Vegas. I wanted to find the name of the author so I could properly reference it. But here's the thing, the book (which I finally found at a bottom of a stack of fantasy novels), which had my name inscribed in the front, written in my messy eight year old handwriting, wasn't called *Call Me Sorcerer*. It was called *Call Me Wizard*. I must have read it fifty times as a child, but sitting there in my parents' house I read it again. And it was completely different. *Call Me Sorcerer*, at least as I recall, was the story of a boy from Los Angeles who goes to Las Vegas to become a sorcerer. *Call Me Wizard*, the creased and worn book I was holding in my hands, was about a boy from Los Angeles who goes to Las Vegas and becomes a wizard. He gradually rises in power until he becomes Archmage of Branch Parthenia and then starts a second Wizard War. The more I read it the more I realized it was, down to the smallest detail, the same story as the alternate future that the shade of Valentine in the OneSpell claimed to be from. I have no idea what to make of this.

3 - What I Learned in Vegas

"Ladies and Gentlemen, for the first time as a married couple, Mr. and Mrs. Rico and Skylar Lopez!"

The room burst into applause as the lights in the room went wild and the stereo played the latest pop song to top the charts. Dancing while walking, Skylar and Rico moved into the reception.

The reception was at *Moneta*, a new club on Hollywood Boulevard built to replace other clubs, like *Ruby Red*, which were knocked down to make way for office buildings and luxury condos. Grant and I arrived together. He went off to the bar while I stood at the entrance for a moment, looking at the sea of faces. I didn't recognize many people, so I felt alone for at least a half minute before I heard a familiar voice greet me from behind.

"So what are you thinking about?"

Skylar looked happier than I had seen her in a while. We hadn't talked much in the lead-up to the wedding. I reached out a hand, but she beat me to it and hugged me instead. She held the embrace for a second longer than I expected, and when I pulled away, her arm lingered around my shoulder for a moment.

"Thank you for being a part of all this," Skylar said. "This isn't weird is it? I mean, you being one of Rico's groomsmen?"

"Not weird at all," I said.

Realizing the time was right, I reached into my pocket and withdrew a small box. I handed it to Skylar, who looked at me questioningly.

"I was going to wrap it and mail it to you, but I wanted to give it to you in person instead. Consider this a joint wedding, birthday, Christmas present. I know how much you like those."

Skylar laughed and opened the box, withdrawing the small gold medallion and chain within.

"It's a token!" she exclaimed. "But Roy, I can't accept this. I'm not a sorceress."

"It's okay. A sorceress gave it to me, and I'm pretty sure she would want you to have it."

Without another thought, Skylar unclasped it and put it around her neck, expertly closing it again with one hand as if she had done it before.

"How do I look?" she asked.

The token glowed golden from its perch against her white dress. It looked beautiful, as if it belonged there.

"You look like a very powerful sorceress," I said.

Skylar looked down. "What does the unicorn symbolize?"

"I can tell you," I said. "But not tonight. It's a long story."

"And I suppose I need to move on to my other guests," Skylar said. "Besides, I think there's someone else who wants to talk to you."

Following Skylar's gaze, I turned my head until I was eye to eye with an unexpected vision of beauty. Maria stood by herself in the middle of the dance floor. In my mind, the music stopped, and everyone (not just me) turned to look at her.

It was as if the Maria I had known my whole life was not the real Maria, but was instead a composite of different possible Marias. She had let herself be defined by each guy she dated, and it was the collection of those different states that formed the whirlwind that was my best friend. But the Maria standing in front of me now was different, confident. The years prior had stabilized her, forced her to choose a single self, and that self was standing before me.

"How's it going?" I asked.

"It's going well," she said, smiling and glowing just like she always did. And she meant it.

It had been months since we truly talked, so we spent a while catching up. She told me about her various adventures around the world, and I told her about my new job. Thanks to social media I knew she was dating Derek, again, but she didn't mention it and I didn't ask.

We talked for a while, at some point migrating over to a table so we could sit down. Then once the standard topics of conversation had run dry, and our reunion reached a natural pause, Maria said, "I'm going to step outside for some fresh air."

I started to say I would go with her, but for the second time that night I heard Skylar behind me and I turned around. The opening notes of Gwen Stefani's *Cool* had just started to play.

"Sorcerer Roy Nakamura," Skylar said, raising the fingers of her right hand to her forehead and tapping them gently. "Would you do me the honor of this dance?"

I cast a questioning glance to my right, in the direction where I imagined Rico must be standing.

Skylar shrugged. "It's a dance-with-your-ex song. It will be more awkward if we don't."

I reached out my hand, taking hers in it, and stepped out onto the dance floor. My other hand reached behind to hold her lower back.

We swayed in place for a few moments. I raised my left hand to twirl her around, then lightly dipped her.

"My, my Roy," Skylar said. "I see someone has been taking lessons."

"It's just a little move a sorceress taught me back when I was her apprentice," I said. "Besides, slow dancing isn't that hard. The only difference between an embrace and a slow dance…"

"Is the soundtrack," Skylar nodded, finishing the sentence.

We danced for the rest of the song.

Maria was standing just outside *Moneta*. She smiled when she saw me walking towards her.

"Roy, what are you doing here?" Maria asked. "Is the reception over already?"

"No," I said, "I just wanted to make sure you were okay."

"Make sure I'm okay? You're the one who just watched your ex-girlfriend get married." I must have looked upset, because she immediately added, "I'm sorry, that came out wrong."

"Don't worry about it." I looked at the busy street, at the cars driving past us. "I suppose I should have known you were okay. You know, there was a time when you would have told me that you don't need me to look out for you, that you can take care of yourself. That it's not my job to save you."

Maria took a step closer to me. "And there's a time when you would have told me that you're my friend. That that's exactly what your job is."

A car drove by, its headlights momentarily casting a shadow across Maria's face.

"There's something I need to tell you," Maria said.

There was a pause as I waited for her to speak.

"I'm engaged."

I looked down at her left hand.

"I'm not wearing the ring. I didn't want to distract from Skylar's wedding, so I'm keeping it quiet for now."

"Congratulations!" I said it a little too quickly, too mechanically, but I meant it.

"I know you had doubts about Derek at first, but trust me, he's a different person now."

"I believe you." Maria didn't know about the Dragon, so she had no idea how truly different Derek now was. "You don't have to convince me."

Maria smiled. "And how about you, Roy? How are things in the relationship department?"

I shook my head. "I've met a couple girls but there are always complications." Thankfully, I hadn't met any additional ex-girlfriends from the future. "I just don't think relationships are supposed to be this hard."

Maria shook her head. "Come on Roy. Anything worth doing, anything really worth it, is always hard. Anything you don't have to work at, that just comes naturally, is probably not that important in the long run."

I shrugged. "I suppose it's like they say in that song *What I Learned in Vegas*. You always hurt the ones you love."

"No." Maria said. Her eyes were warm and soft, like she was explaining the tragic death of a pet to a small child. "No Roy, it's not like that at all. You see, when you love someone, you give that person the ability to hurt you. The more you love someone, the more you open yourself up, the more that person can tear you apart. And it works both ways. When other people love us, they give us the ability to hurt them.

"That song, *What I Learned in Vegas*, it may be catchy, but it's wrong, it's all wrong. You don't hurt the ones you love – you hurt the ones who love you."

Somewhere a block away a police car drove by, its siren calling out a mournful tune. Maria sniffed. She slowly blinked her eyes.

I thought it was something I did, something I said. "What is it?" I asked.

She shook her head. Her arms, still crossed in front of her, dropped to her sides. "It's something I've been meaning to tell you for a while now, but I never quite knew how."

Maria looked out over the street, gazing off into the distance. I waited for her to speak. A moment went by, then another. The police siren grew quieter. I was about to say something, but then she began.

"When we were in Vegas a couple years ago, that time I went for New Year's Eve, right before you moved back to Los Angeles. I don't know if you remember, but on New Year's Eve Derek went missing. You were off looking for him, I think, and I was by myself in that giant hotel suite at the top of Parthenia, all alone, watching the clock tick down to midnight. It was the loneliest I had ever been, the lowest I ever felt. It was like I couldn't accomplish anything in life, like no matter what I did it wasn't going to get any better.

"Then I saw some sort of glow, so I looked up from my self-pitying, and I saw…" she quickly qualified her words, "I *thought* I saw, a unicorn. A unicorn! Just standing there, on the balcony. And it was so beautiful Roy, you wouldn't believe it. It was so beautiful! It disappeared a moment later, but even though it was gone, that one look was all it took.

"When I saw it, when I saw that unicorn, I knew I had to turn my life around. I knew if I kept doing what I had been doing, nothing was ever going to change, but at the same time I knew that if I took a different path, the future couldn't help but turn out the way I wanted."

Maria looked me squarely in the eye. "I don't know how Roy, but I know you're the reason I saw the unicorn. I know you somehow arranged for me to see it. And I never said thank you, so I'm telling you now, Roy." She paused, just a little bit out of breath from her monologue, tears (just a few) spilling out of her eyes. "Thank you."

I couldn't take it anymore. I stepped forward, in one small movement closing the space between us. I put my arms around Maria and she put her arms around my shoulders, folding her face into the nape of my neck. I heaved once, as if about to cry, but nothing came out. A moment later, I felt a single tear roll out of my eye, down my cheek, and onto Maria's back. It was all I had left.

A moment from my past tore away from its mooring and pushed itself to the front of my mind. Maria and I were in my white LeBaron Convertible. It was the Fourth of July, night was falling, and we were driving ninety miles per hour through the desert, leaving Las Vegas far behind us. Maria squealed in delight as wildlife scurried away at the distant promise of my headlights piercing the darkness around them. A familiar love song came on the radio, and Maria sang along at the top of her lungs. Her voice was beautiful, and this time she knew all the words.

> *Remember me*
> *When you're old and gray*
> *There's not enough time*
> *To make me stay*
>
> *My precious love*
> *Time's not my friend*
> *I'll see you when*
> *My journey ends*

As quickly as it had arrived the memory faded. But the song continued to play, at least in my mind.

My throat seized up dry, leaving me almost unable to speak. But I had to speak, I had to tell her. If I didn't now I never would.

I swallowed and tried to form the words with my lips. "Maria, I… I…"

"I know," she whispered. "I know."

The song in my head slowly sang itself to sleep, stranding the two of us alone in the darkness. The only sound was two hearts beating. I started to step away, but I could feel Maria pull me tighter, so I stopped.

We stood there, just like that, for a long time.

Glossary

Aetas – The "essence" of a spell, which a magic user must master in order to cast the spell. Put another way, the correct mental state that a magic user must attain in order to cast a spell.

Amulet – A physical object in which a spell has been bound up.

Archmage – The third in command and head of security for a Branch.

Atlantis – Massive island kingdom that sank in 1012AD. Its inhabitants were the original magic users and spread magic out into the world.

Branch – A clan of magic. Refers to both the literal family at the core of the Branch, as well as the associated allies and business holdings. All ethnic Atlantians are part of a Branch, either by blood or allegiance.

Branch Lord – The head of a Branch. Title is passed down among eldest male heirs.

Chief Wizard – The second in command of a Branch who oversees Branch administrative matters.

EndGame – An annual tournament of sorcerer duelers.

Las Vegas – The last city on Earth where magic still works.

Magician – Literally, any person who uses magic. In practice it is used to refer to a magic user who is neither a wizard nor a sorcerer.

Magic First – A magicians rights activist group that opposes the Branches.

Signed – Someone born with the ability to perform magic. Almost all Atlantians are Signed, as are roughly half of the non-Atlantian population.

Sorcerer/Sorceress – A magic user who has been admitted to the Sorcerers Guild. Not affiliated with a Branch.

Sorcerer's cloak – A black cloak with silver thread that is worn by sorcerers.

Sorcerers Guild – The ruling body for Sorcerers. Swears fealty to the Branches as a whole.

Token – Small medallion worn by sorcerers. Most wear at least two. The symbols on the tokens designate the sorcerer's allegiance or interests.

unSigned – Someone born without the ability to do magic.

Wave watching – The use of magic to determine probability waves in order to win games of chance.

Wizard – A magic user who is trained by, and then swears fealty to, one of the Branches.

The Wizard War – A conflict in the 1980's, originally between Branch Parthenia and Branch Shaskauer, that eventually involved six of the seven Branches of magic, as well as their allied sorcerers and magicians.

The Branches

Branch Cairavel – Lesser Branch. Part of the Alliance during the war.

Branch Daskur – Lesser Branch. Part of the Alliance during the war.

Branch Merkasia – Greater Branch. Part of the Pact during the war.

Branch Padamore – Lesser Branch. Part of the Alliance during the war.

Branch Parthenia – Greater Branch. Led the Alliance during the war.

Branch Primm – The outcast Branch. Remained neutral during the war.

Branch Shaskauer – Greater Branch. Led the Pact during the war.

Cast of Characters

<u>Los Angeles</u>
Roy Nakamura – protagonist
Skylar Trope – Roy's ex-girlfriend
Maria Perez – Roy's friend from high school and college
Grant Chung – Roy's friend and roommate during college
Renée Winters – Maria's roommate in Las Vegas
Derek Hastings – Grant's co-worker
Rico Lopez – Skylar's boyfriend

<u>Sorcerers</u>
Valentine – the time-traveling sorceress
Bastion Edwards – chairman of the Sorcerers Guild Council and former EndGame champion
Roland Tell – member of the Sorcerers Guild Council and reigning EndGame champion
Corinna Windlass – leader of Magic First
Arnold Davidson – wave watcher and dueler

<u>The Branches</u>
Jayden Parthenia – Roy's friend from college and second son of Lord Ricardo Parthenia
Ricardo Parthenia – current Lord of Branch Parthenia, was Archmage of Branch Parthenia during the Wizard War
T-Lock – Jayden's bodyguard
Artimus Cantor – Archmage of Branch Shaskauer
Karl Johnsen – a wizard in Branch Merkasia
Trannanir Shaskauer – co-creator of the OneSpell
Mianna Panashka – co-creator of the OneSpell

About the Author

J.B. Masaji was born and raised in Los Angeles, California. He spent four years on active duty as an officer in the United States Army, and remains a member of the United States Army Reserve. He currently resides in El Paso, Texas with his beautiful wife. Everything he does is by the grace of God.

The Author would like to thank those who read early drafts of this work: Julius, Hannah, Sarah, Jason, Jay, Esteban, Justin, and of course, Lisa.

www.ingramcontent.com/pod-product-compliance
Lightning Source LLC
Chambersburg PA
CBHW072114250626
47159CB00007B/2436